HellBound Books' Anthology of

SUBURBAN NIGHTMARES

Contents:

Moving In
Adam Carlson — 1

Bark
Alayna Frankenberry — 9

The House that Never Ends
Terry Grimwood — 22

Neighborhood Monsters
Paul Lonardo — 36

Twilight Care
Jade Jiao — 49

The Playground
Shawn Montgomery — 59

Colony
Matthew Piskun — 71

As Is
Steve Zisson — 87

In the Cellar
HP Newquist — 104

Unexpected Circumstances
Morgan Fletcher — 117

Eraticator
Dave Davis — 140

Chasm
Bryan Holm — 156

Eye of the Beholder
Carson Demmans — 172

20,000 Steps into the Suburban Vortex
Ryan Dyer — 185

Crabgrass
Damon Nomad — 200

The House on Hideaway Drive
Braden Benzinger — 216

The Killer, the Blood Spatter Analyst, and the OB/GYN
        Alexander Marais   232
The Armoire
        Douglas J. Moore   249
It's a Dog Today
        Tilsen Mulalley   268
The Boyfriend from Beyond
        R.C. Mulhare   283
The Kids Are Alright
        Julie Aaron   312
Comes in Threes
        Danni Bowen   331
Outside Cat
        Colin Adams-Toomey   355

Other HellBound Books   375

Moving In

Adam Carlson

"Wallpaper is a curse on whoever comes after!" Rachel cried as she peeled a piece of green paisley wallpaper off of the dining room wall.

"It's not a curse," Greg reasoned. "It's just a really awful idea."

Rachel shook her head. "The person who lived here before us knew we would have to live with their tacky decorating choices or put in hours of manual labor."

"We could've wallpapered over it."

Rachel paused to glare at her husband for a moment and Greg stifled a giggle.

"It's a curse," she repeated and pulled off the last remnant of wallpaper in the dining room.

"Look at the bright side," Greg said. "We finished a room."

"Not quite." She pointed at the opposite corner of the room. "You missed a spot."

Greg followed her gaze to the ragged square foot of hideous paper that still clung to the wall, which he was sure he had completely cleared.

"I could have sworn I…" He paused to peel away the paper. "There. Now we've finished a room."

Rachel sighed. "Only five more to go."

Greg unplugged the wallpaper steamer and sidled up to her. "We could take a break. We've got the air mattress out in the car."

"Are you serious?"

"I mean… if you don't want to use the mattress…"

"I'm covered in wallpaper glue. We both need like three showers to get clean."

"That's a great idea." Greg wrapped an arm around her waist. "We can try out the shower, see how it works."

Rachel wriggled out of his arms, but gave him a mischievous smile. "This isn't our honeymoon anymore. We have a whole house to take care of. A whole hideously decorated house, and we've only got the wallpaper steamer rented for 24 hours. Let's get started on the spare room. After that we can test out the shower and break in the bedroom."

Greg knew when he was defeated. He couldn't argue against the fiscal responsibility of working within the time constraints of their rental. As unwieldy and expensive as the steamer was, it was a drastic improvement on any other methods they had tried. "Deal." He lifted the wallpaper steamer and felt the water slosh in his arms. "It's mostly empty. We'll have to fill it up again."

"You do that, I'll check out the next room and see how bad the wallpaper is."

Greg gave his last ditch effort: "It'll take at least half an hour for it to heat up anyways…" He let the thought dangle so she could imagine all the things they could do in that time.

Rachel grinned. "It'll be better if we can take our time later."

"What do you want to do while we wait?"

"How about you make a beer run after you get the steamer set up?" She pranced down the hall to the next room.

Once again, his wife's logic was impeccable. Greg carried the steamer down to the utility sink in the basement and filled it up. It was as he came back up the stairs that he heard his wife exclaim, "Dammit!"

He raced to the guest room, where he found her with a piece of particularly hideous wallpaper in her hand: a pattern of silhouetted grinning faces on a chartreuse background.

"What's wrong?" he asked.

She waved the fragment in anger. "I thought this room would be a breeze because I pulled off this piece easily, but then I saw that."

Greg glanced at the wall where she was pointing, but saw nothing but the hideous wallpaper. "What?"

"I pulled away this big chunk, but there's another layer of it underneath! Who does that?"

Greg looked closer and finally saw the rough edges where a section had been ripped away only to reveal the exact same pattern underneath. "That's horrible."

"Did they think, 'Oh, this wallpaper is getting old, I'm going to put new wallpaper over it, but I'll make it the same thing,' or did they do it maliciously? Like, 'The next person who lives here is going to hate this, let's make them work extra hard to get rid of it.'"

Greg chuckled. "Maybe they put up a layer, then forgot that it was there and just did it again."

"This room is going to take forever."

"It'll be fine." Greg pinched a free edge of the wallpaper and pulled until a swath came free, revealing more of the under layer. "See, this comes away easily. I bet by the time I get back with the beer you'll have this top layer down, and then we'll tackle the next layer." He gave her a reassuring kiss, and left.

He climbed into his truck and was about to back up when he noticed a small patch of yellowish-green on the passenger seat. The faces on the scrap of wallpaper were smiling.

"How did you get here?" he asked, as if the wallpaper fragment could talk. It stuck to the fabric of the seat and had to be peeled off. They had been working at the wallpaper for half the day and still had a long way to go. It was inevitable some small scraps would travel with him. He glanced around at the interior of the cab. "I'm going to have to clean this good when this is all over," he muttered. He rolled down the window and threw the small scrap out, then drove down to the corner store and picked up a cheap 12 pack.

The proprietor looked up from a newspaper and eyed him warily. "Looks like you're doing some dirty work today."

Greg nodded. "De-wallpapering."

The salesman shook his head. "I've never done that. Never want to, neither."

Greg handed him the money and smiled. "It's not so bad. Better than some of the other jobs we've got ahead of ourselves, but that's homeownership."

"Sure is." The salesman nodded as he handed back the change. "I've been living in my house for near twenty years and I still have projects I haven't completed."

Greg smiled and nodded as he took his change. The salesman was the third person to tell him the exact same thing since Greg had moved into the neighborhood. He picked up the beer from the counter, ready to be on his way, and froze. On the counter, where the beer had been sitting, was a patch of chartreuse wallpaper, larger than the one he'd found in the truck, with a creepy silhouette grinning up at him.

"What the…" Greg trailed off, seized with an inexplicable anxiety. *How did that get in here? I didn't think I had any on me.*

The salesman glanced at him with a raised eyebrow. "Something wrong?"

"Huh? Oh, no." Greg peeled the piece of wallpaper off the counter. "Sorry about this. You have a trash can?"

The salesman picked up a can from behind the counter and held it up for Greg to toss the trash in.

"I guess I need a shower and sleep more than I thought." Greg smiled as he tried to explain away his anxiety, but he wasn't sure if he was trying to convince the salesman or himself. The salesman went back to his newspaper and Greg walked out to his truck. He tossed the beer on the passenger seat, put the truck in reverse and hit the gas with a crinkly noise. Surprised, he glanced down and saw a small ball of wallpaper under his foot.

"What the hell—"

A horn blared and he slammed on the brake. He'd been so distracted by the damn paper he'd almost drifted back into a little sports car. The other driver laid on the horn again, longer, and Greg picked up the wad of wallpaper, threw it out the window, and gave the other driver the finger. He put the car in gear and sped away.

"Dammit, I need one of those beers," he muttered to himself. "I'm too stressed out, I'm not paying attention."

He pulled into the drive and took a deep breath to collect his thoughts. *I need to relax,* he thought. *We'll have a beer, finish the next room, and then we'll get out of the house. Grab a bite to eat, maybe go see a movie or something.*

"It's not as if the wallpaper is following me," he said aloud, hoping the sound of his own voice would reassure him. "There's nothing sinister, it's just getting stuck to things."

He was about to pick up the beer and get out of the car when he noticed the yellowish paper sticking out of the front door, twitching in the wind.

Part of him wanted to throw the truck in reverse and get the hell out of there, but he knew it was irrational. "It can't be wallpaper," he reasoned as he stepped out of the truck and walked towards the house with increasing trepidation. "It just *can't* be."

As soon as he was close enough, he snatched the paper out of the door and unfolded it. The series of silhouetted faces seemed to greet him with a particularly devilish delight that hadn't been in their expression before.

"Rachel?" he said, his voice too quiet for her to hear from the back room. He licked his lips and tried again. "Rachel?! Did you do this?" He forced a dry chuckle. "This is… funny." He opened the door and any hope he had that it was a prank fell away.

The hallway, which had been painted a hideous yellow color, had sprouted large patches of smiling silhouettes on the walls, floor, and even the ceiling.

"Rachel!" he screamed as he raced through the creepy hallway. There was no response from his wife, but he thought he heard a low, rasping laugh coming from nowhere and everywhere. "Rachel!"

He couldn't see into the room Rachel had been working in; crumpled up bits of wallpaper completely filled the doorway. He hesitated a moment, sure it was already too late.

"Help me!" Rachel called from beyond the barrier and Greg threw caution to the wind. He barreled through the doorway, scattering the balls of paper about as he dug for his wife.

She was standing waist deep in a pile of wallpaper, oblivious to anything except the wall in front of her, which she attacked with vigor. "I'm almost there," she explained, ripping away a vast swath of the paper to reveal another layer beneath. She cut into the wall with a box cutter and ripped away a square. More faces grinned at her. "Damn! I thought that was it." She absentmindedly scratched at a piece of the paper that had stuck to her shoulder.

"Honey," Greg said, "let's get out of here."

"I'm almost there," she reasoned, oblivious to the unreasonable amount of wallpaper she had already removed or its malignant spread. "One more layer."

"We need a break," Greg reasoned, keeping his voice calm out of fear that the wallpaper would sense his panic.

Rachel pulled at the next layer of wallpaper and was rewarded with a sheet larger than herself that ripped free. "Aha!" she cried, trying to push it away. "This is sticking. Can you help me get it off?"

Greg grabbed a free end and peeled it off of her arm, crumpling it as he went.

"Thanks," she said and gave him a quick peck on the cheek.

"Let's get out of here for a bit," Greg pleaded.

"Sure. Just one more layer." Her eyes shone with an unfamiliar wildness.

"But—"

"Can you grab a trash bag?" she asked, motioning vaguely to the rest of the room. "I'll get one more layer and then we'll clean up."

She attacked the next layer of the wallpaper with vigor and Greg wasn't sure what else he could do. He turned his back for a moment to glance out at the hallway, which was now completely wallpapered.

"I don't think we have time," he said over his shoulder. "I think we should go now."

"Greg," Rachel said, "you don't get to just decaud fah aaa…"

Greg turned back to his wife and found only wallpaper. She had stopped fighting the wall, but did nothing to remove the layer of paper that had attached to her face and begun filling her mouth.

"Rachel!" he screamed as he lunged and raked at her cheeks with his fingers. He left the top layer in ragged strips, but another layer of maniacal faces stared at him. "No!"

Rachel gurgled, but even that noise was cut off. In the absence of other noise, Greg noticed the hiss of steam spitting from the wallpaper steamer. He picked up the large paddle, shoved it at Rachel's face, and was rewarded with a loud, piercing scream as Rachel fell to the ground, kicking and flailing.

"It's okay," he assured her. "We got it out of your throat. We just have to get it off your face." He applied the steamer again, then set the paddle down and leaned over her. She tried to push him away as he set his fingernails into the wallpaper that covered her temples, but her effort was pitifully weak. The wallpaper came free with a sickening squelching sound and he fell backwards with the paper in his hands, gratified that Rachel had stopped screaming.

"It's okay," he told her, holding up the strangely rubbery wallpaper. "I got it. Oh." He looked closer. "They used red glue. Isn't that strange?"

She didn't respond, probably because she was overwhelmed with relief at his prompt action.

"Let's go out and get some food," he offered. "We could try that Chinese place we passed the other day…" He suddenly noticed a particularly villainous silhouette face grinning at him from his forearm.

"Maybe we should sell the house," he muttered. "Move somewhere else. I just have to get this off and we can get out of here. Talk about it."

He scratched his wrist raw as he dug at the paper, but couldn't get his fingernails under it. Glancing around he saw, in the midst of the crumpled bits of wallpaper, a small patch of carpet with the box cutter in the middle, as if it had been left there just for him.

"Just give me a minute," he said as he picked it up and prepared for the delicate operation.

The faces on the wallpaper watched and grinned.

Bark

Alayna Frankenberry

Andi heard the dog before she saw it.

WOOF!

The deep bass of it hit her square in the chest. She removed her earbud (she only ever wore one) and listened. The road was empty. She glanced ahead, following the onyx river of new asphalt to where it curved out of sight. Across the street, a sprawling swatch of sepia clay brushed up to the tree line. Ruddy tire tracks quilted its surface, the oldest blurred by rainfall like healing scars. No dog to be seen.

On her right, the driveways were empty. A strip of five townhouses sat before the curve, the newest in the development. (The manufacturer stickers in the corners of the windows gave them away.) She knew what they looked like on the inside. The countertops, the light fixtures, even the paintings with their abstract orbs of cobalt and lapis would be the same as hers.

"Plenty of room to make it your own!" the realtor had promised.

With clothes and linens and cookware unpacked, Andi had spent the late afternoon trying to hang a single framed photo. Carefully, she'd slide a blue canvas from the wall, place her photo and step back. The photograph wouldn't win any awards. It was over exposed, a little blurry. Two little girls sat on the ledge of a wishing well, their putt-putt clubs crossed on the green turf at their feet. Their mother's shadow stretched towards them, frozen forever with the click of a disposable camera. The belly of the well held two pennies, cast by Andi and her sister at their mother's request. That day they'd swum in the ocean for the first time. Andi discovered the vending machine at the motel dropped two Sprites for every quarter. At lunch, their mother let them spend five dollars on the diner jukebox and didn't even complain when they played the same Shania Twain song ten times in a row. By all accounts, it had been the best day of Andi's life. When she flipped her penny into the well, she squeezed her eyes tight and wished that every day could be as good as this one.

When Andi rediscovered the photo many years later, she blew it up and framed it.

"Oh god," her mother winced when she glimpsed it on the mantle. She drew closer, pointing to her shadow, "I can't believe I was ever that big!"

Teenage Andi, already bigger than her mother had ever been, snatched the frame and ran to her room. She believed then what she believed now: that there was still time for the wish to come true. But every day she spent in that house, in that town, dulled her chances. Now, after so many years of fights and failures, breakups and breakdowns, she had finally squirreled away enough money to break free. She'd brought the photo with her to serve as a reminder, and someday, just maybe, to become a trophy for a lifetime of good days. Andi tried hanging it in the living room, the dining room, the kitchen and even the bathroom, but nothing felt right. So, in a huff, she propped Little Andi up in the entryway, slipped on her sneakers, and escaped.

There was something meditative about strolling through Hemlock Hills. Strategic clusters of old growth pine stretched behind the rows of homes, obscuring what lay beyond. White mailboxes, identical but for the black iron numbers marking their sides, stood silent as sentinels while she passed. The longer Andi walked, the more she felt like she was on a treadmill, like she could walk forever and somehow still be steps from home. She guessed that would change. Soon, more buyers would move in. They'd install little landmarks in the form of garden flags and potted plants, holiday decorations and bicycles. Her blank slate would be colored in lot by lot. But this time, she'd be a piece of the puzzle, her house perfectly nestled among all the others. No high school bullies to run into at the gym. No cashiers whispering about her mother at the supermarket. No rumor mill churning the waters with another story about her mom's latest ex, her sister's DUI, the time her dad punched her uncle at Easter Sunday Mass… here, she wasn't one of "Those Andersons." Here, she was just Andi.

WOOF!

A second bark. How long had she been standing there? And why was she being so weird? It was just a dog. She liked dogs. She imagined herself petting a golden retriever while a gorgeous woman with a perfect ponytail chatted and laughed. She pictured an Instagram post, the two of them clinking mimosas over brunch. Back home, in her musty duplex, Andi's sister would see the post and snarl. She'd realize all her sideways comments about Andi's move had been wrong. What had she said? *Your 'new start' is just someone else's hometown.* She was wrong about that too. Residents had only begun moving into the new development. There were no ghosts in Hemlock Hills. Not yet anyway. Andi pocketed her earbud and rounded the corner, smiling.

The road was empty. Up ahead, the asphalt formed a neat circle. A dead end. A twenty-foot-tall wall of chain-link rose behind it. Hanging from its center, a large wooden sign, carved and painted blue and white, read "Hemlock Hills Dog Park."

WOOF!

Finally, Andi saw it. Behind the chain-link, right in the middle of the park, sat a giant white dog. As if satisfied with finally getting her attention, it laid down in the grass.

"What the hell…" she mumbled. Now in the center of the cul-de-sac, she did a slow 360 to survey her surroundings. The road behind her was empty, and aside from the last row of houses she'd passed, no other homes circled the road. Flanking the square dog park, only clay, gravel, and spindly weeds framed the street. Beyond them and behind the park, towering evergreens grew closely together, receding into a fog of hazel shadow. The space looked more like a maximum-security prison than a playground for puppies. She half expected to see barbed wire circling the top of the comically high fence. She thought about calling out, but in what direction? And what would she say? *Hello? There's a dog here?* Shaking her head, she approached the fence.

"Hey boy!"

No response.

"Girl?"

The dog remained in the grass, panting and smiling.

"Um, *they*?" Dog owners in Hemlock Hills might be really progressive or something. Maybe the dog was nonbinary? It laid its head in the grass, looking embarrassed on her behalf. Its fur was long and pure white. She couldn't place the breed, but whatever it was, it looked expensive. Maybe it was hurt? As if on cue, it unfurled a plaintive whine.

To her right, Andi noticed the gate. Standard dog park issue, it led from the outside fence into a smaller four-foot-high box of chain-link with an additional gate. She'd seen setups like this before. About as wide and deep as it was tall, the area provided an added layer of security to prevent dogs from darting past entering visitors. Owners would unleash their dogs here before releasing them to the larger park inside. It was open a crack, and only after stepping inside did she realize why. A pale river rock, big as a grapefruit and nearly as round, was wedged between the gate and fence. With one hand on the gate, she bent down and picked it up. The outer gate clicked closed. Andi tried to push it open again. No luck.

"Wow, really, Andi?" She felt relieved that the only witness to her stupidity was several yards behind her and couldn't speak. It would probably tell the other dogs though. She'd have to alter her walking route to avoid their judging eyes.

A simple metal latch would be far beneath the security standards of Hemlock Hills. Like all the other community areas, this one had an electric lock. Andi dropped the stone doorstop onto the dirt behind her, then fished out her phone to open Hilltop, the official community app. She tapped it to the lock, just like the realtor had shown her outside the community gym. Nothing. She tried again. These things never worked. Again. Again. Again. She pocketed her phone, grabbed the fence, and tried to get a foothold on the chain-link, but the toes of her sneakers were too wide. Even if they weren't, she struggled to imagine herself scaling the towering fence. Behind her, the dog let out an exasperated sigh.

"Sorry, buddy," she said, turning. "The A team couldn't make it. You're stuck with me." She'd figure out the gate issue next. Who knew how long the dog had been trapped here, scared and alone. Before she did anything else, she wanted to make sure it wasn't hurt.

It showed no signs of aggression as she opened the second gate. Thankfully, this one had a standard latch. The dog almost looked relieved as she approached, its tail finally wagging.

"Are you a good girl?" she asked. The wagging grew frantic, though the dog never sat up. Andi crouched to pet the top of her broad head. The dog closed her eyes, melting under her touch. What a strange dog, soft as a rabbit and larger than a wolf. Andi caught a glimpse of black leather nestled into her mane. A collar, of course! She reached inside the fur, feeling for a tag.

"Nice Dog!" Came a voice from behind her.

Andi shot up and whipped around, her breath caught in her chest. A man stood at the entrance, leaning forward with his fingers laced through the chain-link.

"Oh, hey, hey," he said, raising his hands and backing up with a laugh. "Didn't mean to sneak up on you!"

"HA!" She laughed back, way too loudly. *Breathe, Andi*, she thought, clearing her throat. *This is the first neighbor you've met. Try not to come off as a complete weirdo.* "Oh, yeah, yeah she is. That's what I was just thinking."

"Well, I guess it's good that she's got an owner that appreciates her."

"Oh, she's actually not mine," Andi replied, walking closer.

"So…you're a dog walker, or did you just rent her?" Funny. Funny and handsome.

"No, no," Andi blushed, her heart now racing for entirely different reasons. "Rent her, haha, I don't think I could afford her." Did he just smirk? Was she flirting?

"So, you guys just having a meeting or something? I can come back later if you're discussing confidential business." He looked like he'd been plucked straight out of a Hallmark movie. A little too thin to be the lead, maybe, but close. Andi straightened up a bit, tucking a strand of hair behind her ear.

"It's so weird, actually, she was just in here… alone."

"What?" He took a step to the left, peering behind her. "Have you ever seen her before?"

"No, I just heard her bark, but she wouldn't come to the gate. I think she might be hurt or something."

"I haven't seen her before either, but to be fair, I haven't seen anyone really. This place is kind of a ghost town."

"Not yet," Andi replied. *People have to live somewhere before they can abandon it*, she thought. The man was smiling slightly, like he was waiting for her to elaborate. *Don't be a nerd, Andi,* she thought, shifting gears. "Anyway, I kind of locked myself in here."

"You try Hill Stop?"

"Hilltop?"

"Yeah, the app thing."

Andi grabbed her phone from her pocket as she walked toward him, unlatching the inner security gate and stepping inside. She pulled up the app, holding it over the electronic latch.

"Yeah, it looks like it's still not working," Andi sighed between taps.

"Did you add the park to your access profile?"

"My what?"

"Yeah, I didn't know that was a thing either until I tried to go swimming yesterday." He was just a couple feet away now, and Andi tried not to stare as the thought of him shirtless flashed through her mind.

"Let me show you," he said. Sadly, he made no move to peel off his shirt. Instead, he began patting his pockets in search of his phone.

"Damn, I forgot my phone at home. I can just show you if you want, you mind?" As he gestured towards her phone, the wind shifted. He smelled like pine tar and pipe tobacco. *Goddamn.* Andi slid her phone though the chain-link.

"Oh," he held the locked screen up in front of her. It pinged, recognizing her face.

"Well, that was easy!" he said. "Anyway, so you open the app," he began clicking, "you go to settings, go to…places, add place…Hilltop Dog Park… oh damn."

"What?" Andi pressed against the fence, trying to see the screen.

"I think your phone just died." He held up the black screen.

"Seriously?" Andi sighed. "Fuck." The man bristled.

"Sorry," she said. "I couldn't find my charger when I was unpacking, ugh. I was gonna charge it when I got home from my walk. I figured I had enough time left…" The man's open expression returned.

"Don't we all," he replied. Behind her enjoyment of the witty banter, Andi felt her frustration growing. Did he sense it?

"Is this an iPhone?" He examined the charging port. "Well, that's some good luck at least! Don't have my phone but I'm pretty sure I have my charger in the truck. I'll juice it for a couple and be right back." Before Andi could respond, he turned heel, half jogging up the road. A white truck was parked on the bend, its bed tucked behind the trees. Andi watched the man climb into the cab and shut the door. As the lingering scent of pine and tobacco dissipated, Andi felt a fog lifting. *What just happened?*

Had the truck been there when she arrived? She couldn't remember. Inside, the man seemed to be rooting around, probably searching for his charger. The sun was sinking and the golden reflection off the cab's windows blurred everything but the shadowed gestures of his movements. Andi squinted, trying to decipher his shape. He seemed to be sitting still now. Maybe he'd plugged her phone in and was waiting for it to charge? She didn't blame him for not wanting to leave his truck running. Was he looking over here? She couldn't tell.

Shifting from foot to foot, she felt like a schoolgirl. Little Andi on the playground silently studying the girls, longing to decipher the secrets buried under their bouncing hair and trilling giggles, some switch she could flip to make her shine the way they did. Little Andi hunching her shoulders inside a giant threadbare hoodie, wishing at the same time to be noticed and to disappear. She straightened her back, wondering if the man was watching her. She tried to look on the bright side. Maybe the situation had tipped the scales in her favor. Men loved a damsel in distress, right? That could explain why he seemed interested. She wasn't one to charm men on looks alone. Andi pulled her sleeves over her hands and crossed her arms. The wind was picking up, sweeping through the trees. Behind her, the dog let out a whine.

Andi spun around, unlatched the security gate, and returned to the dog. She knelt beside it.

"Are you okay, girl? Are you hurt?" The dog only lifted her eyes. Andi couldn't see any injuries, no blood at least. She gently scratched the dog's head, feeling a little ashamed for ignoring her while she chatted.

"Can you sit up, girl? Can you sit up?" The dog let out a little huff.

"That's okay, baby. It's okay. Can I see your collar?" Still petting with one hand, Andi found the leather band with the other. She began circling the collar, hunting for a tag. Instead, she felt a hard plastic bubble sitting flush against the collar. She tried parting the fur to get a better look. Probably some kind of techy collar that cost more than her car. Maybe this was the clasp? Rich folks sure did love their minimalist designs, no matter how impractical. She wedged a hand underneath and felt two metal prongs, short and rounded. The plastic bar flashed red and before she could react, a hot white pulse shot up her arm.

Andi yelped, yanking her hand free and scrambling back on the grass. The lightning bolt of pain was already gone, but every muscle in her body remained braced for impact. She stared down at her hand in disbelief. No burn marks. No marks at all.

"Oh god," she said, "Oh god, you poor dog." Sprawled beside her in the dirt, Andi felt her eyes well up with tears.

"What happened? Are you okay?" The man was running toward the gate, his truck door flung open behind him. Andi quickly wiped her eyes and stood up.

"Did she bite you? I heard you yell."

"No, the collar. The collar shocked me." Andi approached the gate, clutching her hand.

"Whoa, are you okay? Can I see?"

Andi unlatched the security gate and stepped up to the fence.

"It's fine," she assured him, holding up her unmarked palm. "I'm fine."

"Well, I'm glad, but I feel like a jerk. Sitting in my car playing Candy Crush while you're tussling with Tesla over here."

"I think her collar's broken. I think she's just over there getting shocked. Maybe that's why she won't move. Oh god…" She blinked back tears.

"That sounds terrible. I don't even know how to fix that. Actually, maybe we should run down to the office?" He glanced at his watch. "I hope they're not closed already. I can drive."

Andi didn't want to drive to the office. She wanted to go home. She wanted to call the police, but first, she needed her phone.

"Did you charge my phone?"

"Oh, yeah, sorry!" He pulled a phone from his pocket and passed it through the fence. She looked down at the dark green case in her hand and stepped back.

"This isn't mine."

"Oh jeez, I forgot to grab yours when I ran over here. That's mine." Andi looked up at him, confused.

"Yeah, turns out I didn't forget it at home. I just dropped it under my seat. But hey, maybe our luck is turning around today!" Andi was about to hand it back when her mind snagged on a thought.

"Why didn't you bring it back?"

"Bring what back? Your phone? I told you, I ran over here when I heard you yell and—"

"No, your phone. When you found it, why didn't you just come back and let me out?"

A glimmer of annoyance flashed across his eyes. He clapped a hand to the back of his head in a strained gesture of embarrassment. "Well, I guess I should have. Looks like you're the brains and beauty of this operation, huh?" He waited for her to laugh, but she only managed a thin smile.

"Well anyway, I've got the app too so just use mine. Then we can go to the truck and grab yours."

Once they got to the truck, she'd get her phone and make an excuse to go home. Or maybe she'd stand there and call the police. They could probably take the collar off, maybe she'd even file a report for animal abuse. She hoped they'd catch the owner and throw the book at them. First things first. She tapped the screen to wake up his phone.

As the phone lit up, Andi felt all the blood in her body drop through her feet. The man had a picture of himself set as his lock screen. His pixelated face beamed up at her. His arms were slung around the neck of a big white dog.

The man slammed his fists against the fence just once.

"Sorry," he said, rolling his shoulders back. He shook out his arms and took a deep breath. "Sorry, I forgot about that. Man, that's disappointing. Man oh man." His voice sounded different.

"I don't... I don't understand."

"Well, I'm sure confusion isn't exactly a novel experience for you. You did manage to lock yourself in a dog park." He let out a chuckle. "Sorry, too soon?"

She reached for the security gate. She didn't know who this man was, but she wanted to get as far away from him as possible. The man whistled one piercing note, and the dog sprang to its feet, sprinting for the gate. Andi secured the latch just in time. The dog she'd cried tears of pity for just moments ago bared its teeth with a low growl.

Andi jabbed at the phone. Locked. She tried holding it up in front of her to recognize the man's face. Nothing.

"Look, I'm sorry, I really am. I planned for this to go differently. Lots of empty houses here. Had a whole date planned for us in one of them. A whole night. Honestly, I think you would have had a lot of fun. I know I would have." He looked at his watch. "It was going to be really romantic, but, not to be rude, you kind of ruined the mood and now I'm just tired. Are you tired?"

Andi didn't answer. She didn't know what she felt.

"Yeah, we're both tired. And you know what, you seem like a good girl. So, here's what we'll do. I'm keeping your phone. You've got some nice pictures on there." He winked. "You can try to keep my phone if you want, but if you do, I'm going to let Ghost here hop into your little cage and rip you into ribbons."

Andi remembered the keys in her pocket and the heavy stone somewhere near her in the dirt. What would she do with either of them? Not enough. The man held out his hand, waiting. She crouched down, placed the phone on the ground and kicked it under the fence.

The man picked it up and wiped it off, frowning. He stood there for a while, just breathing.

"You know what? One last trick before we go. Bark."

WOOF!

"No Ghost, not you." He nodded toward Andi. "*You.*"

Andi clenched her jaw.

"Don't make me ask twice."

She didn't move.

"Well alright then. Ghost?"

The dog launched onto its back legs, claws grappling against the chain-link. Its head easily cleared the edge, fangs already close enough to snap through Andi's hair.

"BARK!" Andi's voice croaked. "BARK! BARK! BARK!"

"Good girl," said the man. With a whistle, Ghost got down, trotting away over to a section of fence that bent out slightly above a crescent of clawed dirt. It slid under effortlessly.

Andi would wait a long while before she followed. Eventually, she'd drag her belly through the dirt, the clipped prongs of the fence scraping long red welts down her back. Now she just stood there, the wind whipping through her. She just watched. The dog hopped in the open truck door. The man followed. He closed the door. He started the engine. He drove away. She listened as the rumble of the truck faded, enveloped by the wind, the rustling branches, the distant thrumming of cicadas. Streetlights blinked on. The wind picked up. Somewhere far above her, a jet purred through the clouds. Down the winding road, inside a house that looked like all the others, Little Andi peered up from her wishing well, waiting.

The House that Never Ends
Terry Grimwood

I thought it best to take care of the renovations before moving in to what was to be our first house. No furniture in the way. No carpets to ruin. Nothing to cover in dust, except myself, of course, my wife Gail and my friends who pitched in to help. Two of them, Charlie and Dov, were there that day. I was grateful for them, especially Charlie. He was a builder, so, unlike the rest of us, he knew what he was doing. Dov, on the other hand, was a software engineer, Gail managed the accounts for a transport company, and I was a journalist for a local newspaper, which meant that the three of us knew very little about such arcane items as damp courses, pointing and studwork.

My specialism was local history, so when this house came on the market cheap, following a series of rapid purchases and subsequent quick sales, I looked into its biography. Force of habit, I suppose. What I found not only piqued my interest, but made it imperative that we buy the place. Gail wasn't keen, despite her need to get us away from our dingy, rented flat at any cost. Too much work required, she said. Too damp, old and drafty. Shiny and new was her dream. Bringing her round to my way of thinking required every ounce of charm and persuasiveness I could muster. To my surprise, she relented, but on the condition that the place was gutted and made, well, shiny and new.

This house and its adjoining two-up-two-down terrace dwellings were built in 1902, on the site of a much larger property which had been empty and near derelict for decades. It had been the home of an alchemist, according to local legend. It was a Bad Place when he lived there and remained bad long after he died. A few people had moved in over the subsequent century - then out again in a hurry. According to the 4th of May, 1901 *Sedgemoor Herald*, its demolition was greeted with relief by the neighbours. An evil miasma had been swept away by sledgehammer and pickaxe. Journalists, eh? We do love to make a drama out of very little.

Gail had sighed and shrugged, but here she was, my lovely, loving bride, helping me strip out rotting 1980s kitchen units while Charlie knocked down the wall between the miniscule dining and sitting rooms. The resulting lounge wouldn't be enormous, but it would be *our* lounge, in *our* house.

We had all but gutted the kitchen, except for the sink unit, because plumbing was involved and there was no way either of us were going to tackle that. Charlie, however, knew a guy. He knew a lot of guys.

Dov, meanwhile, was upstairs clearing plaster off the bedroom walls, a dirty laborious job but he was okay with it, headphones on, music filling his head. He slogged away uncomplainingly the way he did everything. Dov wasn't his real name, it was Dovydas, he was Lithuanian. A friend I'd met at work. He was married to, Rose, who was as English as her name suggested. She would have pitched in too, but she was working and was going to call round later with some food.

It was mid-afternoon. Gail and I were dragging the last floor-standing unit across the kitchen towards the hallway door and out to the skip we had hired. We were dirty, tired, but happy. Gail's face was smudged and that made her kind of sexy. She wore a set of overlarge overalls and had a scarf about her head to protect her hair. I caught myself staring at her as we wrestled the unit over the threshold into the hall.

"I still don't think you should be doing that," I said. "In your…"

"In my condition?" she countered. "I'm only a few weeks in, a lot of women don't even know they're pregnant at this stage."

"Yes, but -"

"Maybe this is the right house for us after all. An Edwardian pile for an Edwardian man." She laughed. "Stop worrying, I might be *delicate*, but mother and baby will be fine."

"How are you getting on?" I called up to Dov to change the subject and because I felt guilty about how hard he was working.

"I've just started on the third bedroom."

It took a moment longer for that to register with me than with Gail.

"Dov, we only have two bedrooms."

"No, you have three. Here, I'm in the third. Up here. Look."

Gail and I shared bemused looks. I shrugged, then led the way up the steep narrow stairs. They'd be a bugger when we were old.

On the landing. Three doors, as expected. Large bedroom, small bedroom and airing cupboard. The bathroom was next to the kitchen down in the small 1970s rear extension.

"Dov?"

"In here, Thomas."

It sounded as if he was in the small bedroom. I opened the door. Bright winter sunlight streamed in through the sash window. Dust spiralled through the glow. Dov had cleaned the structural walls down to the bare brick, the others to their wooden laths, which, though ancient, looked to be in good condition. The floorboards had that freshly swept look. The old horsehair plaster was piled into a neat heap to one side of the doorway. The air was gritty.

The room was empty.

"Dov?"

"Thomas?"

"He's out on the landing," Gail said.

She was right. I followed her back through the bedroom door and there he was.

"Where were you?" I asked.

"The third bed…" He looked around and frowned. "But…there was a door. My tools are in there."

"You must have got mixed up," Gail said.

"No, not the door…" He looked uneasy now.

It was infectious. My skin was suddenly alive with goosebumps. "Look," I said, with more confidence than I felt. "The small bedroom." I opened the door.

"Yes, okay."

I went to the other door. "The large bedroom. All done Ready to be replastered."

He nodded.

"So, where is this third bedroom?"

He looked around again, then shrugged. "I don't understand…"

"We're all tired," Gail said. "I'll make a cup of tea."

We had a kettle and mugs in the kitchen.

Gail clattered down the uncarpeted stairs. Dev and I stood on the landing awkwardly. "You okay?" I asked him.

He moved closer, voice lowered. "I did not like the other room."

Those goosebumps again. "What do you mean?"

But he was already on his way downstairs to drink tea. I lingered behind. The whole third room business had unsettled me. I returned to the small bedroom. Nothing but those bare walls. The window. The big bedroom, same except for a built-in cupboard. I looked inside. Just a cupboard.

I was no longer comfortable up here. Which was ridiculous. The air seemed cold and damp. The light was yellowed, stale somehow. I forced myself not to run to the door. Fought off a conviction that the door was going to slam shut on me, then stepped out onto the landing and headed downstairs.

Time passed. The light faded and Gail switched on the kitchen lamp with dangled, bare, from its cord. Dov was back upstairs. Charlie was installing something he called Acrow props, which would hold up the upstairs section of the structural wall he had demolished until he could fit a reinforced steel joist, whatever that was. Gail and I worked at the wall cupboards. My arms and wrists ached from unaccustomed labour.

I heard the front door open.

"Hi everyone. Tea time!" Dov's partner, Rose, had arrived.

She entered the kitchen carrying a bowl of food; curry by the smell of it. She placed it on the wallpapering table we had set up as our refreshment station. She had brought bottles of beer too. Cobra, in keeping with the menu. Dov was a lucky man. but then, so was I. Gail was my soulmate, the most comfortable and loving person I'd ever been with.

"I'll fetch Charlie and Dov," Gail said.

She went out and I heard her shouting their names. Charlie replied straight away and in a moment was in the kitchen, a big, broad character with shaved head and a lush Viking-style beard.

I could still hear Gail calling for Dov. There was no reply. Gail looked worried when she returned the kitchen.

"What is it?" Rose said.

"I can't find Dov," Gail said.

"What do you mean. You can't find him?" Rose asked.

"Perhaps he's in the garden." By which, Charlie meant the small square of long grass and tall nettles that lay beyond the back door. He headed off in that direction.

"I'll take a look upstairs," I said.

Gail caught my arm. "He isn't there, Tom, believe me."

"He must be," Rose said.

"I'll check. Two pairs of eyes are better than one."

I bounded up the stairs, acting braver than I felt. The landing light was on. No sign of Dov. Only the closed bedroom doors. The *three* bedroom doors.

I took a hesitant step towards that third door. It was identical to the others.

"Gail," I called out. "Charlie."

"What is it?" Rose had come to the bottom of the stairs first.

"Tom?" Gail, thank God. I wasn't sure how to handle Rose, given the situation.

"Come and look at this."

I heard her ascend the stairs. There were two sets of footsteps. Rose had followed her.

"There are three doors."

"I thought you only had two bedrooms up here," Rose said.

"We did," I answered before I could stop myself. "Dov," I called out. "Dov, are you there?"

No answer.

That door had apparently disappeared last time we went to look for it. If Dov was behind it, he would be trapped if it vanished again. I found a little courage then crossed to grab at the doorknob. I glanced back, saw Gail, Rose, who looked frightened and confused, and Charlie, who must have come back in from the garden.

I stood there, unable to move. A part of me wanted to go through, to find Dov, but I was too afraid. Then Charlie was at my side. He muttered impatiently under his breath, then opened the door and went through.

I looked at Gail who was on the landing now, trying to hold Rose back. Rose shrugged her off angrily. I made to block her path, at the same time calling out to Charlie.

"It's okay," he answered. "It's just a room, although -"

"Let me through," Rose's face was clouded with anger and fear.

"No, it's…" What? Dangerous? It was *just a room*.

Charlie appeared in the open doorway. He looked shaken. "Dov isn't in there, but there is another door and there's…You need to come in and see for yourself."

How the hell could there be another door? This was a small terrace house.

Rose pushed past me and went inside. Gail took my hand. "Come on, Tom," she said. "Scared?" Her gentle mockery was edged with something that sounded like unease. I nodded and we went in.

Yes. It was a room. There was no window. Charlie had already switched on his phone torch. I activated mine as well and shone it around. The floor was littered with lumps of fallen plaster and broken laths. There was another door opposite to where we stood. I raised the bright, tightly focussed light to play over the walls.

I heard a gasp of shock. It might have been me, I wasn't sure.

The mouldy white plaster, where it hadn't come away from the laths, was covered in writing. The writing was neat, cursive. I tried to read it, but it appeared to be in a foreign language. Its very existence disturbed me, but not in any way I could comprehend. It was if some part of my sub-conscious understood what it said and was repulsed by it.

"The Alchemist," Gail said. "He must have done this."

"We don't know that," I said, although I had no better explanation.

"Where's Dov? We should be looking for him. I don't care about the writing, I want Dov." Rose moved cautiously towards the next door.

"We need to be careful," Charlie said. "We don't know what might -"

Rose opened the door. Then stumbled back, gagging on the stink that billowed out of the darkness beyond. The smell was *cold*. It was redolent with rotting meat, yet, at the same time sweet and flowery. Charlie was there in a moment, which made me feel inadequate and clumsy. Gail joined them almost as quickly. I followed. The going was hazardous. In my restless torch light, the broken laths resembled piles of rotting wooden bones.

The stench from the other room turned by stomach..

We went through, Charlie first, myself last.

More bloated plaster. More bare laths. A swollen bulge in the ceiling. Two doors on the far wall. *Two* doors? Just how big was this place that shouldn't even exist?

And there was more writing. Symbols as well, jagged spirals of what might have been thorns or barbed wire.

I shone the torch up at the ceiling, at the holes left by the laths that had snapped and fallen when slabs of horsehair plaster broke away. The was darkness, beyond. No sign of roof joists or the underside of the tiles. Nothing but impenetrable black.

The floorboards felt soft under my feet. A new fear crept in that they might give way and God knew what was underneath here, because it wasn't my home anymore. This room was huge and must extend far beyond the rear boundary of the house.

"What's that?" Gail said.

I followed her extended finger and saw something on the floor, amongst the dusty web-shrouded debris. Something that looked organic. It steamed a little. For a moment I thought it was a turd, then as I came closer, a snake.

It was, in fact, a roughly coiled length of intestine, blue-grey in colour, surrounded by a dark stain.

Blood.

I stared, my mind grappling with what I was seeing.

"Rose!"

Gail's warning shout was too late.

Rose screamed. The sound was animal-like, primal, primitive. Awful. She screamed her partner's name. In a moment Gail had her arms about her.

"We don't know it's him," Charlie said. He sounded awkward and lost. His voice too rough for this situation.

Gail wrestled with Rose until she was able to hold her tight. She looked at me and I saw the terror in her eyes, made stark by the soulless light of the phone torch.

"Dov!" Charlie shouted. "Dov, where are you mate?"

No answer. Dov would never answer us again. We all knew it. I shone the torch and discovered two more doors. There was blood on the woodwork. There was blood on the floor, a lot of blood, splashed over the fallen plaster, over the tangled laths. Everywhere.

"We should go back," I said.

"Yeah," Charlie said. "I'll call the police, even if it isn't…they're human remains. We have to report it."

"I'm not going back," Rose said. "Nor until we find Dov."

"It's too dangerous," Charlie said. "Whatever…whoever, did this could still be here."

"You go, I don't care. I have to find him."

"Rose -"

She pushed Gail away and was at the doors with surprising speed. I stumbled across in pursuit and almost fell. Rose choose the right hand door. What happened next, happened with awful quickness and yet I saw it clearly, as if time had slowed to a crawl.

Something dark and huge erupted from the doorway.

Rose glanced back. I saw her in the inadequate, but suddenly stark, torch light. There was a terror on her face that was hard to comprehend. It was as terrifying as the monster itself. Then she was yanked through the doorway and into the blackness.

She didn't scream. She had no time.

Gail rushed towards the door, stumbled and tripped and went down. She cried out in pain and what sounded like frustration. I went to her to help her up. The torchlight flickered all over the place as I tried to establish her exact position. She sat on the floor amidst the dust and plaster. A fragment of lath was stuck to her knee. She reached out to touch it, and gasped.

"Jesus," she said. Her voice trembled and was barely audible. "Oh God."

I tugged at the piece of wood. She swore and slapped at me and it was then that I understood that she had fallen onto a nail and it was rammed into her knee.

Gail' face was tight with pain. She made to pull the lath free, but it obviously hurt too much.

"All right, look at me." Where did that come from? Too much *Gray's Anatomy* probably. "Gail, look at me."

She did.

I wrenched the lath free.

"Owwww. Fuck. Ahhh." She grabbed at her leg and rocked back and forth. The nail wasn't that long but it was sharp, old and rusty. She would need a tetanus injection. Her expression changed. "Rose…"

Reality came back. It slammed into my mind with such force it was almost a physical shock. In those few minutes I had forgotten what had happened to Rose.

"We have to find her, Tom."

Through there? Where that thing lived?

"She might still be alive," Gail said. "We can't leave her."

Oh yes, we can, said the cowardly side of me, that tiny primitive mammal hiding from the dinosaurs.

"Tom, Gail." Charlie sounded frightened, which was not reassuring. Charlie was the big, tough builder who wasn't supposed to be afraid. "The door we came through. It's gone."

Charlie shone his torch over the place where the door should have been. There was nothing but mouldering plaster and that infernal bloody script.

"We can't go back," Now there was panic in his voice. "Bloody hell."

"We have to get out of here," I said.

"How?" Gail sounded near to panic. I felt the same. I wanted to shout, scream and pound at the wall until that bloody door reappeared. I wanted to curl up and cry and hope it all went away, but I couldn't. Someone had to maintain a semblance of self-control.

I didn't want to be the one. I wanted someone to come and help me and tell me it was all going to be okay.

I caught up with Gail who was back on her feet and limping towards the door through which Rose had been taken. I grabbed her hand, which was hot. I could feel her trembling. I looked back to Charlie. "Are you with us, mate?"

He shook his head.

"You can't stay here alone."

"The door will come back. Tom. We have to wait for it to come back."

"No, Charlie. We can't stay. We have to find Rose." Gail sounded ominously calm.

Still holding her hand, as much for my own comfort as for hers, I stepped up to the door. I saw blood, on the plaster. Fresh and wet, Rose's blood. It had to be. It had been so quick I hadn't even seen what actually happened to her.

Through we stepped.

I winced, expecting violence, pain, horror.

The room was empty.

I could feel it, long before I waved my phone torch around.

When I did, I regretted it.

The room was a butcher's shop. An abattoir. A charnel house. Surely, the source of the stink that pervaded these strange, extra rooms. Human debris was strewn about the floor, some old and desiccated, some fresh and perfumed with the cold meaty smell of offal. Organs, gut, flesh, hair, ribcages, bones, all mingled with fallen plaster and splintered laths. My strength failed. I grabbed Gail to myself and held her tight as she sobbed into my shoulder.

"Christ." Charlie, now beside us. His breath was laboured and ragged. He turned away out of the small disc of light from my phone torch and ran from the room. His own torch light flickered and danced as he stumbled back the way we had come. In a moment I heard him pounding the walls and yelling. His voice rose towards a scream as he lost control.

No longer wanting to see what was on the floor, I used my own torch to scan the blood splattered walls. There were three doors leading out of this room.

There was also a sound. A scrabbling noise, animal-like. Something was running around beyond one of the doors. Although I couldn't tell which one. It was growing louder, heading our way. Which door? Which fucking door? I played the beam over all three. All identical. All covered in writing.

It was Gail who moved first.

She hauled me to the left hand door then placed her ear against the wood. She jerked back with a cry.

"This one, it's behind this one."

She moved to the middle door, grabbed the knob and wrenched it open. Beyond there was utter darkness. It absorbed my torch light. It was a wall of nothingness, yet so dense that I was sure that if I touched it, I would feel it on my skin.

We had no choice, however.

"Charlie!"

Gail joined in. "Charlie, hurry up -"

The left hand door crashed open and through it came. It was huge in the torch light, made stroboscopic by my panicked retreat. It flowed and changed shape. It was a thing of moving parts, of writhing and pulsing. It was horse-like. It was a worm. Limbs flailed, tentacles lashed out.

One last glimpse of it as it poured through the far door and then Charlie screamed, briefly.

Then there were other sounds; tearing, snapping.

We ran, into the darkness. The torch gave no more than glimpses. Another empty space, no ceiling. I shone the torch upwards and there was only blackness. Horrible and everlasting.

More doors. Three again. We moved carefully now, because the floor was a lethal minefield of upturned nails and slabs of plaster over which we might slip or trip.

We reached the doors. There was no clue which would be right or wrong.

The scrabbling, scuttling sounds resumed. Behind which door? Which fucking door? And how did it get back there from the room behind us? I felt my strength drain. My legs were too weak to support me,

As the thing came into the room.

As the thing flowed through my shaky torchlight and twisted and slithered over the floor the walls. I glimpsed its face, which was unbearably human. I saw its glee and hunger. Its scorn and hate.

"Go," I yelled. "Go, Gail, please, get out." I grabbed a length of wood. It was studded with ancient nails. A pathetic excuse for a weapon, but a weapon nonetheless.

Gail hesitated.

"Save our kid, go on, save her!" Her? It didn't matter. It felt to me as if the child was going to be a girl.

Gail moved then. She staggered away into the dark. She would be making for the door into this room. She would be getting out. If one door opened then the others would too. Wouldn't, they?

I lurched towards the creature to distract it. I saw that face again; blank, formless eyes, wide open mouth, drool hanging from its lips. Wormlike tongue. The stench of its breath was the stink of decay. I grabbed at the knob behind me and opened the door and plunged into the dark. A room? A passageway? I saw walls, I saw a filthy, offal-muddied floor.

And now I feel it behind me. I smell its abattoir perfumes, feel its cold breath and its grasping, groping presence.

I run, splashing through puddles that might be blood, slipping and stumbling over things I refuse to name.

I run in the hope that Gail and our child will be safe. I run into blackness, where there are no more doors. My phone light is growing weaker as the battery dies and the dark is closing in.

Neighborhood Monsters
Paul Lonardo

I drifted aimlessly among the familiar-faced strangers for as long as I could. I needed to get away from the cacophony of voices and the banal expressions of sympathy offered to me by people who didn't know the relationship that I had with my father. Every time someone told me how sorry they were, it was all I could do to keep from screaming. I wanted to tell them that I was the one who was sorry - for having to drive four and half hours from Philadelphia to attend the funeral.

And of course, he had to die on Halloween. Of all the days of the year to come home for a funeral, why did it have to be this one?

Finally, I made it to the kitchen and the backdoor. Everyone was so caught up in their individual conversations and gossip, I didn't think anyone would notice me slip away. When someone gave me a supportive pat on the back, I didn't bother turning to acknowledge who it was. I figured that this person, like everyone else, would just think I was too grief-stricken even for polite social interaction, but they were all wrong. My indifference was genuine, and the fact was that the death of my father was more of an inconvenience than it was traumatic. I hadn't had any kind of relationship with my father since my mother died when I was nine years old. That was when the abuse started, the degrading verbal attacks and vicious beatings with belts, curtain rods, golf clubs, anything he could get his hands on. Although this cruelty had been there in some capacity all along, it became more prevalent when my mother was diagnosed with cancer and placed in hospice. It stopped a little while after she died, and my father married the hospice nurse who worked at the facility where my mother had been staying. I thought I had put all of it behind me for good. If I could just scrub it all from my memory, I would have done it long ago.

The fall leaves, still damp with morning dew, stuck to my shoes as I cut across the side yard. The wind had stopped gusting, but the slate sky threatened rain. I turned up the collar of my pea coat and removed an old pack of matches and a new pack of cigarettes from an inside pocket. I hadn't smoked in a long time, but I needed one now. The first inhalation warmed my lungs as I followed the worn, uneven flagstone path to the street.

I headed east along Tofet Street. It was the first time I had seen the old neighborhood since I left home to join the service as soon as I turned eighteen. That was over thirty years ago. Since then, it seemed I had lived another lifetime in Philadelphia with an ex-wife and a grown daughter. Westenhuck, Connecticut was about as far away from Philly socially, culturally, and just about every other way, even if not so much geographically, but this was where I was rooted.

You can't go home again.

Yeah, right.

Thomas Wolfe didn't know what the hell he was talking about.

As I looked around, I was amazed how so much had changed. Rooftops that once supported TV antennas now had satellite dishes and solar panels affixed to them. Above ground pools were replaced by Gunite and Fiberglass in-ground pools. Few shade trees remained, but there were a couple freestanding plastic speed bumps in the street to slow down traffic. A new cross street, Arcadia Way, had been paved through a portion of the empty lot where I used to play baseball and dodgeball with my friends. The houses were bigger and the lots sizes were immense, with a major portion of the once vast woods along the east side of the neighborhood clear-cut to accommodate the mini mansions.

It was sad in a way, and I felt a pang of guilt deep inside, like I had abandoned an old friend. I quickly brushed the thought away. I didn't owe this place anything. If my father hadn't died, I wouldn't have come back at all.

My ambivalence about the past transcended my apathy about my father's death. My childhood, for a while at least, had been a joyful time in my life, filled with the bittersweet experiences of youth, though that made me wonder if memory could be trusted at all.

It was hard to believe this was the same place where, as a boy, I played barefoot all summer long, my feet and ankles caked with dirt until September. I had walked to elementary school through the woods at the end of the street. It was the neighborhood where on Halloween's past I dressed up as a werewolf, Jack the Ripper, and Mr. Hyde, and went trick-or-treating. There had been a time when I truly enjoyed everything about Halloween; the scary decorations, wearing creepy costumes, the mischief, and the free candy. But that had changed too, hadn't it.

Feeling a little lightheaded from the smoke, I considered walking back to the house, but continued on instead. Although that night was Halloween, none of the houses had a single decoration visible anywhere, inside or out. I approached the faded blue clapboard Cape where Richard and Mike Fortin used to live. I did practically everything with the two brothers. Their house had been the one where all the neighborhood kids congregated, and it was where most of the memorable events happened. When I closed my eyes, smoky images from decades ago winked open in my mind: the crab apple incident with Mrs. DiCenzo; the legendary snowball fight that sent Eric Houston to the emergency room; and my first kiss. Stacey was a cute Korean girl who lived next door to the Fortins. If I wanted, I could still feel the remnants of the bitter sadness I experienced when she moved away, and even though her family had only relocated to the next town over, it may as well have been the moon because I never saw her again. When a black family moved into their old house, I became good friends with Mark, a boy my age. I played sports at school with him. He excelled at baseball and football, and any other athletic activity he tried. Even though I was an awkward kid, all elbows and knees, Mark always picked me first to be on his team.

I smiled remembering the long-ago summer afternoon when me and the Fortin brothers climbed a tree in their backyard and lobbed overripe crab apples over their house into the yard directly across the street where Mrs. DiCenzo's was working in her garden. We couldn't see the old woman, but we could hear her yelling in Italian as the fruit bombs exploded on the ground all around her. Mike nearly fell out of the tree he was laughing so hard.

Eric Houston lived at the very end of the street with his father, who was always home and ready to come charging out his front door to yell at anyone who got too close and touched the chain link fence that penned his modest property. If Eric had a mother, no one ever saw her. Eric was older, and always in trouble with the law, disappearing for long periods of time. When he wasn't at the training school for boys, he was home terrorizing everyone in the neighborhood. I could still clearly recall the snowy afternoon when Eric and his gang suddenly appeared in front of Mike and Richard's house and started a snowball fight that would be talked about for years afterward. It was raised to legendary status when Mikey hit Eric on the side of the face with a rock he had encased in wet snow. The impact tore Eric's cheek open. There was blood everywhere. Eight stiches were required to close the gash.

Stacey had watched the entire incident from the window of her house. She was two years older than me, and I had a crush on her since I was in second grade. She had a brother in high school who spent a lot of time with their father in their garage, either working under the hood on the engine of the family car or repairing some appliance, a phone, lamp wire, or other household item. I would sometimes wander over to watch them, and Mr. Hahn always welcomed me, taking the time to explain what he was doing, and even letting me help on one or two occasions. As a bonus, when I visited the Hahn's, there was also the chance that I might see Stacey. One Sunday morning when I was twelve, I saw their garage door open and I walked over, but her father and brother weren't home. Stacey came out and told me that they had gone to the hardware store. She asked me if I wanted something to drink and invited me inside. She poured me a glass of soda, and then to my complete and utter surprise, she told me I was cute before leaning over and kissing me on the mouth. It probably only lasted a second, but I can still feel it today. Her lips were warm and moist, and they tasted like strawberry. I couldn't remember if I said anything to her afterward, I was in such a state of shock and exhilaration. Her father and brother returned home a short while later, and although nothing ever came from this innocent encounter, my life changed that day. Up to that point, I had been curious about girls, but I never fully understood why older boys made such a fuss about them, until that kiss. She moved away and I never saw her again, but I still think about her from time to time, wondering where she might be, and how her life had gone. Now, I wondered what happened to all of them.

I stopped where the street used to dead end. This was where the new street, Arcadia, bisected Tofet and branched off into a whole new neighborhood. At the intersection was a small copse of trees. It was all that remained of an expansive tract of woods that dominated the entire area when I was a kid. Somewhere beyond the brambles and milkweed was a forbidden cabin and a haunted forest playground, a world of dark, hidden secrets where fear lingered and waited.

I pulled the half-finished cigarette from my mouth and flicked it to the ground at the edge of the woods. Then I took in a lungful of fresh air and exhaled sharply as I stared into the dimness past the stand of trees in front of me. There was no logical reason for me to go any further. I thought this journey had ended decades ago, but before I knew it, I was wending my way through the heavy underbrush.

While it had been my father's death that brought me home, it could only be the lonely child in me that wanted to explore what was off-limits.

The mini forest was shrouded in deep shadow. The sunlight was unable to penetrate the awning of branches and leaves overhead, creating the illusion of dusk. Prickly vines and shrubs snagged my clothes, some of the thorns penetrating deep enough to tear the skin beneath, drawing blood. Progress was slow, but as I advanced, I didn't remember the old cabin being this far from the street. I was beginning to think that it had resigned to gravity and had fallen to the ground, or perhaps torn down by the children who now occupied the neighborhood.

Then I saw it.

Remarkably, it was just as I remembered it, although maybe smaller than it once seemed. It didn't seem to have aged the way everything else in the neighborhood had. It was the same ramshackle cabin composed of warped plywood with a slump-shouldered, single-pitched roof, like a lean-to that didn't abut anything. About eight feet square, it was little more than a shack, but in the preternatural twilight, it took on a more sinister appearance.

The structure was fixed defiantly amid a carpet of decaying leaves and desiccated tree branches. It was guarded in shadow and fortified with the terror of past generations of school children. Seeing it again terrified the child in me so thoroughly that I wanted to run away, just as I had done the last time I'd seen it. But there was nowhere to run this time. I had to face the terror.

Like everything else in the neighborhood, this structure was provincial, with a cryptic nature known only to a few. Even now, its odious presence gave me pause, but I didn't stop. I continued to move forward slowly until I was close enough to peer into the glassless window on the side of the shack. I stopped, unable to see a thing beyond the black square.

I began to tremble remembering that last time I stood on the very spot I was now. It was a raw and chilly afternoon, just like this one. I was eleven, having gone out for my last Halloween the night before dressed as a pirate. I'd worn a bunch of old clothes, rain boots, a red bandana on my head, and an eye patch fabricated out of a black sock. My stepmother gave me a pair of cheap clip-on earrings and smudged some dark makeup on my face to make it look like I had a couple days' growth of beard. Mark was a robot. It was just a big cardboard box spray-painted gray that he walked around in, but it looked cool. Mike and Richard were vampires. They had a set of those plastic glow-in-the-dark teeth in their mouths, so you couldn't hear a thing they were saying. We would ring doorbells and they would yell, "Rick or reet!"

Every house in the neighborhood put up Halloween decorations of some kind, whether it was orange lights strung up around their doors and porches, paper cut outs of witches and ghosts in the windows, or handmade scarecrows in the yard. My house didn't have anything. My father turned off all the lights in the house so no kids would come to the door as he sat in the dark and drank beer in front of the television.

We stayed out for three hours, going around practically the whole town with pillowcases until they were half full with candy. This was in an era when people would give out full size bars, not that bite-size crap that's hardly worth unwrapping to get to what was inside. It was around nine o'clock when we called it quits, and by the time we got back to our neighborhood all the front lights were dark and there wasn't anyone else out. All the while I felt like someone was watching us, and while I noticed that my friends had gotten quiet and seemed to be a little nervous, we didn't talk about it. Mark got dropped off first, and as we headed to the Fortins house, I felt the presence more strongly. Something skulking in the shadows behind us. Once they were safely inside, I felt better as I crossed the street to my house, but the door was locked. I was about to knock when something jumped out from behind the hedges. Before I knew what was happening, my bag of candy was ripped from my hands and a moment later I was struck on the side of the head with it. I actually saw stars. I never knew how painful being hit with ten pounds of chocolate would be, but I was knocked off my feet. When my eyes regained focus, I saw Eric Houston standing over me. He was wearing dark clothes and a black knit cap on his head that trapped the tangles of his long red hair and pushed them down around the sides of his pimply face.

"Don't tell anyone about this," he snarled. "You hear me, loser?"

Before I could respond, he took off across the yard and down the street with my sack of candy. I felt my face already swelling as I got up off the ground and went around the back of the house, raising the window in my bedroom just enough for me to slither through.

The next day I went to school looking like a real pirate from a black eye Eric Houston gave me when he hit me with my own candy. On my walk home, I took the usual shortcut through the woods, following the winding path which took me within a stone's throw of the shack. I could see it clearly through the trees whose leaves were thinning and dropping all around me. It seemed old even back then, probably built by children a generation or two before. Me and my friends always made sure we steered clear of the shack, never daring to venture any closer to it than the edge of the path. The parents warned their kids about an unnamed monster that lived in the shack, and everyone believed them. My father had explained to me years earlier that honest-to-God monsters did, in fact, exist. He said that every neighborhood had one, and that our neighborhood monster lived in the woods at the end of the street, and the shack was where it would lure boys and punish them for being bad. My father laughed through his nicotine-stained teeth as went on further to tell me that our monster was a shapeless and formless creature that could hide anywhere in nature, but it preferred living inside people, and that once it got inside a person it couldn't come out until the person dies, then it would invade someone else.

As I got older, my belief in the local legend diminished, but I still kept away from the shack. At least until that day after Halloween when I was eleven. I didn't know what compelled me to step off the path and walk up to the shack that day, but I recalled feeling nothing at the time, not even fear. It was as if I had been hypnotized, or in the grip of some dream in which I played only an observational role, with no power to act and no free will. As I approached the window and peered inside, I saw my pillowcase lying on the dirt floor and candy bars spattered with blood strewn all around it. Somehow, this sight didn't surprise me. In fact, it was as if I had been expecting it. At the same moment, I became aware that the neighborhood monster was waiting for me. I sensed it lurking in a dark corner. It couldn't see it, but I knew it was there, watching me.

Suddenly the pillowcase began to shift and contort. I told myself that it was a racoon or some other animal rummaging around inside for a piece of candy that it preferred over the bloody chocolate bars on the ground, but I was lying to myself. When something came out of the window and touched the top of my hand, it instantly snapped me out of the semi-conscious state I had been in up to that point. The sudden influx of terror in my system burnt in my gut like acid and I was afraid I might keel over right there. I didn't get a good look at what had reached out to me because as soon as it brushed up against my skin, I turned and ran out of the woods as fast as my legs would carry me. I was too petrified to look behind me as I raced home, across my front lawn, and into the house. Once in my room, I jumped into bed, burying myself beneath the covers.

The next few days, whenever I looked out my bedroom window, I expected to see some hideous amorphous creature shambling out of the woods toward my house.

I never told another living soul about what I saw in the shack that day, just as I never told my friends that Eric Houston stole my Halloween candy. I knew that the neighborhood monster wanted me to go to the cabin alone that day, wanted me to go inside to get my candy. But I didn't go inside. Not then.

Maybe the monster had gotten others to go inside at one time or another, and now, after all these years, the neighborhood monster was calling me back again.

Presently, there wasn't enough light to see much of anything as I peered inside through the dark eye that was the structure's sole window. I drew a deep breath and walked toward the side of the ageless shack where the hinged plywood door was located. As I turned the corner, I could see that no more than thirty yards from that side of the cabin the woods ended abruptly. Where once the cabin had rested in the middle of the woods, it seemed now as if it was trying to escape, moving closer to the edge of civilization. The distinct line between nature and urban development was stark, punctuated by a marked desecration of trees. In the middle of a massive swathe of naked earth brooded the somnolent bulk of a yellow, steel earth mover, a sentinel of destruction awaiting its orders to complete the final phase of construction on a new shopping plaza which would be featuring a pharmacy, a fast-food restaurant, a pet groomer, and a pizzeria.

I realized at once what this represented; it was not the cabin that was vanishing, but just the opposite. The landscape of the entire neighborhood was about to change forever, and the neighborhood monster was being purged along with it.

Facing the cabin door, I approached it slowly. I was prepared to enter, but I hesitated.

What was I going to find inside, I asked myself.

The boogeyman?

I closed my eyes momentarily and told myself I wouldn't find anything because there was nothing in there to find. I understood that childhood monsters were ephemeral, like youth, and only children could empower them. Adults had their own monsters to contend with. Instead of residing in forest cabins, behind closed closet doors, and beneath beds, some monsters dwelled in the human soul, in souls that were corrupted in some way as children. These monsters lay hidden, not in old shacks or in sewer drains, but dwelling unseen and unsuspected behind deceptive charms and the personable guises of relatives, friends, and neighbors. These monsters look like everybody else, and therein lies the greatest danger. Maybe, in that sense, every neighborhood did have their own monster. They're everywhere, but difficult to identify because they are not mythical beasts, but real flesh and blood monsters. This makes sense because it's flesh and blood that drives them. Not surprisingly, the targets of these opportunist monsters are often children, so easy to plant the seed of corruption into, and come harvest time the only thing reaped is further abuse. Because it was this shack where my father sometimes took me to brutalize me so my mother wouldn't see.

Behind me, the tractor shot forward with a jerk, snorting a cable of thick, black smoke from the exhaust stack.

With a creak, the cabin door slowly swung inward. It made it halfway on its rusty hinges and then just stopped, revealing only darkness inside. A moment later, a marble-sized ball of chocolate wrapped in purple foil rolled out of the shadows and came to a rest near my feet.

I briefly closed my eyes again as a vile stench, like vinegar and putrefied meat, assailed my nostrils. When I looked back down at the chocolate, a black, stringy substance was leaking out of folds in the foil. The gummy material exuding from the candy wrapper continued to flow out slowly and spread across the dirt floor, collecting in a large puddle. The miasma it produced made me gag. My gut lurched involuntarily and my throat convulsed as a I made a retching sound. Nothing came up because I hadn't eaten a thing all day.

The inky accretion began to bubble and swell, developing like an alien fetus. It gradually transmogrified into the shape of an amorphous creature. It approximated the torso of a man and the head of a sightless monster, the anatomy of its face indecipherable. Within the semi-solid oozing mass were bits of hair, bone, and sinew. A swirling mass of digested humanity.

Lying prone, with three malformed legs splayed out uselessly behind it, the monstrosity shifted suddenly and began to drag itself toward me on arms that could not adequately support its weight. As it sloshed closer, the middle of its face parted, exposing a maw with no gullet as viscous fluid dripped back down over the cavity, covering it. The thing issued a horrible shriek that produced a bubbling effect throughout its gelatinous frame. The dreadful cry echoed in my head, and I found myself unable to move. It was as if my own skeletal system had dissolved, leaving me an unsupported collection of flesh.

Behind me, the iron machine screamed to full tilt, the bucket of the tractor raised high.

From the darkness at the back of the shack, I heard my father's voice. "Every neighborhood's got one," he said and laughed.

As the tractor bore down on the shack, the laughter grew louder, and the door opened fully.

***

Back at the house, I entered unnoticed, as if I had never left. My stepmother did not say a word about the wet leaves and dirt I tracked in with me, or my soiled and torn clothes.

When everyone else had gone, I gave my stepmother a dutiful peck on the cheek and announced that I was leaving. She nodded and watched me walk out the front door without a word passing between us.

When I got into my car, I peeled the purple foil from the chocolate candy ball. A stringy, dark fluid erupted and ran down my hands. Driving past the older houses on Tofet Street and then the new houses on Arcadia Way, I licked the sticky matter from my fingers until there was nothing left. As I left the neighborhood and got onto the interstate, I tried to recall the sound of my father's voice, but I could not.

Twilight Care
Jade Jiao

Car headlights. Someone was shining them directly through the bedroom window, so bright they were blinding. My head roared. There was noise, I think. Maybe buzzing. A crawling, fluttering thing in my ear. Or, maybe the hum of an engine, or the low chatter of a large crowd. Time seemed to slow to a crawl and, unable to rouse myself, I tossed and turned for hours. I was fitful. Disorientated. As though I were in the throes of a high fever.

In the soft silence of the following morning, I couldn't be sure if there really had been light and noise, or if it had been a dream. I supposed it was probably normal to feel unrested, *disturbed*, after your mother's funeral.

I should have started with that detail, shouldn't I?

I'd probably slept badly because my mother was dead.

Not that I was devastated or anything like that, we weren't close, but the paperwork of a death is always stressful. A hassle. Of course, my brother wasn't going to fly over to deal with all the arrangements, so it was left to me. *As always...* Nobody on the street had come; it had been a very small affair. Half of them wouldn't have known where they were even if they *had* been dragged out. Would have been a waste of time for everyone.

I'd be leaving in a day, once I'd sorted a few more things and gathered the last of the valuables. We'd sell the property (if it could be sold) and *that*, as they say, *would be that*.

I stood in my pyjamas on the cold kitchen tiles, waiting for the kettle to boil. It was very strange to be back. The appearance of the place hadn't changed a jot since I was a child, except for the terrible decay that had encroached on the familiar features of the structure. Damp had seeped in at the corners of rooms, dirtying the wallpaper. Thick dust and grime had settled on the shelves. And in all the dark places were multi-generational collections of daddy longlegs that made me shudder. The neighbouring houses, and their occupants, seemed to be similarly decomposing. I'd remembered them as they'd been forty years ago, when they'd been younger than I was now. When the street was loud with the sounds of children playing. So much life. It had all since rotted away. The children were like me, middle-aged and notable by their absence, and the parents were either at death's door or already through it. The remaining survivors were invariably infirm: mentally, physically, or both. And they were all stuck, isolated on this lonely little estate at the top of the hill, living out their final days. An island unto itself. I couldn't wait to leave.

I should have come more often probably, should have visited her, but life happens. And my brother never bothered, so it wasn't just me. Schedules are busy. Anyway, it hardly mattered now.

I was looking out of the window to the overgrown back garden, unkempt and wild in the morning mist, when something behind a mass of foliage moved slightly and caught my eye. I squinted. There was a foot. Two feet. Greyish and bare, damp in the dew. Still half-asleep, I struggled to process what I was seeing. My eyes travelled upwards, then it hit me all at once. I gasped.

David Greenwood. He stood very still, mostly hidden by a tree. *Completely naked.* For a long, hideous moment, we were both petrified, staring at each other. Then, the kettle came to a boil and clicked, snapping me out of my paralysis. I dashed to the door.

"Mr. Greenwood, what are you doing?" I shouted from the threshold. I shivered. The temperature couldn't have been above zero.

"Is that little Jenny Smith?" he asked. I was, *had been*, little Jenny Smith. I was rather more big Jenny now. I was impressed he remembered me.

I hesitated, then rushed back inside and fetched a large blanket from a bedding chest. I ran back downstairs and crossed the garden as though approaching a wild deer, with slow, nervous steps. Keeping my eyes up, I reached him and placed the blanket over his shoulders like a cape. He seemed so small and frail, a shadow of his former shelf. I knew he'd been going downhill, I had his daughter on social media and I wasn't above having the occasional nosey at her personal life, but I didn't know it was this bad. Dementia is truly a cruel illness.

"Come on, Mr. Greenwood," I said. "You've wandered away from home. We need to get you back. It's too cold for this nonsense."

"No," he whimpered. "I don't want to go there."

"Why not?"

"Not with *them*," he murmured. "They've taken Jan away."

Jan was David's wife. "What do you mean?" I asked. "Let's go and see her now." David looked around like a frightened child, unsure of what to do. "Come on," I said, and at arm's length, guided him through the garden gate and back across the street.

I knocked at the Greenwoods' door. A young girl I didn't recognise answered. She wore a purple uniform and was pale, her hair scraped back into a tight bun that gave her a severe look. Her eyes flicked from me to David.

"He got out," she muttered in a monotone.

"I found him in my garden," I said. "He could have frozen to death. He's got nothing on."

"I don't know you," the girl said, regarding me with suspicion.

"He needs helping right away. He'll catch his death."

"He must have escaped through the back," she said. There was no sign of concern on her face. No urgency at all. I was flabbergasted.

"Inside straight away," I said. "Do you need help running him a bath or something?"

The girl pulled David inside, rather more roughly than seemed necessary. She stared at me blankly.

"Is Mrs. Greenwood in?" I asked, peeking my head around the girl and into the dim hallway.

"No," she said, then slammed the door, almost hitting me in the nose.

I blinked in surprise. *How absolutely bizarre.* I didn't know if I'd ever met someone so ill-suited to their role before. Though, they do say that careers are extremely poorly paid. *Minimum wage, minimum effort?* I shook my head and turned to leave.

It was then that I noticed the van parked on the Greenwoods' drive. *Twilight Care.* "Care" indeed. I wondered if I should look them up and make a complaint. *After I'd finished some more work at the house*, I decided. If I kept wasting time, I'd end up stuck here another day, and that would never do.

I began by going through a fat, unorganised stack of papers and documents, shredding the vast majority. I worked efficiently, flipping my way through wads of slips and receipts, expired warranties, and bank statements. As I picked up a fresh batch, a printed calendar for the month of November drifted to the ground. It was torn, half of it missing, but still visible at the top were the letters *TWI – CA –*. I picked it up for a closer inspection. Someone had written my mother's name, Mrs. Smith, in the top lefthand corner and, on every visible Sunday, Tuesday, and Thursday, this person had placed a large X. I frowned. Had my mother been receiving care? She'd never mentioned it during our semi-annual phone call, and neither had my brother. I wasn't pleased to think it had been provided by *these people*. I sincerely hoped it hadn't been the same girl who was looking after David. She didn't exactly have what I'd call a pleasant bedside manner, or indeed basic competency.

Another *Twilight Care* vehicle trundled by and came to a stop outside the Doyles' house. Two young women climbed out of the front seats, both sporting the same tight bun on top of their heads, slamming the doors behind them in perfect unison. They, too, donned the purple uniform. Sort of like nurse scrubs. It seemed they had quite the monopoly going in this area. Pulling out my phone, I shot off a text to my brother to ask him about it, then got back to the task at hand. I found I kept one eye directed at the window to see if any more of them showed up.

By dusk, I had most of what I'd wanted to do, done, and the house was looking a lot more organised. I checked my phone, and saw I had a reply.

I didn't hire anyone, my brother had written, *I didn't know she had careers. Do I owe you?*

Had I hired them and forgotten about it? No, I'd never had a charge, and even if they do underpay their workers, care is expensive to the customer. I would have noticed if I'd been billed. Had mother hired them herself? I went back to examine her bank statements more carefully. Nothing there. Had she been paying with cash? That seemed unlikely. I went online and searched for the company. Various results popped up, but nothing in close proximity. Looking through the window, I checked one of the… now five… *Twilight*

Care vans parked up, to see if there was a telephone number or web address painted on the side. Nothing. I decided I would go and ask the Greenwoods' girl for the company's details directly.

I knocked at the front door and waited. The sun had set, and I pulled my coat tight around me, bouncing up and down to stay warm. Nobody came. I knocked again, then looked over my shoulder, with the prickly sensation of being watched. My eyes scanned over the various windows overlooking me, but nobody seemed to be there, so I chalked the feeling up to some grief-induced paranoia. Just as I was about to leave, the girl finally answered. I opened my mouth to speak, but then paused, my face turning hot.

There was something almost imperceptibly different about her, though I couldn't put my finger on exactly what. Her hair was the same, that tight bun, but something on her face had changed. It was as if her nose was just a fraction of a centimetre higher, or perhaps her eyes were a millimetre further apart. She wasn't how she had been. My heart sank as some ancient, lizard part of my brain told me to run. To get as far away from this person as quickly as I possibly could. Warning me with all the fury and panic it could muster. But that was ridiculous, of course. It was dark, and I'd only seen her for two minutes before. Of course her face hadn't changed. And yet…

"Yes?" she said.

"Hello again," I replied, doing my best to keep my voice steady and even, to not let the uncanny feeling win. "I was trying to find the contact details for your company but couldn't. Would you be able to give them to me? Please."

The girl stared at me for a moment. I wondered if she could tell what I was thinking. I smiled. Then, she got a pad of paper and a pencil from beside the Greenwoods' house phone and wrote down a number. She tore it off and gave it me.

"Thank you," I said. "Also, do you know if someone from your team was ever working at my mother's house? Number eight. I found a calendar that I think was marking the dates you cared for her, but my brother and I didn't know anything about it."

"We see everyone here," the girl said.

"So, my mother was paying for your services?"

The girl didn't answer. I saw David appear behind her at the end of the hall, barely visible in the shadows. His mouth was moving, mouthing something, though I couldn't make out what. The girl noticed my eyes and she turned to look at him.

"I need to go now," she said, and started to close the door.

"Wait!" I snapped, and pushed my foot into the door frame to stop her. "Can I speak to Mrs. Greenwood, please?"

"She's not here," the girl said, applying a steady amount of pressure to my foot with the door.

"Where is she? I think David is worried."

"She's gone out. Nobody needs to worry. I really have to go now."

Bowing to the literal pressure, I pulled my foot back, and the girl succeeded in shutting me out. My knees felt weak. My brain screamed that there was something very wrong with this girl. It took all my willpower not to run back to mother's house, but walk steadily and sensibly, maintaining a calm and rational mind. Clearly the stress of recent events was getting to me. After all, nothing had really happened, had it? Nothing tangible.

I picked up the landline and dialed the number I'd been given. The phone clicked a few times as I picked up the receiver, followed by a low, rushing noise that sounded like flowing water. I waited as it rang. *One, two, three...*

A shrill, high pitched whining blasted into my ear. I recoiled, almost dropping the handset. "Jesus!" I shouted.

"*Twilight Care*," someone on the other end of the line said, just barely audible over the racket.

"Hello? We've got a bad connection. I wanted to check about someone I think was in your care recently."

More clicking. That awful, grating, high-pitched screech. Growing louder.

"*Twilight Care*," the person repeated.

"Yes, hello? I need to know, did you have a Mrs. Carol Smith as a client?"

"We see everyone here," said the person on the other end of the line.

I shivered and slammed the phone down on instinct, as though swatting away an insect. Could it be, the girl had given me her own number to stop me from reporting her? The voice hadn't sounded like hers, but the turn of phrase…

Whether or not mother was in their care didn't matter, I decided. She was gone, and any snooping would only keep me in this miserable place for longer. And David Greenwood was none of my concern whatsoever. I set my mind to finishing up the last of my tasks and packing my bag as quickly as possible so that I could take off first thing in the morning.

I grabbed a roll of bubble wrap, ready to start packing some porcelain figurines to sell, when there came a knock at the door.

"Who is it?" I called, not moving to answer it.

"It's Mrs. Greenwood."

I went over, and fastened the chain lock, then cautiously opened the door a few inches. On the threshold stood Mrs. Greenwood, accompanied by the girl.

"You wanted to see her," said the girl.

"Oh, hello, Mrs. Greenwood. It's Jenny Smith," I said, eyeing her with concern.

"Yes. Hello," said Mrs. Greenwood.

"Have you just come back?" I asked. I hadn't noticed any cars coming down the street.

"Yes. I've just come back," she echoed.

"Where have you been?" I asked.

"I went to the shops."

"Ah, right." Mrs. Greenwood beamed at me with the most enormous smile, eyes unblinking, with the girl standing slightly behind her. I looked back to the Greenwood house, and saw the silhouette of David in the upstairs window, watching us. "Well, I don't want to keep you," I said.

Slowly, they both backed away, and travelled with small, backwards steps across the street, never once turning around. I watched in horror, our eye contact unbroken, then closed the door and locked it twice.

After a few more hours sorting, I fell into bed exhausted, and passed out almost instantly. More bad dreams, the same as the night before. The bright light. The noise. But I managed to snap myself out of it this time. Managed to move my rigid body and wake up. Groggily, I got out of bed and followed the sound. It was familiar. I tried to place it, then it rose in pitch. I covered my ears with my hands. A horrible whining. A deafening screech.

I crept to the window. Gripping the edge of the curtain, I pulled it back the tiniest fraction so I could peek outside. Looking down, my heart lurched, and I ducked lower out of sight. There were around ten of them. They sat in a tight circle, facing outwards, leaning back so that their hair buns touched in the center. The sound was emanating from their wide, open mouths. As I looked around, I saw my neighbours in their windows, watching along with me, their faces expressionless. And above, in the blackness of the sky, I thought I could make something out. Almost indiscernible in the cloud cover.

I fell. A haze descended. It hurt to breathe. More dazzling light. Then, suddenly, it was cold. Very cold. But there were familiar things to grasp on to. Tweeting. *What was that?* Birdsong. A little, red-breasted robin hopping along a fencepost. A light dusting of snow. I knew this place. *But how –*

I looked down and stared at my pale, bare feet on the grass, my nakedness covered only by scant foliage. A hand reached towards me, and I saw it was one of The *Twilight Care* girls. I pulled back, but she grasped my arm anyway, her skin smooth and moist to the touch.

"Come now," she said. "We see everyone here."

The Playground
Shawn Montgomery

A playground once appeared in the middle of a neighborhood.

Seemingly erected overnight, several immense structures dominated a lot previously occupied by poison sumac trees and blackberry brambles. Nobody saw any construction crews. There were no ribbon cutting ceremonies or news coverage of its opening.

Lucian Graves Neighborhood Park just… *materialized.*

James Ramsay received an early-morning text from his best friend, Billy Halloway, informing him of this magnificent new playground. After breakfast, the boys hopped on their bikes and raced there as fast as they could.

Although it was still morning, an assembly of kids were already climbing along the massive, glistening structures, and for a long moment, the pair stood quietly at the park's entrance, their mouths agape.

A sprawling swing set clutched firmly onto at least ten shimmering swings. Beside the swings stood a hulking dome, intersected by an intricate web of thick climbing ropes. And then the park's centerpiece—a looming tower made up of three sloped tiers, intertwined with tunnels, wooden bridges, and climbing poles. Two radiant kiddy slides stretched from the tower's sides like appendages, while a much larger tube slide corkscrewed down at least twenty feet before spitting kids out at the bottom.

Billy pointed to the lacquered wooden sign. "Who the heck is Lucian Graves? Does he live in the neighborhood or something?"

"Beats me," James said, shrugging. "Probably some rich guy who donated it. Who cares, let's play!"

After climbing across the monkey bars, James pushed himself atop and took in the frenetic scene. It was organized chaos below, no adult supervision to be seen. He initially began looking for Billy, but soon became distracted by a large group of kids playing tag. He watched a few of them race to the top of the climbing tower before throwing themselves into the tube slide in a manic succession.

When the first boy reemerged, he continued running, squealing with laughter. He was followed by his friend, who immediately began stumbling toward the swings before falling to his knees, gripping the sides of his head.

Finally, the last kid tumbled out and staggered to a nearby bench. His face was pallid and sweaty, and as soon as he sat down, reeled over and began vomiting.

James thought this strange, but his attention was quickly diverted to the sight of Billy, shirking under the rope dome and looking utterly overwhelmed. A gaggle of kids scurried around the boy, as he pressed himself against the cables, gnawing on his fingernails.

James was about to call to his friend when he spotted Corey Fielding standing next to the swing set, surveying the playground. The older boy's predatory glare finally settled on Billy, his mouth widening with deranged joy. After hawking out a dark glob beside his sneaker, Corey sauntered over to the dome.

Billy didn't notice the older boy until it was too late.

Slipping through the taut webbing, Corey smirked. "Hey, little shit!" he shouted. "If I were you, I'd start running!"

At first, Billy grinned dopily like he was in on the joke, but when he realized how serious Fielding was, he began to look around the playground with increasing desperation. He opened his mouth to say something, stopped himself, and scampered to the climbing tower instead.

Fielding waited a few seconds before giving chase.

Billy immediately tripped over the metal steps and almost fell onto the first platform. "Help me!" he squealed, his voice drowned out by the surrounding din.

After finally stumbling to the top, he spotted James on the monkey bars. They held each other's eyes for a long moment.

"Help!" the boy cried again.

What do I do? What should I do? James thought frantically. It was too late to run up the structure and do anything now. Even if he had a chance, would he have the guts to confront somebody like Corey Fielding?

The only thing he could think of was to point at the tube slide. "Go down it, Billy! Hurry!"

Billy turned just as Corey stomped onto the platform.

"Leave me alone!" he cried.

Corey released a maniacal, high-pitched laugh, then reached out and pinched the boy's arm. Billy yelped like a wounded puppy, and leaped back against the lip of the slide.

"Go away!" the boy screeched. Corey laughed again and took a step closer.

Finally, Billy shot James a terrified look, then crouched down and lunged, head first, into the tube.

Several seconds passed.

Even though the slide was longer than most, it shouldn't have taken long for Billy to go down, unless he had stopped himself inside. Which is what James thought his best friend had wisely done.

Corey lowered his head and peered inside the chute. When Billy still hadn't reemerged, the older boy shrugged and began hopping back down the tower.

Right as he made it to the bottom, a shrill howl echoed from within the slide.

A second later, it dumped Billy out.

Once his feet touched the ground, the boy ran blindly around the playground as if he was being stung by wasps. The back of his t-shirt had been torn into ribbons, and flapped around his body like wet tendrils. Deep, short gouges zigzagged across his flesh, rivulets of blood spraying several kids who were standing nearby.

"Mommy! Help me!" he wailed, sprinting toward the street.

Some kids began shrieking and ran to their bikes, others fumbled with their phones.

James remained frozen on the monkey bars, overwhelmed with shock.

What happened to him? he thought helplessly. *Why is he bleeding?*

He then made eye contact with Corey Fielding.

With a dumbfounded expression on his face, Corey shook his head in disbelief and shouted, "I didn't do that to him, I swear!"

Three days later, James visited his friend.

Billy's mother answered the door, and quietly ushered him to his friend's bedroom.

He found the boy nestled in a mountain of blankets, watching something on his tablet. Billy looked like he had somehow shrunk, his face ghostly white against the blue comforter draped across his bandaged body.

"Hey, man, how are you doing?" James asked.

"Hey," Billy said, wincing. "I'm pretty sore but I'm alive."

"Do they know what happened?"

Billy shook his head. "The doctors think that I was attacked by something hiding in the slide. There were claw marks. They said I was lucky that nothing was severed or broken."

James recalled the image of his friend fleeing from the playground, his back spurting blood, his voice shrieking.

"Did you see anything come out of the slide after I left?"

"No," James said. "Everybody was freaking out, so something might have run out of there when we weren't looking. What do you remember?"

His bottom lip quivering, Billy's eyes began to well with tears. "I dunno, man," he stammered, his voice sounding as thin as paper. "All I remember is sliding down and thinking that it was too hot inside there. And then I remember going fast…too fast. And then…"

He paused, the words hanging in the air like specks of dust. He then closed his eyes and reached for a stuffed bear that was half-hidden under a pillow.

"And then," he continued, "it got real dark and I couldn't see anything, and then I guess I blacked out. The next thing I remember was sliding out and feeling like somebody was stabbing me in the back with scissors. I really thought I was going to die."

James remained silent, unsure of what to say.

Finally, Billy asked if he'd been back to the playground. James shook his head.

"Good," Billy whispered hoarsely. "There's something wrong with that place. The doctor said I can get out of bed and start walking around next week, but my mom said I can only hang out in our yard, which is fine with me. I don't ever wanna go back to that place. Promise you won't go to that park again, James. Pinkie swear it."

Caught up in the moment, James nodded automatically and lifted his hand, pinkie finger extended. "I won't go back there. I promise."

Despite his intentions, an eleven-year old's nagging curiosity was stronger than the vows made between friends. The following day, James found himself heading back to Lucian Graves Neighborhood Park.

The playground was mostly empty, except for a few kids hanging out on the swings.

To his dismay, James saw Corey Fielding, but didn't recognize the other kid who was with him.

He *was* surprised to find Trina Murphy with them, however. Trina lived two streets over, and although she was in a grade higher than James, they went to the same school.

With sparkling blue eyes, long red hair that was usually braided down her back, and a galaxy of freckles adorning her face and arms, Trina was an object of pure beauty to the boy's pre-pubescent self.

Keeping his eyes to the ground, James warily approached the swings.

"Hello, James," she called out.

"Hey," he mumbled, feeling heat rushing to his cheeks.

Trying hard not to make eye contact with her, he turned to Corey and his friend.

"What's up?" he mumbled.

"'Sup," Corey replied indifferently.

His friend nodded, saying nothing.

The kids exchanged small talk before Trina brought up Billy's accident.

"Were you here when it happened too?" she asked James.

"Yeah," he said, nodding. "It was crazy. Corey was chasing him—"

"I didn't do shit to him and you know it!"

James felt a tinge of panic grip his stomach, but remained calm. "I didn't say you did, man…chill."

The group began sharing theories of what had happened: did somebody put broken glass in the slide? Maybe Billy had somehow slid across shards of plastic?

James shared what Billy had told him about a rabid animal attack.

He then asked if they had gone down the slide.

Corey and his friend scowled, but didn't respond.

"I haven't yet, but I'm not afraid to," Trina said, hopping from her swing and skipping over to the slide. She placed her hand along the plastic shell then jerked it away. "Wow, this thing is really hot," she said, rubbing her palm against her shorts.

"So are you gonna go down it or not?" Corey's friend teased.

"If you're so anxious about somebody doing it, Aiden, why don't *you* climb up here!"

"I will," Aiden replied, his voice cracking. "Right after you."

"Chicken shit," Trina mumbled.

The girl gracefully leaped up the platforms. When she was at the top, she peered over the thin railing. "Okay," she shouted, "here goes nothing!"

She sat down and began shimmying inside the tube, but suddenly stopped.

"Hurry up!" Aiden squealed.

"It's burning my legs, butthole!" she cried. "I don't see you running up here so shut your mouth!"

"You don't have to, you know," James blurted. "We can just hang out here longer or get something to eat?"

Trina stood back up. Her braided hair dangled over the railing, oddly reminding James of a red-headed Rapunzel. "I know I don't," she said, smirking. "But I wanna show these jerks that I'm not afraid of going down a stupid slide. Wait for me at the bottom."

James heard the thudding of her body entering the plastic chute, then a softer thump as she went around the first corkscrew turn.

When she was about halfway down, he heard her release a faint, surprised cry.

And then it was quiet.

The boys waited several seconds, exchanging puzzled glances at one another. Finally, James ran over and peered inside.

"Where is she?" Corey asked. "What's wrong?"

James couldn't see anything other than the reddish-orange gleam from the tube's walls. An odd burning smell wafted out, reminding him of freshly laid blacktop.

He touched the outer shell and immediately flung his hand away. It *was* extraordinarily hot, as if the slide was constructed of tin instead of temperature-resistant polyurethane.

"Hey Trina, are you okay?" he called into the tube.

No response.

"Where is she?" Corey barked again, his voice wavering with panic.

"I don't know," James mumbled.

For the next several minutes, the boys huddled at the bottom of the slide and took turns calling for the girl. They banged sticks along the plastic shell, and peered inside, hoping to catch a glimpse of Trina's hands or feet.

Aiden found a large rock and rolled it down the slide. It banged violently against the walls before dropping to the ground with a soft thud.

After an hour, the boys grew increasingly confused, then afraid.

And as the sun began to set, bathing the playground in an eerie reddish glow, they reluctantly gave up and went home.

Several hours later, James was awakened by his mother, asking if he had seen Trina at the playground earlier. The boy answered her questions truthfully, insisting he didn't know where she had gone.

"This isn't a game, James," she finally snapped, her voice trembling. "Her parents are worried sick! She didn't come home!"

James's eyes began to water. "I'm not lying! She just disappeared, I swear!"

The following morning, James spoke to a detective, then Trina's parents, who took turns drilling him with questions that didn't satisfy either of them.

The Lucian Graves Neighborhood Park was cordoned off with yellow crime tape while the police investigated the playground and surrounding lot. Some of the adults took turns canvassing the neighborhood, and stapling photocopies of Trina's school picture onto telephone poles.

But despite the neighborhood's efforts, Trina Murphy remained missing.

A week later, James awoke screaming.

He sat up in his bed, arms braced behind him, his voice bouncing off the walls. He panicked, not recognizing the shadows in the room, then remembered he was in his bedroom. He was okay. He was safe. Nothing could hurt him. It had only been a dream.

Although the nightmare had begun to drift away, the raw terror the boy felt was still vivid. He knew it was about Trina and the playground, and although the details were hazy, he was gripped by a strong, nagging sense that she was still trapped inside the slide.

The thought of her squirming in that tube in the dark made him feel nauseous. Would anybody hear her? Could anybody help?

Driven by fear and instinct, the boy flung himself out of bed and quickly got dressed.

Going to the playground in the middle of the night was crazy, he knew, but this intense feeling that Trina needed help...needed *his* help...was simply overwhelming.

Not wanting to waste any more time, the boy crept downstairs and left his house.

The neighborhood was eerily quiet, the night thick with humidity.

As he rode his bike, James thought about his parents, his pet cat, his bedroom. I should go home, he told himself. This is stupid!

But then he saw Billy fleeing from the park, his body ravaged…and the blood. He could still hear the boy's terrified screams echoing in his head.

And then he heard Trina's last words—*wait for me at the bottom.*

And her dream voice, begging him to save her.

The playground was predictably deserted, the police tape still stretched across most of the park's perimeter.

Holding his breath, James ducked underneath the tape and entered the park. The shadowy forms of the structures appeared alive and awake, and the boy felt a creeping sensation that he was interrupting something he didn't quite understand.

Shivering, James tip-toed over to the climbing tower.

He tentatively stuck his head inside the tube, and was welcomed by a warm, acrid gust that coated his nostrils and the back of his throat.

"Trina?" he called. "Are you in here?"

Nearby, a dog barked, but it was otherwise quiet.

As if in a trance, the boy crept up the platforms. He briefly peered over the top railing and into the impenetrable darkness, gripped by a feeling that he was hovering over a bottomless pit.

Finally, he let out a low, shuddering breath and crouched down in front of the slide. "Hello! Is anybody inside here?"

Nothing.

In a soft, uncertain voice, he murmured, "Don't worry, I'm coming to get you."

James then sat down and began shimmying himself inside the tube. A gust of stale air wafted out, and he briefly panicked, certain the walls were closing in on him.

After taking several deep breaths, he sighed wearily, and whispered, "Okay, here goes nothing."

Finally, James Ramsey let go of the rim and pushed himself forward.

Just as Billy had described, the slide was unusually fast, and after taking the first turn, the boy dropped sharply. *Five feet…ten feet…fifteen feet.*

James didn't know how far he was plummeting, but felt like he should had been at the bottom already. Instead, he continued dropping.

Veering around the second turn, James slammed hard against the wall as a surge of hot, gummy air swept over his body. An electrical charge began filling the tube, a prickling barrier of static that the boy could feel on the hairs along the back of his neck. He opened his mouth to scream, but instead, released a series of gasping, winded breaths.

Attempting to slow himself, James stretched and pressed his hands and legs against the sides of the walls. The skin in his palms instantly burned and his wrists and ankles snapped back. James howled in pain, but his voice sounded faint, like it was coming from somewhere far away.

Soon, the tube seemed to hum and buckle, burning hot as a furnace, and surrounding the boy in a forge of white heat. The heaviness began to rush in around him, sucking up all of the oxygen.

After swerving around another abrupt turn, James finally collided into something. The force of the impact was immense, as if he had been hit by a car, and his body crumpled into a ball.

Before he had a chance to react, a large and heavy form began to crawl up the boy's legs and onto his chest, driving the tiny amount of air left in his lungs out.

A thousand pinpricks danced up his body, and when he managed to touch his chest, his hand was damp with blood. He opened his mouth to cry for help, but a torrent of putrid air filled his mouth, choking him. The insides of the slide began rattling around him, creating a deafening, thunderous roar that made his skull throb.

As he gasped for breath, a pair of cadaverous, blistering hands emerged from the gloom and wrapped themselves around the boy's ankles. Hot, tiny knives jabbed into his flesh.

James tried kicking at the thing, but discovered his arms and legs were useless now, paralyzed with pain.

A voice, thick and phlegmy, then spoke in his ear: *"You've come back for me! Now we go to the bottom!"*

The impenetrable darkness, and whatever was hiding inside of it, suddenly yanked hard on his legs, and the boy was dragged down to somewhere else entirely.

Nobody heard him screaming.

Colony
Matthew Piskun

The traffic drones on. I'm so used to it I don't even hear it anymore. The hum of engines and vibrating steel are a harmonic undertone to the rhythmic rattle of mufflers. My vision is clouded by monotony and the choking fog of commute, which spreads like a plague. My hands haven't moved off the wheel and my legs are numb from breaking and the vibrations of rubber on uneven road. Can't be late, not ever.

In my rearview mirror I see a black cloud, a slumbering black mass, waiting. The sky above swirls with low lying puffs of gray cumulus as a few rain droplets hit my windshield. I sigh and without even thinking I flip the wipers on.

***

I punch in one minute early, as always. Then I burn the tip of my tongue on the hot, black java, never learning, same as every morning for as long I remember.

My computer hums to life and the desktop picture appears, a toothpick construction of Notre Dame, Paris. I allow myself a moment to appreciate the model's impeccable symmetry. My eyes follow the curves of the three lower gothic arches and get lost in the gorgeous symmetry of the center rose window.

I check my voicemail as my e-mail inbox springs to life. All my work applications come alive, populating my screen, covering the grand toothpick cathedral same as they do every morning. The seat to my left is empty now. Another employee gone with no explanation.

"The least they could do is tell us when someone quits." Marta smiles as she leans over my desk. Raven hair cascades over her left eye. Her white top is tight enough that you can see the scarlet shadows of her nipples. Rumor has it she tattooed them red in Toad Suck, Arkansas last summer.

"Who says they quit? Did you see what they're serving for lunch?" Todd grabs his face with both hands, "Sloppy Joe is people! *People*!"

I look through the tangle of soft black hair into Marta's olive eyes. "Well, I bring my own lunch."

She manages a smirk. I can't tell if it's from amusement or pity. Todd slaps me on the back. "Good one buddy, hilarious. Don't quit your day job just yet."

Before Marta goes back to her desk, she hands me a box of toothpicks. "These have a flat end and a pointy end. I heard you say they were easier to build with."

I tell her they are and thank her with a smile that comes off much too shy. When she leaves, I follow the smooth curves of her ass. "Out of your league, bro. Besides, what would Beth think?"

"We're not married yet. I can look, just not touch." So I look at her, same as I do every morning for as long as I can remember.

It's 9:15 and the day becomes lost in a maze of spreadsheets and data entry, phone calls and answers. I've learned not to look at the clock or it will never move. I eat at noon, pour more coffee at 2:00, shit at 2:30. The toothpicks rattle in my pocket as I walk to my car.

***

I don't even know how I get home anymore. I just get in my car and drive, then I'm in my driveway. Home.

Beth is crushing garlic with a huge knife, chopping and dropping it into a frying pan. She's wearing the same white shirt Marta wore today. I think of her bright red nipples. Moving behind Beth I push her brown hair to the side, press myself up against her and kiss her neck. I can see her smile in the knife's reflection.

"Well, aren't we excited to be home?" She turns around and kisses me. I let my lips linger just a little and pull her into me by the small of her back. "I don't think so," she says, "it's not Thursday."

I've fought this battle and lost every time. It's not worth the energy.

"You know," Beth says, "there's a beehive outside, I think. They seem to be everywhere. Maybe you could get rid of them before dinner?"

"Sure thing."

She wraps her hands around my neck and kisses my cheek. "My hero."

***

The hive is small, hidden away in the knot of a tree. A tiny sphere of honeycomb, its hundreds of equal segments much like the rose window of Notre Dame. It's vibrant, humming with activity. Bees dart in and out, each with their own job to do. I, with my can of spray, have my own job to do.

I sneak closer. The hive is the size of a fist. My finger is pressed gently on the spray nozzle. The buzzing is hypnotic and grows fiercer as I approach. I raise the can of spray. The hair on my arms stands up as goose bumps form. I aim the can. A bee lands on my hand.

Its wings glisten in the setting sun. Huge brown eyes look into mine. Pollen clings to the yellow and black fuzz on its body. It walks up my hand onto my forearm. The insect has a red stripe across its tail from which protrudes a long, sharp stinger. My heart slows and the bee scampers up to my elbow. The chatter coming from the hive is rhythmic, making me drowsy.

It's running its legs across my flesh, tapping, searching. It skitters across a large vein at the crook of my elbow and stops. My finger is still resting across the nozzle of the poison. The bee raises its stinger. I take my finger off the nozzle and the insect strikes, burying its stinger into my blood vessel, releasing its poison. The world goes dark, darker than the storm clouds from this morning. All I hear is buzzing, buzzing and silence. The insect dies on my arm, its stinger still attached to its body connecting us to each other. To my vein. The hive approves, its music ringing in my ears. My heart beats faster and the lifeless bee convulses. The fur on its body quivers, and the bee resurrects. Its wings twitch for a moment then the little Lazarus flies back into the hive.

My arm is tingling. Through the house window I see Beth filling a pot of water to boil the pasta so I know I have time to kill. I drop the can of bug killer in the grass and leave the hive alone, its activity somewhat subdued, no doubt in slack-jawed awe of the miracle of rebirth it has just witnessed. I take the pack of toothpicks from my pocket and go into my garage and there on the folding table is my masterpiece. A burgeoning metropolis created with toothpicks. Several large buildings populate each side of the river I painted on the wooden base on which my city rests, six buildings on each side, a total of twelve. I dump the toothpicks out and envision my next construction, a bridge to bring both sides of my city together.

It will have four catenary arches. It's simple to build. You just use basic algebra for the height ratios and a little engineering. The small pieces of wood lay scattered about and God help me, all of a sudden I can't remember the math. My forearm burns. I scan each side of my city and count the buildings, one-story, two-story, all the way up to six-stories. Six different sized buildings, two of each, one on each side, perfect symmetry.

The bridge should be able to hold the weight of three bricks. The design is from a bridge that spans the Thames River. I hold my head in my hands knowing there's a hyperbolic cosine in my head somewhere. Beth is yelling for me, telling me dinner is ready. My arm hurts and I just stare at the two sides of my wooden city separated by an aqua blue gash that may as well be one mile wide.

***

The next day I drive into work and notice a crack on the windshield. The morning sky is bleeding red and orange.

A car is broken down in the middle lane. The blinking red flashers on the white sedan beat slowly as my heart races. Cars disperse left and right around the conked out vehicle. Into the billowing exhaust commuters disappear, the collapse of organized travel. Into the fray I go, my knuckles white on the steering wheel. The radio says something about an approaching storm. The rearview mirror shows obsidian sky.

I punch in one minute late, for the first time. Ever. Another co-worker's chair is empty. Vanished. I hear Todd in my head, quipping, 'Sloppy Joe, it's people!'

Marta walks over and smiles. "Mornin'."

She's wearing a tight black sweater but in my mind I can see her ruby nipples. I picture them erect. "Mornin'."

Her hand is on my desk as she leans forward, her green eyes looking out from behind a curtain of soft black hair. Without thinking my hand moves closer to hers.

Todd is saying something to me in the background, but my mind is a million miles away, hiding behind a cascade of hair and pressing imaginary lips against Marta's.

The day moves quickly. I plow through my work, my fingers tapping keys, eyes darting. It's 2:00 and I'm not tired, but I get coffee anyway. 2:30 passes and I don't have to shit.

***

Beth is wearing all black. She's putting groceries in the fridge. Milk, upper left top shelf, condiments on the door, etc. Same as always. I come up behind her and whisper in her ear. "It's Thursday." I let my mouth linger by her ear for a few extra seconds. She smiles and her cheeks turn red. "We'll see," she laughs. "There's still some bees outside. Did you get rid of that hive?"

Static raises the hair on my arms and at the nape of my neck. "I didn't find it."

"Well, look again."

"Tonight after dinner, when they're less active."

***

I follow their music. The humming vibrates through my bones. My marrow feels like liquid bubbles, popping to the tune of some great symphony. I could find the hive with my eyes closed. The pale honeycomb has spilled out onto the bark of the tree. The yellow hexagons spread out in every direction, reaching. Disseminating. The sun is a fat, bloated ball of fire that slowly slips beneath the horizon.

The little Lazarus with the red stripe comes out to meet me. His scarlet abdomen can be seen streaking toward me, a jagged blur like lightning. He buzzes as dusk flows in, blotting out the day. My blood hears him calling me and boils just a bit, fizzing in my veins. I put out my arm and he lands on my bicep. He crawls toward my elbow, his stinger lightly dragging against my skin. The bee goes to the same spot as before and plunges his stinger into my vein. Venom runs through me as stars fill the sky. The insect dies still attached to my arm. My heart races, contracting and releasing, as the poisoned blood passes through it. Lazarus performs his miracle, rising from the dead once more.

On my way back to my house I see my neighbor's patio. Red pavers mixed in with slate-colored ones, a giant puzzle of crisscrossing 'X's. It makes my brain itch and my skin gets blotchy. I'll vomit if I continue to stare at it so I go into the house, my hands balled tightly into fists.

Beth is getting ready for bed. "You've been outside for a while."

'Was I? I must have lost track of time."

She's putting on her sweatpants and t-shirt. "Uhm, Beth? We going to do it tonight?"

She smiles weakly. "I really don't feel like it. I got tired sitting around waiting and figured I'll just go to bed early. Maybe tomorrow?"

My heart murmurs and the pumping of blood drones in my ears. There's a whirlwind inside me. I realize my hands are still fists, my fingernails digging into my palms. I take one step toward her. Two steps. I feel filled with insect wings, flapping against my insides. I take in a deep breath and exhale. Every muscle relaxes. "O.K. We'll see. I guess I'll go to bed too."

My pillow buzzes all night long.

***

The crack in my windshield has spread and divided into two jagged lines, one longer than the other. You can almost see it growing one millimeter at a time. The wind is whipping the trees back and forth on the parkway. The black sky is above me now, no longer in the rearview mirror.

In the parking lot I see Marta getting out of her black Jetta. Fat raindrops fall from the sky as I watch her long legs stride. The wind blows her hair back, exposing her neck. I feel pins and needles in my arms and it spreads with every step she takes and every glimpse of her slender, bare neck. Overwhelmed, I put my head down and fall asleep to the rhythmic patter of rain on my roof.

I sleep for an hour. The crack on the windshield has grown. I punch in an hour late and Todd asks me where I was. There's another empty seat four cubicles down.

"I saw you in the parking lot. Why were you late?" Marta's eyebrows are raised and the corner of her mouth is turned up in a devilish grin.

"I fell asleep."

She laughs. "In your car? You need to go to bed earlier I guess."

I can hear the beating of the rain outside. I stand up next to her and brush her hair from her shoulder, letting my fingers caress her neck as they pass. My lips are so close to her ear they're almost touching. "I guess I do," I whisper. Her body quivers.

Back at my desk my hands have a life of their own. I do a day's work in two hours. Its 2:00 and I feel more alive than ever. Instead of getting coffee I go home.

The hive has spread; long tendrils have carved broad sections across the tree as ivy would a wall. In the light of day the pattern in my neighbors' patio is taunting me. The red and grey X's make me sick and I throw up on my lawn.

I take a sledgehammer from my garage and hold it high above my head. A small cloud of bees swarms around my hands and I bring the hammer down. The pavers crack and the sand beneath bleeds upwards. Blow after blow the pattern dissolves into a sea of concrete dust. The group of bees grows larger and soon their buzzing is so loud you can't hear the smashing of steel against brick. Once the patio is pulverized, I stop to catch my breath. A ground-up sea of multicolored dust lies mixed where a neat pattern used to reside.

As I head back to my house, I see the curtains on my neighbors window swing back and forth. Breathing hard I wait for a minute, just me and the swarm that orbits my body. Together we wait. Nothing happens.

I go back to the hive and visit my striped friend. We feed off each other, death and life and the pins and needles that come with it. The insect buzzes past my ear, telling me a storm is coming. I say that I know. I've always known and all you have to do is look and feel. You can see it in the sky. I can sense the pressure mounting in my joints

I go back in the house and wait for Beth, remembering suddenly that $y=\cosh(x)$. I can almost see the soaring tandem arches of my toothpick bridge.

***

Her hands knead the dough, slow and deliberate. She's on her second glass of red wine and her teeth are a slight shade of purple. I used to find that plum shade sexy, it meant I might be getting some action. My forearm itches and my eyes stray to the tree in the back of the yard.

Beth ladles some sauce onto the pizza and I close my eyes and hear the rhythmic static of the bees between the spreading of sauce.

"What're you smiling at?" I open my eyes to Beth taking a long, slow sip of wine. You can almost see the warm trail it makes through her body. "I'm just relaxed is all." I start to pick at the tiny scab made by the repeated entry of the stinger. My fingernail traces it, making circles, loosening each edge, slowly lifting it up.

My girlfriend spreads cheese over the dough and sauce. The sun starts to set and my vision gets a little blurry from the humming in my head. I take a long sip of wine. Beth bends over and puts the pizza in the oven. Her ass is blurry but I can still make out her tight curves. I peel the scab off my arm. It sticks to my finger but I flick it away as I stand up and grab her from behind. She gasps as I pull her pants down. Beth clutches the counter and moans, but she doesn't complain.

***

My windshield is a spider web of cracks. The radio is talking about the possibility of a tornado touching down. There's a large burst of static as a bolt of lightning, more jagged than my windshield, lights up the sky. I count, 'one-one hundred, two-one hundred' and I get all the way to 'eight-one hundred before I hear the soft rumbling of thunder.

Marta is laughing about another empty cubicle. If Todd makes another soylent green joke I swear I'll punch him in his smug face. I do wonder where everyone has gone, though. One worker a day almost, it makes no sense. I try to tune out Todd's chatter, but then he says: "We're like the bees. All the workers disappearing from the hive, they call it colony collapse disorder."

Marta stands up in her cubicle. I don't think she's wearing a bra. "That's because of bug spray or chemicals."

The scab has reformed over my vein. "No," Todd says pointing a finger in the air, "it could be a virus or mites even. Without the workers, the drones, you lose all structure. The hives collapses," he licks his lips, "it dies off."

"Well, what could be the reason for insurance agents disappearing?" Marta asks.

They continue to talk, their chatter droning out even the buzzing of the bees in my head. I pick my phone and dial

3926. Marta bends over to pick up her phone, her raven hair cascading over her face. "Meet me in the women's room," I whisper. She turns to me and I see her smiling through the soft tangles of her hair.

In the bathroom we're kissing. My hands move to the small of her back grabbing her sweater. I have to know. I pull the soft cotton over her chest exposing her bare breasts. Her nipples aren't red. People love to spread gossip. They're a gorgeous shade of violet.

***

I'm waiting for Beth to come home and I stare at my little wooden city. The big swath of blue river looks wider than the Grand Canyon. I draw a bridge on graph paper. It's uneven. I wad up the drawing and toss it away. I draw another. This one would never support any weight. I crumple it up. Then another and another. The toothpicks are spread out across the painted board that is my cityscape.

I hear buzzing, but it's not in my head. A tap on glass, over and over again. I go to the window in my garage to see my little, red-striped friend banging into the pane of glass. I open the window to let him in and I see, through the hedges in my neighbor's yard, the unblinking eyes of my missing coworkers. Our stares mingle until the whites of their eyes disappear into the darkness, leaving only a smattering of black dots that quickly dissolve. Colony Collapse Disorder.

The bee walks up my forearm to his favorite spot and stings and dies and resurrects. It takes off and lands on the painted river of my miniature city. Then it flies over to the smallest building, scaling the side. He gets to the top, circles twice, then vanishes inside. I look for him and occasionally see his red stripe repeatedly appear and disappear from sight.

The buildings all mirror each other. Their images split my mind, like the crack in my windshield. My stomach feels queasy as I view right angle next to right angle, hundreds of squares, triangles and rectangles. All of them made perfect and even. I throw up onto my garage floor, the vomit yellow and thick, hitting the ground with a slap. I reach out and grab hold of one of the smaller buildings. I look at the symmetry, all the fragile, slender toothpicks made strong with math and glue and I crush it in my hand. The pieces of debris fall in different shapes and sizes onto the already scattered loose ones. Then I reach for another building.

***

I can't see out of my windshield. Hundreds of jagged lines crisscross each other, fragments with no pattern. This glass is simply broken, shattered. I pull my knees in to my chest and kick the splintered glass. A few pieces break free and fall. I kick again and again. My feet bust through, scraping my legs. I keep bucking until the glass flops outward onto the hood. Long, serrated streaks of lightning now fracture the black sky. Rain hits my face and blood runs down my shins but I drive. I grab the wheel and wince, noticing I have a toothpick splinter jammed into my palm.

My radio is static, a roar of black and white fuzz much like the buzzing of the bees, like the feeling in my arm and in my head. The clouds are funneling in front of me and behind me, angry, swirling, hungry. The radio spits out words that are easy to piece together. They say the storm is here.

I get to work and of course it's closed due to the weather. I press my face against the cold glass and look at my cubicle, dark and empty. I scan the seats around me and I count the seven vacant desks that are scattered about the office. Seven co-workers gone. Missing. I hear Todd's joke echo in my head and this time it's less funny than ever.

Lightning streaks overhead. Before I can count to one-one thousand, thunder crashes, rattling the window against my face. I leave a skull shaped face print behind that's already fading as I depart to the wailing of the tornado sirens.

***

I park in my driveway. Dripping wet from the rain I hit the garage door opener, my hand throbbing from the toothpick lodged in my hand. The wind is wailing, nearly lifting me off of my feet. I can't hear the straining and creaking of the chain pulling the garage door open.

The street signs are bobbing back and forth. Down the road a stop sign wobbles as if having a seizure. Left and right it swings repeatedly until something snaps. It sounds like a gunshot and hurtling towards me, only its thin edge visible, is the steel octagon. I try to dive, but it hits my face, scraping my right cheekbone, slicing a sizeable piece of meat off.

I hit the ground screaming, louder than the tornado siren. I can see my blood being washed down the driveway along with the severed flesh of my cheek. My face burns hot, the pain nauseating. Tears stream down my face mixing with the rain. Dizzy, I stumble into the garage and hit the garage door opener. The door won't close. The power is out. At the end of my driveway a black funnel dances back and forth on its tip. Revulsion is replaced by panic, turbulent and sickening.

The door to my house is locked and my keys are in my pocket. The rain is pelting off the concrete, its rhythm getting faster and more forceful. The light in the garage starts to blink on, each flash bringing the tornado closer. I reach in my pocket; my fingers fumble for the keys. My face is throbbing and when I bring my hand to the gash in my cheek I feel teeth. Blood starts to trickle from where the bee liked to sting me. Pressure in my head mounts straining against my eardrums. Then everything goes dark. Light bulbs shatter and the black winds caress me.

I hear the table holding my precious city crash to the floor. In my mind I can see the pieces tumble, hitting the ground and splintering, cracking, dying. The used pieces lay intermingled with the new ones Marta gave me, bought for me, because she thought they were special. Ruins are everywhere and the thought of this is more painful than the shreds of sinew that flap against my gums, more soul crushing than losing my home.

A shattered piece of two by four hurtles toward me. I turn away from it and it stabs me in the back. The pain is sharp and terrible. I bring my hand down to my stomach and it's sticking through me. Splintered pieces of wood, wet with blood, puncture my shirt. I contemplate pulling it free when the table lands on top of me, across my chest. I'm pinned down and my heart strains, pushing more blood out onto my chest. The rain is drilling the garage, its beat primal. As I try and push the table, the wind whips at me. My entire garage groans, its structure straining against nature. I can smell fire on the wind. This storm is hunting me, it always has been. In my mind I see a lion with its teeth around my neck, teasing me, playing with its food. I can see it now, the bridge, its arches and framework. The beautiful curves spanning the river, connecting a city divided. The revelation, like the rain washing away my blood, cleanses me of fear, slowing my heart. The walls around me shake and splinter as I'm trapped in a hot pool of my own blood. Then I hear a sucking sound. The entire garage trembles as if inhaling. My ears pop so hard I can feel stuff dripping out of my head and down my neck.

There's a sound like twisting steel, like screaming wood as the room exhales, causing a blast of light as the roof lifts off and disintegrates. The table is lifted off me, sucked into a funnel of grey and black swirls. I start to rise as well but the tornado turns, sucking the garage door away and flinging it across the street as a child would a Frisbee. It slices into a house, sticking halfway into the second floor. I stand and with the wind howling through my shredded face I watch its path. It goes through my neighbor's house, tearing a gash right down the middle, sucking up everything and tossing it God knows how far. I fall to my knees. It hurts, my God it hurts, but I stagger back to my feet. My shirt is soaked now, hot and sticky.

The whistling funnel rips up the remainder of patio I had smashed. Several pavers blur past my head, disintegrating when they hit the side of my house.

The funnel grows darker and thinner as it makes a sharp right, turning into my backyard. It's headed for the tree with the beehive. Dread. It explodes inside me. The hole in my veins spills blood down my arm. I study the waxy hexagons one last time. I notice the tendrils that spill out in every direction like a sprawling galaxy. I marvel at its perfect symmetry and I can see my cities and the bridge between them. The tree shudders and the hive trembles. Realizing my inevitable loss, more tears come. I push the wood from my gut and it falls from my back onto the grass. A fresh gush of heat spills from me as the wind batters the tree and the hive crack and explodes. My vision starts to fade as long, tangled roots are pulled, the earth taking my universe with it. Then it's gone, hive, tree, everything.

***

Beth strokes the back of my head as she sips her coffee. "I can't believe you have to rebuild the whole thing."

I laugh as I glue together a fat end to a skinny end, completing the final piece of my bridge. "It's OK, I can see it all in my head. Clearer than ever actually, not just the bridge, the whole damn city."

Her hand stops moving. "Are you sure you're OK?"

I nod as her fingernails caress my scalp once more. "Yes, I'm fine. I was just thinking that when our place is rebuilt maybe we don't go back."

Her fingers stop moving again, "Oh?"

"I mean I almost died there."

"Well, what doesn't kill you makes you stronger right?"

I finger the scar across my cheek. It's still rough with stitches and several little scabs flake off and float away. Then I rub my hand across my stomach and marvel at the smooth, unblemished skin. They found me face down in the grass; my shirt soaked in blood yet no wounds on my body except for the one on my face. Unconsciously my fingertips are now brushing the sensitive flesh of my forearm and I notice that the scab is gone, having left no trace of injury. "You know it is a miracle I suppose."

She wraps her arms around my chest from behind. "It's settled then, no question we go back." Then she nibbles on my earlobe.

"You devil," I say, "in my condition?"

"I thought you were always in condition?" Her hands move toward my waist and disappear beneath my jeans.

"Geez, hon, its Monday and I don't want to be late for work."

She ignores me and unzips my pants. "Oh, that's right, I forgot, can't be late, not ever," she laughs as she forces herself on top of me.

That's when I notice the small circular scab at the crux of her elbow.

As Is

Steve Zisson

He's wondering if he's caught in a continual loop of House Hunters' episodes with his wife playing the role of the antagonist who only wants a move-in ready home, and him as the protagonist willing to buy a fixer-upper and make it their own. Or is he the antagonist? He's pretty sure he's the protagonist in this episode anyway.

He knows this: They've got to get a house to end this endless episode.

Keagan Penn Brunson is quite certain that his wife Eliot will have to come over to his side to finally snag a house because they can't afford a move-in ready home in this surface-of-the-sun, low-interest rate-fueled, screaming hot real estate market.

He's sure they'll have to settle for making a home their own by using sweat equity. But she's House Hunters' dreaming about move-in ready. He's the *realist* in a sellers' market.

It's with much hope this morning that he fires up his computer to check the new listings online before he starts his workday from home. And he plans to refresh the listing every hour on the hour because homes are going just that fast.

He puts his coffee next to the keyboard, rubs his hands together for luck, and prepares for his first Zillow fix of the day.

Scroll down, scroll some more. He skips by the newer homes. Goes right past addresses on Chestnut Street, the rich part of town.

He's skimming by almost all of Salem's listings in his price range of $400,000 to $500,000, seeking only listings being sold "as is."

He's looking for houses in total disrepair, the homes where the owners just don't give a shit and were convinced to throw it up for sale in a blazing market where anything will be bought at outrageous prices. Sometimes it's an estate sale hurriedly listed by greedy family members who just want to get rid of the property without spending a dime and collect their inheritance cash.

They have no chance bidding on move-in ready homes, despite Eliot's insistence, which will sell for 20 percent over asking after a bidding war that blows them out of their price range. But they've persistently put in bids.

He zips past a blurry image, stops and goes back. $400,000. Check. Box ticked. Right at the bottom of their price range.

He searches for a gallery of pictures because this one is fuzzy.

Click, click and click on the blurry photo but nothing moves. It's just one amateur photo. He squints at it but it's so out of focus all he can make out is that the house is big. Two stories. There's some woods behind the big blurry house.

He checks the property description. Just three words: "Leave as is." *That's it*?

No number of bedrooms are listed. No square footage, or how many bathrooms. What type of heating system? Nothing. AC?

He craves a narrative description about the house but it's pretty much blank.

It could be that "leave as is" is a website mistake, an instruction to the real estate site's webmaster as a placeholder for the listing until the realtor provides further information.

At least there's basic information, the house address! 66 Thompson Lane. You can't sell a house without an address. Thompson Lane. He's lived here in Salem his entire life but he doesn't remember that street.

He clicks over to the map and sees that it's located in an area that he thought was conservation land.

Thompson Lane is off Highland Avenue near the headwaters of the Forest River and backs up to the Salem Woods. Switching to the satellite view, he zooms in but when it stops at its closest shot, the house is still one big smudge.

"Let me see it. Open!" he grumbles then yells out loud. Working from home, he often talks to himself.

Clicking over to the street view, he's back out on Highland Avenue and trying to turn down Thompson Lane but the Google spy video car couldn't or wouldn't go down Thompson Lane when it was mapping Salem.

Back to the satellite view, and as far as he can tell, 66 is the only house on Thompson Lane though it's possible some may be hidden beneath the tree canopy, swallowed up by the Salem Woods, the city's forest.

"What did you say?" calls Eliot from her work area down the hall.

"I found us a house I said."

"Right."

He can hear her trudging dutifully down the hall to see it on his big monitor.

He turns the screen to her. She's still in PJ's, her morning work clothes, and her long dark un-showered hair is pulled back.

"I can't even make it out."

"I think it's pretty big. Like one of those McMansions in Brookside Estates over in Danvers."

Eliot leans in, takes the mouse and clicks about the screen. "Salem didn't build any McMansion developments. All the land here was long gone by the 80s for that craze. You know that."

"I don't know. There's a couple of one-offs on odd streets. I've seen them. They stick out like sore thumbs. They could've built them on Thompson Lane for all I know. But I don't remember ever even going down that street."

Eliot grew up in New York and relies on Keagan for local knowledge.

"The house at the end of the lane," she says, a running joke about her not wanting a house at the end of a dead end or cul-de-sac, cut off from the world.

He doesn't laugh because this house listing appears to be just that. "Yeah."

"I don't want an abandoned McMansion like this one. I want a cozy updated bungalow or mid-century modern in an actual neighborhood. Move-in ready," she says.

"Can we just go see it? What's the harm?"

"It's just a waste of time. And someone will still pay way over asking."

"I bet it has two sinks in the bathroom," he says with fake hopefulness even though there are no interior shots published.

She smiles at another running joke. "You can never have too many sinks. We need three, maybe four for the two of us!" she gives her usual answer.

Then he sees she's growing tired. "I'm really sick of looking. We can just stay here until the market cools."

They've been looking for almost two years, hundreds of houses, two dozen failed offers. It's not the three-house act and then a joyous decision like on the TV show. It's a forever house search.

"The market will never cool. We can't stay in this one-bedroom with your clock ticking. This housing market is killing people!"

"There's plenty of time. I'm only thirty-one!" she says, then stomps out of the room to her office where she monitors adverse events for a biotech company from the kitchen table. He's got the bedroom. Not ideal working conditions. Just another reason to move, in this work-from-home economy.

***

She agrees reluctantly to see the house, the McMansion at the end of the lane.

He calls the realtor, B.D. Dick. He's never seen Dick's name before on a listing so he presumes they are a first-time realtor.

They agree to meet the next day at the intersection of Highland Avenue and Thompson Lane. Dick says the lane is fairly narrow and unpaved so it might be best to walk into the property from there, and also to get a feel for the area on foot.

It's raining when they park in the lot of a Burger King on Highland Avenue. It's one of those late afternoon August downpours when you're going to feel stickier after the rain stops because you got soaked running to the car.

"When is Dick coming?" Eliot asks, not in the spirit of a joke, like all the dick jokes they made last night but because she's annoyed to be at the entrance to Thompson Lane waiting to see a house at the end of the lane.

They're both in lightweight windbreakers, covered in moisture that's steaming up the windows because their AC is broken. Opening the windows won't clear the view because it's still raining hard and rain is 100 percent humidity.

"I can't see out. Maybe we should we make out until he gets here. No one can see in. Remember that time at Dead Horse Beach?" he asks, trying to lighten the stuffy mood.

"Not today. Or tomorrow. Or ever again," she snaps in fake outrage.

A rap on the window and they both jump like it's a killer or a cop trying to clear out lover's lane. A killer or a cop, what's the difference? Either one, *jump*.

"It's B.D. Dick!" he announces himself over the metallic pounding of rain on the car roof.

Eliot wipes the window with her sleeve to reveal Dick. He's bending down with a raincoat hood around his angular face, waving the listing at them. It's disintegrating in the rain, flopping over in his hand.

She cracks the window and Dick tries to shove the wilted paper through the opening to prove it's him. Credentials. But he can't mash it through. It only mushes against the glass like some failed missive from a limp Dick.

"We should take my truck. All this rain has made it too muddy. We'll be up to our ankles if we walk," he shouts through the crack.

Dick waves them over to his truck, which is an old rusted red Ford Bronco. Not exactly a realtor's luxury lease special.

It's a two-door, old school Bronco. Dick opens the driver's side, flips back the seat and points for Keagan to get in the rear. It looks claustrophobic but Keagan really wants to see this house so he squeezes in. His rain-slicked jacket slides him across the worn smooth leather seats until he's behind the front passenger seat where Eliot has settled. He looks for a seatbelt and all he finds is a shrunken lap belt tucked between the seats, atrophied and useless. It's only going to be a short ride so he doesn't put on this alleged seatbelt.

Dick starts the Bronco and jams the stick shift into gear. They enter Thompson Lane sideways as the mud sucks the Bronco down to its axles.

Dick drops the shift into second gear and the truck spins across the road toward the trees and Keagan, beltless, slides across the bench seat into the exposed metal door. "Maybe we should walk!" Keagan yells.

"You don't want to walk through this slop," Dick says, shifting again and grunting.

They skid across the road back and forth with Keagan flying to the opposite side of the truck each time before mercifully the mud weighs the Bronco down into a slow stop in front of the house.

As they exit the car, the rain sputters, the sun breaks through around the dark clouds and humidity explodes.

The house looms over them, as blurry in the clearing mist as it was on the real estate website's listing page.

"Oh," Eliot says, "that's surprising. It looks like more of a midcentury modern than I could see in that one photo. Maybe this was worth it."

"It's really quite a find," says Dick. "Move-in ready I believe."

Keagan wipes the moisture out of his eyes, squinting at the house. He doesn't see it at all, what Eliot has described. That's not a midcentury modern. "I think it looks more like a colonial to me."

"What's wrong with you? You're an architect or something? Let's go in and see who's right."

At the door, Dick removes his hood and Keagan sees that he's really old. Maybe more ancient than his Ford Bronco. He could be eight-five.

Dick opens the front door; it's unlocked. You don't need locks out here in the rural part of Salem? Nice.

Eliot goes in first. "Wow," her excitement echoes through the empty house. "This is something."

"I was right. Now you're happy I insisted."

Eliot turns back to him. "This is mid-century modern. Classic."

"I'm getting more of a Victorian vibe," Keagan jokes in an awful English accent.

Dick closes the door and then steps between them. "I'm just not sure how to define this house. Depending on your perspective, it kind of changes."

"I think we can all agree it does need some work. How long has it been empty?" says Eliot.

Dick tries to revive his sodden paperwork by flapping it in a vain attempt to dry it out. The words and pictures have all run together. "I'm not sure. I can tell you it's an estate sale. Family from Texas contacted me to sell it."

"Maybe we can get a good price. Estate sale!" Keagan says.

Eliot is wandering towards the kitchen, which will definitely need updating with its hardware-less white Melamine cabinets and yellowed, long ago white appliances.

"If we can get it for four hundred, we'll have just enough to fix it to our tastes. Are there any other houses on the street we can compare it to?" Eliot says.

Again, Dick shuffles his wet papers. "I think there used to be a couple. If I remember the records right, they fell into disrepair and were torn down by the city. For back taxes or something. Maybe that land has been returned to the Salem Woods."

"I really like the bones of this mid-century modern. I might be able to overlook that we'd be kind of isolated on this lane," Eliot says as she leans over the kitchen sink to see out the window.

"It's not like it's really rural. We're still in a city off a four-lane road that's a major commercial area," Keagan says.

"Best of both worlds," Dick says.

"When was it built?" Keagan asks.

"There was a major renovation I think in the 1980s. But the records are fuzzy before then," Dick says.

"No problem. The age doesn't much matter. We'd like to put in an offer," Keegan blurts out before Eliot can object. He looks over to her and he's surprised she's nodding in agreement.

Dick drops the wet ball of paper onto the linoleum. "Well, that was easy. My first sale ever."

Keegan studies him. This real estate gig must be a second or third career for Dick. Unless he's a very unsuccessful salesperson.

***

They get the house, as the couple always does at the end of the episode.

There's no bidding war, which seems unusual to Keegan in this hot market. They're so lucky!

They buy 66 Thompson Lane for exactly asking price, $400,000. It seems like a bargain, at asking price, not 20 percent over it.

While 66 Thompson Lane isn't move-in ready, they move in anyway at Keegan's insistence and immediately begin negotiating about the best way to spend their hundred-thousand-dollar budget on renovations.

"Kitchens and bathrooms first," Eliot says. "They're kind of gross. 1980s gross. Like never cleaned since then."

"We can just blast them with bleach for now," Keagan says.

Their focus on the kitchen and baths doesn't stop him from noticing other things that need to be fixed right away. Like the door in the basement that leads to the crawl space under the addition, possibly also built in the 1980s. The addition's something of a sunroom, though it's oddly oriented north. Its metal door is jammed shut, rusted in place. He busted it open with a rusty old crowbar he found in the main house basement on their first morning after the move. Under the sunroom, he finds stacks of videotapes, both VHS and Beta, as well as cassettes and eight tracks. They're all neatly arranged as if by some anal video/audiophile.

But kitchen and baths first.

"It's going to be hard to find a kitchen reno company. They're out straight, too, in this market," he says as they have breakfast in the 1980s kitchen on their apartment kitchen table/work top that doesn't fit with the decor.

"That's your job, Mister Project Manager."

"Yeah, I'm the one who wanted a fixer-upper," he says, just a little weary of the process. To bolster himself he recites his positive mantra: "Make it our own!"

"It just can't be all *your* own," she says.

He puts up his hands in mock surrender. "We're in this together. But one thing I want to do is make this a smart house. I want to replace that funky ancient intercom system with all the latest tech. Did you see that the intercom also doubled as a home stereo system?"

"Can't we just leave the house a little less than genius level. I like the intercom. It's so midcentury."

When they finish their coffee, he pulls her to him for an impromptu 80s dance party in the kitchen, inspired by those 80s tapes he discovered. He put some of them on his phone after he downloaded them, and he plays them now for her. She grimaces at the sound quality.

"The songs sound so tinny through those phone speakers. I can't dance to—" she protests.

But she relents and they dance to songs from bands The Cure, The Go Gos, Psychedelic Furs, The Style Council, Depeche Mode, The Pixies, Modern English, Tears for Fears.

"This was fun but I hate the 80s," she says. "Maybe it was Reagan."

"You also hate my white dude 80s dancing," he says.

"It's really bad. Where did you learn those alleged moves?"

"Eighties films."

After the breakfast/dance party breaks up, and before starting his day job as project manager for a software company, Keegan calls a half-dozen kitchen renovators and briefly describes the scope of the job on voicemails.

Only one calls him back by lunchtime. Keegan wonders if he's shady, desperate for work.

No other contractor calls him back.

***

Eliot is out for an early morning walk in the Salem Woods, which starts behind their house at a small trail head winding between granite outcroppings.

The contractor shows up alone driving an old minivan and towing a small trailer. The minivan doesn't look very professional to Keegan. A pickup truck would be more appropriate. For the estimate, the contractor came in a sedan.

Keegan expected him to show up with a big crew for the demo but he's going to apparently handle it himself. He isn't a big guy. M. Bouchard and Sons Construction. Keegan is hoping for the sons to appear but Bouchard is only in his late 20s so they can't be very old, if he even has any sons.

Bouchard parks his minivan behind the dumpster that's been plopped in the driveway.

Keegan greets him there. "Good morning. Just you today?"

Bouchard is getting his toolbelt on and looks perturbed at the interruption. "I'm all I need. I know how to wreck things. Good help is hard to find. Don't trust anyone else not to screw it up."

"If you need assistance with something big, just holler because I work from home and I'll be in one of the bedrooms, my office."

Bouchard snorts and then spits. "Won't need your help. You'll just get in the way."

Keegan retreats to his office, where he's juggling several projects. He turns on his playlist of 1980s hits that fit with the 1980s frozen-in-time vibe of the house.

It's background noise for him as he answers emails.

Over the low volume, he easily hears Bouchard yelling for him. He didn't expect to be needed so soon. He runs down the hall like he's wanted.

In the kitchen, Bouchard is holding up one of the cabinet doors that he's pried off. "What's this shit? Some kind of joke?"

Bouchard flips the door over and points it at Keegan. Spelled out in blurry red is "Leave as is."

"That's odd," Keegan says.

"Odd? This is bullshit. You want me to do the job my way or not? I've got plenty of work other places."

"No, go right ahead. Rip it apart. Pay no attention to that. The former owner must've left it."

"Right boss," Bouchard says before flinging the cabinet door like it's a frisbee through the opened window where it clangs into the dumpster.

"Back to work for both of us then," Keegan says.

At his desk, he writes down the phrase using a red pen on a yellow post-it. *Leave as is*. Familiar, sort of.

He's staring at the post-it when Eliot rushes in. Another interruption. "You can't believe what I saw out on my walk."

"You won't believe what just happened here."

"Me first. I think I found an old family gravesite or cemetery. I need to do more exploring. It's out there behind some scrub pines in this really hidden spot."

"You sure? Should we report it to the city?"

"Let's just take a walk out there together later. I want you to see it. One thing is for sure I've got to research this area at the historical society. We need to know what's out here. I bet your story isn't as good as mine," Eliot says.

He tells her anyway and it isn't as good as hers or maybe it's in his telling.

***

Though he's been a project manager for ten years, he still possesses hard tech skills and installs a Pest A.I. smart home system when Eliot isn't looking. He's testing it when he hears Bouchard yelling.

Bouchard's shouting turns into a scream. By the time Keegan and Eliot get to the kitchen, Bouchard is immobile, slumped against the lower cabinets, his nail gun at his side, a nail buried like a third eye in his forehead. Blood bubbles up around the edges of the nail and streams down into his eyes, turning them red.

The blood pools in his open eyes before flooding out of the eye sockets and flowing down each cheek.

Keegan screams first even though he's behind Eliot. Then Eliot joins in with her own belated cry.

From down the hall, a song by The Cure plays softly. Something about heaven.

***

It's not until later after the police leave that Keegan realizes the cabinet doors are back up. How did that happen?

Police officers couldn't have re-installed them. They wouldn't alter a potential crime scene, would *they*? He was with them the entire time as they investigated Bouchard's death, which they quickly ruled a construction accident but were still asking OSHA to stop by at a later date to confirm.

"We're going to have trouble finding a contractor now after this incident," Keegan tells Eliot.

"I don't know if I can live here if we don't get the reno done. We've got to get the 80s out of this place and the memory of what just happened," she says as they sit in the living room.

They've moved their kitchen table into the living room because they don't have the stomach for eating where Bouchard died.

"What I can't get over, besides him dying in the kitchen is why he would put the cabinet doors back up. He was ripping them down. He got angry when he saw that writing. The *writing*. I didn't tell you."

"What writing?"

"I'll show you."

Keegan gets up quickly then stops. He realizes they both must go into the kitchen together and *see* things. He can't forget all the blood and Bouchard with a nail in his brain.

Eliot isn't moving. He extends his hand to her.

"I have to show you this."

Eliot rises, pulled along gently. "Okay. I guess. No surprises."

"It'll be all right. It's just writing on a cabinet door."

He takes her by the hand into the kitchen. It looks just like it had when Bouchard died.

In the middle of the kitchen, he releases her hand.

"I'll just open it slowly so there's no surprises."

He eases the cabinet door open.

"Jesus," she gasps.

Keegan jumps back at her reaction and the door opens wider from its momentum. It takes a second for him to focus on it. It's the same message but the letters have bled, dripping and barely dry, as if from a recent massive wound. Yet it's still legible with a clear message: "Leave as is."

Eliot retreats to the doorway. Keegan recovers and motions to her about whether he should open the other doors. She shakes her head. "Leave as is."

"It depends on what the definition of *is* is," he says weakly.

***

"I want out of this house now. As fucking is!" Eliot says, packing up a bag in their bedroom. "I should've stuck to my guns. Move-in ready or bust."

Keegan paces while Eliot is stuffing clothes into an overnight bag, not bothering to fold them like she does carefully on every trip.

"We can't leave. This is where we live. All our money is in this house," Keegan says, watching her pack.

"I don't care if we lose money on the sale. I'll go back to living in a one-bedroom apartment."

"I can't go back there. Those four walls. Just stay one more night here. It will look better in the morning. Things always do in the light of day."

"I won't stay another night. I'll be at the Residence Inn. There's plenty of room for you. It's your decision."

'I'll do the reno myself, Eliot. There was something weird about Bouchard. I think this was about him. Not us or this house."

"You don't have the skills." She hefts the bag and walks out.

***

The next morning, he's perusing YouTube for how-to videos on kitchen demo. He's up early because he didn't sleep well alone in the house. He knows it's up to him to renovate the house to bring Eliot home.

First order of business, he's at Home Depot, buying pry bars of various sizes, a reciprocating saw, a sledgehammer and a battery-powered drill. He can't get Peter Gabriel's "Sledgehammer," out of his head as he walks the aisles. He tries to think of a song about a reciprocating saw to end Sledgehammer banging around his brain, but no song comes to mind.

Back at home at his desk, he studies a video, "How to Demo a Kitchen Like a Pro."

Rule No. 1: Turn off the power supply before any demo. Check.

He wants to do as the video instructs, backing out the screws with an extractor on the cabinet doors first, but that's where Bouchard ran into problems with the cabinets. Or created a problem.

The how-to video playing in his head, he approaches the cabinets, drill in one hand both as his tool and as some sort of protection. He could start at one end of the kitchen as far away as possible from the cabinet door with the bloody message but he decides to go right at it and yank the Band-Aid off.

One after another, he opens three cabinet doors like dominoes before he gets to the Bouchard killer door. All three drip with the same message. *Leave as is*. He feels surrounded.

Instinctively against an unseen killer, he squeezes the trigger on his battery-powered drill for protection and waves it around wildly. Staggering backward, he throws his arms behind him for balance to prevent a fall but slips on the tarp covering the floor. He recovers enough to lurch forward, the drill still whirring at high rpm, with his arms flailing before he goes over. The drill beats him to the floor, lodging under him, impaling him through the heart.

***

Eliot knows she can't go into the house again. She should've insisted that Keegan leave with her on the night before he died. She'll have to live with that guilt.

A week after Keegan's funeral, Eliot researches the 66 Thompkins Lane house at the Salem Athenaeum library on Essex Street. In the dusty old stacks, she finds that no one has lived in it since the 1980s when the family just disappeared.

Then she discovers a *Salem News* obituary that offers a clue. The Thibodeaus owned the house after emigrating from Quebec in the early 1900s to work in the textile mills. In the 1950s, they farmed minks on this rural spot in Salem. In the 1980s, they had a successful run with a three-store mom and pop video store chain before Blockbuster disrupted the industry.

After her research, the only place she wants to go off Thompson Lane is the hidden cemetery. She returns to the house at the end of the lane just to oversee the removal of their possessions by a moving crew. From the outside of the house. The crew leader and she video chat as he goes through the house asking her which furniture or clothes or other possessions can be thrown in the dumpster or taken into her new condo downtown, surrounded by people in houses on both sides of hers.

Once he's got his instructions, she treks out to the cemetery. There, she kicks around the overgrown grass until she finds something hard. She gets on her knees and pulls up the turf before brushing away the dirt on a granite marker that says: "Leave as is."

She scrambles to her feet and runs toward the house at the end of the lane. She needs to warn the movers not to take anything apart, even a door off its hinges if they must squeeze a big item out of a small doorway.

Once she warns the movers, she can't wait to get back to her childless, one-bedroom in the new condo complex. She always wanted move-in ready. She'll always want new forever. She never wanted kids or a McMansion. Sorry, Keegan.

In The Cellar
HP Newquist

Nobody wanted to do this job. Not even me.

I'm sure the other contractors in town turned it down. I couldn't afford to.

That, though, is water under the bridge. Or water in the cellar.

That's where Tim Collins, my partner, is.

In the cellar.

There's probably nothing left of him now.

* * *

I got a message on my phone. Pretty straightforward.

"Repair needs to be done at 233 Merrick Street. Yard flooding. Potential drainage problem."

I'm on the approved list of contractors for the town, but I don't get called too often. A lot of guys are better connected than me, if you know what I mean. I'm like the contractor call of last resort.

No signature on the message. I tried calling the number back, and got a busy signal.

I know 233 Merrick Street. Everybody does.

It's where they found those four kids.

Over the course of a month, one by one, each kid had disappeared. Right off the street. Four all together. Cops had no luck finding them.

Barty Hansen lived at 233 Merrick. He even helped with the searches.

One day he called 911. *Come quick*, Barty said. *The kids are in my basement.*

They found Barty fifteen minutes later in the cellar, hanging by his neck from a pipe on the ceiling. A leather belt was cinched around his neck, and his face was all bloated. His jaw had clamped down tight on his tongue—it was almost bit clean off.

The four kids were lined up at his feet.

What was left of them.

As usual, the neighbors never expected it of him. Barty was a great guy as far as they knew. Nice man, always helped out if someone needed to borrow a lawn mower or a ladder.

But one friend had heard Barty talk about a badness that had come to the neighborhood. It needed to be stopped, Barty told him. The friend said Barty wanted to reinforce his house to keep the badness away. Wall it all up.

Then they find Barty and the kids in the cellar.

Maybe Barty should have walled himself in. Sick fuck.

Anyway, I couldn't get anyone to answer at the number that sent me the message about repairs. So I called George Kolovich at the public works department. He's the only guy I know. Like I said, I'm not well connected.

"Sounds like a county administration number, but I can't be sure," George said over the phone. "But look. That house is a fucking nightmare. No one knows what to do with it."

Apparently, Hansen had no heirs, so the county took it over. However, since the state police had been involved in tracking the kids, the state was claiming jurisdiction over the house. The town council just wanted to bulldoze the place into the ground. Everyone had to wait until all the various agencies signed off. In the meantime, the property had to be kept up, since it was in a residential neighborhood. And now it was flooding.

"Look, I don't know who sent the message. Could have been a county inspector for all I know. But if there's a drainage problem, it's got to be fixed." George let out a heavy sigh. "We'll cover you for it while we're figuring out who has the ultimate say-so." Kolovich knew my situation, vis-à-vis just trying to keep my business afloat. "We'll make sure you get paid for your work. One way or the other. I'll get you on the budget." Good guy, that George.

"How much work should I do?"

George clicked his teeth together—I could hear that over the phone. "The town is gonna tear the house down eventually, so it doesn't matter what you do. Just stop the leak or whatever it is. No one wants that place back in the news."

"How do I get in?"

George put me on hold, then came back with the lockbox combination.

"Keep track of your hours," he said. "And try not to make too much of a scene. Be discreet. Like I said, the town wants to be done with this house. We don't need people starting any more fucking rumors."

Rumors around 233 Merrick never stopped. It was the town's ongoing fascination.

I called Tim Collins. He's my go-to when I need help on a job. Smart guy, graduated from Rice University, but let's just say he wasn't born with career ambitions in his DNA. His Uncle Dave and I went to junior high together, and have been drinking buddies since. When Dave asked about getting Tim a job, I figured I could cut him a break. I didn't need him at the time, but what the hell. He's been a damned good worker ever since.

Tim biked to my house, and we drove in my truck out to Merrick Street. I gave Tim all the information I had, and what we were expected to do.

"There's a reason no one else took this job," he said offhandedly, looking out the side window. "You know that, right?"

Of course, I knew. I heard the rumors like everyone else.

He was quiet for a moment. "I'm not too keen on digging there," he said softly.

He didn't have to explain. All four kids had been found on the dirt floor in Hansen's cellar. But they weren't . . . complete. Parts of them were missing. Mostly hands and eyes. The cops and the coroner dug up part of the basement to see if they could find the body parts. They didn't find anything.

One rumor is the coroner got so sick while looking at the scene that he called off the dig without finishing it up. Another rumor is that there could be more kids buried in there. Hansen was an old guy. Maybe he'd done things years ago that no one knew about.

So, yeah. Digging at 233 Merrick Street wasn't on anyone's list of ways to spend a sunny morning. Which is probably why the job got pushed all the way down to me.

We drove up and parked along the sidewalk. The place was looking worn down, even though it was barely three months ago they found Hansen and the kids. The weeds were as high as the front porch.

Tim walked around to the back of the truck and got the pick and shovels. I grabbed my toolkit: wrenches, drivers, strap. And one non-plumbing essential: a loaded .22. I have a good reason for always having that. My first job ever was to rebuild a sprinkler system for the little department store over on Macomber Road. I think it's a CVS pharmacy now. We had to empty out the entire basement first. Once we got it half cleared of crates and old boxes, all of a sudden rats started scampering out of the walls. Not rats like you see in a tool shed or a garage, but rats with tails as thick as three-ply nylon cord. Almost as big as raccoons. And beady little eyes, if you want to call eyes as big as marbles beady. It shocked all hell out of us, 'cause those damn rats were running everywhere. One latched its teeth into the heel of my boot. It was an old bastard, with little gray hairs and only half a tail. Eyes meaner than a rabid dog's.

I shook my boot hard to get him off, but he wouldn't let go. I started to get a little panicky, to be honest. I tried to hit him off with a plank I found lying on the floor. The rat finally let go, but not without taking an inch of leather stripping from my boot.

After that, I was scared to shit of one of those things getting ahold of my flesh. I figured the only way to keep them away was a nice slug through the skull. That night I went out and got this .22. Ain't been bit by a rat since, but I've sure helped keep their numbers down. Kind of a weird satisfaction to see one of those bastards come running at you like nothing was gonna stop him, and then plaster him to the ground in a furry splatter with a well-placed bit of lead.

I looked over the front yard. There was a large swampy puddle covering most of the gravel driveway. Bubbles were popping up, meaning it was getting a constant stream of fresh water. The runoff was spilling into the neighbor's yard.

My first guess was a break in the water main. That would require a lot of deep digging. It would be a simpler job if a house pipe had cracked and was backing up.

"Kinda quiet around here, y'know?" Tim said, walking to the front door.

"Yeah, well. It's abandoned."

"Not that," he replied, as he opened the lockbox. "I mean the whole neighborhood. No one around, nobody on their way to work. I don't even hear birds anywhere."

I looked around. He was right. The only sounds were our own scuffling feet and the front door creaking open as Tim pushed it in.

We looked around inside. It was a small house. There wasn't any water on the floor, which meant it was probably coming from the cellar. "You want to start downstairs?" he asked.

"Yeah," I said. We walked through the kitchen. Still had a table and chairs, some thrift store paintings on the wall. I don't believe in any of that déjà vu shit, but I felt like I'd been here before in a bad dream. I couldn't shake that feeling as I opened three closet doors before finding the one leading downstairs.

The door was slightly open, and I pushed it all the way. It was thick, about three inches of solid oak. It didn't want to swing open. I pushed it, hard.

As the door opened, I could feel the stench from the cellar before I smelled it. Thick, oily, humid. Maybe the drain had been leaking for months, 'cause nothing else could've smelled that bad in only a couple of days. A real moldy smell, but that might've been more from the age of the house than how rancid the water was. I almost retched from the stink.

I started down the stairs. There were eleven steps; I counted them from the top. They were sturdy, but each time I stepped from one stair to the next I had this feeling the whole thing was gonna collapse under me.

Wasn't a very big basement. There was one little window, and the sky was bright enough outside to light up the cellar a bit. The walls were gray cinder blocks. Three iron water pipes ran across the ceiling and disappeared into the far wall.

The floor was where the problem was. It was packed dirt, dry around the stairs and the near walls. Next to the far wall there was a layer of slime festering like a stagnant pond. That was what smelled, 'cause it looked like a little sea of melting, moldy lime Jell-O with yellow and black colors mixed in it. What a mess. It'd be a bitch just trying to pump it out.

Tim stepped past me and walked to the edge of where the slime was. He placed the tools on the dry ground behind him, and then put the toe of his boot into the muck and wiggled it around. You could see the water underneath move around, but the slime on the surface clung to the boot.

"This crap could be a hundred years old by the way it stinks." He wiped his face with his sleeve. "Give it a few more days and you could probably walk across the top of it."

He walked to where the three pipes entered the wall and took a step into the muck. The scum came about halfway up his boot and attached itself on the leather like a pack of leeches on warm flesh. It quivered as if it was alive. He brought his other foot in. Standing there, he looked like somebody waiting to sink into quicksand.

Tim reached up and grabbed the pipes, one at a time. He gave each a good shake. The third one was loose and wobbly. "This might be it," he grunted, straining to get a closer look. He paused, then bent in closer.

"You know," he said, squinting, "this wall is new. The mortar's not discolored. And look"—he pointed a few feet to his left—"it juts out about eighteen inches from the wall."

He was right. It was like a wall built in front of another wall. I hated to bring it up, but I said, "Supposedly old man Hansen talked about needing to barricade himself in. Maybe he actually got started."

Tim was standing on tiptoe now, looking at the pipes as close as he could. "Well, it appears that he fucked up his stonework." He shook the third pipe again. "I think he either pinched the pipe or actually cracked it when he set that last line of blocks." He traced his finger across the top line of the wall. "The break might be right there."

"We'll have to do some digging. Or some demolition," I said to Tim.

We were gawking up at the pipes when Tim took a step closer and put the side of his face against the cinder blocks. He put his hands on the wall to steady himself, 'cause of the way he was leaning into it. I started to ask him what he was doing.

"SHHH!" he hissed, and held out his hand to silence me. His head rested against the wall.

I didn't say anything.

"Don't you hear it?" He looked back at me. "There's dripping water behind these blocks."

I shook my head. "I don't hear anything." The cellar was silent. "If we have to go wading around in this crap to find some goddamned leak, I think my stomach might volunteer this morning's Oreos."

After a moment, though, there it was, like a leaking faucet dripping into a sink full of water and dirty dishes. I heard it again, about ten seconds later. It was a slow leak, whatever it was.

The sound was coming from behind the wall. I could only imagine how rank the slime was in there if it had already managed to ooze its way through to this side.

Tim plodded out of the water and stomped his boots. The slime seeped off of his soles, like it was crawling onto the ground.

He looked at me and sighed loudly. "'What now?" He made a swinging motion at the wall, making it look more like a tennis stroke than a pickaxe swing.

Even though he asked it as a question, it came out sounding more like "Let's hurry up and do this so we can get the fuck out of here."

All I could do was shrug a little. We were going to have to punch into it. "I guess we got to if we expect to get paid for our troubles," I said. "And the town gave us the okay, so I don't see any choice."

Except for the fact that the whole situation was making me fidgety. It was getting cloudy outside and darker down here, and the room seemed to be a little smaller than when we first came down. Felt colder, too. It would be a nasty place to be caught in after dark.

I pulled out my phone. "Let me take a couple of pictures to show the county. If we're busting shit up, I want them to know why." I snapped a dozen shots, and then started to put the phone back in my pocket. I noticed I wasn't getting a signal.

"I don't know how thick these walls are," I said to Tim, "but they're not letting a signal through. Might have some chicken wire insulation between the blocks, so be careful when you swing."

Tim carried the pickaxe into the muck with him, draping it over his shoulder. I opened my toolbox and started laying tools on the ground. I even laid out my .22 in case rats came out from behind the wall. Then I set back on my haunches to watch Tim chip away at the concrete blocks.

"Well, here goes nothing," he said. I could see the muscles in his neck go tight as he lifted the pick into the air and swung it around against the wall.

No sooner had he hit it than a huge hole erupted open.

It didn't cave in—it caved out, like something had blown up on the other side.

At the point where Tim hit it, chunks of shattered concrete block came shooting towards us, as if they'd been blasted from the other side by a cannon.

I dodged a piece that flew by my head, but didn't see the one that hit me in the stomach. It knocked the wind out of me and I keeled over onto my side, trying to breathe. I could feel blood running from where the concrete ripped into my shirt.

Tim stood there speechless, not knowing why the wall had blown outward. He kept looking from the tip of the pick to the gaping hole in the wall and back again. Words started to form on his lips, but he just jawed like he was chewing gum.

The cellar got incredibly quiet. Cement dust filled the air. The slime rippled.

Tim stared into the space behind the hole he'd made.

He didn't look away. He just peered into it.

I couldn't see what he could.

Then we heard it.

Breathing.

Not breathing like people do. It was a raspy, throaty, sort of breathy moaning. The only time I'd ever heard anything like that was when Don McFeeter's dog got hit outside Minderbinder's Bar by an ice cream truck. We all ran out to see what happened, and there lay Don's Irish setter with half its side crushed in. It was bleeding from its mouth. It was also choking to death on that blood. Every time it breathed you could hear the gurgling in its throat as the blood welled up. There wasn't anything we could do for it.

That's what this breathing was like, half choking and half gurgling at the same time.

Suddenly, I knew Tim and I were in a lot of trouble.

Tim was trembling, like somebody was shaking him. He was still staring through the hole.

At whatever was behind the wall.

He dropped the pick. It disappeared into the water, splattering little Jell-O-like bits over his pants. A droplet of saliva formed in the corner of his mouth. It started to run down his chin.

Slowly, something started to crawl out of the hole.

Not really crawling. Kind of slithering, like a poisonous lizard on a rock wall. It was sort of human shaped.

But not solid.

I could see through it, like a gauzy shadow. Only this shadow had eyes. Bright yellow eyes with no face to match. It tried to stand up, clutching at the wall.

It only managed to hunch over—like a man with a hump.

The thing began to look around. Its eyes flickered in the dimming light of the basement, darting glances from corner to comer, glaring at everything.

Until it saw Tim. Then the yellow eyes arched with a sparkle of glee, like a lunatic who found the key to his padded cell.

Tim just stood there, with his arms at his sides, his hands clenching and unclenching.

The drop of saliva fell off his chin into the slime, causing a ring of ripples around his feet.

The breathing stopped.

The thing made a new sound. At first it was a grunt, but it turned into something worse.

Laughter.

Laughter like you hear at carnival spook houses. High-pitched and screaming. But this was not a carnival. It was real, and the laughter filled the room with so loud a noise that I put my hands over my ears. I thought I'd go crazy hearing it . . . because I couldn't believe what my eyes were seeing.

The thing started to limp toward Tim, shrieking hysterically from a mouthless face.

Tim didn't move. He started to whimper.

It reached out a hand.

It had three fingers.

The longest finger had a broken talon on the end.

It touched Tim's head.

Tim's skull exploded.

Exploded like a little kernel of corn in a popping machine, spurting bits of bone and charred flesh around the room like shrapnel. There was a flash of blue light, and the air filled with static, crackling like the screech from a high-tension wire.

The thing snaked out one hand and clutched at Tim's headless neck. Tim's twitching body slumped into the muck, leaving red and gray brain smattered on the walls.

As the body lay in the slime, the creature started to wrap itself around what was left of Tim, like a dark transparent shell.

Then I could hear it start sucking.

Loudly. Savagely.

Sucking as if it wanted to pull Tim's soul right out of his body.

I saw the gun lying on the ground by my face and grabbed it. I fired one shot and then another into the shadow that was now swallowing whole parts of Tim's mutilated body.

The first bullet went through the thing's back and got lodged in the wall. The second one ricocheted off one of the pipes and ended up in the steps.

I could hear the laughter start up again.

I realized that there was nothing I could do—or anybody in the world could do—to help Tim. Or me. And I wasn't in a good position to stick around.

I pulled myself to my knees and scrambled to the stairs.

I made it up those eleven steps and to that cellar door in all of two seconds.

The door back into the kitchen was closed.

And locked.

From the other side.

That was ten minutes ago.

I've been waiting all this time. Mostly with my eyes closed.

I don't know what I'm going to . . .

Shit. The sucking sounds and the laughter stopped just now.

I can hear the breathing again.

I'm leaning here against the locked door. I don't know how it got locked. Or even closed. Doesn't matter now. I tried shooting the lock off. Twice. All that happened was the door splintered a little. Nothing else.

There's a lot I don't know. I can't begin to wonder at most of it. Maybe Barty Hansen really did find the badness in his neighborhood. Maybe he tried to lock it up. Maybe he found what it had done to those kids, inside his own house.

Maybe he sacrificed those kids to it.

Maybe. Maybe. Maybe.

There might be only one way out of here. I still got two bullets in the gun. I know bullets won't stop whatever it is that's down there. But if that thing comes for me I'll put the barrel in my mouth and use it. Better that than have my skull blow apart like a grenade.

I wonder how long I'll have to wait.

Because . . .

Hold on.

The breathing from the cellar.

It stopped.

Now I hear something worse.

A maniac's laugh.

I think the wait is over.

Unexpected Circumstances
Morgan Fletcher

C arl loved tattoos. He loved collecting them. Just not on his own skin.

***

Alanna awoke in a frenzy, violently tearing at the sheets. In a half awake, half sleep-walking state of consciousness, she frantically searched her bed for something. As she started to wake up a little more, she calmed down enough to realize it was a dream.

She fumbled around her nightstand for her water glass. Even though it was almost pitch black, she found the glass, and the glass found her lips. With every sip (gulp, more like) she felt a little more together.

Okay. She had a dream (no, a nightmare). That was what got her heart so worked up. But what was it about? What subconscious thoughts could have been so grave she woke up frantic and searching for something? *Oh well*, she thought.

Concern now overtook her emotions as she worried, she may have woken Ravi. True, he was a deep sleeper, but she had put on an entire performance as she awoke. Whispering, "Did I wake you?" Alanna got no response. A little louder, "Sorry if I woke you up." Still, no response. "Ravi?" came out now at a regular tone. Nothing. Where could he be this time in the morning?

Alanna gazed towards the bathroom hoping there would be light seeping from underneath the door. She grabbed the phone off her cordless charger, turned on the flashlight, and stumbled downstairs. Ravi wasn't making any noise. Ravi wasn't responding to her calls. She couldn't see Ravi anywhere. Ravi wasn't there.

***

He had no idea how long he had been on his knees, but he was starting to feel them. Rather, his knees were starting to feel him. His thoughts were pounding with alarm, but he had more to be concerned about than his thoughts; the pain wasn't just in his knees.

Physically, the sensation of chains holding him in place was running down his face and neck, into his shoulders and arms, through his stomach (and almost back up and out of his mouth), finally settling on the vice that was his quadriceps. He was only aware of the parts that were in pain, as though every safe, sacred other part of him was gone.

Of course, he had those pesky thoughts. Those weighed the heaviest.

For a brief reprieve, Alanna swam into his thoughts. His thoughts of her were trying to dive through the physical pain, splashing onto the top, creating more than a ripple. He also knew it was little use to think of her right now. She would get swept away. Drowned in the physical realm. A literal realm. No escaping.

A contorting muscle brought Ravi back to truth, to the concrete floor he had been chained to for…how long had he been here? He wondered if his kneecaps could break from the constant pressure of his body weight. He anguished he might find out.

***

Carl had considered this one for a while. This one wasn't exactly like the kind Momma used to bring home, but close enough, and it had been too long for Carl. Momma collected all kinds of things, and she had a special room she enjoyed them in. There were kewpie dolls, old books, and crocheted crosses. One wall supported shelves with coin collections, baby blankets, and picture albums she found at thrift stores, full of other people's pictures.

She loved collecting things that didn't belong to her; not one of her collections started with anything new. She would go to thrift stores and antique houses, garage sales and estate auctions. She would make Carl stay home and fend for himself any time she went on one of her "treasure hunts." Momma would say, "Don't worry Carly, you'll find your own treasures to collect someday."

And Momma never had a problem finding treasures to collect. Including men.

Carl got distracted from his observation by a combination of misery and rage at these memories. These men, no, these *things* were what killed Momma. And it wasn't her fault. She was a generous woman, and they took advantage. They picked up on Momma's occasions of weakness and took what they wanted, which seemed to be a lot. There were some that came back more than once, but mostly they were different, like her other collections. Dark hair or light hair, long or short; tall, short, skinny, chubby— didn't matter.

But they all had tattoos. And Carl had already started a collection.

***

Ravi's cell went straight to voicemail. Not good. She tried his partner in the realty business. "Hey, Alanna. You haven't called me in a long while. What's up?"

"Hey, Mike. I woke up and couldn't find Ravi. I realize I might seem paranoid, but I have a bad feeling about this. He doesn't just leave."

"Maybe he got a call. Business is booming right now, and we're working with those developers who are putting in those new neighborhoods across town. I'm sure everything is fine."

She was getting blown off by him and she knew it. She didn't like Mike, and this was one of the reasons why. Anytime she had to deal with him he treated her like she was an annoying, unmanageable child who should be seen but not heard. He was a misogynist, an egomaniac, and a narcissist. And although she couldn't be one-hundred percent positive, she was sure he was a sociopath (if you separated narcissism from sociopathy, that is).

"He's never left without telling me. He's never walked out the door and forgotten to kiss me. He's never left in the middle of the night and not woken me up. Told me he had to leave, and he loved me. He's never disappeared, Mike. I'm concerned."

Mike intentionally released a little giggle, trying to make Alanna feel like she was being crazy. "He's fine, Alanna. You'll see. He'll come home later today, tell you he was with the developers all day. I don't know. Maybe he forgot to charge his phone. But then you'll feel really silly, won't you."

Through gritted teeth she simply replied, "Thanks for answering, Mike," and hung up the phone.

Maybe Ravi is at the office and Mike doesn't know. Alanna was sure that was it. And sure, maybe Mike was right, and Ravi's phone did die. Maybe he was so busy he hadn't noticed. Alanna called, and as expected, Tammy answered the phone. "R&M Realty. How may I assist you?"

Hearing Tammy answer the phone this way made her happy. For one, it was a miracle Mike didn't bully Ravi into putting his initial first. The only reason Ravi won that one was because it was his money, his inheritance. He wanted a partner, and even though Mike was a douchebag of a person, he was a stellar agent. Mike put in ten percent, and done deal. Aside from that, Alanna liked Tammy.

Ravi and Mike had been through quite a few assistants over the years, many leaving because of Mike, but Tammy was tough and professional. She was also in her mid-forties, so Mike didn't hit on her as much. But when he did, she didn't tolerate his nonsense. Tammy made it clear from the beginning she couldn't be intimidated. In a weird way, it seemed as though Mike respected that. Hearing Tammy's voice and hearing her announce the name of the company her husband purchased and built up in reputation, it made her feel grounded. Like everything was going to be okay.

"Hey Tammy!"

"Well, hello, Mrs. Ghosh! What a nice surprise to hear from you! I hope everything is okay?"

Tammy was that level of professional. No matter what, she only called coworkers by their formal names. Tammy had been with the guys for five years, and it was still "Yes, Mr. Ghosh," and "Not today, Mrs. Ghosh," or during the unfortunate times she had to interact with Mike, "I'd appreciate it if you didn't speak to me like that, Mr. Vandyck."

Sometimes the formality bothered Alanna. Tammy had been there the longest, and Alanna felt as though she should be a part of the family. Or at least Tammy should want to feel like part of the family. Isn't that the way it always goes in books and movies?

"Actually," Alanna replied, "I can't find Ravi. I've spoken to Mike…"

"I'm so sorry, hun…"

Alanna let out a giggle. "Yeah, well, Mike seems to think everything's fine, his phone is dead, and he's busy. But I don't know. I feel like something is off. Maybe I am paranoid. I figured I'd call you, hoping you had seen or heard from him today?"

"Unfortunately, I haven't. What time did he leave this morning? It's still pretty early."

"Yeah, um, I don't know. Something woke me up and he was gone."

"Do you think it was him leaving that woke you up? That might hint at timing."

"Mmm…I'm not sure. But I don't think so. It made me feel weird. He's never done that before. Left without saying anything. Without waking me."

"Well, I'll let him know you're worried, if I see or hear from him. And as much as I hate to admit it, Mike could be right on this one. It could just be an unusual set of circumstances. He'll turn up soon, for sure. You try to have a restful day now. Talk to you next time."

Yeah. Restful.

Maybe she was being a worrywart. If it comes from Mike, it's one thing, but coming from Tammy it's a whole different ballgame.

***

Ravi was trying to remember how he got there. Why he was there. Hell, where even was he? He had a vague recollection of leaving work. Yeah, he remembered leaving work; it was becoming clearer now. A man came in asking about the property on Diamond Drive; said he was interested in building a house there, for him and his wife. Money is money, Ravi decided, even if it was closing time.

Ravi's memories started to become more concrete. "Yes. There was a guy who came in," Ravi garbled out loud.

He had been so dazed that hearing his own voice startled him a little. A chain reaction from his non-consensual jerking movement caused the chains he was in to rattle. He was becoming more focused minute by minute, and that one startling moment of clarity would have brought him to his knees…if he wasn't already on them.

He was dazed. He was in chains. He had no idea where he was. "Help!" Ravi screamed. "Please, help me!" He sounded louder to himself than he thought he should sound. At least he could still scream. It was at this moment of contemplation he thought he heard something in the corner. Scratching…or shuffling.

He swore he saw some type of movement, but the corner was a distance.

And it was dark there.

***

Oops. Carl didn't mean for that thing to notice his presence…not yet at least. And what a presence he was. He liked being in charge. In control. In absolute control. Momma never let him be in control of anything. His stupid sciatica sparked a twinge in his hip that fired right down to the sensitive spot behind the knee; he had to adjust.

Carl had been watching for forty-four minutes at this point, but that wasn't quite long enough for him. He wanted more. He wanted more time with this tattooed captive, getting to know it, seeing how it responds to pain…to fear. Carl preferred being in the shadows, at least in the beginning, but now he might accidentally have a fan. An adoring audience.

"Oh, 'help'! 'Please help me,'" Carl mocked. "Do you think I've never heard that one before?" Carl was a little disgusted at how stupid some of these animals could be. "Next, you'll be saying something dumb like, 'Pleeeeese let me go! I swear, I won't tell anyone!'"

Carl's high-pitched mocking voice forced some viscous phlegm, that he had way too much of, up into his mouth. Momma was constantly onto Carl about how he acted in public, so he was self-conscious about a lot of things, spitting was one. But this wasn't a person who could run and tell others. Hell, it wasn't a person at all. It's not like that "man" could embarrass him.

Carl had thought too long about all of this and was forced to spit the chunk out on the floor or swallow it back down. No time to get to the bathroom and take care of it properly. This was when Carl realized the thing in chains couldn't *see* him—it had only *heard* him adjusting. Although he couldn't wait to get started adding to his collection, he realized there was more fun to be had.

***

They had plans that day. Granted, sometimes Ravi did have to break plans for work related issues, but it wasn't typical. He hadn't made it home for dinner yesterday either. She hadn't thought about it until now. No dinner, no phone call, nothing. She had no idea what time she fell asleep last night, but she did so while waiting for him to get home.

When was the last time she heard from him?

They had lunch together over the phone; that was around one. *Did I talk to him after?* Alanna tried to remember if there had been another phone call, if he had told her he was on his way home, but she was pretty sure there hadn't been. Now it was lunchtime again, but no phone call this time. It had been twenty-four hours since she spoke to him.

She wanted to call the police but knew she would feel stupid if Ravi showed up. But at the same time, if something happened to him and she didn't call she would feel worse. She wanted to call Mike again and ask him which site Ravi might be at, so she could drive by and see if his car was there, but she also didn't want to talk to Mike. She compromised with herself and sent him a text.

Alanna: I know you think I'm being paranoid, but it's been twenty-four hours since I last spoke with Ravi. Would you happen to know which site he might be at today?

Mike: Why? The sites don't have landlines. What's your deal?

Alanna: I don't want to call; I want to drive there.

Mike: Jesus Christ! What, are you stalking him now?

Alanna: Mike, will you help me out here? I'll quit bothering you. I want to drive by and see if his car is there.

Mike: Fine. He might be at the old car lot. There have been some interested developers talking to him about that place and the land surrounding it. There's also four acres off Highway 50.

Alanna: Thank you.

Alanna threw her phone in her purse and sprinted out the door.

***

Typically, he would let this game run its course and it would be over quickly enough. But there was something different about this one. Maybe it was the build of it. Maybe it was the tone and frequency of its pleas for help. Didn't matter. Carl wanted this one to be special. He wanted to take his time with it. See how long it begged while Carl flayed the tattoos from its skin.

He had never put one on its knees, so he was curious as to what would happen. Carl wondered if the thing on the floor wondered about that too.

Carl would love it if he could hook some kind of T.V. up to the thing's mind and have all of those worries create pictures on the screen, for him to watch, of course. There would be a glory and joy of being able to see what was going inside of the minds of his victims (not *victims* but *things*); no longer guessing or asking about it, watching as the fears came into view.

And he would make them watch.

He would make them watch their own darkest fears come to life. Fears they never knew they had. Depravity they never knew existed. And he would gift them with not only living through reality, but also watching their fear of the unknown. He would bring their worries to life. If they thought about something, feared something he hadn't thought of — yet— he could act it out for them. Let them see how cool their idea is.

But if they were boring, or too far gone perhaps to come up with any original ideas, he could at least let them watch as he removed their tattoos.

***

She decided to drive out to Highway 50 first because she and Ravi lived out in the county anyway; it was a closer drive.

Alanna didn't have a lot to do with the business side of things, so she didn't know a lot about what was going on, but as she neared the site off the highway she was confused. There was barely anything going on at that site. There were no machines or concrete blocks. There were no cones or sawhorses. There were no people. Alanna drove all the way up the gravel road, hoping she would see something that could give her a clue. "Oh well. Off to the old car lot."

She tried Ravi's cell again, just to be on the safe side, lest she be seen as insane. Still nothing, so she continued the drive. When she arrived at the car lot, she was more curious than anything. This was the second site she had been to, both given to her by Mike, who should know what's going on, and both sites were empty. This one did have some machinery, but the building was still standing. None of the ground appeared to be grazed, and it didn't appear as though that was happening anytime soon.

A sick feeling started to heat her inside from her toes to her brain. Was Ravi cheating on her and Mike covering? Logic told Alanna that would never happen. Hell, emotion told her Ravi would never do that. But…there was that other emotion. The, "What if I'm wrong?" emotion. The sense of unbalance that most, if not all, women have experienced at some point in a relationship. "This isn't one of those relationships though," she convinced herself. Or, at least, she thought she had.

***

Carl hated everyone except Momma when she was alive. He especially hated the tattooed ones that took advantage of her.

Even if he was sleeping, Momma would kick Carl out of his room, always having to remake his bed when she let him back in. He wondered what kind of garage sales were going on that late at night. But he knew where she was really going.

He could hear the men laughing at him, he was sure, judging him. They had no right to do that to him; they were no better, but they thought they were. They must have had money because they were out doing things. They had friends. They probably got their panties bunched up at the thought of having a job and paying for their own things. Losers like that didn't have a right to judge him.

Momma had him practice driving since he was twelve. If she needed to go to the store, he brought her. If she needed to go to a doctor, he took her. If she ran out of alcohol, he drove her. And mother ran out of alcohol a lot. It wasn't her fault though. If it weren't for all those bad men she dated, those bad *things*, she wouldn't have had a problem with alcohol at all. They made her like that, drove her to it—haha—no pun intended.

She would give them whatever they wanted, whether it was money, drink, or food. She was an angel. But it seemed like what they wanted most of all was sex. That's what made Carl hate them because angels didn't have sex. Sex was dirty and gross, and they made Momma do it.

They were worthless creatures. Demons that coerced Momma into doing things she never wanted to do, with their meaningless purpose and manipulation. They were the equivalent of old, run-down, used objects that should be destroyed, removed from permanent resale.

Things.

He knew it was his purpose, his meaning in life, to remove such things from existence. Take away their ability to manipulate other innocent mothers into doing things they didn't want to. No, he didn't hear voices, that only happened to stupid people. Every idea, every new torture method, was all his idea, and his alone. And he wanted it to be that way. To stay in control.

There was one more thing Carl would need to start having fun. "I've got to go back upstairs to the garage to get a different toy out of my car. Don't worry, it might take me a little bit to choose which one I want, but it shouldn't take too long. Don't miss me too much," he scoffed.

***

Ravi was going to lose consciousness soon. Or at least that's what he hoped. It wasn't just the physical pain; it was the knowing. Knowing the damage that was being done and that there was very little that could prevent that damage from being permanent. And knowing was also causing psychological pain, also more than likely permanent.

Had Ravi seen this man before he entered the office? Had Ravi wronged him somehow? With thoughts becoming more and more clear, Ravi couldn't remember any interaction with this stranger at all.

Perhaps this guy interacted with Mike and didn't realize there were two agents in the office. Mike probably hit on this guy's wife, or something, and this guy was doing this as retribution. Mike makes a lot of people angry, so it's entirely possible that this guy, this psycho, had grabbed the wrong person. Not that it mattered; Ravi was stuck nonetheless and knew he was in trouble.

He was hoping that however long he had been held prisoner here, someone would notice and call the police. Left with his horrifying thoughts, Ravi contemplated how long "a little bit" would be. If he didn't come back, Ravi might have a chance of escaping; he didn't know how, but there could be a chance. If he did come back, the torture would begin. Ravi's weighted thoughts were interrupted by the creaking of the basement door.

***

Alanna's internal debate was interrupted by a notification; it was a text from Mike.

Mike: I still think you're being a freak about this, but I remembered another spot. We've been working with a housing developer. These guys are moving incredibly slow, but they're putting houses up. It's more of Ravi's deal, but I think there's one street in the upcoming neighborhood that's done, or almost. The street is Diamond Drive.

Mike: I'll send the location.

Alanna didn't bother responding; she sat there and waited for the directions. This was her last hope before making a fool of herself and calling the police. Hopefully, making a fool of herself. She had to find a way to slow things down. She had taken too long to realize anything was off, so she rushed to make calls, rushed around to empty work sites, and she supposed, rushed to judgement. She decided to stop at a gas station and get some vanilla flavored crappuccino, as she called it, and a Slim Jim.

She sat in the parking lot partaking of snack time, attempting to breathe deliberately and with intention between sips and bites. Clearing her mind of every sensation other than taste, she convinced herself not to obsess. It hadn't been that long. She was being ridiculous. Taking as much time as her mind would allow, she finally finished, threw out her trash, and drove towards Diamond Drive.

Her emotions had been capricious since she awoke from the nightmare, and this was the exact moment those emotions decided to let go. Trying to continue to stay in the lines, she gripped the steering wheel so hard her palms were becoming sore, while tears rolled down her blouse.

Everything is fine. You are being stupid. Look at you, crying! For what? She continued to internally chastise herself while pulling onto Diamond Drive.

Oh my God. What if he leaves me because of this? Alanna tapped on the brakes, slowing gradually so as not to be noticed immediately. Just because her worry was clamorous didn't mean her car needed to be.

Alanna turned around in a driveway a few houses away, parking her car facing the opposite direction; she wanted to ensure she could make a quick getaway if the break-up happened here. As she started walking towards the house Ravi was supposed to be at, she at once noticed something odd: no real-estate lock box on the doorknob.

No one in the business of showing houses would leave property unsecured. Anyone could walk in and tear up the place. Thousands of dollars would be lost, and more importantly, reputation. Ravi wouldn't leave a house like this, not even for a few minutes, yet there was no lock box on the door nor a vehicle in the driveway.

She pulled her phone from her pocket, readying herself to have a voice conversation with Mike, when she was unsettled by something.

Was that rattling?

She couldn't be sure, because if it was, it was faint.

Moving out of view from the front windows, slinking alongside the house next door, she edged closer. Still and barely breathing, trying to focus everything else out, she heard it again, only this time she also saw the garage door shake with the noise.

It's the sound of the inside garage door being opened and shut.

But was this rattling the opening or closing of a door? Was someone, at that exact moment, standing inside of the garage, looking out, looking for a vehicle they swear they heard driving up just a few minutes ago? Or was that the sound of someone leaving the garage? Going back inside.

Alanna knew she had to peek. She waited another minute to listen for any other noise. Inhaling then holding her breath, she exhaled while moving just enough to see what was in the garage. Her pulse quickened as Ravi's car came into view…and the car next to his.

***

"Why are you doing this to me?" Ravi's strength came back to a shout. "I don't know you! I haven't done anything to you! I'm not Mike, man. If that's who you think I am, I'm not him. I'm happily married. I've never cheated on my wife. I've never been with another man's wife. What do you want?"

Carl loved the begging, but not questions of rational thought. Who did these things think they were, questioning him? He didn't owe this thing any type of response, but there was something Carl liked about it. "So, you think it makes it okay because you're married? So were they. Oh, but you don't cheat. I call bull. But let's say you haven't ever cheated on any woman in your life, ever. Does that excuse how you treat them?"

Ravi was more perplexed than frightened. What was this psycho talking about? "How I treat who?"

"Whom."

"Whatever, you sick bastard. Look, I don't know what you're talking about, or who you think I am. I've never cheated on anyone, and I don't know how you think I treat people."

Carl laughed, "You don't know? That's my point! You don't even think about how your behavior affects other people. Look at you. You have no regard for the temple that is your body. Of course, you don't have any regard for others.

"Wait. You kidnapped me because I have tattoos?"

"I took you because your kind shouldn't be allowed to roam around, without any thought to the harm you're causing, taking advantage of people."

"I don't take advantage of people! You don't even know me. You're nuts!"

"I know your kind well enough. I watched you people take advantage of Momma over and over again. You caused her death. You did that to her, now your kind has to pay it back."

"Pay back how? Killing me? I never knew your mother," Ravi certainly hoped, anyway.

"With your tattoos. I want your tattoos."

"How is killing me going to give you my tattoos?"

"It's not the killing. To preserve them the way I want them, I must take them while you're alive and alert. Death is not caused directly by me. Death is secondary."

Ravi realized what was going to happen to him. He knew wherever he was it wouldn't matter, but a combination of fear and hopelessness took over, and with that came a most guttural scream.

***

What the hell was that noise?

Although she couldn't for sure identify it, it caused a most visceral reaction. Alanna's pulse now threatened to tear through her skin. Sweat ran down her forehead and soaked the top portion of her shirt, yet chills covered her like a blanket. "Oh God. No. Do not vomit right now."

Her mind was blank with terror; there was something off about that noise.

***

"When are you going to realize screaming doesn't matter," Carl stated rhetorically, as though he was a philosophy major at an Ivy League University. "Why do you think I chose this place."

Carl grabbed something glinty off his chair.

"I like you, so I'm not going to lie to you. This is going to hurt. A lot."

"Why are you doing this? I don't know your mother."

"You wanna know why? I'll tell you why. Momma was an angel; until she was corrupted by things like you. They were all different, like everything else she collected, but they all had tattoos. All of em'. There was no respect for the body as a temple. Especially her body. I had to keep her clean. I had to…they killed her. I saved her soul.

"As soon as I cleansed Momma, I knew I had to help rid the world of the filth that defiled her. Filth like you. Momma always said I'd find something of my own, and here I am. Kill a few birds with one stone. I keep your marks of worthlessness as a reminder of what I sacrificed for my whole life, what I sacrificed for Momma, and I get rid of scum like your kind."

Carl meticulously sculpted a layer of flesh from Ravi's calf. Ravi's scream hammered at the concrete that was the unfinished basement.

As though he were holding a class for a group of first-time hunters, "Ya know, this knife I'm working with is called a skinning blade?" It was obvious Carl was amusing himself with that piece of knowledge. "I chained you up this way so there'd be less blood. I hate blood."

Attempting to assuage his deranged jailer, "I'm sure those men who hurt your mother deserved to be tortured. They were terrible people."

"Oh! You think you're going to be my buddy now?"

"But I've never even met your mother. And I'm not like that."

"Friends, are we now?"

Ravi's chin fell to his chest in despair.

***

Alanna slinked through the front door. A few feet inside, her body ceased to function normally; every muscle fiber strained from rigidity, every nerve ending hyper-vigilant. It was more than just screaming. It was a growling, like an animal that's been injured; nausea again overtook her senses.

A part of her wanted to tear into whatever space Ravi was, and wrest him from whatever monster held him imprisoned, but she knew that would yet again be rushing, and that wasn't just a bad idea right now, it might mean life or death.

She delicately traveled her course in reverse, taking refuge in her car for both safety and sound. Keeping watch on that last house on Diamond Drive, Alanna's fingers flitted the emergency number across her phone's keypad.

"Talbot County 9-1-1."

"Yes, I need help. I believe my husband is being held captive and tortured. I'm at the end of Diamond Drive. Please come soon…"

***

Alanna spent a few minutes on the phone with the operator, giving details of both the location and situation. The operator implored Alanna to stay in the car, justifying the request through the repetition of heartened but stereotypical phrases. *Sure. I'll stay in the car. It's for my own safety. The officers will be right here.*

Clouds started to darken the stratosphere around her, adding to her already heavy mindset. Rain that started peacefully enough escalated into a deluge of precipitation, enhancing her frayed deportment. She knew she wouldn't have been able to hear him from her car anyway, but the deafening rain made her feel more removed than she was comfortable with. And she was feeling very uncomfortable as it was.

Alanna decided the downpour might be creating enough noise that she could sneak back in. She didn't have any weapons, so it was a stupid idea, but if she could at least hear what was going on. She could…*What? Go save him? Beat up the bad guy?* She couldn't justify her illogical thinking, but she knew she'd feel better if she was inside. *Telepathically support him while a lunatic is doing God knows what?*

She tenderly pressed her hip against the car door to keep the latching as quiet as possible.

Reenacting the steps of her first journey towards the house, it dawned on her the downpour might muffle her skulking about, but equally, it might muffle the sounds of fiendish footsteps coming for her.

The door was still slightly ajar from when she left. She was immobile, listening for anything that could be an indication of impending danger.

Groaning noises sent her on sensory overload. *It's just the hinges on the door. Of course, it would happen right now. Stupid.*

Uncontrollable shaking was gifted from stress-induced, hyper-stimulated muscles. B*reathe.* Every breath was coming in ragged wisps.

Eyes as wide as the sockets would permit, mouth agape to help regulate respiration, Alanna floated through the threshold. Her heart abused her chest cavity with trepidation as she guardedly inspected the room she was in. Reminders of the storm beaded down her forehead, mixing with sweat, obscuring her vision. Her clothes, saturated, worked tirelessly to decrease any warmth she had left.

She was out in the open. Vulnerable. Easy prey.

Slipping down the nearest hallway, she entered a room that would serve as both home base and a hunting blind. Alanna recognized she could not tell the difference between torrents of rain, and what could be sounds of suffering. *This was such a dumb decision.*

A scuffling sound turned arctic what was already chilled. *Oh my God.*

Alanna crept behind the door, placing her back against the wall, hoping it was open enough to block anyone from finding her. The scuffling transformed into a scurrying. The scurrying became a shadow that slinked past the door, creating an unnerving jingling as it shifted.

Succumbing to the logic of her five-year-old self, she held her breath hoping it would make her invisible to whatever was out there. She tittered at the irony.

A light danced menacingly back towards her sanctuary. It heard her.

Drawing more memories from the well of childish fairy tales, she inhaled to hold her breath again, closed her eyes, and stood motionless.

Frantic with hopes of the charade working, she continued to discipline her need for oxygen, but knew soon it would turn into a punishment. Keeping her eyes closed and every other part of her body still, she slowly exhaled through pursed lips.

The hairs on Alanna's arm alerted her to the proximity of the shadow; the dancing light it wielded burned the thin skin protecting her eyes. Without rational thought, the animalistic nature of humankind brewed from her bowels, ready to screech out a last stitch effort to survive.

A large, calloused hand covered her mouth and nose completely, diminishing her primal scream. The body attached to that hand, equal in every way, deleted the small gap between her back and the wall, pinning her. Adrenaline demanded she fight, or at least breathe, but neither was an option.

Her mission had failed. The fairy tales were lies.

"I'm not going to hurt you, but you need to stop making noise," came from the voice of a stranger who was fighting for control as much as she was. "As soon as you calm down, I'll explain." The stranger tightened his grip just a little, pushed her just a little more into the wall. What difference did it make at this point? He was either being honest, or she was dead, either way.

Alanna stopped her scream from escaping; stopped trying to fight off this unexpected visitor to her haunted attraction. She took steadying breaths to sequester that adrenaline.

"My name is Detective Marshall, Easton P.D. I'm here with my partner Detective MacDonald. We saw you weren't in your car. When we came up to the house, we heard noises. Do you know where your husband is?" Alanna shook her head.

The detective put up hand signals that universally mean 'stay put,' then did a thorough check of the room. She could hear the detective communicating with his partner through his shoulder radio, but the voices were too low, and the rain too loud for her to figure out what was being said. He signaled for Alanna to come to where he was. "I need you to hide in here. Don't make a sound. We're going to look through the rest of the house. Do you understand?" Alanna nodded.

Through a tiny crack between the closet door and the frame, she could see who she assumed was Detective MacDonald. The two detectives had a brief conversation, then Marshall walked out of the room while MacDonald stayed at the door. After a few minutes of fixed stillness, Marshall came back whispering something about the basement, then off they went.

Alanna had no idea how long she had been there. She heard violent noises other than rain: Screaming; objects falling or being thrown; other unidentifiable but frightening sounds. Uneasiness draped over her when one of the detectives bellowed for an ambulance. The wrestling of good versus evil was making its way up the staircase, out the front door, and into an unmarked car.

Alanna wasn't sure if she was calling on forces of bravery or naivety, but she walked out of the closet. Not sure if it was safe yet, she tip-toed to where the basement door was open. Also, not sure if she wanted to see what was down there, she carefully placed a foot on the top step.

Detective MacDonald hurtled herself to the basement, grabbed Alanna's arm, and yanked her back up. "You don't want to go down there, Miss. I know you want to see him, but not right now. The ambulance is already here."

"Is he okay?"

"He's alive."

In rushed the ambulance workers. Pushing her and the detective out of the way, they glided down the staircase, and eventually advanced back up, assiduously slow. Ravi didn't look good. He didn't look like himself.

Alanna clutched the side of the gurney he was on and kept pace with the EMTs. They let her ride in the front with the driver because both of them needed to be in the back to take care of Ravi. They made sure she knew that wasn't typical procedure.

The whole ride was fraught with fear. His pulse was weak. His heart rate wasn't steady. "Please don't die, please don't leave me," were the only cries in the ambulance.

***

"Now, Mr. Ghosh, what reason did the defendant give for kidnapping and torturing you?"

Ravi admired his lawyer. "He said, basically, to avenge his mother's death."

"Did the defendant tell you how his mother died?"

"Well, not how per se, but he said he had to kill her to save her. Something like that."

"And why did he try to skin you alive?"

"To collect my tattoos. He said he kept them to remind him of his purpose."

"Thank you, Mr. Ghosh. No further questions, Your Honor."

***

"So, Ravi, did you read the article about psycho Carl's conviction?" Mike was full of himself already.

"I don't need to read it. He's in jail. I lived it."

"No, man. Apparently, after he got back to the prison, he confessed to doing it a whole bunch of times."

"Yeah, he more or less said that. We all kinda figured."

"He told them about some storage place. Out on highway 50. The police found an entire shed full of people's skinned tattoos."

Ravi shivered. He was glad to be done with everything. Perhaps, he darkly chuckled to himself, he should be done with the real estate business too.

Eraticator
Dave Davis

Jon was losing his sleep, energy, health, mind. His vitality was being extinguished on all fronts. Anxiety, hypertension, arrythmia, insomnia, hematochezia, and melancholia culminated in a miserable existence of gloom. The petulant neighbors refused to curtail their incessant hellraising. He was being terrorized with near daily bombardment of penetrating bass from their hip hop, and raucous yelling, cussing, and laughter. The activities would persist from early evening, throughout the entire night, into early morning hours consistently. He had moved to the quiet coastal community of Seabrook to escape the roaring hustle and bustle of Houston. By all outward appearances, and during tours of the property with a real estate agent, Jon would've never surmised that his future dwelling was anything but tranquil. Almost all of the surrounding homes were inhabited by geriatrics, retirees, or respectful families, so it seemed.

Despite involving the police on a half-dozen occasions, when he had reached the end of his wits, no action was taken. This didn't influence the hellions to curtail their tyranny; it only emboldened them, with a renewed malice. The degenerates, rats as Jon had come to refer to them, seemed to enjoy employing their endeavors now as retaliation, and with a zest for inducing suffering.

Not only was regular, or any type of sleep impossible, with the obnoxious voices and body reverberating soundwaves, but anxiety and fury insured deprivation of rest and rejuvenation, as the bass induced heart palpitations, and the audible yelling fits included verbiage pertaining to assaulting Jon. "Hit them from the side!" and "Catch him in the streets!" were particularly unnerving exclamations, in addition to the perpetual cursing about him and his wife, which were readily discernable with full on penetration of the habitat's walls.

The neighbors from hell would always go dark and quiet upon spotting an arriving patrol vehicle, and then lie profusely to the reporting officer about the circumstances, while displaying contemptuous attitude. The rats would confront the policemen, and attest vehemently that they weren't doing anything. After being informed by the authorities that no legal options were available with the current identifiable, existing evidence, Jon began to feel helpless, and doomed to torture in his own abode. The disrespect and sadism of these 'people' was hard for him to fathom. He just could not believe that anyone, much less an entire clique of so called civilized human beings, would volitionally, intentionally, willingly, engage in such ambitious disrespect, directed at their goddamn neighbors, of all targets, for fuck's sake. Immediately upon reentering the confines of his home, after repeatedly forcing himself to engage with the police and hoodlums in the middle of the night, Jon would be left in his supposed sanctuary to endure the boiling blood pressure, headaches, tinnitus, and adrenaline shakes; and, more often than not, he would spend an unreal amount of time suffering prolonged diarrhea, with profuse loss of blood flowing into the toilet along with it, which only added to his dismay. This would further delay any return to sleep, and collectively robbed him of rest, health, and sanity. Under the influence of ongoing neurotic apprehension, leading to paranoia, leading to rage; coupled with the absence of sleep, and distraught that his peace and sovereignty were under attack, his mind broke.

One evening, while lying in bed, with ear plugs inserted, white noise employed, and with blankets and pillows strategically placed surrounding his head in a vain attempt to doze off, Jon suddenly noticed flowing waves of ambient darkness sifting throughout the airspace encompassing his bedroom, predominantly along the left side of his bed and room. Expecting causation from the neighboring backyard, Jon turned to inspect the window area rightward. Not only was a heavy curtain blocking the probability of penetration, but nothing could be spotted to blame for the anomalous visualizations. As he returned his view to the opposite side of the room, close examination confirmed that these slow-swirling shades seemed to be emanating out of thin air. The light from the rats' yard was peeking through the topmost aspect of his curtained window, yet the supreme darkness existed. What he perceived to witness was even more coherent, via the disparity in darkness across the room, enabled by the unwelcome infiltrating light, which the hateful rats had purposely concentrated onto Jon's sleeping quarters. The active, formless things were clearly much darker than the blackest side of the room, and didn't seem to be translucent. They weren't solid, but couldn't be seen through either. Jon had never had this experience, nor this sight, invade his visual field. Just as he began to wonder about the nature of this event, 'Was it hallucinations, a stroke, shadow people?' his attention was stolen to a vastly different observation. The mobile amorphous clusters vanished, and his mind now interpreted a dark blue and black tunnel of sorts. Now he was really concerned of cerebral vascular or psychiatric pathology. 'Am I suffering from hypertension related exudates occluding my retinas, or an infarct to the occipital lobe?' he further pondered. 'Am I becoming schizophrenic?' After some trusty deep breathing exercises, and calculated calming thoughts, consciousness left him.

He awoke the next morning, surprised to have been awarded more sleep than he could recall acquiring in over a year. It was pleasing to actually awaken rejuvenated for a change, never mind that this shouldn't have been deprived of anyone, who otherwise didn't intentionally avoid sleep to pursue volitional endeavors of their choosing, but not from those who meticulously arranged their life in order to guarantee regular, sufficient sleep. To pass the time while relaxing in the living room, Jon pulled up YouTube on his smart TV, selected a recent live concert from his favorite band Belphegor, and then began perusing eBay on his Android phone, while savoring the grinding riff of "Conjuring the Dead" emanating from the soundbar. An item presented itself almost immediately, which really piqued his interest.

The knife was the most beautiful object he had ever laid eyes on. The functional art was expertly designed and crafted, promising effortless efficiency and flawless performance. The vendor had it listed for $550 - buy it now, but there was an option to make an offer. Later that afternoon, Jon was ecstatic to find, that the Busse kin, Swamp Rat, Eraticator knife purchase was awarded to him, for $500.

Friday

The rat commotion began as usual, with numerous vehicles appearing throughout the late afternoon, bringing hollerin', cussin', bangin' doors, and the like. As darkness neared, the bass emanating from the garage, where they always congregated, drifting between there, the car port and back yard, permeated the neighboring properties. The shearing noise of glass bottles being hurled into the dumpster between Jon's house and their nest, was accompanied by repeatedly slamming barbeque pit lids and other ruckus. After peering through his front window to surmise the extent of excess to be expected this night, Jon took a brief glance at the revolving Kemah boardwalk Ferris Wheel gleaming in the distant dusk, before situating himself at his living room coffee table. He stared at the elegant cutting tool laying before him, admiring its beauty, its potential, its thirst for use. Instinctively, Jon scooped the generous blade up into his dominant hand, which fell automatically into a comfortable natural grip. Gradually, though his eyes remained fixed on the newfound prize within his grasp, the dark tunnel he had viewed previously while in bed, returned to consume his vision. Abruptly, his mind's eye was now enamored with a vast landscape of mounded offal. Sweet innards originating from the human mediastinum and peritoneum lay glistening about. The beautiful anatomical architecture of the viscera brought a pleasant sense of tranquility to his being, dichotomous to the pervading putrid exteriors that the rats exuded, exclusively! More than a couple of hours slipped by, before Jon snapped to, and came to realize that he had been zoned out, or rather zoned into, the new friend, the new helper, the new extension of himself. A smile crept across his face, as he had a sudden thought, but the voice, although originating from within his own mind, seemed foreign, 'Can't have barbeque without butchery…'

Jon was able to slip over the short cyclone fence, into their backyard undetected. The pitch-black night, abusively loud hip hop music, gangsta rap, or whatever the hell you wanna call it, and inebriation of the rats, only made this feat easier. It wasn't long before the rat with a limp staggered into the yard to piss, just out of the garage's escaping light, emanating from the back door.

'Oh, how I hate that son of a bitch!' He would show up every freakin' week, sometimes more than a couple of days. Always leaving his car stereo thumping obnoxiously loud, to the point of rattling the crappy vehicle's dilapidated panels and bumpers, as if this was an impressive spectacle for presentation to his fellow miscreants; additionally, the bastard would make sure to slam the driver side door upon exiting each and every single goddamned time, to announce his arrival. The thug would, without fail, initiate an onslaught of boisterous, high volume, spewing of verbal nonsense to his cohorts throughout the proximal carport, as if they couldn't hear him from that close, and alternately directed to those accompanying pricks within the farthest confines of the garage hangout, ensuring that no one had to miss out on his shenanigans. He must believe that he is so important, or amusing, that he's doing them all a favor by gracing them with his appearance and performances. It was baffling. 'What was so good, or entertaining about leaving the distorted, scrambled, shitty car 'music' remaining on for an extended period, while the just as loud, or often louder garage boom box was simultaneously spilling out through the yard, and everyone else's for that matter?' That arrogant fucker must consider it as his supporting theme music for his unsolicited, impromptu show-off extravaganzas. Only filth escaped this sorry waste of skin's voice box, while mostly talking shit, with false bravado, about inflicting violence on whoever the targeted topic of the day was: commonly coworkers, but often as of late, exclusively the object of their sadistic infatuation, Jon.

As Jon suspected, the filthy rat went into the deeper recesses of the dark, to leave his bottle on a table, where they dependably would mound debris. The foul-mouthed creature didn't even get a sound out, as Jon exploded up from crouching around the house's farthest back corner, while simultaneously slashing completely through the soft tissue and between the lower cervical vertebrae of the beast, with a fluid backhand horizontal, hacking cut. That one dropped into the dark, unnoticed, by the self-absorbed mob.

Tilting the knife into his view, Jon stared in wonderous satiety at the wet blade, as a voice, not so different from his own, rapidly amplified from the deepest recesses of his mind, 'Look how beautiful!' Pleased with the first test-cut of the long, sharp, balanced, ergonomic Eraticator, he awaited the next victim. The trial implementation proved his original impressions; with the thick spine, recurve blade profile, grip contours, and surprisingly light weight for its size, the planned tasks were going to be, simple. The blade was hungry. Jon was elated, and encouraged.

Several minutes later, the mustached rat strolled into the yard. "Hey you crippled fuck! What, already pass out, you light-weight? Better not be jerking it!" the most despised of rats exclaimed, as he snorted and chuckled with slobbering drunkenness.

Although the limper was in close contention for the Most Hated Varmint title, it was the mustache sporting rat whom Jon despised the most. Afterall, it was he who operated the tyrannical machinations; he who orchestrated the plight and sufferings which Jon came to know. It was that hell spawn who officially resided at the wasteoid encampment. That's the motherfucker who could care less about the rights, dignity, and peace of the surrounding mortgage paying and tax paying residents, who displayed the proper neighborly respect one would expect, and kept to themselves. He's the one who casually lied to the police officers about the infractions they had committed (not that the others wouldn't readily jump in frequently, declaring that this was a case of crying wolf, as if multiple lies made a truth, as if the numerous voices were more credible than the one), and had no problem supporting his act with instant, coordinated concealment of the reported violations, so that they may resume their onslaught of torture, with gusto, immediately upon the officers' leaving, as the attending law enforcement representatives couldn't dispense justice without directly observing the alleged infractions themselves. Never mind the circumstantial evidence and track record.

Jon would relate to the police, on several occasions, with agitation, "Do you think I enjoy getting out of bed at two, three, or four in the morning, getting dressed, standing outside to wait for y'all, and having to hash this out over and over again, especially while getting stared at, intimidated, and yelled at by the perpetrators across the way, while waiting for your arrival?!" As usual, the attending policemen would give the typical response, as if on replay. The original offending activities would never have been endured by Jon, his progression of psychosis would never have been catalyzed, if not for this most hated rat. The only one who could actually organize the torment, invite the torturers, provide the tools of sadism, facilitate the application of tyranny, and manage the whole abhorrent operation.

Stache-rat stopped suddenly when his boot impacted something on the ground during mid stride, that nearly made him topple over in his stupefied, as usual, state. Peering into the darkness, he leaned forward to see his comrade motionless, mutilated. His eyes bugged out, and he spun on his heels to run back across the darkened yard, only to be instantly met by the Eraticator, which plunged into his spleen from a forehand diagonal power thrust. The angle of delivery, combined with the blade geometry and driving force, ensured massive perforation of his descending aorta concomitantly, as the gargantuan flesh gobbler of a knife overcame the superficial viscera, and passed beyond, into the deepest recesses of his trunk. The torturer had now become the tortured. That sadist should have reconsidered his careless sense of amusement at others' expense. It now seems, the tolls for his delights, and blatant disregard for those who endured the waste product, were too expensive. The main maestro of rat-land festivities, had now become the waste, as he had no chance in hell to escape the speed of violence, with which Jon determinedly appeared within his vector of escape, and penetrated his presence. 'Now you gotta face the music!'

A short yelp escaped his lips, before Jon violently crowbarred the knife out to his contralateral hip. The stunned rat saw his viscera slip out to the grass, propelled by an accompanying copious gushing hemorrhage, prior to tipping over like a felled tree, supine. Instantaneous hypovolemia, due to the severed primary blood vessel, expedited his expiration. 'I wish it could've been a more prolonged agony accompanying your demise, but there's no time; more rats need killin',' a voice passed through Jon's mind. He peered over his shoulder at the garage portal, unsurprised to discover lack of any presence, or interruption to the boisterous festivities. He knew that even if they had heard the transient chirp from the doomed, it would be regarded as typical jackassery. Verbal abuse and otherwise nonsensical hoopla were only expected of the group, as egocentric flamboyance was the norm. Besides, they weren't to be bothered with concern for others, especially since they had to 'get their swerve on.'

Jon had only just finished dragging the vermin back around a lawn equipment shed, when he heard one of the female rats call out to the mustached rat, as she poked her head out of the light portal. With no immediate response, she sauntered out through the yard rapidly, looking for a chance to clown them, or hopefully bust them partaking of prize drugs they were hoarding, so that she wouldn't have to miss out.

This bitch had the nerve to insert herself in Jon's formidable escapades with the police visits on a number of occasions. As a non-resident, she unapologetically took it upon herself, like she had any business or right, to interfere with official police investigations, and gladly aided in the continued deprival of resolution, and perpetuity of Jon's misery. She had the nuts to dare not only contributing false testimony, but actually try intimidating the authorities with threats. "You know, this is bordering on police harassment!" she threw in the officers' faces. What arrogance? What false sense of entitlement? She displayed no qualms about utilizing the popular cancel culture tactics and misplaced fears of the myriad '-ism' assignments, to unjustly force herself on anyone who would deprive her of any old damn thing she wanted to do, no matter what, or who it affected. Emboldened with this false sense of security, she believed she could bully the world to her will. My way, or the highway. Well, the tables were about to be turned. You get what you give. What's good for the goose, is good for the gander. Turnabout is fair play. All's fair in love and war.

'Enough talk!'

She got all the way to the trash table, paused in confusion at the voidance of attendance; then, as she began to slowly turn her head and shoulders leftward towards the space between the shed and fence, her mind was perplexed, which figured her face into a paralyzed horror stare, due to the sudden presence of the Eraticator, buried vertically from beneath her mandible, clear through her sinuses, and into the apex of her cranium. Jon smiled at the protruding tip of the impervious knife directly beyond the skull's sagittal suture. The dazzling show of strabismus her eyes displayed, was only enhanced by the hot, red waterfall simultaneously dancing along the wonderous hilt and his wielding hand, which added accompanying delectable adornment. During the satisfying sanguine shower, the retribution claimer couldn't conceal a devious toothy grin, as the twat twitched helplessly. After allowing a few seconds to admire the art display, Jon yanked the grip downward, another fantastically easy feat owing to the superbly crafted knife handle palm-swell, another attribute of the superior knife specimen's design, to spare wasting any more energy supporting the lifeless rodent, and observed it crumble to the ground, like an accordion. And oh, how that was music to his ears. Although these expedient vanquishings were satisfying, Jon was happy that more fodder was available, to further discover the wonderful applications of the glorious, edged instrument.

The two remaining rats must've been convinced that something was definitely amiss now. The thunderous bass music suddenly ceased, but the macabre dance would continue. They appeared in the small rear door threshold of the garage concurrently. Jon had traversed halfway there from the black before they presented themselves. The tall middle-aged rat pulled a Karambit-style knife from its IWB (inside-the-waistband) Kydex sheath. Jon held the Eraticator cocked and locked at guard position. They couldn't judge the breadth of the knife from this perspective, nor were they aware of the wielder's abilities, much less his fortitude, commitment, nor state of mind. Feeling emboldened with stature, armament, and liquid courage, the statuesque fleabag hustled toward his doom, followed abruptly by the second in staggered formation.

These sleezeballs gratuitously amplified the animosity previously as well. On one particular occasion, stache-rat put them up to an attempted display of hostility and intimidation, in which they overzealously accepted the opportunity to entertain his whims, aiming to please the mischief, the plague, the colony. Upon hearing Jon exit his front door during one of their congregations, surmising that he was going to intervene with police presence for the umpteenth time, the booze buddies hurriedly scampered out from the open garage that usually serves as the locus for their revelries of self-degradation, to confront Jon just as he reached his front porch. In lieu of proper engagement, via the actual vested interest individuals, namely the residents, these surrogate lackeys must have had no problem seizing an opportune chance to flex on the unfortunate, seeking possible gratification, ego stroking, and bragging rights from harassing any potential party pooper. This ante-up directive, sent by the spiteful head varmint really drove the nail home for Jon. The coward chose to escalate the enforcement of their encroachment on his existence, with implied tandem brutality. "You lookin' for some kind of trouble?!", barked from the short rat, while his cohort stood menacingly beside him with his posture bowed up, echoed within Jon's mind for the remainder of that night, and the nights of weeks to come.

The Karambit was delivered with a looping horizontal swipe at neck level, only to find the hand steering it amputated, as Jon countered with a ballistic synchronized body pivot and hack through the wrist. The shortest, youngest rat froze in his tracks the instant this was witnessed. The giant rat screamed upon losing his dominant hand, and Jon followed up with a horizontal snap thrust into the squealer's open mouth. As the wide belly of the knife cheek severed the rat's spinal cord between the atlas and occiput of his vertebral column, his legs crumbled. DEAD.

In terror, the last remnant pleaded, "What do you want?!"

Jon calmly stated, "Silence," before lunging at him with a vertical power slash to the face. The gash exploded his forehead with ichor, continuing on to bisect his nose, lips, and chin. This trauma caused the 'shorty' to reflexively lurch erect and backwards, but Jon was already finishing him off with a horizontal power slash to the lower abdomen, as one contiguous motion, allowing its wet, steaming, putrid entrails to plummet onto its feet. 'Find some trouble?'

Before returning inside his residence, Jon hosed the Eraticator and himself off in the thick grass. He then stripped all his clothing off, and placed it into a heavy black plastic trash bag, the kind made thick enough to endure containing tree branches and other yard debris. Slipping stealthily through the house, Jon passed by the bathroom to towel himself and the grail knife off; then, he returned it to the coffee table with gracious acknowledgment, before moseying down the hall to the bedroom.

As Jon slipped back into bed, his wife inquired, "Where were you for so long? I thought I heard the back door open. Is everything alright?"

"I heard some commotion in the rats' backyard, so I wandered through the back to take a peek, and make sure they weren't vandalizing our property, trespassing, or putting our property and lives at risk with combustible apparatus again. You know, like when they set that fire pit ridiculously close to our wooden fence for some ungodly reason, and then let it get out of control, or when they were launching fireworks directly over our roof. Looks like their craziness has been suppressed tonight; just the typical racket that they're incapable of self-regulating. Let's try and get some rest."

Saturday

The police knocked on Jon's door at 7am. He was greeted by officer Hernandez, as taking notice of the multiple cruisers parked along the street, juxtaposed to the previously vexatious habitat. His visage displayed no emotion; the facial muscles weren't recruited, weren't innervated, and laid dormant, despite the inward elation he rolled in, which was only heightened upon viewing the still-holstered weapons of the law enforcement gaggle. She empathetically informed him of his neighbors' demise, and wanted any potential helpful information in solving the massacre. An elderly woman and two young children survived the incident unharmed, and were completely unaware of what had transpired beyond the walls of the domicile, since they merely occupied the deepest and farthest recesses of the habitat's confines, opposite the backyard, for the entirety of the evening, until they awoke to find the patriarch missing. Unfortunately, the senior citizen stumbled upon the carnage upon searching him out, but the juveniles were spared viewing the traumatic atrocity.

'Fucking old maid knew they often passed out on the couches in the garage, and always turned a blind eye to the inappropriate environment the poor kids were forced to be immersed in, but the corruption enabler at least had the impetus, the guilt, the miniscule obligation, to ensure the developing future hoodlums were ensured some breakfast.'

With feigned dismay, Jon related how they had initiated their common carnival like clockwork the previous evening. He furthered his response detailing how he was particularly fatigued from the accumulating sleep deprivation, and knew that calling the police out once again was futile based on the prior trials, so he decided to take an Ambien, utilized headphones concurrently, and turned into bed early. The very few times that he awoke, random hollering and perfuse bass music were observed, which was nothing out of the ordinary to his plight, so he ignored it to the best of his abilities, and tried deep breathing to restore his slumber.

The neighborhood was always absent of anything overtly audible in the early morning hours, once they blacked out, so he wouldn't have been concerned about absence of motion or activity, on any typical post-party day. They were the only trouble makers after-all, as the rest of the community was peaceful and respectful, continually.

Jon tried to display concern about the revelation unfolding of such a heinous crime in such close proximity to his perimeter, but the peace officer of course relayed that no details could be revealed at this point with an ongoing investigation newly being undertaken. With official police duty tact, Officer Hernandez told him, "That'll be all for now," as leaving her card, with instructions to make contact if anything else useful came to mind.

Jon added as she turned to leave, "You know, they probably got themselves mixed up with the wrong crowd! What, with all the comings and goings of non-residents, and blatant disregard for authority when y'all would make noise complaint calls here. They never even so much as tried to be discreet about their partaking of illicit drugs. It concerned me that the children of the residence were subjected to this influence and exposure so unashamedly. I almost never saw hide nor hair of the old woman. She never partook in the goings on, but never intervened in the child corruption neither. Contacting Child Protective Services had occurred to me. But, since y'all had been over there so frequently, I figured you must have been aware of the situation, and that nothing was too far amiss, or not crossing the threshold for allowing the department to act in any way at least. Calling CPS would just make me look like a vindictive 'Karen' as far as I was concerned. I didn't want to ruffle any feathers, nor give my contemptuous neighbors any more motivation to inflict further abuses upon me neither. I would commonly catch glimpse of them consuming copious amounts of junk. It amazed me on occasion, for various visitors on multiple dates, to meet my gaze as approaching my own front door, in the middle of taking a huge hit, with a glaring, 'I dare you, bitch!' look directed squarely at me."

She merely smirked, and continued unceremoniously spinning away as replying, "Thank you, sir."

Monday

Felicia browsed her favorite pawn shop on 146 in Kemah, as she ritualistically would each week, just to get out of the apartment, if for nothing else, hoping to find something special on this particular visit. A new inventory item snatched her gaze, barely, as the urban camo coated blade, and black micarta grip slabs, weren't gleaming out like the surrounding chrome or stainless-steel pistols, nor brilliant jewelry were, in the glass display case.

"Ewww!" she blurted out, "can I take a look at that…?" The shop-keeper proudly presented the phenomenal 'short-machete' to her, as Felicia enthusiastically awaited the opportunity to inspect it, with the look of a child in a candy store on her face. She was instantly dazzled, upon taking hold of the metallurgical wonderment.

With a devious Cheshire cat grin, the proprietor imparted, "Don't see many of those around. I've had another specimen from the Busse family of blades in here once before; a Scrap Yard Knife Company DB 721 model, prototype at that. It's the one with a sheep's foot tip, kinda like a meat clever. It didn't last long in here. But I've never had one of those around here, much less got to handle one myself before. And I'm a knife guy!

"Swamp Rat Knife Works, custom shop Eraticator; proprietary SR 77 steel; special blade coating. Sparsely used at that! The original owner said he only test cut with it a few times, and that it worked like a charm. However, he wanted to acquire a polished-finish Eraticator instead, and didn't realize some of those were available upon initially shopping around. The prior ownership, and light usage will help with the price, but you won't be compromising on the quality or performance one bit. Busse kin are known as indestructible knives, after all! With tax, it could be yours for $400."

While readily finding the glove-like fit of the user-friendly knife, as she assumed a natural hammer-grip, like a tractor beam had seamlessly pulled it into place, her mind instantly reflected on her petulant neighbors that resided in the apartment beneath her supposedly peaceful abode. She internally fumed as rapid flashbacks of never-ending, argumentative yelling and banging rattled her cage. Her sanctuary, her only accessible domain for tranquility, where she was supposed to have unconditional, relishable solitude, that she painstakingly worked so hard to pay for, was robbed of her with everlasting torment. That little voice she, and only she, had been atypically hearing of late sent notice to her with, 'Time for some rat extermination!'

Felicia turned her gaze back to the merchant. "I'd like to do some test cutting of my own! Will you consider taking $375?"

Chasm
Bryan Holm

They had been drifting apart. Diane knew this, and she wondered if Eric felt it as well. A numbness had insinuated its way into their lives, building a wall between them. Still, it was a great dinner, and a great night overall. Eric had been putting in an effort lately, resurrecting date night on Saturdays. They were finally checking off the seemingly endless list of new restaurants around town. Diane appreciated the effort.

"Should we do another bottle?" Eric asked.

Diane looked at her empty wine glass, "It is really good."

"That's why we Ubered, right?"

Diane smiled, "Why not?"

Back home, Diane embraced Eric as he fumbled off his shoes in the back hallway. They made their way upstairs, losing items of clothing as they went. Afterwards, in the dark, Eric snoring next to her, the room spun for Diane, a sickening lull, smothering her to sleep.

Diane dreamed of a dirt tunnel, enormous, dark, endless. She was crawling through it, frantic. The wet soil was cold, anise, slivering deep beneath her fingernails. The oxygen in the oppressive space was evaporating, her breath ragged. Behind her, a dark shadow grew.

Diane awoke to bright sun and a pounding headache. As her eyes focused, the room was still spinning. Diane barely made it to the toilet. When she finished, Eric was behind her with a glass of water and stifled laughter.

"When's the last time you threw up?" Eric asked.

Diane snatched the water from him, pounded it down. "Sophomore year? Good God." Round two was suddenly upon her.

Diane finally made it back to bed, a lurching crawl. Eric started to sink beneath the sheets. Diane stopped him. "Blinds," she whispered.

"What?"

"Bright light."

Diane closed her eyes and grimaced dramatically, a hand over her eyes, a vampire at dawn, before disappearing under the covers. Eric got out of bed and banished the sunshine from the bedroom. An hour later, their phones started going off. First Diane's, then Eric's, two calls in a row.

"Go away!" Diane pleaded with the ceiling.

Eric's phone rang again. Groaning, he leaned over, grabbed it. "Shit, it's my boss."

Eric sat up straight, answering it. "Sir? What do you mean? It's Sunday…" A long pause, Eric put his hand over the receiver, mouthing to her, "Your phone."

"What?"

"Your phone, the date," he hissed.

Diane fumbled for her phone while Eric stammered, "No, sir, just a bad joke. My wife and I, we have a horrible case of food poisoning. I thought I sent you an email this morning. I can't make it in." Another pause. "Yes sir, I'll be there tomorrow, no matter what."

On Diane's home screen, a text from her boss. *'Everything okay?'* She looked at the date. It was Monday.

How was that possible? Her stomach dropped, a cold sweat on her neck. Eric was still stuttering. "Yes sir, won't happen again, see you tomorrow."

He hung up, and they sat in silence. The room spun again for Diane, but she wasn't sure it was the wine anymore. They went over it again and again. Did they both really just sleep for nearly 36 hours? Could they have been drugged? If so, why, and by whom?

They walked the house. Nothing was missing, nothing was misplaced, nothing out of the ordinary. The doors and windows were locked, their clothes from Saturday night still scattered across the floor. They both checked their call logs, messages, emails. Only Eric had a missed call on Sunday, from a blocked number. They finally collapsed on the couch.

"We should see a doctor. Maybe I can get us in on a cancelation," Diane said.

Eric laughed, "I don't know if that's necessary."

"You need to be more disturbed by this. This isn't normal. We're missing an entire day."

"It's messed-up, no doubt about it, but we've both been really stressed out lately, right? We got way too drunk, and we slept for a long time. That's it. It's not that big of a deal."

Diane left the room, exasperated. That night, they went to bed in silence, a line in the sand between them. Diane hated to do that, made a point of it never happening, but her frustration with Eric warranted it. How could he just blow this off? Just forget about it? This was typical of him, never deal with a problem, just bury it. The tension between them, that had been smoothed over as of late, came rushing back. It was hours before Diane could fall asleep.

Once she was, Diane was in the tunnel again. The passageway was smaller, the floor softer, muddier. Her arms were half-buried in the soil, she had trouble keeping her chin above the muck. Behind her, the shadow grew larger. Softly, a boy cried in the darkness. Diane twisted her head, peering into the inky depths. The shadow shot forward, consuming her, turning her world to midnight.

***

Diane awoke the next morning alone. Eric had left early for work without a word. After a long, hot shower, Diane made their bed. As she pulled the sheets over on Eric's side, she noticed a dark spot, the size of a dime. She scraped at it with a fingernail. Crimson flakes broke free from the sheet. She brushed away what looked like dried blood.

Diane rushed out of the house, late for work, a flurry of spilled coffee and dropped keys. Out of the corner of her eye, she caught sight of her elderly neighbor, Janet, shuffling down the street behind her ancient basset hound. Diane pretended not to notice, loading her laptop bag into the car.

"Diane, Diane!" Janet yelled.

"Shit." Diane finally turned around, her best fake smile on display, "Morning!"

This was Diane and Eric's first house, a modest starter home in a first-ring suburb. Diane didn't miss their cramped one-bedroom apartment in the city, but she did miss the people. She had no idea how cliquish and vindictive the suburbs could be until they moved to one. Every time she made it from the front door to her car without speaking to another person was a win in her book.

Janet approached her, ignoring any reasonable sense of personal space. Diane knew this meant she was about to be privy to some neighborhood gossip. Gossip, in Janet's case, likely meaning someone hadn't cut their lawn in two weeks. Diane leaned on her car, bracing herself.

"Can you believe what happened, in *our* neighborhood?" Janet asked.

"What happened now, Janet?"

"I wondered if you two were out of town! You were the only ones not standing in your front yard gawking. The Miller's boy, he's gone."

"Gone? What do you mean?"

Janet told her the whole sordid story. The Miller's son, Hunter, only five years old, went missing sometime Saturday night. When his parents awoke on Sunday morning, his bedroom was empty. There were no signs of a struggle, but a backdoor was left open. Mr. Miller insisted he locked it before going to bed. Janet was not convinced of this detail however, on account of his drinking problem. A drinking problem Diane was confident only existed in Janet's head.

"It was a circus, Diane. Cops all over the place, news crews too. They're still out there." Diane looked past Janet, down the street. Sure enough, two news vans sat idling at the intersection. "I'm sure they'll want to interview you. Channel 5 interviewed me, and I gave them *tons* of useful information, and they didn't even air it!"

Diane did not have a productive day at work after that. She scoured their newspaper website, but it offered nothing in addition to what Janet had already told her. She texted a link to Eric, and it was an hour before he responded, '*sad*.' It took considerable willpower to keep Diane from flinging her phone against her cubicle wall in response.

That night, Eric cooked dinner, a peace offering, and they began speaking again. As Diane expected, he did not seem rattled at all by this new piece of information. He was even mystified by Diane's reaction to it. In his mind, there was simply no connection between the missing child and their missing day, even though they happened to overlap. Diane clutched her fork tightly to keep from screaming.

"Did you cut yourself?" Diane asked.

"What? Where?" Eric reached up, touching his face.

"There was blood on our sheets."

"Weird. Not that I know of." Eric got up and cleared the table. Diane continued to pick at her food.

That night, Diane was back in the passageway. The mud underneath her was a soup, and swimming in it were thick, cold nightcrawlers. The worms were in a frenzy, a slime-covered orgy. She twisted her body to see behind her, the walls of the tunnel pressing down on her. The shadow of a child crawled towards her, crying in the dark, piercing, overwhelming. She cupped her ears with her hands. Her brain was pulsating, a slithering pressure growing, pushing against her skull.

Worms spilled from her nose and mouth.

Diane woke up screaming, her sheets wet with sweat. She raced to the bathroom mirror, convinced the worms were still inside her head, a wet echo of the dream following her into the light. The sight of her normal self did little to calm her nerves. After an excruciatingly hot shower, she put on a pot of tea, and called in sick to work.

It was later that day that the smell came. It was subtle at first, and Diane mistook it for mustiness that could be remedied by opening the windows. Then the smell turned pungent, sour. A mouse had crawled under their front steps to die the previous winter, and Eric assumed that's what it was again. Diane was unsure. This smell was different, more multifarious.

Eric took a hose to the space underneath the front steps, sprayed some Lysol, and called it good. The next day, when Diane got home from work, the stench was nauseating, permeating the entire house. Eric was working late, so she took it upon herself to root out the source. Armed with a flashlight, she ruled out the front steps, and made her way through every room of the house. As she approached the basement door, the smell became overwhelming.

Diane liked to call it their horror movie basement. She hated the wooden stairs that creaked with each step. She hated the cinderblock walls, covered in cobwebs and water stains that appeared every time it rained. She hated the single bare light bulb, which seemed to create more shadows than light. Most of all though, Diane hated the floor. There was no cement, only tight, packed earth.

The smell was overpowering in the small space. She had to choke down bile as she gingerly stepped onto the soil, sweeping the flashlight back and forth. In one corner were the rotting remnants of an antique firewood bin. Did something make a home in there? As the light pierced the darkness, something caught her eye. The dirt in the back corner seemed darker than the rest, fresh, as if recently tilled.

Standing over it, it was indeed an inch higher than the earth around it. Diane tentatively pressed a shoe down on it. It was soft, loose. As soon as she disturbed the soil, another wave of the awful smell clamped down on her nostrils. Above her, the floorboards creaked. She almost dropped the flashlight.

Eric was home. He had picked up a pizza. As they ate, Diane told him what she had found. As she predicted, he didn't seem overly concerned.

"It's probably nothing," Eric said.

"You didn't do any work down there recently?"

"No. It's an old house, I'm sure the foundation just shifted a bit with all that rain last week."

"The smell is horrendous."

"You're too sensitive. I didn't smell anything when I got home."

Diane kept thinking about Eric's response as she washed up the dishes. He couldn't smell it? It was an outright lie, it had to be. It was still there, the stench, deep in her nose, clinging like bleach after a deep bathtub cleaning. Eric had agreed to take a closer look, but not until he returned home later that night. Diane had forgotten, he was meeting a college friend for drinks. He said he wouldn't be late, but he took an Uber rather than drive.

***

Diane sat on her front steps, scrolling through her phone, making her way through a bottle of white wine. Condensation rolled down the glass, a wet circle on the cement step beside her. It was a beautiful night outside, the humidity of the past few days had finally evaporated, and the rising chorus of insects seemed to agree. Children were playing in immaculately landscaped yards up and down the block. Dogs were barking from behind screen doors.

A car door shutting down the street broke her from her spell. Someone was leaving the Miller's house, another visitor in the endless parade of well-wishers. Diane felt a pang of guilt, she hadn't reached out to them in any way. She had gotten to know Hunter's mom, MaryAnn, in a neighborhood book club that had fizzled out after warring politics tore it apart. Diane wanted to stop over earlier in the week, but Eric had claimed to be too tired. The liquid courage warming her cheeks, she decided to get it over with.

Diane knocked on the door, carrying a basket she had hastily put together from odds and ends in the fridge, a bottle of wine, crackers, cheese. After a few seconds, she knelt to set the basket at the base of the door, planning a quick retreat. The door opened, and MaryAnn stood in the doorway, eyes puffy, looking shorter than Diane remembered, as if the weight of her current horror had already diminished her physically.

"I'm sorry. I know it's late, and you're probably exhausted," Diane said.

"No, thank you for stopping by."

Diane handed her the basket. "I wish it was a lasagna, but I'm not much of a cook."

"This is great. We could use more wine around here."

MaryAnn's attempt at a joke nearly crushed Diane's heart. After an awkward hug, MaryAnn invited her inside. Diane sat on the couch and listened to MaryAnn tell her story. Most of if she already knew from the news, but the thought of any silence between them terrified her, so she kept asking questions. Their son had simply vanished, and there were still no leads, no evidence of any kind, no suspects at all. Diane's eyes wandered to a framed photo of Hunter, posing with a baseball bat, a giant smile on his face, two front teeth missing. MaryAnn followed her eyes. "This summer was his first year in T-ball."

"It's an adorable photo," Diane replied.

"What am I going to do? It's been three days, and you know what they say about the first 48 hours…" MaryAnn faded into a quiet sob.

All Diane could say was how sorry she was. The silence she was dreading emerged then, an unwanted guest sitting between them. Diane's insides twisted; her stomach lurched. The room suddenly felt off balance. A creeping nausea rose in her guts. "I'm sorry, but can I use your bathroom?"

Diane stood at the sink, her face gaunt under the harsh light. She splashed cold water on her cheeks, hoping to avoid vomiting in their house. What was wrong with her? She didn't have that much to drink. After several deep breaths, she dried herself off with a towel, still wet and slightly musty from the steady traffic through the house.

As she headed back to the living room, she passed Hunter's bedroom. The door was slightly ajar. Before she knew what she was doing, she was standing inside it, surrounded by sports posters, toy cars, everything you would expect to see in a young boy's room. The silence of it felt like a tomb. Diane had a vision of this room, exactly the same, years later, covered in dust, a fading memorial for a vanished son. On a dresser was a worn baseball mitt. Diane reached for it. As she turned it over in her hand, she was struck by the familiarity of it. The leather was dyed black and red, in alternating stripes. Where had she seen it before?

"That was so nice of Eric." MaryAnn was right behind her. Diane jumped, her heart racing. She almost dropped the glove on the floor.

"I'm sorry, I don't know why I came in here."

"It's okay!" MaryAnn placed a hand on Diane's shoulder.

"What do you mean, Eric?"

"He was walking by one night, and Hunter was in tears because he had left his mitt at the little league field. When we had gone back for it, somebody had already taken it. Anyway, later that night, I heard Hunter talking to someone on the front porch. I found Eric, on a knee, laughing with Hunter. He had gifted him his childhood glove!"

"I didn't know about that."

"It was really sweet of him, and Hunter was elated!"

Diane imagined that scene in her head as she lay in bed that night. Eric still wasn't home, hadn't even texted a preemptive apology for being out all night. The interaction with Hunter seemed so out of character for him. He was always awkward around children. When they occasionally had to babysit her niece, he came up with every excuse imaginable to leave the house. Neither of them had ever wanted kids. It was something they had bonded over early in their relationship. Why did he not tell her about it? The noxious smell hit her again as she sunk into her mattress, and she pulled the sheet over her nose.

Diane kept sinking as she fell asleep, back into the tunnel. The shaft was even smaller now, and the passageway felt much longer, a limitless space ahead of her in the darkness. It was so tight her arms were pinned to her sides. A wave of rot enveloped her from behind, along with a child's cry, even more distraught now, more panicked.

"Hunter?" Diane asked the dark.

There was only deep silence in response. Then, small, cold hands gripped her bare feet. Diane tried to squirm forward, but the fingers dug in, impossibly strong, the tiny fingernails gouging the flesh around her ankles. Diane screamed but could not break free.

Diane awoke, gasping. She was sitting on the floor of the basement. Her hands were full of dirt, black soil caked under her fingernails. Her ankles were scratched and bloody. The smell was even more foul, alive. She fled up the stairs. Eric was in bed, snoring, undisturbed. Diane scrubbed her hands and ankles clean in the bathroom, then slipped into bed beside him. She could smell the liquor oozing from his pores. Diane knew sleep was off the table for the rest of the night.

***

Diane spent her workday stifling yawns and downing black coffee. She was tired, cranky, and a little behind, and she was afraid it was being noticed. She hoped hiding at her desk would do the trick, at least for one more day. Eric had woken up late of course, and they exchanged less than a dozen words as he scrambled out the door, a loose tie around his neck.

Eric had to work late again that night. Diane texted him that she was taking a valium and lying down. She included a friendly reminder that the basement smell was worse than ever, and could he please find a solution. Diane justified self-medicating because of her recent lack of sleep, but deep down she knew she was trying to avoid another night in the tunnel. The pill worked, along with two glasses of wine, and she slept soundly, dreamless.

The front door shutting woke her up. Still in a Diazepam fog, she checked the clock, it was three in the morning. Eric was not beside her. She crept to the window and looked out just in time to see Eric close the trunk of his car. He got in and drove away.

Diane made her way downstairs. Her head felt heavy, a slight wobble in her step. The door to the basement stood open, faint light filtering up the stairs from below. Diane made her way down, one hand on the wall for support. As she reached the bottom, she realized the smell was gone. In the corner, a hole had been dug, a shovel laid against the wall.

Diane couldn't see anything inside the hollow, only darkness. She stood at the edge, waiting for her eyes to adjust. The hairs on the back of her neck stood up, a cold trickle of fear moving through her chest. She was being watched; she was sure of it. A shadow moved inside the hole. Something was in it, breathing. Diane leaned closer. A child's hand shot out, pale, bloody. It gripped the edge of the opening, digging into the soil. Another hand joined it, feeling for something to hold onto. Diane fell backwards, hitting the floor hard. Everything went dark.

Diane awoke on the living room couch, a blanket over her. As she sat up, Eric came in, carrying a cup of hot tea. "Are you okay? You scared me."

"What happened?"

"You tell me. I found you in the basement passed out. Wasn't sure if I should call 911."

"I'm okay. I think. Just a bad headache."

"You shouldn't take those pills anymore. They really do a number on you."

Diane nursed the tea he brought her, tried to clear her head, remember what happened. She asked Eric where he had gone in the middle of the night.

"You were right, about the smell coming from the basement." Eric replied. "Craziest thing. I found a dead raccoon down there. Must have dug itself under, looking for a place to die."

"A raccoon? How did it get in?"

"I found a hole up in the rafters. Chewed right through the insulation."

"Where did you go?"

"It stunk so bad, I drove over to the park off Vernon, dumped it in the woods."

Diane sipped more tea. It tasted different; she couldn't quite place the flavor. She felt herself growing tired, her headache worsening. Eric helped her up to their bedroom. As she laid in bed, she felt the room tilt again, off kilter. She was sure she wouldn't sleep, but within seconds she was out.

***

Diane yawned and stretched in the morning sunlight. She glanced at her alarm clock. It was after ten. Diane bolted upright. She was late for work again, and Eric was gone. Why hadn't he made sure she was awake? Or at least set her alarm? Her phone wasn't on the nightstand. She made her way through the house, finding it on the kitchen counter, nearly dead.

On her home screen were dozens of texts and missed calls from her boss. *'Where are you?' 'Are you okay?' 'We need to talk.'* Diane's heart raced. She checked the date, but she already knew what it would say. It was Thursday, and it had been Tuesday night when she had collapsed in the basement. She was missing another day.

Diane called Eric. Waiting for him to answer, she realized her hands were filthy, dirt caked under her nails again. She held the phone between her neck and shoulder and scrubbed her hands in the sink. Diane turned off the water. Eric's ring tone was playing faintly, somewhere in the house. Diane redialed his number, following the sound.

She found Eric's phone lying in the center of the basement floor. His home screen echoed her own, missed calls and texts from an irate boss. She entered his passcode to see more, but it was rejected. She tried again and was warned she would be locked out. When did he change it? Eric's car was still in the driveway, his keys in the front hall. Diane grabbed them, slipped on her shoes, and went outside.

It was a brisk morning, a warning that fall was around the corner. Dread filled Diane as she approached the car. What was she scared of? What did she expect to find? Diane pressed the fob and popped the trunk. She stood there for a full minute, the trunk ajar, before opening it. The familiar smell hit her before dispersing into the morning air. The trunk was empty except for a crumpled blue tarp and a shovel. Diane leaned in closer. There were spots of dried blood on the shovel, a few brown hairs. Diane shut the trunk and went inside.

Diane sat on the couch, contemplating calling the police. What would she even say? She knew they would tell her she jumped the gun. That her husband would probably show up in a day or two with a bad hangover. Instead, Diane retreated to the kitchen and opened a bottle of wine. She went to bed alone that night, tripping as she crept up the stairs. The bottle of wine had not lasted long. As she fell into bed, she prayed she was too drunk to dream.

Her prayers went unanswered.

The tunnel was freezing, her ragged breath a cloud before her. Her arms were pinned against the tunnel walls. She rocked back and forth, kicking her feet. Diane slowly shimmied ahead, inch by inch. Her body shook from the cold, the mud like ice against her skin. A wind rose, hitting her in the face. She stopped, her heart pounding in her chest. The crying came soon after, like she knew it would, but this time it was ahead of her. She fought back tears, peering into the darkness.

"Hunter, is that you?" Diane pleaded. "I, I don't know what you want, but I'm not going to hurt you. I want to help you."

The crying stopped. Diane felt dizzy. She took rapid breaths, unable to find oxygen. Hunter slowly crawled out of the darkness toward her, his face pearly white, his cheeks sunken, bloodless. Diane screamed as his pale hands clawed at her face. His long fingernails gouged her cheeks, digging in. His mouth opened impossibly wide, his throat a shadowy abyss.

Diane woke up choking, gasping for breath. She was lying in the hole in the basement, her mouth filled with wet dirt. Screaming, she pulled herself out and sprinted up the stairs, vomiting in the kitchen sink, rinsing out her mouth with water. Her cheeks were on fire, cut to shreds, blood dripping down her neck. Diane's hands were bloody, chunks of skin deep under her fingernails. Diane threw up again.

The days merged together after that. Diane didn't leave the house, didn't answer her phone, letting it go dead on the counter. Her days were fueled by caffeine to stay awake, and her evenings were fueled by copious amounts of alcohol to stave off the night terrors. It didn't work. She wasn't even sure if she was awake or dreaming anymore, and she wasn't sure if she had lost any more days. She was too scared to keep track.

Diane was hunched over her kitchen sink, rubbing her temples, waiting for her coffee to brew when the smell returned. The odor grew throughout day, becoming unbearable, even worse than before. It was everywhere, invading her clothes, her pores, her hair. She could taste it when she swallowed. The dark urine she left in the toilet smelled like it. She flushed three times to be sure it was gone.

By nightfall, she had finally drunk enough whiskey to face it. Diane crept down the basement steps, a shovel in hand. Each step down was a horrendous assault to her senses. She coughed and gagged as she stepped onto the dirt floor.

Diane began to dig.

Inches turned to feet; minutes turned to hours. Diane kept digging, a heap of dirt next to the hole. The dirt was alive; worms, centipedes, severed roots bleeding green. Diane was soon covered in mud, a mixture of soil and sweat.

The mud was soon joined by blood, her palms splitting from the punishing work.

The smell kept getting worse and worse, as if she was mere inches from uncovering something ghastly and rotten, but it never materialized. Diane knew it had to be there, somewhere in that cursed basement, just out of her reach. As she struggled lifting a shovel full of dirt high over her head, Diane realized that she was probably too weak to climb out of the hole. She was several feet below the surface, and hadn't eaten anything in a long time. Instead of terrifying her, it only hardened her resolve. She dug deeper and deeper, a furious pace, her hands ragged and raw.

Diane stopped to catch her breath, leaning on the shovel. A cold draft hit her neck, chilling the black sweat running down her back. A small portion of the muddy wall had collapsed, revealing an opening at the bottom of the pit.

Diane knelt in the dirt. It was freezing, her breath a cloud in front of her. It was a small tunnel, its clay membrane crisscrossed with tree roots. Diane leaned forward, peering into the darkness. The smell coming from it was overwhelming.

Diane crawled inside, shimmying into the skintight passageway. Behind her, the walls of the hole began collapsing, a chain reaction of tiny dirt avalanches filling the grave she had dug for herself. Darkness soon enveloped her, the oxygen vanishing rapidly.

"Hello?"

There was no reply, but Diane felt Hunter in the tunnel with her. She felt his soft breath on her face, his small, icy hands reaching out for her in the dark.

Diane closed her eyes for the last time, ready to embrace him.

Eye of the Beholder
Carson Demmans

L isa Lipke was pissed off, Andy Henson was terrified, and they were both going to her bedroom. It was her idea, not his.

The teenaged girl had dragged the eleven-year-old boy into her bedroom. He was almost twelve, but in the eyes of the law he was under twelve and therefore only eleven, an important age for those who know they can't be charged with criminal offences yet.

She liked looking at herself in the mirror but was realistic about what she was looking at. She knew that she didn't win the genetic lottery when it came to her looks, but she felt she was at least comparable to winning a free play instead of a million-dollar jackpot: not a great prize, but still a prize, and definitely not a losing ticket. She didn't mind some male attention from some males. This little twerp, she had decided, was going to have to learn that he was not some male.

She had made sure that nobody had seen her take him off the street. He was a neighbor and therefore usually nearby, which was one of many things about him that she hated. Theirs was a relatively quiet neighborhood and what people did live there were either usually inside their small homes or in their backyards, which were almost as private as their homes. It was an older neighborhood with many tall trees so that the backyards were almost impossible to look into.

As she had found out though, the tall trees also made good observation posts for creepy little boys with high powered binoculars. She had seen a glint of reflected light one day in a tree, and then saw it move. Curious, she started looking for such glints and became expert at spotting them even in the trees with the densest leaves. Keeping hidden that morning, she had watched one such glint for several minutes until she discovered it reflected light off his binocular lenses. When he had finally come down out of the tree, she had pounced on him and dragged him into her empty house and bedroom. He was offering no resistance. As always, he was curious as to why she did certain things. He felt the same way about most people. He was still terrified but also puzzled as to how she caught him. He was as vain about his intelligence as she was about her looks.

With her bedroom door closed she let go of his arm and slapped him hard in the face.

"How long have you been watching me with those damn things?"

"Since I got them on my birthday. Before that I had toy ones and before that just with my eyes."

She looked at him dumbfounded. She was vain about her looks and dieted, exercised, and used makeup to look as pretty as she could, but she was not stupid. There were better looking girls than her nearby, with better faces, busts, or butts, depends on what the little pervert was into. Why all the effort to spy on her? The expression on his face was scared but not lustful. What the Hell floated his little toy boat? She pulled off her t-shirt and stood before him. She was still wearing her bra.

"Is this what you wanted to see?

"No, I've seen you without your shirt before, but don't worry, I've never seen you naked. I'm not asking you to show me either. That is your prettiest bra though."

She was a little taken aback.

"What? This plain white one? What about the black one?"

"Too much padding. It looks fake, almost as bad as the dark-haired girl on the corner."

"What? Becky wears a padded bra?"

"She shoves socks in a bra way too big for her."

"Tell me more!"

Lisa was still angry with the ugly little jerk, but she was also amused. He knew things, but not what she expected. If a couple was making out in a parked car or a kid was sneaking a cigarette, he wasn't that interested. Those things were too obvious. He wanted to know about other things that people tried to hide.

"So why all the effort to watch me?"

"It started in the spring. You were wearing shorts and you had a bandage above your hip. A couple of weeks later it was still there. It's always there."

"That's it? You wonder about my bandage? Why not just ask me?"

"Would you have told me?"

"Of course not, but if I tell you now will you stop spying on me?"

"Yes."

"It's a mole, you idiot! I have a mole I don't like so I put a bandage on it if I'm wearing something that might show it. Satisfied?"

"Yes. Can I go?"

"Not so fast. Any reason why I shouldn't call the police or your parents?"

"Because I'll say you hauled me into your house and slapped me. I'm too young to get charged for anything. You're not."

Lisa shook her head. The little bastard had a few brains even if he was a jerk.

"Get out of here. Wait! Not so fast. What do you know about the weird Greek lady?"

"Who?"

"Ms. Steno or something like that. She rents the Louis place. They're in Europe or something. When she does come out of her place, she's always wearing something wrapped around her head."

"That end of the street doesn't have as many tall trees as around here. I've never seen her."

"I've only seen her a couple of times. She's had to drop some stuff off for my mom that got dropped off at her house instead. It used to happen all the time when the Louis's were there too."

Andy had a thoughtful look on his face as he left. Lisa started smirking as soon as he turned to leave and it had turned into a broad smile as she watched him head down the block towards the Louis house. Good. The Greek woman was a bitch and resentful as Hell for having to drop off a couple of stupid Amazon boxes. Lisa had offered to give her cell number to Ms. Steno so she could just get anything else that was delivered by mistake and the old witch had made a face that looked like a Halloween mask.

"I don't have a phone. When I was your age, we didn't have such things!"

"They probably didn't have the wheel either, bitch!" Lisa thought to herself. How old was the bitch anyway? She looked to be about her mom's age but sounded older than her grandmother. At any rate, now she'd be the little jerk's next victim. Hopefully, she'd catch him and really lay into him. She had a bad temper and would do more than just slap his face. Afterwards, Lisa could pump him for information.

Maybe the little jerk could spy on a few other houses on the block for her too.

Andy approached the Louis house like it was a math problem. He wasn't very good at basic math questions because they were too boring. One set of numbers multiplied by another set of numbers. Who cared? But story problems were different. He loved those.

A woman is behind a fence that's eight feet high. There are no trees high enough to look over the fence without being too close to be seen. He could sneak into a yard that had a suitable tree in a different yard, but then he faced two risks: being seen by her and the people who owned the yard he was in. That had happened before, more than once. People had stopped believing his excuses for being caught in their yards.

That was the solution. Other people had stopped believing him because they had caught him more than once. Ms. Steno had never met him and didn't talk to other people, so she wouldn't have heard about him.

Another story problem solved.

He walked down the alley that went behind the Louis place. The fence was high but had a couple his favorite type of braces; some of them ran at a forty-five-degree angle to give additional support to the middle of the fence boards. Not only did it help prevent boards from warping but made it a lot easier for him to jump the fence. Getting out was harder without being seen, but most of the time that wasn't necessary. If he was seen, he just said he'd lost his ball, which he really had hidden in his hand and could produce it as "found" quite convincingly. Then he could be let out by the angry homeowner. That usually took a few minutes, and observation at close quarters was always better than from a distance anyway.

He was peeking over the top and froze. She was lying on the grass in her back yard naked except for a kerchief wrapped around her head. There were no signs of hair creeping out from underneath it.

"Either come in all the way or get back down on the either side," she said. Her voice was emotionless. "You look stupid just frozen there."

He could've run but she gave him the option of going in. If she wasn't serious, he could always claim he hadn't understood. He threw himself over the fence and landed in the backyard awkwardly. He wasn't used to being watched doing that.

'You're smart," she said as she got up and put a bathrobe around herself. It was Mrs. Louis's robe. Andy had seen her wear it a few times as he looked back over his shoulder while being chased. "If you had knocked on the front door I wouldn't have answered. Did you get a good look?"

"I was looking for my ball," he said.

"Look in your hand then. I spotted it as you were climbing over the fence. You wanted to look at the old Greek lady. How was it?"

She was smart and observant and apparently used to being spied on. That intrigued Andy. People like that usually had something interesting to hide.

"You're not that old."

She laughed.

"So it wasn't that bad then. I guess that's something."

"I wasn't spying on you."

"Then why do you have binoculars with you? In case you throw your ball a long way away and you can't see it?"

Crap. She was good. But she also wasn't angry. Why? It made no sense.

"Follow me. We'll go through the garage."

"So, you're Ms. Steno?"

"Stheno. You must be friends with that Lisa thing down the street. She's the only one who calls me that. Friend of yours?"

"No."

"Well, she must talk to you sometimes. If you're not friends it means she was only talking to you because she was mad at you, probably for spying on her too. She immediately thought of someone else she was mad at, and that was me, right?"

Crap, crap, crap, crap. She was very good. Too good. He was in over his head. He had to get out of there quick. She was too smart for him.

"I know the way myself," he said as he headed for the garage. Her surprisingly strong hand on his shoulder stopped him cold.

"What were you expecting to see? There was no way that the girl knew I like to lay out here and enjoy the sun and pretend I'm still in my homeland. I didn't tell her, and she is too wrapped up in herself to bother finding anything about anyone else. There's nothing worth stealing that you could carry off yourself. My art's too heavy. What were you trying to see?"

"Art?"

"Very good. Trying to change the subject and make me try to talk about myself instead of you. Did that trick work on the girl?"

It had and it was his best trick. Crap. People always assumed the worst about people. His truth probably wasn't as bad as she was assuming it was, so out of desperation he resorted to telling it.

"She told me how you always covered your hair."

"I have lots of hair. I don't believe in shaving. You just saw that for yourself. Try again."

Her grip was getting tighter. She was hurting him deliberately.

"You have very strong hands."

"That trick didn't work the first time. Why try it again."

"She told me that you cover your head all the time. She didn't know why."

She relaxed her grip slightly. He couldn't run away but at least he wasn't in pain. The truth did hurt, but at least it hurt less than some other things.

"So, she tricked you into coming over here to find out. She didn't care if you got punished. I might have to worry about her more than I thought."

"Are you going to tell me why you do that?"

"Because I want to. Come. Through the garage."

She was gripping harder again as she pushed him forward so he couldn't break free and run ahead of her. She wanted to show him something. She opened the garage door with her free hand and unceremoniously pushed him in, turning on the light once they were inside. She shut the door behind them.

The garage was no longer a garage, at least in the conventional sense. She obviously didn't own a car because there was none outside, and the garage was now a workshop of some kind. There were hammers and chisels of varying sizes, including a sledgehammer that looked far too big for her to lift let alone use. There were pieces of stone everywhere, and on one bench there was a cat. At first, he thought it was real and about to pounce, but it was made entirely of stone, sculpted as if it were horrified and about to pounce.

"That's a sculpture!" He said excitedly. "Did you carve it out of stone?"

"Well, I made it. But it's not done yet."

"But it's perfect! Every detail is perfect."

"I think that's your problem, young man. You want to know all of the details. Details aren't necessary. What does matter is how things make you feel. The blonde thing down the street is attractive. That should have been enough for you. It doesn't matter if there's some detail you don't know. Did you like seeing me naked?"

He froze in horror, and it was the first time he saw her smile.

"I'll take that as a yes. Then, that should be enough. The physical details of this cat are accurate. So what? To make it art, it must reflect how I see it. Watch."

She was a flurry of motion as she took a hammer and chisel and attacked the stone cat with greater speed and strength than he thought was possible. In minutes the cat's expression had changed to one of hatred. It no longer looked terrified. It was terrifying.

"I think I knew this cat. I mean, the real one. It used to be in this neighborhood. A stray, I think."

"Very good. But you see, this is its true essence. You did not recognize it before, but you do now. I'm letting you go. I mean you no harm. See me as a neighbor who likes her privacy and will be nice to you. Don't go looking over my fence or in my windows and maybe sometime I'll make a nice sculpture for you. Maybe something small like a bird. You could put it in your room. How does that sound?"

He looked at her closely. She seemed sincere. He had to admit that he had liked looking at her nude body, but now all he could think of was the scarf on her head. He stared at it continuously while she had chiseled the cat but was smart enough to stop when she was talking to him. He had to find a way to continue the conversation.

"Do you sell your art?"

"I do. It's how I make my living. My sisters and I made our living that way in Greece a long time ago, along with potions we made for people. Then, like you did, young man, a stranger came into our life. He killed one of my sisters and the other one has blamed me for it ever since. She wasn't as strong as the two of us, and we always tried to protect her. We failed. I've lived alone ever since. I still have to live in cities and deal with people to survive, but I don't like strangers. Does that make sense to you?"

He nodded.

"Good. You see? You asked a polite question and got a polite answer. If you ask me about my scarf, I will politely say no, at least the first time. Anything after that and you could get dealt with the same way I dealt with that cat."

He shivered slightly. He had no desire to be carved with her hammer and chisel. Still, would she? He couldn't stop thinking about her head scarf. He had seen quite clearly that she had hair, and a lot of it, on other parts of her body. He had heard of sicknesses that could make a person lose all their hair, and she clearly didn't have that. Did some women just go bald on their head the way some men do?

"Don't get me wrong. You and I will never be friends. But we don't have to be friends, you know? We can just exist side by side, not hurting each other. That's how it used to be in the old country. That was a long time ago, and I miss it, you know?"

Her eyes were focusing on some memory from long ago and not on him. She was distracted, and Andy saw it as his moment. He could snatch the scarf and be out the door and over the fence before she knew what happened, and they would never have to speak to each other again. She was still staring off in the distance as he moved slowly behind her so he would have a short path to the door to the backyard. His hand moved as fast as he could make it, but it was too fast. If it had moved a little slower, he might have had a split second in which he could have saved himself. He might have been able to realize how much jeopardy he was in, shut his eyes and begged for forgiveness. Instead, his hand moved like lightning and the scarf was off her head and he had no time to realize what he was looking at, but it had enough time to look at him.

One look was all it took. One look where its eyes locked with his, and the feeling began The feeling was actually a lack of feeling as Andy's cells, one by one but in an incredibly fast progression, ceased to alive. But they simply weren't dead. They were now a different material entirely, which could look like something alive but was totally inanimate, hard and unyielding except when shaped with hammer and chisel.

Andy felt no pain, but he did feel terrified. His brain was able to react fast enough automatically to feel emotion even if it didn't have enough time to think of a logical plan to save him. His brain had just enough time to twist his face into an expression of pure fear before his face couldn't move at all because it wasn't made of flesh anymore.

Stheno the Gorgon sighed as she turned around. The snakes that covered her head where mere humans had hair were already looking at the piece of stone that was once a human child. The snakes were part of her in the sense that they were attached to her, but they moved independently without any conscious thought or control by her, and she didn't see what they did. In a way, they were an automatic defense mechanism. Because they acted independent of her, each one could look a different direction at the same time, and turn anyone who looked at one of them into stone.

But as she had already told the boy, she had to live among humans in order to live, and that meant keeping them covered most of the time. She had no love of humanity, but she was still fond of eating, which she had learned she couldn't do if she turned everyone she met into stone.

"It was easier to get by when there were three of us," she mused to herself as she ran her fingers over the stone surface of what used to be the young voyeur "But Medusa has been dead a long time and my one remaining sister has blamed be for her death for centuries. I can only count on myself. Perhaps I can at least turn you into a sellable piece of art. Then at least you didn't die for nothing, eh?"

She picked up her hammer and chisel and began to work. She reshaped his face, so the look of horror was gone and it was now a smug grin as if the boy was thinking yet again about how much smarter he was than everybody else. The end result reflected the truth of what he was.

She looked at the statue with a critical eye. It reflected the truth of his soul, and was definitely art.

"But true art doesn't always sell," she sighed and picked up a well-used sledgehammer. "At least between him and the late owners of this house I'll have enough gravel to sell to a landscaper."

It was days before anyone came looking for the boy. He had apparently taken off in the past when engaged in one of his stakeouts, but he had been gone longer than ever before and his parent had notified the police. She was used to dealing with police at times like this, so she was surprised to find Lisa Lipke at her door instead.

"Can I come in so we can talk?" the blonde girl whispered. This amused Stheno. There was nobody in sight and if anyone had seem them whispering it would have made them more suspicious, not less so. She let the teenager into her home and Lisa showed her a MISSING poster with Andy's face on it.

"Oh the little peeping tom!" Stheno said with a smile. "He looked over my fence and saw me sunbathing in the nude. He started running and is probably still doing so. Perhaps I should tell the police that, eh?"

"No!" Lisa pleaded. "Don't! I was afraid something like that happened and I was the one who told him to come over here! Honestly, I wanted to get him into trouble, but I didn't want anything too bad to happen! I knew he was no match for you, but I realized I wasn't going to get any sympathy when people found out I hauled the little brat into my bedroom and took my shirt off!"

Stheno laughed and then put a comforting hand on Lisa's shoulder. There was no point using her snakes on the teen because her brain was already lifeless stone.

"You did nothing wrong," the Gorgon said in a comforting tone. "But, we will say nothing, eh? If people don't learn he spied on me, they will never know you gave him the idea, eh?"

Lisa's eyes brightened and she tried to make amends.

"I'm sorry I made a fuss before. Is there anything I can do around your house to help you?"

"You can help me haul some bags of gravel out of the garage to the front curb. A landscaper is coming by for them. They are what is left of some art projects that didn't work out so good."

Lisa struggled to help with the heavy loads and was breathing hard as she carried one bag versus the two Stheno handled with ease simultaneously. She hadn't needed the help but the girl needed to be punished in some minor way. She was afraid for a second that the punishment would have to be increased when Lisa picked up a small piece of rock from the top of one of the bags.

"An eye! This piece of rock looks just like an eye, doesn't it?" Lisa said in a pleased tone. Stheno smiled. The girl had no suspicion at all, so she could live, for now.

"You can keep it. We used to have talismans like that in my old country. It is a good luck charm. If you wish no harm to ever come to the person who gave it to you, no harm will come to you."

And Stheno would have kept her promise if the stupid blonde thing hadn't knocked her head scarf off when she hugged the Gorgon in thanks. On the plus side, Lisa would have been proud of the high price she fetched.

20,000 Steps into the Suburban Vortex
Ryan Dyer

He opened another tab. He had around ten open now, of different Japanese pornographic films via the site missav.com. He clicked on the first tab open - *MIAE 195 (Rim Job Licking Maid)*. The porno depicted two females dressed in maid costumes teaming up to lick cock and ass. It was a great porno - one he had watched several times, though, so the luster was beginning to wear itself out. He practically knew every lick, so he spent the night searching for similar-themed JAV videos to see if they could arouse him in the same way. He had picked up a liking for Japanese porn while living in Hong Kong - he liked the inventiveness and quality of the releases, and the actresses were of course beautiful. He had been up for hours now - watching these videos, jerking off. Basically, killing time until he felt tired enough to sleep.

Okay, one more toke and then I'll get busy and hit the sack.

He stood up, walked to the window and opened it, hearing the trickle of light rain outside. He took the half-smoked joint from the ashtray on the table and the lighter beside it. He stuck his head out of the window and lit up, looking at the sleeping city outside of the window. He took a long puff of the joint and exhaled the smoke out into the misty air.

Alright, let's get this over with.

He sat down again and pulled down his pyjamas. He put his earbuds in. He squirted some lotion into his left hand as the right controlled the mouse. He pressed play on the video and then opened the other tabs, checking the other titles. He listened to the opening advertisements on *MIAE 195* while opening up a new tab and then clicking on Tinder from the list of most visited sites on the bottom of the web page. Tinder opened up and he saw that he had a new match. He clicked the *MIAE 195* tab once again and pressed pause.

Doubt this will be anything worthwhile but let's check it out before I finish the job.

The message was from a girl in his city. She had three different pictures on her profile. She had brown skin and was maybe Indian. Aside from the photos, her profile was blank.

Probably a scammer, but fuck it, I'll humor myself for a minute.

"Whas up? U awake?" her message read.

Why yes, I am. I've been awake all night. He looked at the clock. *Fuck, it's four in the morning. I can't waste any time.*

"Hello! Yes, I am awake. Are you? What are you doing?"

He looked at her photos again. Nice smile. Dark skin. Her pictures were closeups of her face. It was hard to tell the shape of her body.

"I was drinking. Going to airport tomorrow at one. What are you doing? I like your Bruce Lee photo." She was referring to his main profile picture, which had him standing beside a Bruce Lee statue at Avenue of the Stars in Hong Kong.

What am I doing? I was getting ready to jerk off. "Thanks. Nothing."

"Wan come over? I'm horny."

Come over? Is she serious? It's pretty fucking late... He then started closing the porn tabs and put his focus on the Tinder conversation. *It's not often that a girl will just ask you to come over. This could be a scammer by all accounts...but what do I have to lose? I'm leaving the country in three days. Either I try to get laid now, or wait until I get back to Hong Kong.*

"Where do you live? The address."

It took a few minutes before the reply came, "614 Sage Peak come nowww."

He copied the address and then pasted it into Google and then loaded up the Google map. From his location in the city center, the destination reached out far into the North. It would take one hour to get there by train or 30 minutes via car, which he didn't have. *Shit, it's on the edge of the city. What community is this?* He zoomed out on the location to see the community's name. *Sage Hill. Suburbia. Great.*

He wasn't really a fan of suburban neighborhoods. For his 30 years, he lived mostly in the city. He did have experience with going to these neighborhoods on the outskirts of the city - a few of his prior girlfriends lived in these communities. He recalled taking a bus for an hour, going through the maze of nearly identical yards, vehicles and houses, to find a single stop with no one around it. He would leave the bus, walk another block and find his girlfriend's home - humanity and familiarity within this expensive building surrounded by other buildings that could or could not have humanity within. He didn't understand why people would choose to live so far outside of the city. So far away from a corner store. So far away from a shopping center. A restaurant. A school. A park. Anything. The only way in and out was via car. His girlfriend's parents had bought her own car. A privileged life. It was a privilege to live there. It felt like a nuisance to him. He picked up his phone and snapped a photo of the map.

"Okay but it will take me an hour to get there," he wrote.

His phone was at 56% battery power, and he did not have data. Since he started working in Hong Kong, he had bought a phone there and had a data plan for that region. He had also forgotten his portable battery charger in his apartment in Kowloon. He had come back to visit his family two weeks ago and that's where he was now - sitting in the tiny spare room watching porn videos, masturbating, waiting for the days to trickle by before he went back to his teaching job across the ocean. He had two days before he had to catch his plane.

"Just come. I'm tired. Guna lie down."

It was late though he knew one thing - if a girl wants and asks for sex, you'd better say yes at that moment because you'll never be sure when she's ever going to ask again. He had also never been with an Indian girl, so the prospect interested him. His phone was at half battery power, though, and he knew finding the place would be a pain in the ass. He could take the train to the final stop, an hour away, and then search the area for the house. He didn't want to waste money on a cab either. Regardless, he had to go now.

"Okay, coming."

He closed his laptop and then put on his clothes. It was still dark outside, and he was starting to feel tired, but the idea of getting with this mysterious Indian girl woke him up a tad. Even if nothing came of it, it was better than sitting there watching another porn movie, ejaculating onto his stomach again, wiping himself off, going to sleep and then repeating the same routine the next night.

He turned off the lights, closed the door to the spare room and then went out into the hallway to put on his shoes. His parents were sleeping in the next room. Maybe they'd still be sleeping by the time he got back. When his shoes were laced, he looked at his phone one more time - 52%. He softly shut the door and then locked it as quietly as he could. He turned around and walked down the building hallway until he got to the elevator. He pressed the elevator button and waited.

The elevator door opened, and he walked inside. He pressed the ground floor button and then took out his phone again. He turned on one of the songs he had saved on the device, an atmospheric John Carpenter track he felt fit the mood, "Vortex." He closed his eyes and got lost in the ominous synths.

Ding.

He opened his eyes when the elevator reached the bottom floor. The foyer was predictably empty. He walked over to the apartment building entrance door and then exited the building, feeling the light spray of rain from the still-dark sky. The streets were moist and empty - most were still sleeping or had maybe just woken up for their early shifts. He wondered how many people in the world were living the scenario he was living at this moment. *Who was up all night jerking off? I guess I'm lucky. At least I got a message.* He soldiered on, thinking he should have maybe brought an umbrella, to the closest downtown train station.

He arrived at the empty station, an elevated concrete slab which went around 50 meters. He knew that the trains started at four so it wouldn't be a problem getting to the neighborhood. He just didn't think the fare price of $4 was worth it. Luckily, you didn't need to pay a fare before getting on the train and it was rare that transit officers monitored the trains, especially that early in the morning. He looked inside of a trash can for a ticket, then thought that the idea was stupid. *From last night? It would be expired, idiot.* He decided to just hop the train and ride it down to Sage Hill.

He looked at the train schedule on the monitors hanging in the station. *Five minutes, alright.* He looked at his phone again. 48%. *Fuck, must be because I'm listening to music.* He turned down the volume on the current song being played, Umberto's "Night Fantasy." The lower volume, he thought, wouldn't waste as much battery power and it also allowed him to hear the rain, which actually added to the atmosphere of the track.

By the end of the song, the train emerged out of the darkness of the city and beckoned him to come in, to go through with the trip. He didn't think twice, pressing the button to enter the car and going in. It was nearly empty aside from a man in a security uniform and a homeless individual sleeping. The train took off and he looked out the window, seeing the city's empty streets - a few pieces of discarded trash gave the sense that someone had been there before, but not now. Maybe not ever again.

He looked at the photo of the map that he took. It only showed a closeup of the neighborhood she lived in and the house location within the neighborhood, but not the area outside of that neighborhood and how to actually get into it from the train station. There might be a bus that goes near it, but maybe it's too early.

Why didn't I ask for her phone number? Fuck. Fuck it, I'm already on my way. He shut his eyes again, letting the music relax him. It would be a while before he arrived at the stop.

Ding. Dong. The next stop is Sage Hill.

He opened his eyes. *Shit, must have fallen asleep.* He checked his pockets. *Phone. Wallet. Okay, nothing was stolen.* He stood up and looked at his phone - 26%. *Uh oh. The volume must have fluctuated or maybe a button was pressed accidentally.* He turned off the music and turned off the screen. He'd need every second of power.

The sun was just starting to peek out from the darkness of night as he walked off of the train and out of the station. The comforting blanket of blackness now gave way to the reality of the new day - the sun was coming, and he had to follow its pace. Light rain continued to drizzle down. Expressionless citizens walked past him, on their way to the train. On their way to their regular jobs. Doing things in their regular schedule. He didn't like the feeling of being an irregular being that contrasted with their order, but that was what he was now - a tired, irregular, horny night owl who was now facing the morning world.

He looked around him. There were communities on either side of the train station, which was situated next to a freeway with a bridge crossing over it, connecting the communities to the station. On one side was the community of Soft Hill, while the other was Sage Hill. There was a bus station beside the train station, though he didn't see any buses and knew he didn't have any time to waste. She might be sleeping right now and would be catching a flight later. He looked at the photo of the map again, looked at a street going into Sage Hill which seemed like the right direction, and decided to put caution to the wind and to just start navigating until he found the right street.

24%. He entered Sage Hill, which began as a long road with two white fences which looked impossible to climb on either side. Roofs of houses, houses he'd never visit. Houses which probably held people - wealthy people, important people. He walked and thought about that old *X-Files* episode, the one about the monster in suburbia. It came to be because the suburban neighborhood was built on a landfill, at least that was how he remembered it. He wondered if Sage Hill and Soft Hill were also built over landfills.

After five minutes of walking, he came to the end of the road, which split off into three separate roads going into different mini communities in Sage Hill. Sage Street. Sage Way. Sage Crescent. No Sage Peak yet. But which one to take? He looked at his phone again. 20%. He didn't see any of these streets on his little map, but tried to imagine what street would connect to Sage Peak and decided Sage Crescent was probably it. He continued on.

The houses looked new. The neighborhood was new. The city was always expanding. Always building new neighborhoods to catch up with the ever-growing population. Each new neighborhood was that much more far apart from what he knew. The city center. It looked even more vacant as compared to what he knew in Hong Kong - perpetually crowded streets. Cockroaches roaming in and out of cracks. No private place to even take a piss without someone watching, even though they wouldn't have cared.

Some of the houses had garages with cars inside. Or maybe they weren't. Maybe they didn't own a car. Maybe the house was still empty. It was hard to tell. Some did have cars in the driveway outside. Some had two. Who owned these cars? It was impossible to tell as no one was outside, just him walking through this suburban neighborhood like a sleepy zombie.

He thought of that one episode of *To Catch a Predator*. He often watched reruns of the show on YouTube in the wee hours of the morning to pass time. The episode featured a man named Jean Pierre Michael Wehry, who came to the sting house with a sweaty face, a backpack and a sack of lies. The host, Chris Hansen, had his chat logs, of course, and knew he was looking to meet an underage boy. Wehry had travelled for several hours to get to the house, which was in the middle of a suburban neighborhood. He tried to construct a scenario for Hansen, that he had received a phone call saying that if Jean Paul wanted a job, he was to go to that address. The name of the person giving the phone call and the person Wehry was to meet at the house changed a few times in his story. Hansen famously asked Wehry about one of his quotes from the chat log, "Can I taste your nuts?"

"That's not my style," said Wehry.

He thought of the Tinder profile. Her age was 27, so that wasn't the problem, but he felt as pathetic as Wehry going through suburbia. He wondered how lost Wehry got before finding the actual house. Still, he continued on with nothing except his perverted desires to motivate him. He must have been relieved to have finally stopped walking.

He felt a bead of sweat start to form on his forehead. He looked at his phone - 15%.

He reached another fork in the road - either cross the street and continue down Sage Crescent or go down this new street, Sage Road. Sage Crescent looked to twist and turn up ahead, while Sage Road went straight down. *Fuck it, I'll go down Sage Road and if I can't find it in five minutes, will go back here and up Sage Crescent.*

The sun was beginning to now illuminate everything. He was no longer shrouded in the comfort of darkness. Instead, the sickly-sweet sound of birds chirping accompanied him. Did they see him? He looked at the houses as he walked by them. *Who is awake? Who is looking out the window? Do they see me?*

After another three minutes of walking, he reached another street to cross as Sage Road continued on after it. He looked at his phone - 12%. He tried to picture the original map he saw on Google in his head. There were a few twists and turns before Sage Peak. *Peak.* He yawned. *Was it on a hill? This neighborhood looked as flat as an ironing board.* Fuck it. He couldn't turn back now. He went down the new road, Sage Lane.

At this point he started to get thirsty and again cursed the suburban neighborhood. *Why don't they ever build any stores in these places? What if I was a kid who lived here and just wanted to get a bottle of Pepsi from the store and we had no Pepsi at home? Would I have to ask my parents every goddamn time to drive me into the city to buy something?* He thought of Hong Kong, where two corner stores were on every street and street food vendors were outside in the dozens. He thought of the skyscrapers - the denseness of the city area - the constant swarm of people. Upon first arriving in Hong Kong a few years ago, it was jarring, but he soon accepted it as comforting and secure, as opposed to this ghost community. *Thank God I'll be back there in a few days.*

A single car drove past him with tinted windows. As no one else was on the street, they had no doubt seen him trudging along. He thought of hiding his face, but why? *I could have jerked off happily and be sleeping right now. Right. That's my motivation. Once I get there, I'll be welcomed in, we'll hit it off and then we'll get into bed. This will all be worth it.*

Sage Lane came to an end and there were another two roads to choose - Sage Drive and Sage Hill. Sage Hill. This has got to be in the same vicinity. He looked at his phone - 9%. The map showed that Sage Hill was connected to Sage Peak. It just went on for a few hundred meters first. *Jesus, finally.*

Sage Hill was an elevated hill road, and despite his being thirsty and exhausted, he quickened his pace to get to Sage Peak. There were less cars in the driveways now and the houses looked plain and spotless, as if untouched by humans or animals after they were built. They all shared the same color pattern -white with black doors and black window frames. *She must be rich to afford one of these.*

After another few minutes of walking, he arrived at another turnoff - Sage Peak. He looked at his phone once again - 5%. *God, at least I made it here before the battery ran out.* He looked at the first house on the street - 203. Hers was 614. He started to speed walk down the street. The time was now seven in the morning. If he got there shortly, there would be at least three or so hours until she had to get ready to go to the airport. He felt confident. *Hopefully she's waiting for me and didn't fall asleep.* His mind drifted to another thought. *Hopefully it isn't a scammer or murderer. Hopefully it's the right address that she gave me. But why lie? Girls want to get laid too.*

He had to piss. *Well, I'd better do so before arriving.* He looked at the house number of the one closest to him - 413.

The house looked as bare as the dozens he had walked past before. Everything was so wide and out in the open, but he saw a bush next to the garage. He quickly rushed over to the bush, went behind it, pulled down his pants and let the steaming river hit the grass. He looked around to make sure no one saw him. He looked up into the window of 413. Nothing was there. He looked across the street at the other houses. Nothing as well. *Does anyone live here?* He shook the last drops of urine out of his penis and zipped up his pants, then looked at his phone again - 3%. It didn't matter now. It would die soon but he was nearly there. He continued on down Sage Peak.

500, 502, 504, 505, 506. He continued walking, looking at each house now - staring at the black numbers on each door. The numbers before seemed to be slowing down somehow. He was sure that the next one he looked at would be 506.5.

He started to jog and counted the houses as he went by in his head. *I'm tired. I need to lay down. Once she lets me in, I'm going to have to ask for a nap.*

590, 591, 592. He felt the vibration of his phone in his pocket. He knew it was the "Your phone will shut off in 30 seconds" warning. He continued jogging. 599, 600, 601. He slowed down. He caught his breath. He felt his pocket. *Cigarettes, yes.* He pulled one out of the pack and lit it. He took a big puff and continued walking towards his destination. 608, 609, 610. He took the last puff of his cigarette by the time he reached 614.

There was no time for shot nerves. He walked up to the door and knocked. He waited. He knocked again, louder this time. He waited. He knocked again for a longer period of time at the same volume. He waited. He rang the doorbell. He waited. He rang the doorbell again. He waited. He closed his hand into a fist and pounded on the door. He waited. He sat down on the front steps. *Fuck. She must be asleep. I've gotta rest. I've gotta…no, I need to keep trying.* He stood up again and continued to pound on the door.

"Hello!" he yelled out.

He kept pounding and yelling for another few minutes. The door opened.

A musky, sweaty smell came from the slowly opening door. Out of the darkness inside, he heard a voice.

"What?"

"I messaged you on Tinder a few hours ago. You gave me your address. I'm here." It sounded stupid, yes, but it was the truth.

"You'd better go home," the voice said.

"I travelled far to get here. I'm really tired. Is it okay if I just sit on your couch for twenty minutes?"

"You'd better go home," the voice said again. The door followed the statement, closing. The sound of a lock being activated followed.

He stood there for a minute. *Was that her? I couldn't see who it was. The voice did sound female. I'd better go home? Yeah, I should. I should. Was that her? I wish I could message her right now. Fucking phone. Data. Wi-Fi. Ah shit.* He sat down on the steps again. He lit another cigarette and smoked the whole thing, contemplating what he would do next. He stood up again and lightly knocked on the door. *It's no use. This was so idiotic. What am I doing here?*

He started to walk back. There's gotta be a bus stop somewhere. He didn't have any change, but he'd explain to the bus driver that he was lost and had to get back to the train station.

You'd better go home? I should go back. She invited me there! He started to walk back to the house, then stopped. *What if it is a warning? If I go in, something terrible might happen.*

He turned around again and continued back down the street. His eyes felt as if they had five-pound weights hanging off of each of them. *I'd better go home. Back to*

Hong Kong. He walked down Sage Peak in silence - no birds chirping, no rain drizzling, no planes flying by in the sky or dogs barking in yards. *I'd better go home.* The house numbers dwindled down as he walked. Dwindled down to under two hundred now. Didn't this street start at number 200-and-something? He got to the end of the street. There was no street sign. There was an option to go left or right. He took a right.

I'd better go home.

He looked at the houses. Now, they had no numbers. He continued on and some of them were now unfinished, though there wasn't any heavy machinery or building materials beside these houses. Some were without a roof. Some were without a door.

I'd better go home.

He came to another crossroads. He took a left. He walked for what seemed like an hour with his head bent down. He saw an open yard without a house belonging to it at all. *I need to sleep. I need to go home. Jesus Christ, where am I? I can't take it anymore! I'm just going to lie on the grass...*

He woke up and saw that he was just about 100 meters from a bus stop. *Thank God. Any bus should go to the train station. Once I'm there, I can finally get out of here.* He sat at the bus stop for what seemed like an hour. There was no way to tell time, but the sun was now in the middle of the sky. He guessed it was around three in the afternoon. Finally, he saw it coming. *Yes, I'm out!*

He got on the bus and saw a driver in sunglasses, "I'm lost. I just need to get to the train station. I'm really sorry."

"It's okay, get in."

He saw a woman with two babies sitting in the front seat. He went to the back. The bus started to drive through the suburban neighborhood, taking a right, and another right and another right and then a left. One baby started crying. The bus took another left. And another. And another. And a right. The mother shushed the baby as the second started crying. *Shut the fuck up.* He felt his head start to throb. *I'm going home. It's okay. I'm going home.*

The bus drove through the suburb for what seemed like 40 minutes. Finally, the station was in view. The bus stopped at the station and the woman took her crying babies off.

"Sorry, could I have a transfer to take the train. I have no change."

The driver silently ripped off a transfer and handed it to him. He got off the bus and walked towards the station. Once in the station he looked at the monitor. The next train would come in five minutes. He sat on a bench and closed his eyes again.

The train arrived and he forced himself up and got on, finding an empty seat inside. The train was full of excited tourists going to the local carnival that took place every year. They excitedly talked about their plans for the day and asked each other what stop they should get off at. He knew which stop but said nothing to them. He felt his head throb as he closed his eyes and listened to the stop announcements as the train made its way towards the city center.

DING DONG. Sage Peak.

He woke up. No, not Sage Peak. It was his stop downtown, Center Street. He got up and forced his legs to push themselves forward. He stepped out of the train and walked towards his building. Once at the building, he took out his key and pressed it against the magnetic lock. The door opened and he went inside and then walked to the elevator. He pressed the button to activate the elevator and waited for it to come down. Once the elevator was at the ground floor, the door opened, and a few residents walked out. He went in and pressed the number for his floor, 20. He sighed and waited for the elevator to make its way up. When it got to his floor, the door opened and he walked out into the empty hallway. He went to his door, took out his key, put the key into the keyhole, unlocked the door and then opened it.

"You'd better go home," said a voice from inside.

He woke up on grass. There was a house next to him. He looked at the house number - 614.

I'd better go home.

Crabgrass
Damon Nomad

Tyler turned off the highway onto a narrow winding road. The entrance to the neighborhood was marked with two large boulders on each side of the entry. "We're here." He slowed down so they could enjoy the cruise to their new home. The top of the two-seat convertible sportscar was down on this warm spring day and there wasn't a cloud in the sky. The narrow lane meandered nearly a mile, with four roads branching off along the way.

Tiffany gestured at the large stones and read the name aloud, "Serenity Park." She smiled as she clapped her hands. "What a beautiful day to move in." She kissed him on the cheek. It was Friday and Tyler had taken the day off work.

She pointed as they went past the clubhouse, swimming pool, and tennis courts to the right. "We are going to be so happy here."

Tyler glanced at the clubhouse and nodded in agreement. "Yeah."

It was an easy drive. The entrance roadway dead-ended in a large cul-de-sac. Two roads branched off to the left and two on the right. Each of the branch lanes also ended in cul-de-sacs. It was a small community with acre lots for all the homes. They weren't mansions for the wealthy, but people in Serenity Park were well off and seemed to be living the American dream.

Tyler chuckled as they came into the large cul-de-sac where their new home was situated. He nodded at a neighbor on a lawn tractor towing a cart tossing out fertilizer. "Someone should tell him those plaid shorts went out of style about fifty years ago." The guy looked like he was probably mid-fifties, crew cut, with black horn-rimmed glasses held in place by a retaining strap. "He looks gung-ho."

Tiffany giggled. "Tyler, don't start in. He looks like he might not have much of a sense of humor. Watch yourself, okay."

He pulled the car up to the garage. "Yeah okay. The movers should be here in an hour or so. They have your car on a trailer." He got out of the car and watched the man on the mower. The guy snapped a salute at Tyler as he zipped along. *Okay general.* Tyler saluted back and then followed Tiffany towards the front door.

***

Tyler answered the doorbell early Sunday afternoon. A man and woman were standing side-by-side on the front porch. He guessed they were in their mid-forties, ten years or so older than Tiffany and himself. The man was rail thin and kind of short, with thinning black hair combed straight back. The woman was probably an inch or two taller than the man and chubby was a nice way of putting it. Her short brown hair was held in check by two flowery barrettes.

They glanced at each other as if they expected the other one to speak. Tyler smiled and broke the silence, "I'm Tyler Noble. Nice to meet you."

Tiffany came up beside him. "Hello, I'm Tiffany."

The man cleared his throat. "The Gibbs's. Well, I'm Barney and this is . . ."

"I can speak Barney. Geez Louise. I'm Helen. I brought a homemade apple pie. We wanted to welcome you to the neighborhood. We thought we would give you a couple of days to settle in."

Tiffany waved at them. "Please come in. Would you like a glass of wine or beer? Or maybe you don't drink. We have sodas."

Helen moved in quickly with Barney following. "Well, if you're sure it's okay. Oh, my you have nice furniture. The movers did a good job. Wine sounds good."

They settled into the great room with each couple on matching sofas with a coffee table between them. Barney took a sip of red wine and spoke up after Helen had been chattering for a while. "So, no children? Not meaning to be personal."

Tyler leaned back on the small sofa next to Tiffany. "No, just us and the cat. How about for you?"

Helen answered, "Lucy is sixteen and Dan is fourteen." She glanced at the cat curled up on a footstool. "A dog, Sherlock." She nodded at Tiffany, "You said you don't work anymore. You look familiar. Were you on television? You're so pretty and petite. I hope you don't mind me asking."

Tiffany smiled as she fluffed her blond hair. "Thank you. I did some modeling after college. For nearly ten years. I made a few covers for women's fashion. You might have seen me in some of those."

Tyler got up, filled everyone's wine glasses, and sat back down. "Barney, what's the deal with the guy next door? He gave me a salute as he rode on that big lawn tractor. Like Patton aboard a tank."

Barney snorted a laugh and took a drink of wine. "Patton, that's funny. He was in the military. Retired as a major, I think. Kenneth Kramer. Don't call him Ken or

Kenny. He can be intense. Lives there alone now, kids are adults and live out of state."

Helen shook her head. "His wife left him three or four years ago. He's a bully. Especially when it comes to people and their yards."

Barney sighed loudly. "Yeah. Did you notice the small sign as you come into the cul-de-sac? First place street for lawn care in Serenity Park. He takes it very seriously."

Tyler chuckled, "Contest for the yards in the neighborhood. Whose idea is that?"

Barney frowned, "Kramer runs the whole thing. Judge, jury, and executioner."

***

Tyler sipped a cup of coffee as he stood at the window of the front parlor early in the morning the following Saturday. Kramer was standing in the road at the edge of Tyler's front lawn. *What's he doing?* He put on a ball cap and headed outside.

"Hello, Ken, is it?" *Let's see how he reacts to that.* "I'm Tyler. Can, I help you?"

Kramer clenched his jaw and growled in response, "Kenneth. It's Kenneth." He gestured at Tyler. "Tyler Noble, I've got that intel." He waved a hand at the lawn as Tyler got close. "You know what you got here?"

Tyler shrugged. "Grass."

"No sir, that's what the women folk might say." He squinted as he stared at the ground. "This is a battlefield. Yes, it is. This is Bermuda grass, and it's in pretty good condition." He paused for a moment. "For now. But it needs to be fed and watered and protected from its enemies."

Tyler chuckled, "Enemies?"

"Yes. Dandelions, clover, thistle." Kramer hissed, "The worst of the worst, crabgrass. Many others." He waved a finger in Tyler's face. "I suggest ten, ten, twenty. Sometime in the next month. Get a good model spreader."

"What are you talking about?"

"Fertilizer boy. Nitrogen, phosphorous, and potassium ratios. Herbicide for the weeds when it gets warmer. I'll point you in the right direction."

Tyler shook his head. "Naw, I'm gonna rely on Mother Nature. Rain and vitamins from the sun." Tyler turned to leave.

Kramer grabbed him by the arm. "Not on my watch. Get with the program."

Kramer was a good-sized man and in good condition. Tyler had been a linebacker on the football team in college, he rode the bench, but he was athletic and stayed in shape. Bigger and much stronger than the older man. He pulled his arm loose and instinctively put his hand on Kramer's chest and pushed him. "Don't get physical with me, Kenny." The older man stumbled and fell to the ground.

Tyler heard Tiffany's voice from the front door. "Tyler! What's going on?"

He turned toward the house. "Just a misunderstanding." He turned back towards Kramer to help him up. Kramer was marching back toward his house. Tyler met Tiffany on the porch. "He grabbed me by the arm. I just reacted."

"Why did he do that?"

Tyler sighed, "He's crazy. Said the lawn is a battlefield." He headed inside.

***

Nearly a month later, Tyler was on the back patio putting burgers and bratwurst on the grill. Tiffany and Helen were inside drinking chardonnay and laughing wildly about something. "They're having a good laugh."

Barney was on an Adirondack chair not far from the gas grill. "Yeah, probably about one of us." He took a slow drink from a beer bottle. "I see you broke down and started watering the lawn."

Tyler grabbed a beer from the cooler and popped it open. "Yeah, Tiffany complained and said I was being childish. She was right, I guess. What's the deal with the other two houses on the cul-de-sac, I haven't seen anyone but the lawns are in great shape."

"The Spaldings and Rouseaus. They are both retired and were one of the first people to move here, maybe twenty-five years ago. Rouseau is from a wealthy family that has an estate in France. The Spaldings went to stay with them. They both have lawn services and caretakers that check on their homes. They will be gone all summer."

Barney finished his beer and got another one from the cooler. "You talked to Kramer since that morning?"

"Nope, it's on him to make the first move."

Barney sat back down. "I don't see that happening."

They talked about sports and work until the meat was ready and headed inside. Helen and Tiffany were just finishing setting the smaller table in the breakfast area. Tyler saw that they were onto their second bottle of wine. "You have time to do some cooking between your storytelling."

Tiffany giggled and patted Helen on the shoulder, "Mixed vegetable salad, corn on the cob, baked potatoes, and homemade cherry pie from Helen. We are all set."

Barney took a seat at the table. "What had you laughing so hard?"

Helen sat down next to Barney. "Tiffany told me the story again about Kramer and Tyler." She took a drink of wine. "I would have loved to have seen when he hit the ground." She waved at Tyler. "Tell us what he said again, about the battlefield."

Everyone laughed as Tyler finished the story. "Crabgrass. That seemed to set him on edge." He paused and took a drink of beer. "I've been doing some research on crabgrass. About how it gets hold and spreads."

Barney laughed and then went quiet. "You're serious. Why you been doing that?"

Tyler smirked as he continued, "Kramer's lot is sandwiched between our homes. It's about time for herbicides for weed control. A few plantings of small trees near the border with Kramer's yard on your side and my side. The soil around those trees is a perfect germinating site for crabgrass. We both skip the weedkiller and Kramer has a war on two fronts."

Tiffany shook her head. "Tyler, no. Barney's not gonna do that. Neither are you."

Helen squealed, "I love it. Just this one summer. You can get it under control and kill it off, right?"

Tyler nodded in agreement, "Just this summer."

***

A few weeks later, Tyler and Tiffany were sitting on the back porch in the early evening. Tiffany jumped out of her chair. "What was that?"

Tyler bolted out of his seat and ran toward the front of the house. "That was a gunshot."

Tyler spotted Kramer in the middle of his own yard holding a semi-automatic handgun. Barney was ten feet away holding a baseball bat. Helen was standing in the street sobbing. "What the hell is going on?" Tiffany crept up beside him. He whispered to her, "Stay back."

Kramer waved the gun. "Stay off my land, Noble. This state has a hold-your-ground law when it comes to guns and trespassers. Your scrawny accomplice has a weapon. I'm within my rights to defend myself."

Tyler gestured at Barney. "Barney, what's going on?"

"He killed our dog. The vet said there was weed killer mixed in with his outside food bowl."

Helen screamed, "You're a monster. That dog never harmed a soul."

Kramer chuckled, "Herbicides can be dangerous to pets. He must have come over here and got into mine. I keep the garage open sometimes." He sneered, "Since you two haven't used any this year. Kind of a curious coincidence. You always stay with the program, Gibbs. Not this year."

Kramer back peddled towards his front door. "You two want a war. If I find any weeds migrating into my lawn from your territory, you got one."

Tiffany ran to Helen and Tyler shuffled over to Barney. Tyler put his arm around Barney and they met their wives in the street.

Tyler shook his head. "I'm sorry. I didn't think he would get violent. We can undo this."

Helen nearly shouted, "No it's on him, not you. Don't back down. I'm calling the cops."

A few hours later, a county police officer knocked on the door at Barney's house. Barney answered the door and escorted the officer inside. Tyler, Tiffany, and Helen were seated in the den as Barney and the officer entered the room.

The young policeman shrugged with a sigh. "I talked to Mr. Kramer. He admits he fired a warning shot." He gestured at Barney. "But you admit you had a bat and were screaming at him while you were on his property. He was within his legal rights. I can't arrest him."

Helen's voice cracked as she brushed away a tear, "What about our dog?"

"Sorry mam. There's no way to prove how the dog got poisoned. There is nothing we can do."

***

Nearly two weeks later, Tyler came to a slow jog as he headed back to his house from an early morning Saturday run. Kramer was in his yard examining the decorative flowering shrubs and flowers in the plantings in front of his house. Tyler stopped about halfway up the driveway and shouted, "Hey Kenny, your friends are looking kind of sickly. I hope you read the warning on that herbicide. It's poisonous for most flowering plants."

Kramer bolted toward Tyler but stopped a good five feet away. "It's taken me five years to get these established." He shook a fist at Tyler. "You did this, last weekend when I was gone."

Tyler stepped a few steps closer. He sneered, "Got any proof?" He waved at Kramer. "I think you're on my property. Get back on your land."

Kramer shuffled back several steps. "Yeah, sure. You know war is hell." He headed back and continued to examine his ailing plants.

Tiffany opened the front door as Tyler came up onto the porch. "What was that about?"

"He's worried that some of his plants are dying."

"Did you have anything to do with it?"

Tyler looked down. "Not that I can remember." He slipped past her and headed into the house. "How are Helen and the kids doing? I know they loved that dog."

Tiffany closed the door and followed Tyler towards the kitchen. "You're changing subjects on me." She sighed, "The kids are heartbroken. They both are gone for a few weeks; Dan is gone to Helen's brother to visit with cousins. They have a farm about three hours from here in the hill country. Lucy has some sort of college preparatory camp. I think Helen is okay, she said they might get a puppy in the fall."

***

Late that night, Tyler awoke to Tiffany shaking him. "Tyler, something's wrong. I smell smoke."

Tyler jumped out of bed and headed down the hall to the front of the house. He opened the guest bedroom door and saw that something was lighting up the darkness outside.

He ran to the window. His car was on fire in the driveway. He ran down the stairs, put on some sneakers, and ran out the front door. Barney was running out his front door and shouted. "You got a garden hose?"

"Yeah!" He dragged it toward the driveway and Barney turned on the water. Tyler could see that someone had smashed the front driver's side window. Probably poured in gasoline and dropped in a match. As he sprayed it down, he saw Kramer standing in the darkness on his front porch. Kramer saluted and went inside.

Late that morning, a county police lieutenant and the young officer who had come to Barney's house finished taking Tyler's statement. The officers sat at the kitchen table with Tiffany and Tyler. The lieutenant sighed with a shrug. "This has always been a quiet neighborhood; it's been more than ten years since we have had any kind of call out here. That was about smashed mailboxes. I hope whatever is going on here gets settled, soon."

He stood up and gestured at the young officer to follow him. "I can't imagine we are going to get any kind of forensics and there are no security cameras on any of the homes. We will talk to Mr. Kramer but I don't expect to get much. Our report will say malicious vandalism. We will email you a copy for the insurance." He shook a finger at Tyler, "I hope I'm not back here again."

***

Early the next morning, Tyler heard Tiffany shout from downstairs. "Tyler! The back door is open."

He raced down the stairs in gym shorts, a tee shirt, and slippers. Tiffany was at the bottom of the stairs waving toward the corridor that led to the back door. He shuffled slowly down the hall and looked in the pantry, laundry room, and powder room. "Everything looks okay." He walked out onto the patio and looked around. The patio furniture and everything was right where it should be. He closed the door as he came back into the house.

Tiffany followed close behind as he pushed the door open to the kitchen and crept in. They walked all through the downstairs. Tyler shrugged, "Could we have left it open?"

Tiffany shook her head. "No way, it's the last thing I check before I go to bed. So that Flash doesn't get out at night." Her voice got panicky, "Where's Flash?" Their three-year-old gray tabby cat was bonded to Tiffany like a mother. Tiffany rushed through the downstairs making a sound with her tongue that was a call for the cat. "He's gone!"

Tyler chased after her as she ran upstairs. He was attached to the cat as well and he had a sinking feeling they were not going to find him upstairs. "Calm down, he's got a collar with a tag. Our phone number is on it."

He followed as Tiffany raced back down the stairs to the den. She went to the cat's favorite bed next to the fireplace. She picked up the collar lying on the cat's bed. "That psycho took him."

Tiffany raced out the front door and Tyler followed, not sure of what to say. He stood next to her as she pounded on Kramer's door. She shouted, "Open up."

Kramer opened the door after a few moments. "Why are you pounding on my door?" He had a baseball bat in his hand.

She waved the collar and tag in his face. "Where's our cat?"

Kramer chuckled and answered with a sneer, "You people can't seem to take care of your animals. Haven't seen the creature. It will turn up somewhere." He gestured at Tyler. "Maybe it got into some of that herbicide that was on my plants." He smirked, "Make sure you check the side yards, never know where it might be hanging out." He slammed the door shut.

They raced to the side yard. Tiffany screamed, "He hung him. Oh my God."

Tyler continued to the tree. "Wait. It's not real. It's just a stuffed animal." He pulled it down.

As they came back into the house Tiffany came to a dead stop. "Quiet. You hear that?"

"No, I don't hear anything." He followed as she moved toward the corridor and she stopped at the door to the garage. "You don't hear that?"

Tyler closed his eyes for a moment. "Yeah."

They found Flash in the trunk of Tiffany's car. Hot and barely breathing, but alive. Tiffany carried him to the kitchen, got a bottle of water, and poured it into her hand. She spent an hour slowly bringing Flash back to life. They didn't talk about it, but they both knew that Kramer had come in through their unlocked back door. He was tormenting them and hoped they would find Flash dead in the car trunk in a day or two.

Tyler said the obvious as Flash curled up on his bed, "We need to start locking the doors."

***

The middle of the next week, Tyler pulled out of the driveway in the new car he had picked up the day before. Same model and color. The insurance company had paid up quickly and he had the old one hauled away. Kramer was standing near the edge of his property near Barney's yard. *What's he doing?*

Tyler eased the car out of the driveway and Kramer turned and stared at him. Tyler glanced in the rearview mirror as he drove away. Kramer stood there staring until Tyler couldn't see the cul-de-sac as he got further down the road. He put Kramer out of his mind as he headed onto the main highway, it was about a forty-minute drive into the city and his office. He had a busy day packed with meetings.

***

Tyler had forgotten about Kramer and the dispute during his busy day. It was early evening when he got back into his car for the drive home. He had forgotten to call Tiffany and tell her he would be late. His mobile phone buzzed with a text message from Tiffany when he was about ten minutes out of the city. *Get Home Now!*

Tyler felt a knot in his stomach as he called her mobile. It went straight to voice mail. He tried Barney and Helen; they were both off work this week. But neither of them answered their mobile phones. He was in a near panic as he mashed down the accelerator and hoped he didn't get stopped for speeding. He saw brownish smoke as he drove down the entry road. He could tell it was coming from near his house as he got closer to the cul-de-sac. Not a lot of smoke and not like a house fire. But something was smoldering as the sun sank below the horizon.

He was confused about what was burning when he got to the cul-de-sac. He stopped the car in the middle of the road and got out. He moved a few steps toward Kramer's house. Kramer's entire lawn was smoldering and burnt. It smelled of gasoline and it was torched from Barney's property to his own property. The fire had wandered a bit across the property lines but didn't get far. *Did Barney do this?*

He looked towards Barney's house and saw someone lying in the driveway. *Barney!* Tyler raced over and found Barney lying on his back in a pool of blood with a baseball bat lying next to him. *Oh God. So much blood.* There was no pulse and he wasn't breathing. Barney's eyes were wide open and his skin was ashen white. It looked like his throat had been slashed and there were several stab wounds on his chest. Tyler's pulse pounded in his ears as he reached into his pocket for his mobile phone. He realized he had left it in the car.

He heard a faint moaning sound and saw Helen lying on her side on the front porch. She grabbed Tyler's arm when he got to her. Her voice was weak and raspy. "Is he alive?"

"I'm sorry, I don't think so." Her blouse was soaked in blood. He asked, "Why did Barney set a fire?"

She answered in a near whisper. "Kramer started the fire. Barney saw him and grabbed his baseball bat. I heard the door slam and screaming and came out to the porch. Kramer was ranting and shouting about helping the enemy. He had one of those big military knives."

She sobbed and struggled to catch her breath. "Barney swung at him but missed and Kramer just kept stabbing him. Then he saw me on the porch and came after me. He muttered something about collateral damage. I must have blacked out when he stabbed me. But only for just a few moments. I was on the ground when I woke up and Kramer was standing over me. Then he said . . ."

She coughed up some blood and took a few deep breaths. "You need to . . . you need . . ." She went silent and slumped to the ground. Tyler couldn't find a pulse and she wasn't breathing.

This is a nightmare. He saw her mobile phone lying a few feet away. *I need to call the police.* He picked up the phone that was smeared with blood. He saw a text message that she must have sent shortly after Kramer left her for dead. A message to Tiffany. *lock the doors Kramers coming after you.*

Tyler forgot about the police and dropped the phone. He ran back to the spot where Barney was lying and saw that the front door to his house was open. He grabbed Barney's ball bat and ran towards his house. He moved without thinking and was fueled by adrenaline. The same as a football game during intense action. He saw that the frame of the front door was broken and a sledgehammer was lying on the porch.

It was getting dark as Tyler crept into the house. He saw that a light was on in the kitchen. He braced himself for the worst but hoped that Tiffany had not met the same fate as Helen and Barney. His first reaction was relief when he saw that she was alive. That quickly turned to panic when he realized the circumstances.

Tiffany was tied to a kitchen chair and her mouth was gagged. Her eyes were red from crying and wide with fear. Kramer was standing behind her and he was decked out in military camouflage and combat boots. A blood-covered combat knife was on the counter next to him. He was holding his semi-automatic handgun in his right hand. His eyes looked wild as he put the gun to Tiffany's head. "Drop the bat."

Tyler was ten feet away from them; there was no way he could rush Kramer. He dropped his makeshift weapon. His only chance was to make a trade. "Tiffany had nothing to do with any of this. She asked me to stop." He moved a few steps closer. "Let her go and take this out on me."

"Stop right where you are. There is a chair against the wall. Take a seat." Kramer paused a moment. "You are on trial for war crimes. Giving aid and comfort to the enemy. This woman supported you so she faces the same charges."

Tyler sat in the chair. "What are you talking about, aid to the enemy?"

Kramer shouted, "Crabgrass!" He waved the gun at Tyler. "I found it in my lawn this morning and traced it straight back to your yard as well as Gibbs."

"That's why you burned your own lawn?"

"Sometimes you have to destroy the village to save it. That is a lesson of war." Kramer kept the gun aimed at Tyler, picked up the combat knife with his left hand, and pressed it tightly against Tiffany's throat. "Admit your plan!"

Tiffany closed her eyes as tears rolled down her cheeks.

Tyler took in a deep breath. *He's going to cut her throat either way.* He closed his eyes as he searched for an idea that could save Tiffany.

POW.

Tyler's ears were ringing from the sound of a gunshot as he looked at Tiffany. She had blood in her hair and on her forehead but Kramer was the one falling to the ground. A shot to the middle of the forehead. *What happened?*

The police lieutenant rushed into the room with the young officer following behind. The lieutenant holstered his firearm and felt for a pulse on Kramer. Tyler's ears were ringing but he could make out the orders from the senior officer. "Call in the status. Armed suspect down and out. Get the crime scenes secure when the other units get here." The young policeman rushed away.

The lieutenant looked at Tyler. "We got a call about smoke."

Tyler rushed to Tiffany, untied her, and took the gag off of her mouth. He could feel she was trembling as he pulled her close. "It's over. It's all over."

A few hours later, the lieutenant was met by the chief of police near his cruiser in the middle of the cul-de-sac. The chief patted him on the shoulder, "I've read the other responding officers' statement. It's a clean shooting. The guy had already killed two people and had a knife at the woman's throat. I would have taken the shot without a warning. I know it's your first shooting, hopefully your last."

"Thank you. I hope it's my last."

The chief sighed loudly as he gestured at the homes. "It's like a war zone. Drugs?"

"No sir. Crabgrass."

The House on Hideaway Drive
Braden Benzinger

No matter how much Serenity Mason tried, she was never the kind of girl that could get into the Christmas Spirit. Whether it be from the foreboding atmosphere of the barren trees coated in icicles and depressing dark bark or the abysmal weather that was enough to make anyone want to move to Florida, she didn't know. Getting away from the place's mood is exactly why her hair was now a bright pink. But she certainly wasn't happy in Westerash, Illinois. Living alone was quite the challenge and all she could afford after college graduation was a single bedroom apartment. Her family did their best to support her and tried to convince her to come back to live with them. That she would not do. Deadwater Swamp in Georgia was a disaster itself. It had some kind of insect problem with all the heinous buzzing that went on. It just wasn't a place for an artist to thrive and the idea of going back was not appealing even five years later.

Life in Westerash could entertain from time to time, but the city lacked true inspiration. The oddity it was best known for was a horrific stone sculpture of some hideous bird that an unknown man made back in the 1800s. But Serenity was able to use it, as reviewing it led to the launching of her YouTube career. She did well for herself on the site, amassing a decent platform of nearly 15000 subscribers. She used her platform to discuss artwork from some of the greatest artists of all time like Da Vinci, Michelangelo, Van Gogh, Monet, and others as well as show off some of her own watercolors, sketches, and other pieces going into local shows. Sometimes she didn't know if her subscribers were genuinely interested or just liked her looks and precious pink hair.

She loved to explain her style of painting. Serenity never liked to paint things she didn't have a high level of understanding of. Being a part of her piece was of vital importance and that process included learning about her subject. This meant any piece could take more time to finish, but the ones she applied this method to were pieces she relished in creating. The con was the money wasn't coming in as fast as it could.

Commissions from YouTube and some local patrons were not in short supply, but not steady enough to quit working. Being an Art and English double major certainly didn't mean jobs were being flung her way out of college, but she knew it was time to find at least something full time. As a result, she knew she wanted to quit her job at the Henning Family's Gold Rush Amusement Park and become a freelance writer or something along those lines.

But her dream was to make it big and get invited to an art exhibition in New York. Serenity didn't care which one, but New York was the place of dreams. If her career was to be a success, she knew that's where she needed to be. Living and putting on a show there would be better than anything in the world and would help set her and her family up for life.

But these bigger dreams of grandeur would have to wait as she floated through the most boring parts of existence in Westerash, Illinois. As Christmas came closer, Serenity knew that she would have to at least keep the job for some extra money to afford the needed presents for the season. It would all need to be bought, packaged, and shipped down to Georgia by at least the 15th for it to arrive timely. The claim that she would have to work on Christmas saved her from having to actually go to the event, and the lack of a boyfriend meant she wouldn't have to endure any Christmas celebration.

But Christmas always had its way of finding her. The unfortunate fact was that she had to see it on her drives to and from work every day. Exiting her small apartment and heading to the nearest possible way to get on the main road would take her across the entire street of Hideaway Drive. This would mean that she had to pass the daunting Acrea House that sat on the lonely road.

The people of Westerash were normal enough around Christmas time. Some had some blowups that they'd put on the lawn. Others had lights that wrapped on their porches, doors, and other mundane things. But the Acrea House of Hideaway Drive had a more theatrical approach. The Acrea family seemed to take Christmas one step above the others, going above and beyond with the most elaborate Christmas setup of all.

But the strange thing was that their dedication did not mean optimization. For their setup was not at all beaming with any elegance or sophistication but was rather crude and seemed downright unrefined in areas. Decorations enveloped the lawn to the point where they looked like Black Friday shoppers toppling over one another in some hurry to acquire some hot product. It was hard to see the ones behind them because the damn things would block one another and be so smushed, they'd spread disease if capable. Each part of this display was filled with various licensed properties, as well as those more rudimentary in design. Some older specimens were losing their paint or had such odd expressions that looked to be the absolute antithesis of their intended function. Penguins appeared bizarre and bereft of senses. Gingerbread men looked unaware with uncoordinated eyes.

But it was the snowmen that were the most queer. Seemingly the oldest and cheapest decorations on the Acrea House of Hideaway Drive, it was they that suffered the most from deterioration and the loss of the black paint that once covered their eyes. The severity of these losses varied to the individual decoration, though keen observation could note a distinct set of commonalities shared among groups of them. Some came off as weeping, while others frightened. But the worst of them had to be the ones with those sickly smiles plastered to their hideous faces. They curved their faces in just the wrong way to give off the abhorrent quality that made the more mature folk turn their heads. Serenity never dared stare as she drove past the house and all its odd commodities and trinkets.

It was at night when things would be most active. The Acreas seemed to relish at lighting up their absurd blob and sharing it with the world, a ritual likely encouraged by their electric company. Every night, their Christmas cottage glowed like the North Star itself, looking to guide a group of sinners into its firm embrace.

As Serenity would pass her neighborhood's most famous landmark, she would often wonder of the Acrea family and what they were like. Stories regarding the old couple were shared throughout Westerash. Some said they'd spoken of a son in some passing conversations while collecting groceries, but no one could verify this beyond hearsay. They were also a newer addition to the area, making factual information scarce. The lack of facts led Serenity Mason to obtain a sense of curiosity that would only be furthered, as colors glistened from the house at night from her bedroom window.

Other residents of Westerash, Illinois seemed to share this notion of unspoken curiosity with her. Many would flock to at all times a day to get a glimpse of the weird surplus of decorations. Children were especially fond of the house, lacking whatever judicious quality adults possessed that made them more weary of it. No one really knew quite what to make of it.

These thoughts are the ones that dwelled inside Serenity as she sat in her room drawing a picture of Mt. Everest in her sketchbook with a glass of wine at her side. She liked the sketch, but knew it just wasn't the time to pursue it beyond that. That Acrea House just wouldn't leave her racing thoughts. Unable to resist their call further, she took out her computer and looked up anything she could find, leading her to discover a local media story which included the house. It was an awkward piece of writing displaying some of the top houses that were decked out in what they called, "Christmas gear."

"I wouldn't be caught in any of that crap," Serenity said, bringing the wineglass to her lips.

Unamused by the basic prose of a white man that was likely paid too much to write it, she simply wanted to see the Acrea house within the article. Her search ended rather quickly as it ended up being the seventh house in an article of 25. Upon seeing it in the photos, she was more impressed with it. Whether it be the local news fixing it in post or the fact that she missed a few things avoiding the haunting gazes of the snowmen, Serenity knew that this house and its peculiar Christmas decor was going to be her next project.

Armed with a desire to paint the odd house and a curiosity of the Acrea family, Serenity knew that she would want their approval before starting, as it was ethical.

Daylight seemed as if it would never come, but the minute the sun peaked out, Serenity was awake. She needed to make sure she looked perfect when she met the Acreas for the first time. She tried on a few different outfits, but none seemed as if they were fit for the occasion. Some felt too casual, while others too professional. There was a balance she needed that she didn't feel she had to make a good impression on the older Acrea family. She finally settled on a pair of jeans and a striped button up top. She brushed her bright pink hair and took a deep breath before driving the brief way down to the Acrea House.

The house wasn't any easier to look at outside of a car. In fact, being closer to it made Serenity even question her idea. How was she to paint what she couldn't even look at? But for now, she ignored the gazes of the unintentional instruments of terror and gave the door a knock. When she exhaled, she saw her breath leave her mouth and hoped that anyone would answer before she froze to death alongside the grinning snowmen.

After a second knock, a response from the other side was finally audible.

"We're not voting for him. Thank you though," a man's firm voice said.

"No, sir. It's nothing like that at all. I just wanted to talk to you about something."

"Yeah, and we're not buying your girl scout cookies either."

"Ugh," Serenity began, surprised at the tone. "Sir, I'm just an artist. I studied at the University of Westerash. Please, this will be just a second."

"Oh, come on, John. I think she's perfect," a softer female voice said.

The door finally opened to reveal an older woman in at least her fifties. She had a pleasant smile, a distinct birthmark on her arm, and blonde hair that was in the process of graying.

"Hello, dear. I'm Andrea Acrea. How are you?"

Serenity smiled and ran her fingers through her distinct pink locks. "Hi ma'am. I don't mean to bother you at all. My name's Serenity Mason. It's just that… Well, I'm an artist like I said. I live at the apartments down that way. I pass your house every day and I find it fascinating. There's just so many unique decorations and I was just wondering if I could maybe paint it for you and take that painting to a few local shows."

Serenity winced as her words left her mouth and regret instantly filled her. Why did she even bother coming here? This was a bad idea. The older couple was probably judging her to an extreme degree. Mr. Acrea didn't seem too excited based on his aggression when she knocked. But Mrs. Acrea's expression couldn't have been more jovial, and her bright brown eyes lit up like a candle.

"Wow, that sounds like a swell idea. Please, come in, darling."

Mrs. Acrea waved Serenity and guided her into the house. Unsurprisingly, there was an equal amount of Christmas cheer in the house as well. Pictures and reefs covered nearly every part of the house to where the entire thing, like its outside counterpart, lacked grace or beauty. Among the decorations inside, however, were a set of intricate porcelain dolls, each wearing their own elegant dress that extended to the floor. This set of dolls had the unique distinction of being organized and well-constructed as opposed to the awkward setup of Christmas characters. While their stares were equally blank as those within the mess on the outside of the house, the amount of detail on their faces, like their blush, lips, and just the most fashionable hairstyles proved the immense dedication of their creator.

"Do you do this every year?" Serenity asked, approaching the dollhouse.

"Why yes, dear. It is a very important time of year for the world. It is worth all the work."

"Your passion is contagious. When did you finish putting everything up?"

It was at that moment that Mr. Acrea returned to the room with another box containing ornaments and other trinkets that didn't seem to have any specific function rather than decoration.

"We haven't," Mr. Acrea barked in response to the question.

"My goodness," Serenity said. "Well, if it would help warm you up to me painting the house, I would love to help you in any way that I can."

Mr. and Mrs. Acrea didn't react at first, something that Serenity didn't anticipate. But they were quick to get back on track after a glance at one another.

"I think that would be just wonderful. We've had little help this year. It would be nice to get an extra set of arms. Maybe we'll be done by Christmas if you help. I like that very much. What do you think, John?"

Mr. Acrea shrugged. "Maybe she could help with the smaller stuff. I have to get on the roof soon and she can't help with that."

"It's a deal then. We will pay you too. It makes no sense for you to work for free."

"Oh Mrs. Acrea, that's not-"

"We can even make cookies! Have you ever made them before?" Mrs. Acrea asked.

Serenity shook her head, laughing. "Only when I was a kid. I don't think I've done it in 15 years."

"Well, then we'll make some and I might even give you the recipe so you can make them when you have kids. What do you say?"

"Yeah, that would work," Serenity said, forcing an awkward smile.

"Delightful. Let's start by putting out some candles so we can light them up tonight."

Serenity went over to the window to observe the blockade of snowmen from another angle. The vile things looked to be from some other world with the angles of their smiles and the distance between their eyes. The light colors of their bodies contrasted with the dull bark coming from the lifeless trees they were projected against. The fading paint gave off the impression that they were melting, sinking back into the ground where they could only grin at the sky.

"You like them?" Mr. Acrea asked from behind, startling Serenity to her core.

"Uhh, yeah. They look like they've been used for a long time."

"They've been around awhile. Truth is that they come from my father. He actually liked Christmas more than anyone else in the family, if you can believe that."

"I don't know if I can imagine what his house looked like."

"Simpler than ours. But that's because he had less decorations. I like to think we're moving the needle about as much as he did in the day."

"I think you're succeeding, sir," Serenity said, bowing her head.

"Yeah, yeah. Go get the candles out. I'll go get ya a glass of water."

Serenity nodded and went back to assist Mrs. Acrea with the candles and helped her get her candles aligned in the way she wanted. Mr. Acrea came over and gave Serenity the glass of water before heading outside presumably to tinker about with the disorderly decor on the backside of the house.

"Walk with me, dear," Mrs. Acrea said as she began a slow walk out of the kitchen and into the living room. Serenity took a last look at the dolls and their deadpan glares before following Mrs. Acrea who was in the process of picking up a decently sized book which she sat on a nearby table before sitting down on the couch. Serenity raised the glass of water to her red lips and took a drink, a bigger one than she thought she would before looking at the book.

"This is how John and I record just how many people have helped us over the years. As we get older, it becomes harder and harder to put out all the decorations on our own.

This year has been a lot slower because no one has helped us yet."

Serenity picked it up and sat it on her lap, flipping it open to see a plentiful number of names on it. Some people opted to put their first and last names only while others put their middle names too.

"Why do you dye your hair pink?" Mrs. Acrea suddenly asked.

It was an unexpected question and one that threw Serenity off when she heard it since it didn't seem like the right time to talk about it. She had answered it a great many times before, usually to unimpressed family members. But Mrs. Acrea wasn't like that. The way the old woman's gaze was glued to her locks indicated an awkward fascination with it. Mrs. Acrea studied her hair the same way Serenity looked at an incomplete piece of art.

"Well, I-I used to live in Deadwater Swamp in Georgia. I hated it down there. Everything was so dark and dreary. I always called it a permanent night when I was a little girl. So, when I was a teenager, I knew I wanted to show that I was different from the place I grew up and black hair would never help me do that. So, I changed it. I've done a lot of colors before. Blonde was the first. I thought it contrasted the area most. I moved to a light blue, then yellow, then some combinations throughout college, and now I'm trying pink."

Mrs. Acrea nodded and listened to the story with great enthusiasm, which made Serenity give an uneasy smile. Feeling a bit odd about herself, she picked up a nearby pen and flipped the pages until she could find the one that hosted the first blank space. She filled out her name as Mrs. Acrea spoke again.

"I see many kids today who like to dye their hair. I think if I was younger, I'd be like that too. Ways to express yourself have advanced a long way since our time. I believe you're the first person I've seen who decided to do it to stand out from where they lived."

Serenity shrugged. "I get told that a lot. Goes to show you how bad Deadwater was." She picked up the water and drank it again, finishing it.

"Well, I think it is just beautiful like that. I hope you keep it that way."

"I like it for now. It's hard for me to stay attached to one color for so long. I just won't do green or black. Okay, maybe I'd consider a light green, but I'd have to be in a very different place in my head."

At this point, Mr. Acrea came into the room and announced that he was done with the outside for the day. It was just too cold to continue. Mrs. Acrea stood up and helped him take his jacket off while Serenity studied the odd book she had signed. The amount of names within it, like the decor, was plentiful. Although since the Acreas were up in age, it's likely that a lot of the names contributed in the same year as each other.

Still, it was a correlation that was hard to ignore. The Acreas always just seemed extra about each thing they did. It had to be as big and over the top as possible. As Serenity thought about her painting and the best way she could replicate the over the top nature of the house on the canvas, Mrs. Acrea gave off a wide smile.

"I think it's time we make those cookies now. What do you think?"

"Sure," Serenity said.

"I'm gonna leave that to you two. I'm about to watch the news and learn more about why you liberals are ruining the country," Mr. Acrea said.

"Oh you're exaggerating it, John. Change is good."

"Yeah, yeah. I hear you."

Serenity and Mrs. Acrea went back into the kitchen and began to get out the ingredients for what she described as "the best sugar cookies in the state of Illinois."

"Dear, will you preheat the oven to 375?"

"Yes, ma'am."

Upon Serenity going to the oven, a wave of pain blasted through her stomach. It started on her right side, but it didn't take long for it to go to the left. She let out a grunt of pain while preheating the oven and returned to Mrs. Acrea as she stirred a mixture of some ingredients, hoping the elderly woman would not sense her newfound discomfort.

"So, if you and Mr. Acrea aren't on the same side of the spectrum, how do you get along so well? I've never seen anything like it. College was always fiery with debates."

"Well, I think what helps us is the fact that we share a lot of core values. People think that can't be done in today's age. But I assure you it can. We think that the left and the right exist to complement each other, not to attack each other in the way that many people do today."

Serenity held her hand close to her stomach and looked at Mrs. Acrea. "I think that's a wonderful way to look at life. It can be hard, but I think that would help a lot of people be better."

"It also helps that John and I have a couple of mutual interests."

"Like what?"

"Can't spill all our secrets, dear."

Whatever affliction Serenity felt worsened at a rapid rate and conversation did little to distract from it. Her stomach growled and seemed to gurgle as if some unholy organism that once lay dormant in her innards was now very much awake and actively trying to burst out of her abdomen. Her tightening grip was ineffective at causing any real remedy for it.

"Excuse me, please," she said, running out of the kitchen.

There was only one room that she cared about and that was the bathroom. Even that room was filled to its maximum capacity with Christmas decorations, with a little reindeer rug and Santa candles aligned at the sink. The Santa candles themselves were another atypical asset to the house. They had no eyebrows and eyes that were completely blue. Their positioning was deliberate as they stared holes through the poor soul in an awkward situation. Uneasiness filled Serenity as she sat in silence.

What came out of her was not at all solid except in a few chunks. Serenity could discern that by the way it exited. She did not dare take even so much as a glance inside the toilet or else drop dead from the embarrassment it may give her. The situation was only worsened by the fact that when she thought she was done; it started again. Upon the gruesome process finally coming to a close, the unfortunate discomfort was the fact the release did nothing to cure the affliction in her stomach.

It was quite the opposite. The horrific process made her feel worse rather than better. She wiped and flushed before stumbling out of the room, barely making it to the kitchen in a straight line. Upon her arrival, the only thing she could do was slump limply into the chair and curled into a ball, looking over to see that the collection of porcelain dolls had been moved from the living room to be leaning against the wall of the kitchen. Further scans of the room revealed the dolls to be all over the kitchen. Their tiny bodies sat along the wall, some on the stove, and others on the kitchen table.

"What's wrong, dear?" Mrs. Acrea said with a smile that mirrored the worst of the snowmen in the front.

"I don't know. Everything hurts," Serenity replied weakly.

"Oh, my. How terrible. Maybe you should sleep here tonight."

"We have a guest room," Mr. Acrea called from the other room.

"That's nice of you, but I'll just go home. I can make it," Serenity said as Mrs. Acres crept closer to her inch by inch.

"No, dear. You mustn't," Mrs. Acrea said.

"But…" Serenity said looking over. "I just want to go home."

"You said you'd help with getting the house ready. We need you."

Mrs. Acrea reached out and glided her index and middle fingers across Serenity's smooth skin. Goosebumps formed on Serenity the instant their skin touched, as her fingers were cold.

"I'll come back. I just need a night."

Mr. Acrea came into the room. "Why don't we get her upstairs into the guest room?"

"In a second, John." Mrs. Acrea said, bending over.

Serenity began shaking as Mrs. Acrea got close to her. "Stop, please. Let me go home."

Mrs. Acrea slid her fingers into Serenity's pink hair, bringing it to her face and sniffing it from the tips to her scalp. Her hands wiggled throughout, and she took individual strands of it within her wrinkly hands, observing the length before going to her notebook and scribbling some details in it.

"Do you ever curl it?" Mrs. Acrea asked.

"Stop."

"You're just the cutest."

Her hands went down to Serenity's face where she pinched her cheeks and rubbed her finger along her lips. Without a moment to spare, she turned to Mr. Acrea

"John, get me the scissors."

"Can't you do this after she's-"

"John, get me the scissors."

Mr. Acrea rolled his eyes. "Alright. Don't bite my head off."

He then went over to the cabinet and pulled out a pair of scissors and handed them to Mrs. Acrea who gave them a few snips in front of Serenity's face. The woman yanked a much bigger chunk of Serenity's hair than previously and placed the scissors on the top of her head so that she could feel just how cold the steel felt upon it. Serenity looked around the room frantically before her gaze landed at one of the porcelain dolls as it gave its blank stare forward at the other end of the table. Its bright hair shined as lifelike as her own. Before Mrs. Acrea could continue, Serenity reached out for her life and was just able to grab the doll by its leg and used it like a whip to deliver the most powerful strike she could manage on the old woman's skull. It was enough to force a scream and she dropped the scissors, which gave a thud as they hit the ground.

She scampered over and picked them up with the fresh burst of adrenaline she now had within her. Mr. Acrea's arms slithered around her stomach, and he hurled her against the fridge causing her to about knock it over. She coughed again before looking up at him, her vision blurred, but still feeling the scissors in hand. Acting on nothing but instinct, Serenity thrusted them into Mr. Acrea's shoulder, making him flounder to the door.

One hand on her stomach and the other hand still in possession of the scissors, Serenity limped over to the front door and flung it open to be greeted by the faces of the several wicked sneers of the snowmen decorations that had been moved to the porch, blocking the door from opening. They sat, ever still and their grins wide. The blurriness of the vision caused them to distort and seemingly combine to form some wicked beast.

Serenity's stomach pain returned, and she fell to her knees, coughing and gagging as she stared into the faces of the many snowmen, she had avoided on her various drives past the Acrea house on Hideaway Drive. Coughs turned to dry heaves which eventually became brown, chunky vomit. Serenity slumped up against the wall, feeling blood smack her lips that had no doubt come from her innards.

Both Acreas were now standing above her. Mrs. Acrea looked down over her with rage in her eyes. In her hands was a massive knife. She leaned in to seemingly use it, but Mr. Acrea stopped her.

"Let her pass in peace," he said, rubbing his wound.

Serenity felt a tear in her eye after the words left his mouth. She held up her left hand and placed her right index finger in her mouth, getting blood on it. Using it, she made the stick figure sketch of a little girl on her hand before closing her eyes and letting fate take her.

Hours later, Mrs. Acrea came into the room and saw the corpse laying against the wall.

"She's gone," she said. Her husband followed and they stared at her body.

"She seemed like a good kid," he said.

"Well, I'll make sure when I finally use her, she'd be proud of what I make."

The two stood in silence for another minute as they stared at her lifeless body.

"I'll order another snowman then," Mr. Acrea murmured, leaving his wife to collect her thoughts.

The Killer, the Blood Spatter Analyst, and the OB/GYN

Alexander Marais

"*L*ex, please…"
My eyes stared coldly at her, someone I was doing my best to misshape perceptually. To remove any sense of sentimentality towards.

Between us, on the pale white tablecloth, was a plate of cookies.

I made sure they had nuts.

The woman before me was older, pushing seventy. From the sounds I'd heard coming from the bedroom, she was able to inexplicably maintain one hell of a vagina. The minority of times she went at it with various gentlemen callers confirmed it. They were all spaced out, though, reminding me of something equivocating that level of passion – however not just physically – that I decided, along with certain individuals she so cruelly asphyxiated. The plate of cookies between us was a gateway, one I knew she'd never be able to cross. The anaphylactic shock would put an end to that. Now it would be interesting, perhaps even amusing, to see what she did next.

"Eat a cookie. I made them myself. Then maybe we can reconnect. You said it yourself. If you want a relationship that works, well...it takes just that. Work."

The words coming out of my mouth betrayed the cold, sinister demeanor I'd been working to maintain. They were fraught, raw with distinctive emotion. I hated that. But I managed to negate any attempts at hurting myself by refocusing my attention on the plate. As soon as she was out of the way, I reasoned, the assets would be mine and phase two of my plan could begin. That's when the real fun would commence. Psychologically torturing my mother by simultaneously playing upon her love and guilt was one thing. But the next woman in my life I would dispatch of proved a visceral goldmine. If the woman before me was the solidifier of why I cut my face, the next one was the crux of my anger at being alive.

"Just eat one..."

That was better.

My voice was calmer. Almost soothing, even. Such emotiveness was welcome. It probably made my delivery, in some ways, stronger.

"No."

"You said one needs to put in the work..."

"Lex, if I eat one of these, I could die."

Her eyes were leaking, though. The water works on full and cataclysmic display. It was wonderful to see that, honestly.

She wasn't saying anything from a place of self-determination, or respect. She was simply saying it earnestly, visibly so. My eyes looked down on the cookie at the top of the heap —with the most almonds. I had arranged it in a pattern like how we used to bake together, back when I was young and still had much masculinity to strip. I liked towing an uncanny valley line between that little boy she craved such interconnectivity with, and the "scarred" man a walking rejection of her values.

I waited, holding the berries.

Sure enough, she slowly started coming home. I saw that sort of faraway look in her eyes. The kind of thing overtaking sense and reason. In contrast, her face began to crumple – the tears starting to fall and fogging up her thick, faux-sophisticated designer glasses. The tips of her fingers danced a couple inches from the nuts, before hurriedly sinking themselves into the baked, doughy part of the treat.

I sat there, smiling slightly. I couldn't help feeling a slight pit in my stomach at the sight. How far she'd go for love, even if there wasn't any to give in return. This wasn't how I would deal with the other one – the vicious cunt who, to paraphrase Thunberg, 'stole (my) dreams and childhood.' I wasn't quite sure if I'd dispatch of her messily, although I decided to bring along a few tools just in case.

***

Alina's eyes opened slowly.

She leaned forward in the car, pressing herself tightly against the steering wheel whilst convincing herself no one could see.

Don't be weak.

Don't be weak.

Slowly she rose her head, leaning back into the driver's seat, as if being pulled by tremendous weight. Her mother's voice was dancing in her head again, all endless pontificating and finger-wagging. It was such a goddamn cliché, really. The kind of thing she was used to making fun of and acting unflappable towards. Only now it was her reality too, regardless of the rather morbid line of work she decided community college best prepped her for.

"Keey-*rist*."

Making her way out of the car, Alina was quick to adopt the equivalent of the customary smile in that line of work. Simply put, the usual nine-to-five poker face.

"What have we got, guys?" she said, dropping her voice a couple octaves and adopting a slight, masculine swagger to her movements.

The three men turning around to face her didn't display friendly expressions. Except for the lead detective, Thompson. He had nice eyes. At least, Alina liked to think so.

"It's bad," he said, with characteristic bluntness.

His eyes moved to the large camera hanging around Alina's neck.

"Isn't it always?"

"Not like this." Thompson gestured towards the interior of the tall, San Franciscan high society abode. "The wife's a fucking hysteric, the husband well…someone's blasted him six ways to Sunday. You better be ready to get down and dirty with that thing."

Alina forced a grim smile. Once again, the typical plays in an arena like this one.

"Of course," she said, somewhat huskily.

Slowly she proceeded past the men, trying not to notice one of them conspicuously brushing against her as she moved.

Stepping into the arched grounds of the property, Alina turned to her right and subsequently ventured through a tall, imposing doorway leading into something even throwing her for a bit of a loop.

"*Jesus H. Christ*," she heard herself say.

Lying in front of her, in stark juxtaposition to the grand, ballroom-décor, was what remained of a decidedly *defiled* figure. Hysterical, bereft screams – likely belonging to a Dr. Martha MacIsaac Martin – echoed audibly in a room up a flight of stairs on the second floor.

Alina stepped forward slowly, stopping short when she took full, objective stock of the damage. The body had been stripped naked, its genitals removed and bloody, cavernous holes where its eyes used to be. The worst part was the skin missing from its back, exposing in gruesome, anatomical fashion tissue and bone underneath. It was sitting in somewhat slumped pose, presenting worst of both worlds. As she put the camera to her eye, the young woman couldn't help but feel that familiar, dreaded split.

The part of her assuming automatic function, the part of her retaining some semblance of humanistic trauma…

The white flashes illuminated the body's unhinged, presentational quality.

The reddened back, the thing you could no longer call a face. The now emasculated, sexless disposition of its privates.

Instantly what came to Alina's mind, although she had by no means a detective's instinct, was rage. Simply put, pure and unfettered rage. Whoever did this was making her feel some sort of twisted version of what he or she had been feeling. *Maybe for years.*

She stepped closer, making sure her white shoe didn't touch even a millimeter of the blood pool surrounding his form. Enough time had passed that much of it solidified anyway, as if the murderer had splashed red paint, rather than drawing blood. But someone with this level of animalistic savagery likely just got started. Despite her youthful naivete, Alina had been around enough to know what qualified as a crime of passion, and what was the start of descent. Whoever this person was, they had crossed that line. The kind of unhinged deviancy before her implied release. And with that kind of externality *when* released, there was no knowing what they would be up to next.

"Easy there, Hernandez. Don't dirty your shoes or pollute the scene."

Alina swallowed audibly, hiding a scowl as Thompson materialized behind her – staring despondently in the cadaver's direction.

"What are we looking at?"

Alina took a moment to respond, briefly viewing damages through the lens and focusing on the wounds prevalent on the backside.

"Given the direction of the blood spurts, whoever this was stood over the guy – likely a surprise attack. Spontaneous, clearly – I mean, you have a streak in the front, you have a second large spill in the front, on the opposite side. Given the markings on the wall behind him to boot, there's no question this wasn't planned…"

Alina slowly lowered the camera and rose to her feet, turning to face Thompson and another one of the men from outside.

"Getting in here, though, no records – no trace. Had to be planned. I suppose, for whatever reason, our guy didn't expect to run into the husband. He must have been coming here for Dr. Martin."

A smirk formed on the man's face standing behind Thompson. The latter remained expressionless.

Except for his eyes.

"You doing my job for me, Hernandez?" he said.

Alina bridled slightly, then shook her head – keeping her expression equally indiscernible in spite of the hiccup.

"No sir."

"Photograph some more, then we can send in the rest of forensics."

Thompson turned on his heel, moving past the man behind him. The latter stared at Alina for several seconds, then licked his lips with deliberation.

"Nice one, *teacher's pet.*"

Alina took the hit, this time without even bridling. It was simply part of the job. Something to piss about when she was home with a bottle of scotch, her trusty handgun locked in the safe beneath her bed.

"Asshole."

Slowly she turned as the rest of the team moved into the premises, the anguished shrieks still materializing from up the stairs. Making her way out of the tarred home, through the archway, and back onto the street. It was only when she felt rather than thought she was out of sight Alina allowed her pace to quicken.

Leaning against her car, a familiar nausea threatened to overwhelm. But as quickly as it happened, it was over. Certain aspects of on-the-job training had become thoroughly embedded. It was only as she turned the young woman jumped a foot in the air, the forensics camera round her neck hitting her hard in the chest.

"The fuck?!"

Her eyes squinted as she tried to make sense of the gentleman standing before her. In his outstretched hand was a cigarette carton.

"Smoke?"

Alina's eyes narrowed again, taking full stock of the situation and her defenses visibly on display.

"Who the fuck are you? You don't just sneak up on people, you goddamned creep."

The man in front of her, probably around his early thirties, remained unfazed.

"Sorry about that," he responded, matter-of-factly. "You just looked like you needed a smoke. I sure fucking do."

Alina looked between him and the carton in his hand. Letting sense overpower reason, she grabbed at one of the smokes, the former somewhat cornily hoisting a plastic lighter up to her face with the other hand.

"I can't believe what happened to Dr. Martin in there. The whole neighborhood is talking about it."

Alina looked at him with renewed suspicion. "Yeah, well, if you're reporter – you're not going to bum me for a story," she shot back. "Besides, I'm not the man in charge to talk to. That would be Detective Thompson."

"I'm not a reporter," the man said, as he lit his own cigarette. He blew a gust of smoke out of his nostrils before continuing. "I'm just a concerned civilian. I knew Dr. Martin and his wife back in the day. They had a…you could almost say…profound impact…on my life."

Alina looked at him curiously, clearly gauging the nature of this interaction. However she was quick to relax, assured by her perceived common sense there could be no synchroneity.

"How did you know them?" she asked, practiced edge in her voice.

The man blew another gust of smoke, this time from his mouth.

"His wife Mrs. Dr. Martin was my mother's OB/GYN. Naturally, of course, they were both OB/GYNs, it was a different time I suppose when attending medical school."

He let out another breath.

"They both serviced a lot of clientele here in the San Francisco Bay Area. Not to mention, of course, Dr. Adam Martin was a scion of the city's top family. A match made in Heaven, the papers said. Now it's all so terribly wrong. It's a very tragic thing."

He looked in Alina's direction, the latter staring at him curiously.

"I'm sorry," he was quick to defer. "I know this is all very awkward. Clearly you don't look like you associate with such people."

"Well, you've just made it worse," Alina said, staring back in the direction of the Martin house.

"Sorry, didn't mean to do that either."

It was the first, slightly less pretentious statement out of the gentleman's mouth. Alina decided she'd let it hang.

"Who are you?"

"Lex, Lex D'Antonio," the man awkwardly stuck out his hand, positioning himself next to her.

"Nice to meet you, Lex."

She never took her eyes off him, refusing to let a half-smile form on her face.

"What's your name?"

"*Alina*."

She grimaced, unsure of why she just spat that out without hesitation.

"Alina," the man echoed. "*Alina*…Interesting. Well, Alina, tough night for you folks, I'm sure."

"Yeah."

Alina breathed in heavily, then pulled the cigarette out of her mouth and held it by her side. She subsequently let out a deep breath, obscuring their view of the Martin household.

"It's funny, you never quite get used to this job," she found herself off cuff again. "I've been doing it for over a year, and there's actually a surprising amount of shit that happens out here. There's something about photographing someone's shit they…what am I saying…Never mind…"

She shut up and shut down, adopting a stonier expression as she reexamined Lex by her side. If there was one thing the job had taught her, rule of thumb, it was not to converse with the passersby.

Lex stared back at her earnestly as her features hardened, appropriately unperturbed.

"Thanks for the cigarette," Alina said coldly. She looked back at the Martin house again, prying her back off the car. "You best be getting on your way."

"Of course," Lex said, dropping the cigarette and stamping it out with a bourgeois set of shoes.

As Alina made several paces toward the grounds, she cast a quick glance back. Antithetical to things getting obvious, Lex had already disappeared from where he was standing. He was making his way back down the street, headed toward several other gawking residents nearby.

Turning back to see where she was going, Alina stopped short at Thompson – materializing under the archway.

"Who was *that*?"

"Just one of the neighbors. Apparently the news has broken out about Dr. Martin…"

"Yeah, well, that's bad enough," Thompson said, an uncharacteristic edge beginning to enter his voice. "The last thing we need is one of the forensics staffers spilling the tea on an active investigation."

"I'm sorry," Alina said, instantly shrinking under his gaze. "I didn't talk to him about…"

Thompson wasn't having it though, already raising his voice. Doing his equivalent of shouting. "Do your fucking job, and don't mingle with the color here," he said. "I want several more photographs of the walls now that they're moving the body. When you're finished, give *me* your camera – I don't trust your conduct."

Alina flushed, diverting her gaze from Thompson and quickly making her way past him. Heading back into the front of the home, the nausea distantly struck again. Its duration was mitigated slightly, now that Dr. Martin's body had been moved. The streaks of red almost didn't look legitimate in their origins, providing something of a pacifier to intrinsic repulsion.

Slowly, Alina put the lens of the forensics camera to her eye.

***

My husband is dead.

My husband, my life partner. The co-founder of our practice.

I'd like to think in the face of something like this, I would have been stronger. I was always the taciturn one. At least, that's always what Adam said. I remember how my father always would make me do a man's work. He always used to say that he wouldn't raise a weak girl.

Now, I am that weak girl.

I am broken.

I suppose that is a natural response to coming home, with your husband. Then hearing his screams, hearing the sound of something like skin being scraped off a chicken. You heard that right. You know that sound, when you're peeling the skin off cutlets? That's what it sounded like. By the time I made my way towards him, by the time I actually even heard the screams…it was all over.

I had made my way to the top of the stairs.

I looked down.

I saw him.

I saw…him. Even today, I recognize those eyes.

Those soulless, black dots. The kind that stared at me many, many years ago. The kind initially displaying a literal lifelessness, when he was finally induced at the forty two week period – covered in meconium. One of his lungs collapsed. The parents naturally were apoplectic, at least the husband appeared to be. Limp little thing. Something asphyxiated from life seemingly from the moment it was born. But it was not to be.

He looked at me. It wasn't like one of those scenes from the thrillers Adam liked to watch. The horror tripled, quadrupled what such evocations induce. There was no gleeful sadism, at least none visibly. I do think he enjoyed taking out on my husband what I believe I understand he intended for me. But staring into those eyes, staring at that pale, Aryan face, I saw unbridled hatred. Not some unfeeling cruelty. A bottomless pit of induced rage and psychotic tempestuousness, something developed and metastasized over years and years of simmering. I'm not a spiritualist. I worship at the altar of the Hippocratic Oath. But if the concept of the aura can be used here, however analogously, what was emanating from this man was black.

He was the black.

He stared at me, and I stared at him.

Not a word was said.

There was no need to say anything.

I knew he would come up those stairs for me. I know he would enjoy cutting my throat and defiling my form. Just like what he did to my husband. It wouldn't just be about the killing for him, it would be about the carnage. Perhaps an externalization of whatever he felt we had done to him. And we had done something to him.

I by no means sympathize with this young man. He got his revenge. He destroyed my life, utterly. I don't know if I'll ever physically bring myself to practice again. The tremors in my hands are getting worse. If not because of severe trauma, then perhaps because of the haunting realization that he is not done. Not done with me.

Not yet.

***

Then, he opens the door.

He's standing there, smiling at me. He's not prepared. He'll be dropping skin flecks and DNA all over the place. He's dressed casual, his hair slicked back. I look at him, but I don't scream. I know why he's here. I'm more scanning for anything that can be a weapon, anything that can be an escape.

"Hello Martha, do you remember me?"

He closes the door behind him, slowly making his way towards me.

My body is rigid. I don't move. Only my eyes dart frenetically to track his movements.

"You found me," I hear myself say, breaking into a smile that's more showing my teeth. My voice wavers – I sound more like the quintessential damsel in distress. That's all I am now.

"I never thought San Francisco's elite would choose Bolinas of all places as a rural escapade."

"It's untouched," I spurt out. "It's supposed to be a place people won't look."

"Good."

He's sitting on the bedspread in front of me. His face is almost kind, it's such a strange juxtaposition. I feel my hands starting to move.

"Don't get any ideas."

He reaches into his pocket, withdrawing a handgun.

"A little elaborate, don't you think?" I freeze.

"Well," he says. "I come prepared."

He holds the gun by his side, but I know any sudden movements and I'm likely dead, or severely maimed. I go through my mind the options, but can find none.

"I am a doctor," I finally hear myself say. "I perform a service. My patients will need me. Surely you can understand that."

The kindly disposition on Lex's face is gone. Now, I see that familiar, Aryan stare. Except this time, there's nothing behind the eyes. There's nothing human – even malignantly so – to connect to. Honestly, that's more frightening to me. It means whatever he winds up doing, it won't be motivated or flawed by emotional inclination.

"Tell me at least what you intend to do with me…"

Now I'm lying down on the bed. He's standing over me.

He doesn't answer, though. And those eyes – those, terrible black pinpoints – they're dead. The hate, the spark of wrath – it's gone. What he's doing here is completely automatic. Maybe not even driven by impulse. My eyes move to the gun in his pocket, then to the metallic glint of what's in his other hand.

It's a…cheese grater.

I don't understand.

"What are you going to do with that?"

There's almost a mortified amusement in my voice. A sort of hopeless, depleted laughter hints at the peripherals of my psyche.

Lex opens his mouth to speak, but when he does so – I know it's not in response to me. He's monologuing, yet his attention remains entirely on me. The cognitive dissonance of this stance only makes the unnerving nature that much more unbearable. It permeates my veins, penetrating deep. I don't understand what, exactly. I can only surmise the level of shock I've been in, now multiplied with abject terror, will bring on many things.

Or, nothing at all.

It's not that I've accepted what is about to happen to me. It's more I simply see no logical way out. I am stuck at a never-ending crossroads, and I'm seeing the sign moving in on me.

"I've never been exactly well-adjusted..."

He's speaking emotively, despite that face remaining coolly blank.

"I've never understood. Is it the brain damage? Or is it the years I've spent being told I have such a condition? I really don't know. But what I do know is this."

He moves the cheese grater down towards my arm.

"That study you and your husband ran, that Faustian bargain my mother made, that damned research initiative at the hospital...the black stick that left me in utero for over an additional month...It's taken everything."

His tone flattens, but I know the affect belies what he actually feels. Now his face is starting to replace what he's not communicating verbally anymore.

"My life. My aspirations. You made me into something...worthless."

All of a sudden, he's tearing at my morning blouse. This is when I start screaming, actively struggling. He jars me with a slap, but I keep trying. Then he's actually straddling me, slapping and punching me repeatedly. The actuality of what might befall me is taking full effect. I will not let this happen to me. I can't.

"You are worthless," I hear more than actively say the words.

One final slap and tear at the fabric rips it off, revealing my bare, naked form in front of him. The horror of this gives way to a rage I didn't think I had. I'm clawing at him. I'm trying to knee him in the balls. I see him reaching for the gun in his pocket. I start actually roaring a bit at him, no longer just screaming. There's blood coming out of my mouth. It's primal, it's visceral. I know what he is about to do…

***

I put the gun to the woman's head.

I appreciated her tenacity, I must say.

In the moment the barrel pressed itself against her forehead, I realized for a split second I would miss this. It moved me, deeply. As she clawed uselessly at my side, I clicked the safety catch and pulled the trigger.

It fired, she jerked – then moved no more.

Her eyes stared blankly ahead, her face suddenly relaxed and submissive. I continued straddling her, panting and instantly aware this bird was baked in terms of trying to keep things low-key. My eyes dropped to the cheese grater in my other hand.

Was it really necessary to do what I was going to do here? The bitch was dead. Along with my mother.

I looked back at the body, and just decided. For once, there wasn't a sense of deliberation, just vexation. I ran the cheese grater down her arm, hard enough blood flowed freshly from the permeated surfaces. She hadn't reached the point where it would turn black. I ran the grater down her arm again, then again. Her form jerked with each assault. More delicious streaks of red splashed against the clearly expensive sheets, despite the home itself appearing deceptively modest in terms of exteriors.

Goddamn, medicinal marijuana latte liberals. Such environmental auspices obviously beneath the sanctity of Dr. Martin's perfect marriage. Or so the papers said.

It was only when I was practically finished picking the skin off her nude form I heard the click of a safety catch. Then, naturally, the sound of a harsh voice telling me to put my hands up.

I turned slowly, grinning from ear to ear – feeling the strands of deliberate action being pulled from me much like how I pulled the flesh off Dr. Adam Martin's bones. The rookie staring back at me – yes, *clearly* a rookie – had unabashed horror on his face. Clearly, in this part of town, he wasn't used to seeing a young man straddling a reddened, bloodied corpse of a middle-aged woman.

Someone still sharply handsome, despite her epidermis now being entirely nonexistent.

"Hey man," I said.

"Get off the body," his voice wavered. "Get off…"

Right around the same time, a voice – *female* – materialized a couple paces behind him. "This is my goddamn *Airbnb*," it was saying. "I deserve to know…"

Now it was my turn, ironically so, to stop short.

"*Alina?*"

Right as she materialized behind him, the rookie proceeded to fire.

She then screamed. Hands on her mouth.

A hole subsequently appeared in my chest, beneath my breastbone. It took a minute for me to *feel* it. *Jesus Christ, I'll be right back where I started.*

Still grinning, I fell backwards onto Dr. Martin's form, the bloody cheese grater falling out of my hand and slamming against the floor.

I lay there, for the first time in my life – how can I put this? - feeling peace.

I felt something almost tender about the squishy feeling of lying upon the body of the woman. But my thoughts were starting to become shapeless around the edges. I also was starting to become confused about the majority of whose blood coated me.

Dr. Martin's, or mine.

Did it really *matter*?

I was fighting the world around me becoming more and more blurred, in every sense of the term. Then, all of a sudden, and most inexplicably and improbably, I saw Alina's face materializing by mine. She was staring down at me, all ashened features and unbridled horror.

It was kind of nice, that being the last thing I'd ever see. I certainly would leave an impression, I suppose.

"*Found me*," I heard myself say.

The Armoire
Douglas J. Moore

They had considered leaving the city for some time, on exiting New York for a less stressful, more bucolic environment, with the haste, heat, and hate of Manhattan and Brooklyn a constant test of endurance.

But, when to go, where, and how?

As such a topic frequently fomented an argument it was routinely neglected, with Daniel keen on a final promotion before an exit and his wife, Charlotte, casually indecisive as she held a languid appreciation of her career at the museum.

The *force majeur* was the pandemic, with the horrible images of the refrigerated tractor-trailers occupying the South Brooklyn Marine Terminal finally terrifying Daniel into action.

It's spring he thought, and this virus isn't subsiding. That little spike protein is still out there killing people and I'm stuck on the F-train breathing it all in. Even before the Covid the overall air quality in the city was terrible, something we all mostly ignored. Sure, the department of health monitored for pollutants, but that didn't matter, all of Manhattan a toxic morass of diesel exhaust, lead, dust, raw sewage and heavy metals. Group One Carcinogens swamped the city. A slow death guaranteed in each breath.

Covid wasn't going anywhere, the virus an invisible, airborne noose. Who cared, parts per billion, parts per quintillion? Nanoscopic measurements didn't matter to the virus, you were a cadaver either way.

"We've got to get out of Brooklyn." He exclaimed to Charlotte one night, the Astoria sky absent clouds and Persephone warm, the metropolis surrounding them a hushed zone of the huddled fearful.

"Like, the marine terminal." Charlotte replied as she finished her third glass of wine. "It's insane to stay. You can work from home. I can switch careers, or work part time- or whatever. You always talked about Vermont. I'm good with winter. Plus, it can't be much colder in Burlington then it is here."

Immediately they strategized their escape, the internet affording them endless views of multiple properties across northern New England, the pair eventually deciding on a full dormered cape with a two-car garage in Hillsboro County, New Hampshire.

"It's got a new roof." Daniel said as he studied pictures of the interior of the property, the ugly bathrooms, worn wooden floors and a dated kitchen with its saturnine walls and boxy appliances demanding renovation.

"Yeah, good bones." Charlotte replied. "Inside though, a train wreck."

Daniel nodded, with one bedroom capturing his attention, the walls a rancid yellow that made him think of dimly lit 70's Hollywood, a series of fetid images from The Exorcist in his mind as he imagined scraping the old wallpaper loose and painting the room a delicate eggshell white, the space clean and sleek.

"We can do the remodeling. It'll take some time, but I can run a power saw and you know tons about painting."

Daniel casually concluded. "I'm going to put in an offer, tonight. We're getting out of here."

***

The move was arduous, the rented van stuffed to capacity with their apartment and their 16th Street storage unit. To their surprise Mr. and Mrs. Chen gave them sandwiches and bottles of water for the trip, their final farewell issued from behind a closed door. Then it was northbound, the stubborn traffic its usual snarl, the border of Connecticut a welcome relief to Charlotte, her New York life now suddenly behind her.

"We're doing it." She anxiously sighed as they rumbled through Danbury towards Woodbury, her hand atop Daniel's shoulder as a dismal longing panged in her chest. "It's done. We've left Gotham."

"Are you scared, or excited?" Daniel tentatively inquired.

"I don't know." Charlotte hesitated. "I'm not sure."

"Don't worry." Daniel cheered. "We're going to be fine."

"I hope so." Charlotte inconclusively shrugged. "I hope so."

***

Charlotte smiled at the street names, Farmhouse Lane, Autumn Ave, Bogart Street, Chort Way. This was their new neighborhood, the development a postwar automobile suburb, with the properties well-tended and the streets lush with bulbous maples alongside sleepy pines, each sprawling lawn a bold emerald patch that exuded nostalgia.

Unpacking was tedious, the couple thumping box upon box into their new home, the garage an impromptu staging ground as the main bedroom, kitchen, and their separate offices demanded priority.

Daniel's trading terminal was situated on the first floor, his monitor as well as his private modem and security jumper all tucked under his desk. There was profit in the pandemic and Daniel was mostly unconcerned about income as the chaos of the supply chain pulsed with opportunities to short or bundle trades, with the prices of health care stocks as well as the commodities futures of beef, wheat and petroleum as unpredictable as a mass shooting.

Within a month they were mostly settled, their days running a new rhythm, with Charlotte working mornings on her laptop before preparing their lunch, her afternoon a long bike ride, with gym visits still considered an unnecessary risk.

Alone, Daniel would compose trades while the markets gyrated, his attention scattered between his three screens, with all his incoming news concerning the ongoing pandemic terrible.

Gordon Levi-Maldon, a trader still down in the city, was relentless with his texts, each message a regurgitated headline followed by Gordon's own grim, idiosyncratic analysis.

¼ of the population might die from this. You seen India? Over A billion people there – if that # is right that about 250 million dead. Basically the entire population of this country.

It was dreadful, death running wild, the market impossible to predict and no sense of control or response to remediate the carnage. It drew Daniel weary, his afternoons soon less than productive as his mind wandered and he absently drifted away from his terminal.

It was overwhelming, the news, the market, and somehow the new house as well, with the amount of work to be completed across the property a nightmare.

Yes, the roof was fine, as was the siding and the chimney. However, the basement was terrible, the real estate agent as well as the photographs of the home on the internet conveniently overlooking the fact that the cellar was filled with junk.

Of course, they discovered this when they'd first moved in, the basement overstuffed with wreckage, the space swamped with battered carboard boxes, overflowing plastic bags and innumerable plastic tubs stacked high into lopsided piles that ran tight to cobwebbed encrusted joists.

This was what greeted Daniel each time he stepped away from his terminal and into the basement, his mind quickly numbed by a basement filled with a prodigious mass of consumer detritus.

Maybe a yard sale. No, a dumpster, a big blue one, filled to the brim and then carted away. Or, to save money, a rental truck and some dump runs. It was all shit down here too, stacks of faded newsprint, soggy boxes of mismatched teacups and saucers, rusty cutlery, old cans of paint, broken tools, ruined furniture, boxes on boxes of moldy books and damp magazines.

It was a rotten hoard right to the boiler where the sweet stink of diesel exhaust staked claim on Daniel's nostrils, a trio of desiccated dead mice stuck there beside the burner, their tiny brown forms mummified by heat and time, Daniel wrinkling his nose as he routinely wondered how many mice continued to infest his home, the little rodents perniciously persistent.

Rats in the walls and a junk filled basement. This was better than living in Brooklyn? There were rats there too, oddly aggressive cat sized creatures, each ugly one foul with sharp, sallow teeth.

Looking about the basement, Daniel sighed.

Maybe a backyard fire he speculated. Why move all this trash around when paper burns easy? Yeah, a good old-fashioned book burning.

Smiling, Daniel imagined a roaring fire in his backyard, some fresh snow falling, the heat comforting and welcome.

It would be good, a fire, forget moving all this trash to return to the trading desk, the true command post.

But no.

The Covid trades would wait.

Here was a mess here, one that demanded attention. Plus, what else was there? There was nothing to be done about the virus but mask up and remain distant, the Covid untamed. It was now a waiting game, and by far it was good to clean things up, to focus on the basement and forget the virus and the trading desk.

Likewise, it would be easier here in the basement, skulking under the dim light of the uncovered bulbs, the pandemic distant from this musty world of sodden boxes and mouse shit. Quite possibly too there was something great down here, an antique or an obscure collectable, say, a dusty old canvass that Charlotte would recognize as something painted by 19th century New England eccentric and landscape enthusiast LPH, the piece eventually auctioned off to cover a hefty chunk of the mortgage or to establish a future nest egg.

Adrift in such thoughts Daniel began to shunt boxes about, a trio of ash-colored spiders fleeing a malodourous box that contained a collection of damp paperbacks, with one mustard hued volume in near pristine condition catching his eye.

As he briefed the book Daniel laughed. *"Witchcraft: The Astral Plane & Ethereal Contact."* I could give this to Charlotte he playfully thought, his reverie interrupted as he noticed a large wooden structure just behind the mess he'd been trying to sort, this sizable *thing* well hidden by a faded crimson tablecloth.

Intrigued, Daniel pushed aside a few more boxes and then pulled the tablecloth free, an ephemeral cascade of swirling dust making him sneeze.

Before him waited an armoire, the huge, caramel hued piece large enough to contain a sizable collection of winter clothing. Take that C.S. Lewis Daniel smugly thought as he studied his discovery, the dulled veneer suggesting faded daguerreotypes of long dead Union soldiers.

But, no, there was more here, the double doors of the massive cabinet fastened tightly together by a trio of heavy bolts, this hardware long rusted shut, Daniel suddenly running his index finger and thumb over the cold metal of the old locks while he wondered why an armoire required such ugly, heavy duty bolts.

Deliberately, Daniel tried the middle bolt, the thing stubbornly stuck. Annoyed, he swore some and immediately doubled down on the obstinate bit of metal, his force shaking the armoire until he unexpectedly slipped, a pang of bright pain racing through him as a large red gash appeared on his thumb and hand, his fresh blood now streaking the wood and rusted metal of the cabinet.

"God damn!" Daniel raged as he put pressure on his zigzagging laceration, the unwelcome thought of a fresh tetanus irksome. "This is bullshit!"

Dismayed, Daniel slipped into a Kurt Cobain wallow of self-pity, his thoughts overwhelmed by the possibility of going to the walk-in clinic, his cut liberally bleeding despite his best attempts to staunch it.

Of course I'm cut he silently lamented as blood oozed down his palm towards his wrist. God, we'd better have some Band Aids.

Shaking his head Daniel gazed at his hand, his thoughts percolating self-absorbed until he heard it, the sound low and distant yet distinct, his eyes sliding up to the armoire as the hair on the back of his neck stood on end.

THUMP THUMP THUMP

This is crazy Daniel thought. Something is knocking from inside the armoire. This can't be happening.

THUMP THUMP THUMP

This can't be real. A sound, from inside that cabinet?

On the knocking continued, the terrible banging now impatient and demanding, the ugly, rusted bolts on the exterior of the armoire suddenly squeaking and twisting aside with an agonized groan, Daniel growing even more fearful as the armoire rattled and then opened, a stinking gust of fetid air stinging his nostrils as an ugly little creature now appeared between the open doors of the armoire.

Daniel cringed, the reek of stale urine making him cough, his mind racing. This can't be happening. I must be hallucinating. No way that armoire opened up with that *thing* right there inside of it.

But the creature was there, the biped short and bulldog sized, the thing looking very much like a simian crossed with a racoon, it's unkept fur matted silver and black, it's paws humanoid yet defined by stubby thumbs alongside four dirty, slender fingers that ended in foul, crooked talons.

Dumbstruck, Daniel stood there immobile, the little monster before him stretching some while staring at him, it's yoke like eyes mean and vindictive and it's torso somehow covered in a threadbare burlap tunic that was cinched by a gleaming silver belt buckle, a sheathed dirk dangling from its belt like a gunslinger's pistol.

For a moment Daniel thought of Yoda from Star Wars, this idea quickly dismissed as the creature before him offered no sense of benevolent wisdom or noble tutelage. Instead, this thing was very much the opposite, its temperament clearly chaos, vulgarity, and maliciousness, its yawning mouth revealing a long line of milky white incisors.

"What the fuck?" Daniel sputtered, incredulous.

"What the fuck!" The creature instantly mocked. "You what the fuck! Ho- ho!"

Now animated, the creature did a little dance, its ugly black paws with their crooked nails tapping a horrid click-clack atop the wooden armoire, the imp like thing laughing as it gamboled about.

"Ho! Ho!" It sang. "What the fuck! What the fuck!"

Horrified, Daniel stood there paralyzed, sweat cascading down his back. This isn't happening he thought. This can't be real. I've gone crazy.

"Me home." The things growled before it bared its sharp, tiny teeth. "You what the fuck! Me home. Not you."

"What are you?" Daniel wondered aloud, the creature shaking its head.

"What you?" It barked back before it sat down inside the armoire and tapped its ugly feet against the wood.

"This is insane." Daniel said. "I must be going crazy."

"Ho ho! Crazy- ho ho!" The creature cackled before it coughed some and spat a viscous daub of pink and yellow phlegm to the floor, Daniel cringing at the site.

"Me home!" The creature shouted before it held up its gnarled clawed hand and directed a spindly middle finger at Daniel. "You go! Me home. What the fuck! Another you? Go! Go away!"

With a cruel laugh the creature slammed the armoire closed, Daniel's terror now breaking like a wave as he knew he had to flee, his heart thundering adrenaline as he ping-ponged between boxes and bins, one box splattering glassware across the basement floor, Daniel blundering across the fragments before falling face first into the shards, a spiderweb of fresh lacerations now riddling his cheeks and forehead, the bleeding profuse.

With his tumble Daniel's fear reignited, a wild flailing atop the floor eventually getting him onto his feet and up the stairs, the basement door slammed and locked behind him as Daniel wondered what in the world had just happened.

***

Charlotte found her husband on the couch with a tall glass of bourbon in his hands, his face a mess of cuts and his agitated story mostly incomprehensible.

Her concern was immediate, and Charlotte wondered if Daniel needed stiches and an MRI, with his lacerations quite gruesome and the mottled purple bruise on his forehead also alarming.

"Slow down." She cautioned as she sat beside him and helped herself to a massive sip of his drink. "I mean, what you're telling me is insane, like, crazy. There's a little goblin, no, a gremlin or something in our basement?"

"Not in the basement." Daniel countered. "In the armoire in the basement. I saw him. He gave me the finger and told me to leave, to go."

"He talks?" Charlotte asked and Daniel nodded.

"He talks, he walks, all of it." Daniel stated. "I mean, I know this sounds crazy, but, down there in our basement is this thing, a little imp. I saw it."

For a moment all was silent between the two, Charlotte uncertain on how to respond until her husband finally said, "Come on. I'll show you."

***

"It was here." Daniel stated as they stood beside the armoire, his drink empty, the glass still in his hand. "That the thing, that creature, simply opened the armoire and came out. He was like a Muppet or something. It was nuts."

Charlotte nodded, her husband once more reiterating his tale of a vexing gremlin, her attention keen on the details of what had happened, her worry now that her husband had slipped down here in the dark and had become concussed.

"So, that little creature, the gremlin," Charlotte inquired, "you're saying he just jumped out of the armoire?"

"He didn't jump." Daniel corrected. "He opened the door, popped out, said some stuff and slammed the door closed."

"Sounds like that *Twilight Zone* episode." Charlotte countered. "You know, the gremlin on the wing of the airplane, the Cold War version of the show, the one with a pre *Star-Trek* Bill Shatner."

"It wasn't like that." Daniel protested. "This was real. I saw that thing. I don't know what it was but I saw it."

"Well, the armoire is a gem. A great find." Charlotte stated as she ran her finger over the piece, Daniel suddenly proud of her curatorial expertise, her lifelong work in the rare air of Manhattan's museums and the McGill University Archeology Department one of her greatest strengths.

"Two doors, well hung, all of it still plum and level." She continued. "I'd bet that it's probably veneered in cherry or walnut. The profiled cornices and ebonized columns are great. If I had to guess I'd say that it was most likely made between 1870 and 1890, probably with local oak or maple. You said there were locks on it, three big bolts? I don't see any of that hardware here Daniel, or holes or anything else. All I see are the original brass knobs, hinges, key frame."

"Well, that's not how it was two hours ago." Daniel sulked. "I'm telling you, there was a creature in our basement, a gremlin, or whatever. There were locks on the armoire too."

"That sounds pretty fantastic." Charlotte soothed as she stole a glance at her husband. "Your story sounds crazy."

"It's not crazy." Daniel belligerently countered. "It happened. That thing is down here. I'm telling you the truth."

"OK." Charlotte recanted. "I believe you. Still, you've got to go to the doctor. You need stiches."

"To the doctor?" Daniel snapped as he shook his head. "Now? With the virus out there killing everyone? No way. That's like signing your own death certificate."

"Alright." Charlotte back peddled. "It was just a suggestion."

Worried, she pulled Daniel into her and hugged him, his body tight with tension as her hand wormed into his.

"Daniel, I love you, but this all sounds crazy."

"It happened." He replied with conviction. "I saw that thing. It's still down here too. I don't know where he is, but, I'm sure he's here."

Quiet anguish seeped across Charlotte, her husband somehow spinning away from her, this gremlin, or imp, or whatever, well- who knew?

"I believe you." She whispered, Daniel hugging her even tighter, her words empty as she had no idea if her husband was telling the truth, his story utterly bizarre.

"It was down here." Daniel lamented as he began to sob. "You've got to believe me."

"I do." Charlotte soothed. "I do."

But she didn't.

***

The pandemic continued, Charlotte taking even longer cycling trips that frequently left Daniel at home alone, his earbuds apocalyptic with the news as his trades waned incomplete or unobserved.

There were times when he'd outright miss a trade and stare blankly at his monitor, his mind hazy as a silent emptiness haunted him, the scrolling ledger that defined his success or failure a radiant cascade of meaninglessness.

It was the Covid he thought, the virus still lurking about like an airborne toxic event. Likewise, that little imp was still out there too. Or, well, maybe the imp wasn't, with Daniel sometimes wondering if he'd really seen that little thing down in the basement after all.

In retrospect it was hard to know if that little monster was real. Had he really seen it? For the last few Daniel had grown unsure, and as a matter of fact he'd stopped talking to Charlotte about it. There was no point in such a discussion.

She'd think he'd lost his mind.

No, it was better to try to focus on work and avoid the basement. The basement though, dear God, there was still so much to be done down there, so much to clean up, to pick through! Where was Marie Kondo when you needed her?

Still, the basement would have to wait. The trades mattered, they needed attention, and after a coffee it was back to the desk, with all that remuneration vanishing into the black hole of automatic debit transactions. Was this better than Brooklyn?

Daniel stretched, a cup of coffee, yes.

Yawning, Daniel abandoned his monitor for the kitchen, his path abruptly halted as there in the living room was the creature, its crooked form flopped atop the couch while its ugly feet kicked against the creamy upholstery, a shiny red apple in its curled, clawed hand, its garish, toothy maw tearing delightfully into the sweet fruit.

"You!" It garbled as it gawked at Daniel. "Ho! Ho! Apples to apples. Get cider! No, get beer! Drinky-drink!?"

"What the fuck?" Daniel sputtered in disbelief. "You! How is this possible?"

"What the fuck, you?" The creature laughed as it expelled a mouthful of half chewed apple across the living room, the pieces spewing forth like a foul volcano, Daniel stepping left to avoid this nasty projection.

"You are real." Daniel gasped. "And you were locked in the armoire. Somehow though you got out- how?"

"How out? How you in?" The ugly creature speculated as it glared at Daniel, its porcine eyes thoughtfully hostile.

"This is crazy." Daniel whispered, the creature suddenly cocking its head high so that Daniel could see its floppy, feline ears, a rancid odor of wet earth and rotten leaves filling the space between them.

With a shrug the ugly imp hopped from the couch and stretched, the cruel sound of popping bones echoing across the living room, Daniel suddenly frightened as he tried to deny preternatural reality before him.

"Beer!" The creature demanded as it stomped hard on the floor. "Beer, cider! Drinky-drink! Go get!"

"You're not real." Daniel replied. "This isn't real."

"Real real, ho-ho!" The creature shouted. "Get cider, get beer!"

"The hell I will." Daniel protested. "Get out of my house!"

The creature shook his head, it's yoke like eyes shimmering wickedness.

"Get beer." It hissed. "Get cider."

"Get out." Daniel replied. "Get out of my house."

"Get out!" The creature parroted. "No out! Go get beer, get cider!"

Before Daniel could say anything else the imp was at him, its mouth roaring a raw, feral growl as its teeth snapped at his legs, Daniel skittering backwards to avoid the attack, an ugly set of claws besides the foul jaws of the creature just missing his upper thigh.

"No!" Daniel cried as he ducked behind the love seat, his awkward motion knocking the accompanying side table over with a loud crash.

"Get beer!" The creature barked. "Get beer! Get cider!"

Enraged, the creature hurled what remained of its apple at Daniel, the gnawed fruit just missing his forehead before it exploded against the wall, the debris cascading about like shrapnel.

"Beer, cider!" The creature wailed as it dug its talons into the love seat, the fabric ripping with an awful tear, Daniel jumping sideways to avoid further battle with the imp who continued to claw at him.

"Beer! Cider!" The imp bellowed before it drew out an ugly little knife, the crooked blade cutting harshly though the air as Daniel backed away, his jerky skuttle knocking the standing lamp to the floor.

"Ho-ho! Beer! Cider! You get! Get!" The imp cheered as it waved its knife about. "Go get! Get!"

Overrun with terror Daniel raced towards the kitchen, the creature's little knife just missing his knee as he grabbed his keys from atop the counter and then out the door, the imp howling behind him.

Within seconds Daniel was in his car, the imp dancing in the doorstep as Daniel backed up his car and raced away, his mind a jumbled fear and confusion as the howling laughter of the callous little imp echoed hard in his head.

This is real Daniel concluded as he fled down the road. I've got an imp in my house.

God help me. I've got to get rid of him.

***

The hatchet was rusty, the blade a pitted orange. This didn't matter to Daniel as he knew what had to be done, the armoire in front of him and the ax ready. He swung the tool with purpose, the first blow connecting but failing to penetrate the wood, Daniel doubling down until the blade finally bit, a tremendous joy thrilling him as a massive gash appeared in the dead center of the cursed wardrobe.

On he went, the ax coming down again and again, the dark wood cracking some before abruptly splintering into a mess of long, jagged pieces, a burst adrenaline thundering though Daniel before he paused to examine his destructive handiwork.

That's right troll he thought. This is my house. Not yours.

Soon enough the once majestic double doors of the armoire lay in pieces, Daniel smiling, a great sense of accomplishment inspiring him to continue to hack away, the rotten reek of ancient urine as well as musky soil filling the basement as Daniel steadily reduced the armoire to pieces.

***

Still, there was more to do.

Buzzed by accomplishment Daniel lugged the ruined wood from the basement to the backyard, the pieces soon a jackstraw pile beside a box of old newsprint, a new spade, a gallon of water and a bottle of vodka, Daniel extemporizing a wish for some jet fuel or a gallon of gasoline.

No. This will all burn. I'll see to it.

Although he had never been a boy scout, Daniel carefully crafted a stubby teepee of armoire wood atop a crumpled base of yellowed paper, his dénouement a wild splattering of vodka across the entire pile before he satisfied himself with a long pull from the bottle.

Gleefully Daniel flicked the lighter, the golden butane flame smelling sweet as he leaned into the pile and grinned. *Burn baby burn* he thought as the aged, damp newsprint resisted the applied flame, a few orange embers sputtering and swirling sluggishly about until the paper caught, the wood soon following, with some of the hard fragments blazing like cheap cigars, the smell terrible, the fire delightful.

Fucking burn Daniel bitterly ruminated as he gulped again from the bottle. Fuck this house. Fuck this little gremlin. Fuck the Covid. Fuck all this shit.

"That's right bitch!" Daniel shouted as a spiral of hot embers radiated high. "I burned your shit! Where are you now, fucker? Come on out! Come out and see that I've wrecked your shit!"

Daniel watched and hoped, the fire now brighter and warmer as he drank once more, a foul line of sooty black smoke cascading upwards as the rancid reek of ancient decay simmered from the burning timbers.

"Come on out Tom Thumb!" Daniel laughed with abandon as he gulped down more vodka, a belligerent mania capturing him. "Come on bitch! I've got something for you! Come out and face me you troll under the mountain!"

"You Tom Thumb!" An angry voice bellowed from behind him. "You troll!"

Before Daniel could turn around the creature was on him, Daniel roiled by pain as he felt teeth and claws tear into his lower legs and backside, the assault so furious that Daniel fell flat to the ground, his wind gone.

Stunned, Daniel struggled to breathe, a fresh round of pain ripping through him as the imp's sharp fangs tore away, Daniel's arms flailing about until he accidentally struck the creature on its head, the imp sprawling backwards and away with a yelp of unexpected pain.

"That's right!" Daniel catcalled as he stood up and fumbled for his shovel. "I'm going to kill you!"

"No!" The imp shouted as it drew out its knife. "You kill you! Me home! You go!"

The two foes then raced at each other, the ensuing combat brief as teeth tore into flesh and metal shattered bone, the two grunting and swearing as muscles worked with rage and potency until one collapsed face first onto the muddy lawn, the fight abruptly over.

***

In the distance Charlotte saw a line of wane, black smoke coming from her backyard, this ugly, sooty streak telling her all that she needed to know.

Daniel was in trouble.

Alarmed, she dialed 911 on her Bluetooth, her legs suddenly working her bicycle with a tremendous force, one she'd never expected.

"Nine-One-One," a pragmatic voice answered. "What's your emergency."

"I think my husband is having a break down." Charlotte puffed as she pumped her legs even harder. "I think I need an ambulance. I think he's hurt himself, or, he's about to hurt himself."

"You need an ambulance?" The indifferent operator inquired. "Has someone been injured?

"God, who knows?" Charlotte replied as fear surged through her. "I mean, yes, I need an ambulance, right now!"

"And your address?"

All blurred to Charlotte, the 911 operator asking questions that she hardly heard, her own mind overwhelmed by tragedy, her thoughts racing.

Work it bitch. Get home.

Save Daniel.

***

Her husband looked terrible, his arms and legs a labyrinth of fresh lacerations and his clothes torn and caked with dirt and blood. In his hand he carried an ugly old ax the blade bloody.

"Daniel," his wife asked from a distance as she anxiously eyed him. "Are you OK?"

"I did it." He stated flatly as he stared down at the fire.

"Did what?"

"I killed him." Daniel replied as he absently swung the ax about. "That little imp. I got him."

"Honey," Charlotte soothed, "can you put down the ax? I want to help you, but I need to know that you're going to be safe, OK? Will you let me help you?"

"Go and see." Daniel sputtered as he gestured behind him. "Go and see what's left. He's right back there. He was tough, but I got him."

Charlotte nodded, and ever cautious she kept her eyes on Daniel while she tiptoed by him, the stink of ancient decay and fresh blood high in her nostrils as her eyes grew wide with fear.

Here, just behind the fire were the remains of what looked to be an animal, or perhaps the carcass of one, Charlotte cringing as she gazed at a mess of bloody gray fur, snapped bone and spiraling entrails, a dozen fat, black flies buzzing about the ghastly remains.

Disgusted, Charlotte shuddered, her eyes spying what looked like a skull in the bloody pelt, a long jaw like bone still displaying a line of sharp feline teeth, Charlotte sure not to touch anything, a bright fear of rabies or contact with a fresh zoonotic virus corralling her.

"Daniel, what happened?" She called out. "What happened here?"

"I told you." He absently stated. "The imp, the gremlin. The thing. Somehow he escaped from armoire. He was trying to kill me. He would have killed you too."

Daniel had dropped the ax and was drifting towards his wife, his misty eyes distant.

"I did it." He sighed. "I got him."

In the distance Charlotte could hear sirens, the noise of forthcoming aid making her all the more fearful as she did not know what to expect, her husband's bloody hand now tight in hers.

"It's OK." She said as they hugged, her tone gentle as if she were trying to comfort a frightened child. "Whatever it was, it's over. No one is going to hurt you. No one is going to hurt me. Some paramedics are coming. They're going to help us."

"Help?" Daniel sputtered as he began to cry in earnest.

"Yes, they're going to help you." Charlotte concluded.

"Ho-ho." Daniel sputtered. "You help you."

It's a Dog Today
Tilsen Mulalley

I.   Morning.

"It's a dog today." Judith Wench's grating voice reported the current state of *it* over the phone before the receiver had even touched Edie Vonavich's ear.

"Good morning, Judith," Edie sighed. She was careful to keep her voice low so as not to wake Jefferey.

"Morning." Judith sounded distracted. Edie could picture her now: glowering disapprovingly over the prim and proper lawns of Hawthorne Street, peeking through the blinds above her crystalline pink kitchen sink, and minding everybody's business but her own.

"Didn't you hear what I just said?" Judith sniffed.

Edie stifled another sigh; the shrill little woman's voice reminded her of the high notes on an untuned piano. She removed the hard-boiling percolator from the stove, pouring a steaming black stream of coffee into a speckled green mug that matched her lime kitchen.

"I heard you," Edie replied, taking a sip of coffee and savoring how it scalded her tongue. She looked out of her own window, toward the corner. She couldn't see *it* from here, of course. Judith's house was in the way. Still, the presence of the thing was palpable. She knew it was right over there, just out of sight, and Edie had a feeling it was aware of her as well. Despite the luridly hot coffee, Edie shuddered and snapped her blinds closed. "It's a dog today. So what?"

"What do you mean so what?" Judith asked.

"I *mean* that it's usually a dog."

"Yeah? Well other times, it's a greasy-looking teenager loitering on the corner, or a newsstand with nonsense headlines!"

Edie pinched her brow, trying to keep her voice measured; she could feel a migraine coming on. "Yes, sometimes it is," she said, "so what?"

"You've got some nerve Edie Vonovich! How are you and Jeff not bothered by this?"

"Of course, we're bothered by it, Judith," Edie said exasperatedly, "but it's been sitting there for a year now, and it hasn't hurt anybody. We all agreed at the last HOA meeting to just leave it be and let it run its course."

"I was *stonewalled* out of that meeting and you know it!" Judith snapped. Edie heard a sharp slap over the line as Judith slammed her bony little hand down on her pink granite countertop.

"Well you were making a scene, Judith," Edie replied.

"Only because I care about our neighbors, unlike *some* people apparently," Judith screeched. Edie ignored the jab, and after a moment of tense silence, Judith sniffed haughtily.

I'll bet she's got great big crocodile tears in her eyes right now, Edie thought.

"What if it's some kind of weapon from the Soviets, hmm?" Judith continued.

Edie bit down on a derisive chuckle. "On Hawthorne Street? I doubt it, Judith."

"Well, it's something, Edie! And I'm gonna do something about it."

"Oh, why don't you just–" Edie began, but Judith slammed the phone down hard, cutting off Edie's protest and leaving her ear ringing.

"Goodbye, Judith," Edie said to the cut connection, hanging up herself. Jefferey would be waking up soon. He'd be cranky if breakfast wasn't on the table.

Even after a tantrum, Judith always called back; Edie was the only one left on Hawthorne Street who'd still put up with her, after all. Today though, the phone didn't trill again. After she'd carefully packed Jefferey's lunch and sent him off to work, Edie tried calling herself. She hung up after a dozen rings. Perhaps Judith was actually upset with her this time. Wearily, she supposed she might have to go over there and apologize.

Jefferey had indeed been cranky this morning, despite his favorite breakfast— a bacon sandwich on rye with one runny egg in the center. He was simply unavoidable some days. Edie checked her concealer carefully in the mirror by the door. She'd gotten quite good at hiding the marks, and the swelling had been skillfully subdued by icing in just the right places, but the broken blood vessels in her left eye were still visible. She slipped on a pair of pert little shades; it was supposed to storm later, but as of now, the day was sunshiney and clear. She'd use the early summer weather as an excuse to lure Judith outside so she wouldn't have to take the glasses off.

The sun felt good on Edie's skin as she stepped outside. A cool breeze caressed her as it rolled by, carrying the scent of lavender and laundry, and Edie inhaled it deeply. The fresh air slowed the anxiety that thrummed in her blood as she took off.

She didn't like walking near *it*. Most days, she avoided this end of Hawthorne Street altogether. That thing was on the opposite corner from the Wench house, in front of a vacant lot the neighborhood kids had used to play in before *it* had appeared. Where the thing had come from, nobody really knew, nor could anyone remember exactly when *it* had first begun squatting on the corner. One day, *it* was just there. Edie's view of the thing from her yard was obscured by the profile of Judith's house, several yards from her own home and across the street. She was thankful for that. Judith's front door faced the thing's corner. She could see *it* from her kitchen window. Maybe that was why she was so obsessed with *it*. On days when Edie didn't have to go in this particular direction though, she could almost forget that the thing was there. Almost.

Edie walked the three-house distance between her own abode and Judith's, crossing the street and moving quickly. She kept her eyes down as she rounded the corner of the Wench house, branching off from the sidewalk to their paved walkway. Edie could feel *it* staring at her from across the street– if the thing *could* stare. She was fairly certain *it* could. Worse than that, she could *hear* the thing.

The closer one came to *it*, the louder the incessant, ringing hum that seemed to come from the thing became. It was high-pitched, on the edge of human hearing, and decidedly unpleasant. It forced the brain to search out the source, convinced that danger was afoot. Edie plugged her ears as she approached Judith's front door, trying to block it out. As she neared the porch, she couldn't help but cast a backward glance at the thing on the corner.

Judith had been right; *it* was a dog today. At least, *it* was if you didn't look too closely. The thing was more like the vague idea of a dog. The longer one looked, the more one realized that *it* was only pretending. As she stared, Edie could feel the anxiety begin to race toward her heart once more. She turned and quickly stepped onto the Wench porch. She knocked urgently, trying to ignore the feeling that the thing was specifically watching her. As her flurry of knocks began to quicken, Sean Wench answered the door mid-pummeling, nearly receiving a tiny fist to the chest for his trouble.

"Oh, hi there Edie, what can I do for you?" he asked. He wore a torn-up t-shirt and grimy jeans. His hands were greasy, and as he spoke he wiped them off with an equally greasy rag. His smile was friendly, but his uneasy eyes flickered back and forth from Edie to the 'dog' on the corner as he spoke.

"Hi Sean, sorry to bother you," Edie said, plastering a fake smile onto her face. "I called a moment ago." She did her best to discreetly peer past the square-framed, ginger man and into the house but failed to see much at all past the shadowy landing.

"Sorry about that," Sean said, stuffing the rag in his pocket and leaning on the doorframe, "I was out in the garage doing an oil change on the Mercury."

"I see. Judith home?"

Sean's eyes fell to his feet. "No, she's… at the store. Getting supplies."

"Supplies for what?"

Sean looked uncomfortable. "She's gonna make signs. To boycott that… thing over there."

Edie's jaw dropped. "W-what?"

Sean sighed. "Yeah," he continued, "She's… protesting it."

"Oh for the love of Pete." Edie rolled her eyes and crossed her thin arms tightly.

"I told her to just leave it be," Sean said, shrugging and shaking his head. "Judith always was an independent one."

Edie scoffed. "She is going to look just like one of those dirty hippies on the news," she said, turning away and descending the porch steps. In her fervor, she momentarily forgot *its* presence. As she walked crisply down the sidewalk toward home, she continued to grumble. "Wait until that silly little woman gets back," she mumbled under her breath, "I'll talk some sense into her."

II.   Noon.

Jefferey called on his lunch break, as he always did, to inform Edie he would be going to the bar after work and would be late, as he always was.

"Jefferey, Judith Wench is out protesting *it*," Edie told her husband.

"Protesting what?" Jefferey's bored voice was muffled by a bite of the lunch Edie had packed him.

"*It*."

"Oh. This sandwich you packed is dry as hell."

"I used extra mustard like you asked—"

"That's two strikes counting breakfast, Edie. Dinner best be something else, or I swear to God."

His sentence needed no final point. Edie knew what a bland dinner would entail, and whenever Jeff swore to God, he meant it. He was a Christian man, after all.

"It's meatloaf tonight. Like you asked. I'll make sure it's not dry, I'll... I'll use fewer breadcrumbs–"

"Use extra barbecue sauce on it too. The last time you made it I thought I was eating packed sand. Just don't make it dry. Anyway, I gotta go."

"Jeff," Edie said meekly, coiling the phone cord around one finger, "Did you hear what I said about Judith?"

"Yeah? Who cares?"

"What if she provokes *it*?"

"Maybe it'll eat her."

He chuckled cruelly at his little joke, "Wouldn't that be just fine?"

"Jeff, I don't think it's a good idea for her to be out there."

"Leave it *be*, Edie." His words had a venomous bite, and Edie's protest coagulated in her throat.

"Yes, Dear. I'm sorry."

The line was silent for a moment, except for Jefferey's greedy smacks as he downed another bite of his dry sandwich.

"Damn Judith, getting you all riled up," he mumbled through crumbs, "That Sean needs to get a handle on his woman. Maybe I'll have a word with them. After work."

Edie forced a tight smile onto her face and hoped it would translate well over the phone. "That would be nice, Jeff," Edie said, "I love–"

But Jefferey had hung up.

III.   Afternoon.

Jefferey had said to leave it alone, and Edie tried. She cleaned the house thoroughly, prepped the ground beef for that night's meatloaf, and ran a load of laundry, making sure to do Jefferey's whites separately so that she didn't accidentally stain them again. She had let a red sock get by her the week before. Jeff had wrenched it from her hand so hard that her wrist was still fairly swollen. Although she hid it well with her mother's gold cuff, Edie didn't feel the need to repeat the scenario with the other wrist. She was hanging the clothes out to dry when the chanting drifted down to her from the direction of the Wench house and the thing on the corner. It was offkey and haranguing, definitely Judith. Hanging the last of the sheets, Edie couldn't help but traipse up the street to see how much of a commotion she was truly going to make.

The thin little wretch was out on the street, standing next to *it*, goose-stepping in place and throwing together badly rhymed shouts of protest. Neighbors were peeking out of their windows, and a brave few even opened their doors to observe a moment before shutting them again.

"Judith, what are you doing out here?" Edie whisper-shouted as she approached. The last thing she needed was to draw attention to herself. If one of the neighbors let slip to

Jefferey that she had been out making a fuss about Judith's fuss, after he had told her to leave it be, well… that was best to be avoided.

In Judith's grippers was a hand-painted sign emblazoned with the words "Make Hawthorne Street Normal Again!" in thick black paint. At Edie's voice, Judith turned, her pale blue eyes glowing with determination behind coke-bottle glasses.

"I am picketing here until the city gets involved," she cried.

"The city did get involved, Judith," Edie said, throwing her hands in the air, "They even brought a crane in, remember? They couldn't budge the darn thing!"

Judith didn't miss a beat. "So now we'll get the county involved!"

"What's the county going to do? Bring in a bigger crane?"

"They could call somebody!"

Edie planted her hands on her hips. "Yeah? Who?'

"I don't know! The President? The Army? Somebody who could get rid of this thing!"

"Hell's Bells, Judith, it's just a dog!" Edie could hear herself getting louder. The realization began to lightly fry her nerves and only loosened the control she had over her voice even more.

Judith threw her sign to the ground now. "It's not just a dog, Edie," she said, pointing in the thing's direction. As she did so, the ringing that emanated from *it* changed pitch, as if it had taken notice of somebody acknowledging it. Judith didn't seem to notice.

"Look at that thing and tell me it's a dog," Judith shouted.

Slowly, the muscles in her neck creaking like rusted machinery, Edie forced her gaze over to *it*. The thing stared back at her with both too many and too few eyes, watching her intently. Edie could have sworn its head cocked at her curiously. She was suddenly acutely aware that though she had mixed the beef for dinner over an hour ago, this *thing* might still be able to smell the scent of raw meat on her. Edie turned back to Judith.

"It looks enough like a dog that I can ignore it," she said.

"And what about tomorrow?" Judith stomped her foot. "What if tomorrow it's a… a… a homeless man raving in another language? Or some kind of bomb set to destroy us all, hmm? What if it turns into something that you *can't* ignore, Edie?"

"Judith, you're being foolish. Go inside!"

"I am not leaving this spot until something is done about this! Someone has got to hold the line around here, and I guess it's me!"

With that, she picked up her sign once more and continued to chant and holler.

"Fine!" Edie said, turning on her heel, "I've got a meatloaf to make anyway!"

As she walked away, she did not notice the humming of the thing change register one more time. *It* almost seemed to squeal, like the squelch of radio static. Too low to be heard over Judith's chanting, something almost like a word seemed to slip from the hum.

"Meatloaf."

IV.   Evening.

Suppertime came and went without Jefferey pulling into the driveway. As the purple summer dusk gradually drained from the darkening sky, Edie delicately wrapped a plate of meatloaf and mixed veggies in cling wrap. She placed it in the fridge on the second shelf. On a miniature yellow legal pad, she carefully wrote a note to Jefferey, telling him his dinner was in the fridge and that if he microwaved it with a paper towel on it, it wouldn't be dry. She stuck this note to the fridge door with a magnet. God, she hoped he'd read it.

The clouds had begun to gather over Hawthorne Street, throwing an ever-blackening blanket over the stars. Edie had opened the bedroom window before lying down to try and stir the stagnant, stuffy air of the house, but the hot breeze that blew in was thick and humid, making sweat spring from her pores whilst carrying the heavy scent of the impending summer rain. Thunder began to rumble faintly in the dark heart of the gathering storm poised above. Still, if she lay quietly and strained her ears, Edie could just hear the faded chants of Judith Wench as she marched on in solitary protest down the street. She secretly smiled, tickled at the thought of the little busybody getting soaked in the imminent downpour. Hopefully, she'd still be awake when the storm broke and let loose. She wouldn't be able to see Judith from her window, but surely she would hear her screeches of distress.

V.   Night.

At some point, Edie fell asleep to the thought of her nosy neighbor ending up waterlogged. She rarely dreamt anymore, but when the sudden, brilliant flash of white light shocked her from the dark recesses of sleep, she thought for a moment that she might be in one. Lightning that close always made a sound after all, and the strobing, sterile flashes that pulsated periodically along her walls were entirely silent. Gradually, though, the chill of the room touched her bones, and she realized that she was no longer asleep.

The storm had broken the heat of the day, pushing it out of the house through the open window on the other side of the room. The breeze had sharpened into a cutting wind, sending the curtains flailing. The smell of the furious rain that beat against the house was metallic in Edie's nostrils. She felt toward the other side of the bed with her hand and found it empty. Jefferey wasn't home yet.

Edie lifted herself out of bed, traipsing carefully across the room so as not to stub her toe. As she reached the window and began to slide it shut, another silent flash erupted. This one seemed brighter than the others, illuminating the entire room and momentarily blinding Edie's tired eyes. She rubbed at them, forgetting the blackened one that Jefferey had given her and wincing in pain as she touched the delicate, purple skin. When sight returned, she finished shutting the window before peering out of it and into the storm. The lightning had seemed lower than it should, as though it had come from street level. A moment later, a peal of thunder erupted, loud enough to be heard through the double panes. Instead of a low roar though, it was high-pitched and shrill. Edie's tired mind took a beat of calculation before realizing that what she was hearing was a scream. After another beat, it hit her just who that scream belonged to: Judith.

Not bothering with clothes or shoes, Edie burst from her front door barefoot into the pouring rain with only her nightie. The downpour was a spattering cacophony, but behind it, she could hear something else: a constant, humming whine, as though high-pitched radio static had been sharpened into a spear. Monotonous and unrelenting, it stabbed at the eardrums and dimmed the sound of the rain. Ignoring it, Edie beelined toward the Wench house. Another flash erupted on just the other side of it– from the corner where *it* was. This time, the light did not fade, though. It remained on, blindingly bright. The street lights of Hawthorne Street all turned off at once, convinced that the day had come early. Edie hustled on, her lime-painted toes slapping through the rivulets in the gutter.

As Edie came upon the corner proper, the incessant whine grew louder. She shielded her eyes as she came upon the heart of the brilliant white light, so encompassing that it made it impossible to move any closer to it. Something in her nose popped, and a hot trickle of blood erupted down her face. Desperately trying to peer into the engulfing whiteness, she thought that she could just make out three silhouettes–two human, and one so entirely vague yet defined that it defied description. She tried to scream and found that the sound was taken by the ringing. Compressing her eyes to slits and shielding her face, Edie watched as the vague silhouette moved toward the humans. It appeared to reach for one, extending itself in an ever quickening motion.

"Judith!" Edie mouthed in horror, the words muted by the tinnitus-like ring.

"*Meatloaf.*"

The reply seemed to come from both the center of the light and from within Edie's own mind. Before she could fully comprehend this reply, the light receded into a pinpoint on the corner where *it* had been for a microsecond, plunging the tangible world into rain-filled darkness. Then, it silently exploded. The blast put Edie on her back, soaking her through whilst bleaching Hawthorne Street featureless. White nothing enveloped everything. As the world dematerialized around her, Edie closed her eyes and waited for reality to end.

Minutes ticked by like hours. Gradually, Edie realized that the whining ring had dissipated, leaving only the pattering rain. A few more minutes passed, picking up the pace now, and finally, Edie dared a peek. Prying her eyes open, she found herself lying half-submerged in an ever-deepening puddle. The night was black again.. A shiver erupted violently from the middle of her spine, and Edie shakily picked herself up just as the streetlights began to tick back on, one by one. Edie wiped a hand down her face and looked at it. The blood from her nose had been thinned by the rain, smearing her hand pink. She tried to step from the puddle and stumbled. The arms of a neighbor caught her; she realized then that a crowd had gathered.

Where *it* had once perched on the corner, there was now only a charred mark on the sidewalk. Sean Wench was gathering up Judith, who lay in a crumpled heap beside it. She was wailing, high-pitched and dreadful like a banshee, clutching her protest sign desperately to her chest as her husband led her away through the silently parting crowd toward their house. Something else was on the corner, too– something familiar. Crookedly against the curb, the driver's door hanging open, was Jefferey's Chrysler. Its engine was silent, but the headlights were on, lancing through the darkness and the rain.

I'll have a word with them. Jefferey's voice echoed in Edie's mind. Silently, peering through a soaked rat's nest of hair in front of her eyes, she scanned the corner for any sign of her husband. There was none except for the car.

Without a word, Edie shook off the hands of the neighbor who'd caught her. He said something as she walked away, but it was lost on the wind. Edie approached the car and slumped into the driver's seat. The keys were still in the ignition, and when she turned them, it started right away, the engine still warm. The growl of the engine seemed to snap everybody back to reality, and the crowd began to disperse as Edie shut the car's door, put it in gear, and slowly rolled down the street to her own house. She parked in the driveway and went inside.

As the door shut behind her, she became viscerally aware of the humming whine; bladed tinnitus. A flickering white light emanated from the living room, and as Edie approached she could feel the warm dribble as her nose began to bleed again. Yet, there was no dread like before.

She rounded the corner to the den, delicately clutching the molding of the doorway as she peered in. Crouched in his easy chair and finishing up the meatloaf she'd left on a plate in the fridge, was Jefferey. At least, it was if you didn't look too closely.

"The meatloaf was delicious darling," 'Jefferey' said. His voice sounded like TV snow bent into words.

Jefferey doesn't like my meatloaf, Edie thought.

"It wasn't too dry?" Edie's voice squeaked from her throat, just above a whisper.

'Jefferey's' lips(?) curled into something like a facsimile of a smile. "Moist," *it* said.

After a moment, Edie smiled back. "Good. Welcome home, Dear."

The Boyfriend from Beyond
R.C. Mulhare

I first met her in the back of an ambulance in East Manuxet, a girl in her twenties so small and slight she could pass for twelve, covered in blood that didn't come from her, and soot from a fire of at that point unknown origin. She sat shivering in the mid-March cold, a paramedic draping a thermal blanket over her bare shoulders. The girl tightened her face as if she tried to keep from crying.

I knelt before her. "Hey. Hey, you can cry. I don't mind. I'm here for you."

She lifted her head, her gaze staring through me. "Are you police?"

"No, though I've worked alongside them." I showed her my press badge and the Leica on a strap around my neck. "I'm Carton Tillinghast. I'm a news photographer."

"That's an odd name." She stopped herself from laughing.

"Go on and laugh. Kids at school used to call me 'Cardboard', till I reminded them how useful and versatile cardboard is." Gospel truth, and I think my parents wanted to name me Charlton after the dude who played so many powerful leads in so many Hollywood epics, but someone in the East Manuxet records department goofed on the birth certificate and it stuck.

That night, I'd ridden along with Al Wyzhard, the high school chum to one of my nieces, now one of East Manuxet's folks in blue. The night started quiet and we'd spent it keeping each other awake by trading stories of weird stuff that had happened at our respective work while we sat in his squad car parked in the lot of a disused middle school. He'd started telling me about the time a selectmen had gone missing after he'd voted to change the night of the town's trick or treating and a manhunt involving the FBI ensued. An East Manuxet fire truck roared by, drowning him out, followed by another, then followed by three more from different towns. Then the radio quacked with a call to the Davenport section of town, where the wealthy business types had their million dollar McMansions alongside with the old money families, far away from the cracker box ranch houses where their accountants and office workers lived south of Route 38, where we'd set up for the night. Someone had heard screams coming from the house of Marcus Whitford, an old money man who'd revived that old money via canny tech investments, followed by the reek of smoke. Wyzhard snapped on the lights and sirens before pulling away and roaring in the same direction as that battle line of fire trucks. I made sure I'd loaded fast film into the Leica.

A row of firetrucks and ambulances filed along the street in front of our destination. Smoke filled the air and firelight reflected from the windows, casting shadows on the house across the way and the old pines and oaks surrounding the nearby houses. A line of cars blocked the circular drive which had likely served as a carriage path in the grand old days of the house, long before the McMansions sprouting up. A gout of flame erupted from the roof of a converted barn connected to the renovated Victorian, devoid of the usual picturesque details. A figure completely engulfed in flames ran from the rear of the house as the firefighters had their hoses trained on the roof. Wyzhard got out to assess the situation. I held back, taking shot after shot of the scene.

The burning figure sprinted across the lawn before bouncing off the side of a fire truck and collapsing. Two paramedics approached, one with a fire blanket, throwing it over the fallen figure.

I popped open my door, holding up my camera.

"Sir? Ma'am? Can you hear us?" the paramedics kneeling over the figure asked, as they carefully removed the blanket. The reek of burned flesh rose and the patient groaned. The medics carefully lifted the patient and helped him to a waiting gurney by the nearest ambulance.

Folks from the neighborhood had gathered along the opposite sidewalk, staring and whispering among themselves. One person waved to me, but finding Wyzhard, I dogged his heels as best as I could.

Another burning figure ran from the front door, clad in what remained of a violet bathrobe, now melted to their skin where it hadn't charred, before dropping to their knees and crawling toward the street.

"What's going on in there?" Wyzhard asked one of the firefighters, helping man a hose connected to a pumper truck.

"We don't know. Neighbors thought they were hosting a party, but around midnight they saw smoke coming from the barn," the firefighter replied.

"Shindig at the Whitford house? We sure of the occasion?" Wyzhard asked.

"No idea. Given the season, I'd say it's a happy spring party. They aren't Irish there and it ain't Easter just yet."

"Happy spring party? Who does that outside of nursery school?" another firefighter asked.

"Fluffy nature worshiping pagans might," I offered.

The firefighter blinked at me; Wyzhard tilted his head. "Right. You've covered the woo-woo beat in Salem and

Arkham. They do that kind of thing there."

A naked middle-aged man ran from under a carriage porte-cochere repurposed as a carport and stumbled up to Wyzhard. "Officer, you gotta stop her, you gotta!" he begged.

"Stop who from doing what?" Wyzhard asked, taking the guy by the shoulders, but holding the guy's sweaty, oil-slathered body away from him.

The naked guy pointed into the house. "The High Priestess. She called it down."

"Called what down?" Wyzhard asked.

"Called down fire," the naked guy said, breaking down coughing before dropping to his knees.

"Medic!" Wyzhard yelled in the direction of the closest paramedics. Two EMTs approached with a stretcher, quickly assessing the man and lifting him onto it before carrying him toward the row of ambulances, which I swear had grown longer.

"This is nuts. This like one of the cases you talk about," Wyzhard muttered. Looking right at me, he asked, "You ever see anything like this?"

A window blew out from the side of the house and a tongue of fire billowed from it. "I've covered fires this bad. I've seen some pagan gatherings get out of hand."

"What do you mean by 'get out of hand'?" he asked.

I cranked the current roll of film to the end, dropped it into a 35mm container and put it into one of the many pockets of my canvas fishing vest, closing the snap on its flap before loading a fresh roll. "Usually nothing worse than public meltdowns or a bonfire catching nearby flammable materials. Maybe an odd case of deliberate public nudity. The worst was the guy who kicked over an altar and tried to beat people with a large crucifix. But a house catching fire and people running out burning? This is a first. I'm guessing a candle tipped over and caught something flammable. But then there's the guy yelling about the High Priestess."

"Could have been hopped up on something."

"Or he could have spoken the truth."

The fire soon hit the walls of the barn, forcing the firefighters to fall back, alongside the civilians, if they weren't working to keep the house from catching fire. The hose crews sprayed down the walls and hosed down the house. But the walls soon collapsed, sending up sparks which managed to jump to the house.

By daybreak, the ruins of the barn had burned down to smoldering ashes and the fire crew had kept the house from burning completely. The fire marshal came to examine the wreckage, which reeked of burned flesh, like a barbecue from hell. I hadn't smelled anything that bad since Sarajevo and I'd prayed I'd never smell that again.

I'd gone home to scan and upload my shots to my boss at the East Manuxet *Ledger*. The news would have gone cold by the time the paper went to press later that week, but the Manuxet *Daybreaker* would have an interest as well, considering some of the fire crew had come a house on the town line between them. Once I finished, I caught a cat nap, then fortified with some espresso, drove myself back to the scene.

I arrived in time to witness one of the fire marshal's assistants limping away from the wreckage before he stumbled toward one of the privet hedges, dropping to his knees and shoving his head among the branches before hurling. I turned away respectfully.

"Really bad there, hey?" I asked.

The tech looked up. I approached them, offering them a handful of Dunkin Donuts napkins, which he used to wipe his mouth. "There's at least three bodies in the wreckage. There's another in the back garden. They must have crawled out there and died from their injuries."

The coroner's van arrived shortly, with a reefer truck in tow. Someone must have given them fair warning.

"How the hell many people did Whitford invite to this

party?" I muttered, as I took careful shots of the workers, taking care not to show any charred carnage.

"Probably at least six, and we have three injured people in the hospital," Sherry Birch, the marshal said, stepping beside me.

"Are there any police over there?" a woman's voice called from the street. Marshal Birch looked at me with a "Who the hell is this now?" crumple and relaxing her face, went to meet the woman at the fence, me at her heels.

A well-dressed woman in a gray skirt-suit stood there, a woman who looked like her maid beside her, looking around with wide eyes and murmuring in Serbian. "My God… she scared me."

"What can I do for you?" Marshall Birch asked.

"My housemaid, Katia, found something in the shed behind my house, across the street," the homeowner said, pointing to the McMansion with the asymmetrical roof immediately across the street.

"What scared you? Can you tell us?" I asked, in my wonky, just north of conversational Serbian.

"A girl. A naked girl. She's in the shed near the kitchen, covered in blood and soot," the domestic replied in the same, clasping and unclasping her hands.

"She must have escaped the fire," I said. The domestic nodded in agreement.

Marshal Birch got out her cellphone and called for an ambulance, then she and two of her assistants approached the house across the way. She led us around the back of the house to a shed which stood open. Katia led us inside, past a stack of wooden Adirondack chairs, to a table covered in a dusty blanket. She lifted the blanket aside.

A girl, no more than eighteen, lay underneath, curled on her side, arms hugging her torso, her head bent on her chest, naked and covered in blood and soot. I looked away, respecting her space.

Marshal Birch knelt beside the table. "Hey, hey, miss?

Are you awake? Are you all right?"

I heard the girl shifting; she crawled out on hands and knees, her ash blonde hair falling about her face. Once she'd cleared the table, she sat back on her heels, looking up at us, her brown eyes unblinking. Marshal Birch met her gaze, offering a reassuring smile. The girl blinked and managed a wavering smile before looking past Marshal Birch's shoulder at me.

"Miss? Are you all right? Can you hear us? Can you speak?" one of the medics asked.

"Are you with him?" the girl asked.

"Which 'him'?" I asked, gently.

In a quiet voice, the girl asked, "...My father. His coterie."

"That the group in the house across the way?" Marshal Birch asked

The girl nodded, dropping her gaze.

"Are you in any pain? Did your father or part of his coterie hurt you?" the second medic asked.

"He can't hurt me anymore, can he?" she asked, still staring past us.

"She sounds shocky," the first medic said, looking at Marshal Birch.

"Where's her father?" the second medic asked.

"We're presuming he's one of the charred bodies," Marshal Birch replied. Turning back to the girl, she added, "No, he can't hurt you. We're here to help you."

The girl hugged herself. "I need warmth."

"It's warm in the ambulance," the first medic said. "Do you think you can walk, or do you feel like you need some help?"

"I can walk." The girl rose. I took off my coat and draped it over her shoulders. As short as I stand, the coat hung nearly to her knees. She pulled it close as the group walked her to the ambulance. The medics dug out a thermal blanket as well as some heating pads and a towel to wrap around the girl's hips.

"Is there anyone looking out for you? Do you have any family worried for you?" one of the medics asked.

The girl shook her head, her eyes starting to glaze over. I met her gaze, introducing myself properly.

"So what's your name?" I asked.

"I've had so many names," she said. "The High Priestess will do."

I tried to keep my stomach from flipping inside me. It must have showed in my face because the female medic tossed me a sideways glance of concern. "The High Priestess, like tarot card?" I asked.

"The High Priestess of ...something," the girl said,

"Are you the High Priestess of your father's coterie?" I asked.

"I am, if the circle still holds," she said.

The medic glanced at me. I wagged my head. Not the right time for her to learn the bad news.

"Do you want something warm to drink? We have canned hot chocolate," the medic offered.

"Canned hot chocolate?" the High Priestess asked.

"It's self-warming. It's a bit weird but it's not half bad," I said. One of the medics dug in a bin and found a can, popping the top and offering it to the High Priestess. The girl looked back to me, before accepting the can and holding it close to herself, warming up before taking a sip from it.

"Would it be all right if we took you to the hospital?" one of the medics asked.

The High Priestess frowned up at the medic. "No. No hospitals."

"Are you sure?"

"No. Hospitals."

"All right, is there any place we could take you where you'd be with people you know or feel familiar with?" one of the medics asked.

"Can you take me through the Gate?" the High Priestess

asked, with almost a wry lilt.

"The Gate of what?" the medic asked.

"If you have to ask, you probably don't know," the High Priestess said.

"There's a women's shelter in Manuxet. Could we take you there?" one of the medic asked.

"You may take me there," the High Priestess replied.

"Mind if I tag along?" I asked.

"Are you family?" one of the medics asked me.

"We're both part of the human family," I said. "I might have a human interest story here: 'Fire Consumes Private Ritual Space: One Alone Survives'."

"No press," the High Priestess said.

"Would you accept me as a friend?" I asked.

"I have a boyfriend beyond," she said.

"Seems to me you could use a just-friends kind of friend," I said.

"You'll do," she said.

I put aside my press pass and stowed my camera in my carryall. "So, you want to talk about what happened? I promise I won't write any of this down or release it to the press."

"My father had lit the spring solstice fire. Another girl was supposed to enact the Great Rite, the Marriage of Earth and the Beyond. I offered to act in her place, as I had performed it before and this would have been her first time.

"Then my father decided to serve as the High Priest, the channel for the Gate Who Is The Key. I refused. He insisted. That's when my boyfriend intervened. He summoned the fire from beyond."

She stopped and shuddered, looking away. "That's when the ritual space caught fire. My boyfriend picked me up and carried me out. The barn was on fire and the yard was full of police and fire fighters. I hugged the shadows in the rear of the yard and slipped past everyone as best as I could. I found the shed open and so I went in to take shelter. I must have fallen asleep at some point. I didn't notice the sun rising, or daylight, until the maidservant opened the door and startled me awake. I hope I didn't scare her too badly?"

"She didn't expect someone in the shed, much less someone in the state you're in."

She looked down at herself, a small, sad smile crossing her face. "I must be a sight."

"We can clean you up, if you like," one of the EMTs offered.

The medics brought her to House of Mercy Women's Shelter in Manuxet. Imelda Merkesian, the director and main caretaker, met us at the door with a set of clean clothes for the High Priestess. The girl eyed them, then started to pull them on. Imelda guided her into the office, closing the door discreetly. Sometime later, the two emerged, another caretaker guiding the High Priestess up to the rooms on the second floor. I almost didn't recognize the High Priestess in the baggy pullover, blue jeggings and slippers they'd found for her.

Imelda looked at me with concern in her eyes. "Carton, do you know much about her?"

"I know she's badly shaken after last night," I said, giving her the Reader's Digest of what had gone down.

"I figured something dire had happened. She has some suspicious though superficial injuries. Some of her behavior suggests she's experienced some form of abuse or trauma, possibly of a religious nature. She may have some form of stress induced amnesia, which is why she can remember some of what happened, but she can't remember her given name, only her title."

"Or she might never have had a name, at least since she joined Whitford's circle."

I hitched a ride back to the firehouse with the ambulance crew. One of the fire crew claiming he needed to check on something gave me a lift back to the burn site on West Street where I could meet up with a police detail,.

Marshall Birch sat in her own car, tapping on a laptop. I approached, gently rapping on her window. She glanced up and buzzed it down.

"How's the girl doing?" she asked.

"She's in good hands at Hands of Mercy, but I get the feeling she's stonewalling us, unless she's genuinely in some kind of altered state after last night. She told me a few things that I hesitate to pass on. Promised her I wouldn't give this to the press."

Birch smirked slightly. "I ain't press, so you wouldn't be breaking your word to her."

I gave her a longer version of the Reader's Digest account. "Damn. That poor kid. Sounds like cult abuse stuff, never mind just having an odd belief system."

"I'm no expert, but I'm a total agreement." God knows I've seen the kind of madness a person can embrace when someone latches onto an idea that ends up poisoning their mind rather than bringing them close to the sublime.

"I'll pass on some of this to the boys and girls in blue, though I'll try to avoid naming names, even if we don't know the name involved."

"That works." I still had to find a way to learn more, even unofficially.

***

"How ethical is this, Uncle Carton?" my niece Molly asked, side-eyeing me.

"You've been hoping to get some volunteer work in. With your creds, I'm sure they could promote you to a paid position," I said. We'd gone to The Copper Coffee Cauldron in Manuxet, her favorite coffee shop, in a mall on the fourth floor of a converted mill building.

"You didn't answer my question. I'm getting a sneaky feeling about this."

"All right, I need you to keep an eye on a particular

client they're looking after. I'm not sure the personnel appreciate me hanging around the place too often, though the High Priestess doesn't seem to mind me."

She breathed softly yet audibly through her nostrils, glancing aside. Then she let out a slightly exasperated sigh. "All right, as long as you don't name me as a contact or a source or something, in case this goes sideways." She looked right at me. "Do I have your word?"

I raised my right hand. "I swear on your great-grandfather's grave in Normandy."

"All right then."

After lunch, I dropped her off at Hands of Mercy, giving her sufficient money for bus fare home. I drove to the East Manuxet Police Station, where I found Wyzhard in the middle of filling out paperwork at the end of his shift.

"Any news on our suburban cult?" I asked. "I could use some backstory to go with the fiery shots I took the other night."

"Nothing we can share with the general public just yet. You know it's an on-going investigation."

"How about a crumb to keep an especially squeaky mouse quiet?"

Wyzhard growled under his breath. "All right, but I see this in the *Ledger* next week, that'll be the last time I let you ride along."

I raised my right hand. "Scout's honor, I won't print a word or a photo of this til we get to the bottom of it."

"All right. We've interviewed some of the neighbors. Most of them have nothing bad to say about Whitford. He's quiet and respectful. Family comes from old money, so he's blended in easily with the older crowd. But this gets interesting: Most of them barely knew he had a daughter, much less one who's the High Priestess of his circle, which raised some eyebrows. He might have done a little canvassing, trying to recruit new acolytes. A few may have dabbled, but no one admitted to doing more than that."

"Obviously none of them showed up for the spring fling, and just as well. Speaking of which, you identify any of the DBs found in the wreckage?"

Wyzhard consulted a file. "Had to pull the dental records, but Whitford was one of them. The other two were acolytes, a businessman named Halsey from Salem, and a college student we think worked for Whitford as a domestic worker. We're interviewing the survivors in the hospital. They aren't saying much. They seem to think they're under arrest, though we haven't a reason to arrest them. It's just that they're too injured to leave the hospital.

"Burns, I take it?"

"Burns, broken ankle, severe smoke inhalation. One got discharged with only superficial scratches. You think your High Priestess is willing to talk to someone about what happened?"

"Between you and me, she's took shaken to say much now, and maybe not for a while yet. I suspect Whitford and his cronies did a number on her head, but not enough to make hospitalization a necessity to help her clear it up."

"Think if we sent a female detective to talk to her, she'd be more willing to talk?"

"Very highly doubtful. To give you an idea how bad off she is, she's vague about her own name."

"Sounds serious. But we still need to figure out what happened there first."

I left a few minutes later, a small part of me putting some faith in my own deception. Maybe my own soft touch had gotten to me, or maybe something in the High Priestess's own arguments had hit a chord. A part of me regretted getting Molly involved.

In the meantime, I didn't let moss grow under my bootheels. I knocked on the doors of the houses nearby the Whitford house. I got a few doors slammed in my face and got mistaken for a repairman at one house. One housekeeper mistook me for an immigration agent and refused to talk to me, while one lady of the house threatened to call her husband and have him beat me up. Most of the ones who spoke to me didn't know much about Whitford, much less that he had a daughter, however defined. Until I spoke with Marie Jeanne-Baptiste, a housekeeper who let me onto a back porch out of a rain shower.

"There was bad stuff going on in that house, very, very bad stuff," she said, shaking her head, her pendant earrings brushing the sides of her neck.

"Define that 'bad stuff', if you can?"

She looked past me as if expecting interelopers, then looked me in the face, her dark eyes concerned. "I heard screams coming from the barn one night. Several people in the neighborhood called the police. But Mister Whitford told the police that a fisher cat got into his yard. Except fisher cats don't come into this part of the town. Not enough trees for them. He had a different girl at that time, not the one who escaped the fire, but after that night, I did not see her again. Not long after, he found the one who escaped the fire."

"Did you know her name?"

She wagged her head. "Hester? Esther? Some name like that."

"Did you talk to her much?"

"At first, I did. We'd meet on the street or in the store. She lived in the house, but she did not come out often. Even when I saw her in the Market Basket, she did not talk to me much, especially after she had worked there for a time. She stopped speaking to me or to any other domestic worker she met. She never carried herself high and mighty, not like in a silly TV story. She would act cool toward me and the others."

"Sounds like she got a promotion and it went to her head, but she's astute enough to keep her composure."

"I would commend her for that, but it bothered me."

"You felt like you lost a friend?"

She wrinkled her lips. "Not a friend, but a co-worker,

even at a different job site."

"A colleague?"

"Yes, that's the word."

"She ever talk about what went on in the house?"

"I asked about the things that went on in the barn, especially after the night of the screams. She told me her master did real magic there. I was not sure if I took that seriously. I have an aunt who *sevi Iwa*, who serves the *Iwa*. I'm familiar with real magic. Many white folk play at magic, but they would not know real magic if it hit them. I have worked in houses where the lady of the house collected crystals and taroque packs and called herself a witch. But I don't think any of them are brave enough."

"So you think she was just playing at magic?"

Marie-Jeanne looked around us, as if making absolutely sure she could see no eavesdroppers. I spotted one older woman in a window of a nearby house watching us, but she moved away, likely just watching the world and passing on to something else.

Marie Jeanne continued. "I think she is working with real magic. She did not have the same air about her as those who play at magic. She spoke at times like my aunt who spoke with spirits and let them speak through her." She looked at me with concern. "You don't think I'm crazy or dangerous or that I mess with demons?"

I shook my head. "None of the above. I've seen plenty of odd things in my time. In my experience, there's dangerous humans on this side of the spirit world and dangerous entities on the other side, just as there's neutral or harmless ones. And some people overestimate their own capability when they mess with things they shouldn't."

"That's good to hear. But I think she is one of those people who overestimate their capabilities. The entities she spoke of, I don't think are helpful at all."

"I don't think so, either. She claims that the fire that damaged the house and destroyed the barn wasn't from this world at all."

She sucked in a long breath through her teeth, crossing herself, then softly murmured something in Kriol that sounded like a prayer in my ears. "I hope we are both wrong, that it came only from this world. But I think she called it into this world."

"I think so too. Thanks a lot, Marie. You've been a huge help."

"I hope you can help her find her way out of this. If she plays with such things, if they can use her to destroy things, it could destroy her as well."

I got up, preparatory to leaving. "Let's hope someone can help her pull back from it before it does."

***

I didn't have to worry much, as it took a couple of weeks for Molly to report back to me. The times she came to my apartment to crash for the night or to make sure I hadn't fallen prey to eldritch fire, I didn't bring it up, figuring she'd tell me about it when something outstanding happened.

Finally, one night, as she folded her laundry, she opened up, "You gave me a tough assignment."

I looked up from stirring the Mulligan stew I'd tossed together from some canned soup and canned vegetables from my cupboard. "Has someone been able to get through to the High Priestess?"

She folded a pair of pants. "She's thrown up thick walls between herself and the world. She's still uncertain about her name. The shelter counselors have encouraged her to find some family, if she can remember their names and contact, and reach out to them. But she seems content to stay put for the time being. She helps out around the shelter, washing up and sweeping and vacuuming. I've wondered if she was a domestic when she wasn't tending to her priestessly duties."

"Priestessly? Is that a word?"

She piled up a small stack of tee shirts. "It is now. You've seen some things in Salem and Arkham. You seen anything like this?"

"What, cult stuff? Nothing like this. Not to say I haven't run across some odd groups on the North Shore. I photographed some fish folk coming to shore last year. I'm sure they have some practices we'd find peculiar. But nothing this weird." I shut off the burner and steered the pot to the table, setting it on a cork trivet before dishing the soup into two bowls. "Anyone cooking for her?"

"You suggesting I try my hand at your weird stew and try to loosen her up through kindness?"

"It's an idea."

"I'd try it, but she's a bit of a particular eater. She'll eat anything that grew out of the ground, but if it came from anything that once walked around or swam, she has no interest."

"Heh, wonder if it's something she chose, or if it's something the cult imposed on her."

She set aside her basket and came to the table. "That witch-fortuneteller-psychic in Salem, the one who sometimes takes people under her cloak. You thought of bringing her around to meet the High Priestess?"

I hadn't seen much of Irena since I'd had more work in East Manuxet, but I internally cuffed myself upside the head for not thinking of her sooner. "Good call, though considering Irena's practices are earth-based rather than beyond-based, I wonder if Irena could help our confused cleric?"

"What have you got to lose, as the cliché goes?" Molly said, with a smirk.

***

I paid a visit to Irena's shop, buying some incense before broaching my question to her.

Irena, minding the counter between psychic consultations, looked me up and down as she rang up my purchase. "Long time since I last saw you, Carton. You in town visiting Sibyl?"

"Not this time, though I might grab lunch at her cafe. I did have a huge favor to ask of you."

"Does this have to do with the Whitford cult fire?" she asked, cutting me off at the pass.

"You read my mind?"

"No, I read the article in the East Manuxet *Ledger* when I saw your name on the photo credits. I can't tell you much about the more eldritch groups, but I can tell you a bit about how they operate. And to be honest, it's best if neither of us knows much about them. That lot messes around with the proverbial things no man – broadly defined – should know about."

"So HPL and his crowd weren't kidding when they spoke of the dangers of calling up what you can't put down again."

"Most eldritch beings have little to no interest in us. But if you open the door and let them through, their very nature can raise hell in this world. It's nothing personal. It's like dragging an elephant into a studio apartment. It's going to wreck the furniture just by moving its feet to get comfortable. But there are others who find us interesting in ways that don't bode well for us."

"We are as insects to them," I said in an ooga-booga voice. More serious now, I added, "And some of them are kids with magnifying glasses and no sense of empathy and with too much time on a sunny summer's day."

"Exactly. If either of us tries to pry into that, we'd better be prepared for what's lurking under those rocks."

"All right, what if I told you there's a girl in a shelter who might have had her brain broken by those eldritch entities or something far more mundane and human?"

Irena shifted her weight from her back foot to her front

foot, leaning closer to the counter. "All right, I'm listening."

I told her what I could about the High Priestess. She listened, her dark eyes dubious but softening with concern. "Have they brought in a spiritual counselor who can speak her language to talk with her?"

"Not as far as I know. It's a nondenominational shelter, but I'm not sure they're that broad-minded."

"One way to find out: I could go with you to see if I could speak to her."

"All right, you got a free day?"

She dug up a planner from a desk behind the counter. "I have a half day coming up next week… The 14th."

"Hrrrm, I'm busy that day."

She scanned the calendar. "I could tweak it to Saturday."

"Still nope: it's Easter Vigil."

"You're poking at rocks that may be masking entities that some lunkhead cultists have poked at, but missing Mass is a bridge too far?" she said with a teasing smirk.

"I'd rather keep the register for not-great stuff short, even when I've done it for the greater good."

"What about Saturday of Easter week?"

"I got my grand-niece's First Communion."

She nodded. "Family, however you define it, matters most. Especially when she's having one of her rites of passage."

***

I spent Easter Sunday with my brother's family, hoping I'd pick up some grace and protection. I hoped the All Mighty understood my work-induced tardiness from Mass and would recognize my attempts at protecting the greater good through helping – or at least offering help – to a trouble young person who might not even understand the gravity of messing with things greater than us.

Molly button-holed me while I helped load the

dishwasher after Easter brunch, while her mom my sister Eileen, along with great-aunt Myra coached the younger cousins through an Easter egg hunt outside.

"I think I need a crash course in cult deprogramming before I work anymore with the High Priestess," she said, while carefully loading salad plates.

I scraped bits of grated carrot into the compost bucket. "I was afraid of that. What's going on?"

"I won't say she's trying to recruit me, but she's definitely trying to get me and anyone else who'll listen to hear her side of things. I'd go into detail, but I worry I'll start to sound like I'm recruiting you to the side of someone radicalized."

"Except we're talking about people messing with weird god-alien things, not people trying to blow up Federal buildings or breed a master race."

"No, but imagine someone going on about restoring the Earth to a race that supposedly once had dominion before humanity did. I can see her ecological angle – humanity has been terrible stewards of this world. But to give this world back to them?"

"Some kind of weird transference of guilt?" I asked.

"More like projection or reversing the order of victim and aggressor." In a phony histrionic voice, she added, "I'm not harming the earth, you were harming it first!"

"Please tell me those weren't her exact words?"

She loaded the last of the silverware into the basket and slid the loaded rack in. "No, thank God. She can be...unsettlingly rational, but there's times when I feel like her seeming fragility hides something more."

"If it's any consolation, I may have a specialist coming to help."

She slammed the door shut. "Please do: the staff wants to bring in someone as a spiritual consultant who matches her belief system, but so far they haven't had much luck. First, they brought in a Unitarian minister, who had no clue on any of what the High Priestess was talking about. Then they brought in an occult studies professor from Misk U, but that went even worse." She shuddered and glanced away as she turned on the machine.

"Do I want to know?"

"The High Priestess flipped a table at him and called him a dilettante unworthy of the material he studied, in so many words."

"Sounds about right: She lives that sort of thing, so no doubt, she'd find those types distasteful." A thought crossed my mind. "Is she trying to share her beliefs with the rest of the residents?"

"Thankfully without much luck. A lot of the other clients are Christian or not religious. There's one woman I'd class as anti-theist, since she likes needling anyone with a belief system. One of the kitchen workers follows something they call 'the left-handed path'. The anti-theist – let's call her Martha, even though that's not her name – likes to sneer 'Not today, Satan' at them, or make devil horns on her forehead with her index fingers." Molly demonstrated. I stifled a laugh. "No, go ahead and laugh. Amaranth the kitchen worker laughed at it saying it looked dumb."

"Do I want to know what Martha does to an eldritch god-worshiping girl?"

Molly rolled her eyes upward. "Worse. She does this tentacle-arm-waving thing while making cracks involving the Flying Spaghetti Monster." She demonstrated, waggling her arms like octopus tentacles flopping around in front of her torso and face.

"I bet the staff aren't cool with her attitude."

"She generally behaves in front of the staff, but she slips and gets told off."

"Let's hope she doesn't seriously antagonize the High Priestess, in case it backfires on her hard."

"For her own good and everyone else's."

***

The following Saturday, when I put in an appearance at Arya's First Holy Communion. I made sure to fortify myself with the Sacrament. I insisted I had to bow out of the party, due to work-related stuff.

I met Molly and Irena at our mutual friend Sibyl's coffee shop, then the three of us drove to the shelter, Irena dressed a little less fancifully, in a conservative black A-line shirt and a gray button-down blouse.

I introduced Irena to the staff as "a specialist in esoteric belief systems". Not a lie. Leslie regarded Irena curiously, bur she allowed Irena to come in. She led the three of us to a common area at the back of the ground floor.

True to the cult cliché, the High Priestess sat on a floor cushion, two other women sitting beside her.

"High Priestess?" Molly said.

"You may call me Hestia. I don't think it's my real name, but it will suffice if you need to address me," she replied.

"Hestia, Carton and I brought along an old friend of his. She knows a lot about esoteric belief systems, so we thought she could help you puzzle your way through whatever's blocking you recollections," Molly said.

The two women excused themselves, giving us some space. Hestia looked at Irena, her eyes going from curious to impassive to outright cold. Irena met her gaze firmly but evenly.

"We've met elsewhere. I remember that much. It happened some time ago," Hestia said, coolly.

"Hestia is one of your names, or at least one Craft name you'd used, to use 'Craft' loosely," Irena said, gently.

"Yes, since I reach toward far higher beings than you do," Hestia said, with a vague lilt of superiority. "Why limit yourself to lifting your hands to the genii of this world when you could reach toward beings far greater and stronger and able to bend this universe to their wills?"

"Because I've seen what many of those beings can and will do when they take notice of beings as small as we," Irena replied.

"Yes, to those too afraid to reach beyond the bounds of their provincial lives, bounded by their fear."

Molly glanced at me, taken aback. "This is...very unlike her."

"It's like Irena rattled her and put her on the defensive," I murmured. Out loud, I asked, "Hey, uh, is this some kind of denominational difference I wasn't aware of?"

"That's not a completely inaccurate comparison," Irena said.

"Oh, it's a completely inaccurate comparison," Hestia said. "Our practices are nothing like each other, except that we don't shy from the unusual and the eldritch, if I had to use a word worn out by a certain author who exploited our practices for his scribbling."

"You still came to my circle for help some time ago, when you wanted to leave Whitford's coven," Irena said.

"Before he adopted me as his daughter and successor, before I surpassed him and truly harnessed these beings' power."

Irena clasped her hands loosely before her, her tone cautious and free of credulousness. "How did you accomplish that?"

"How do you think? Some would go so far make it saccharine and call it 'the power of love', but which I see only as sentimentality fueled by weakness." Hestia turned away from Irena, who did not try to follow her.

"Maybe some forms of attachment, but it sounds to me as though your 'boyfriend' has changed you through the power of indifference," Irena said.

"Which people have a weird habit of turning into hatred or at least spite," I mused.

Hestia scoffed, looking sideways at me as if an insect

had just said hello to her and started soft-shoe dancing. "Only because of those pesky things called emotions."

"Which you're showing a fair amount of," Molly pointed out.

Hestia went still, almost freezing in place, almost like a kid with her hand in the cosmic cookie jar. Her expression went flat, and the shockiness of the High Priestess as I found her returned, like she'd pulled on a mask. She looked away and raised her hands, shifting her fingers in some kind of ritual gesture, though to me, it looked like a one-person version of the secret handshake for some kids' clubhouse. A whisper of smoke trickled from the substance of the ceiling.

"What's she doing?" Molly whispered to me.

"She's invoking the entity," Irena said, raising her hand to her shoulder level, palm upward, and keeping her voice low. I felt the air around us tighten like some kind of force field.

"He's coming, my boyfriend is coming!" Hestia cried, looking to the ceiling, her tone at ease, but hopeful and welcoming.

The smoke roiling from the ceiling intensified. I grabbed Molly and Irena by an arm each, as Irena raised a stronger field around us. A tongue of strange-colored fire burst from the ceiling. It smashed into a half dome several feet across above our heads, lighting it with an electric blue glow. *It held,* I realized. The tongue of fire wrapped around Hestia, sending her up like a living torch. She screamed. The reek of burnt flesh and hair flooded the room. I tugged on Molly's arm, but she knelt frozen.

"Run, you idiots! I can't hold the shield forever." Irena roared over the scream of the fire alarms. Molly broke from her trance and let me drag her from the room.

Someone had called emergency services. Fire trucks blocked the street as the three of us fled the building, joining the rest of the residents fleeing the blaze and gathering in the parking lot. Smoke poured from the upper windows, already glowing with eldritch light.

"Someone go back and get Hestia! Molly cried.

"You saw her go up1 You think there's anything left of her to rescue?" Leslie yelled.

"Irena's in there, too," I cried.

The front door burst open. Irena rushed out, hair and clothing singed and eyes streaming, but unharmed. "I'm here." A medic approached her, but she waved her off.

"Is she…?" Molly asked, as Irena joined us.

Irena looked her in the eye, shaking her head. "She wouldn't have gone with us, even if we could have saved her. She was gone before the flames took her."

"How do you know?" Molly asked.

Irena looked at the windows. The roiling blaze had shifted to the orange glow of earthly fire. "It took her mind, and then it took her soul. The body remained for the fire to consume. I wonder of they'll find even a trace of her when the fire dies down."

"What a waste."

"She made her choice. If she found her bliss with him, it is what it is, though we can't understand it," Irena said. "If not, the entity deceived her and there's no argument there."

"But from an entity which made promises it wouldn't keep. You saw how she cried out," Molly glared at Irena. "All that pain, all that sense of manipulation, all that letting that thing blind her and twist her mind, for what? For her to end up dead in a heap of charred bones."

"I suspect we meant well. She did what she could with what she had."

"Don't sugar coat it, Carton. I've met girls like her far too many times, girls who escape one trap, only to fall into another and worse trap," Irena snapped.

"And for what, for a thing that offered itself to her as a boyfriend? I've argued about women turning their own backs on themselves for the sake of a man, but the thing we're dealing with isn't even human," Molly growled. "This isn't some kind of 'Mars Needs Women' sort of thing, is it? That rubbish can't be real, can it? Please tell me no."

Irena gazed across the parking lot at the burning building, the firelight golden on her tanned face. "There are beings from beyond which find humans fascinating, who find our emotions and desires easy to manipulate. I'd also lay blame on her father. He opened the door to this entity, thinking he could control it. Instead, it manipulated his daughter into helping it turn on their would-be controller."

"Isn't that victim blaming?" Molly asked.

"It's more like a case of 'play stupid games, learn stupid prizes', or the victim also being one of the perpetrators," Irena said. "Both her and her father thought they could control the uncontrollable."

"And there's nothing harder for a human to control than a thing that can reach across universes and probe for places where humans have cut a hole through the wall of our world," I said.

"As if that would keep someone cutting a deal with an entity that powerful," Molly said. "So is this where the whole 'making a deal with the Devil' thing came from? Are these things the devils that Christians ascribe as one of the sources of evil?"

"They could be. I'm not about to argue either way," Irena said. "As far as I or anyone else can tell, the worst demons were her father and his circle and the rest of the humans who exploit others, and who themselves are at risk of being exploited."

"It's exploitation all the way down," I said, bothered by the lugubrious quirk I felt in the back of my throat.

The crew managed to knock the blaze down before it consumed the rest of the building. Even still, the clients had to relocate to another shelter across town.

"I tell you, this is why we're all better off without any religion whatever," "Martha", the anti-theist said, as I sat with a group of clients gathered, for the moment, in the common area of a family shelter.

"From my experience, I'd say we're better off without any money whatever," I said, nursing a cup of bad coffee that tasted good, if just for the way it warmed my insides. "I've seen enough cases where someone killed someone else just to get their life insurance money. Stuff like that happened almost the moment life insurance was invented in the 1800s and a group of old ladies decided to poison their friends and family, ala *Arsenic and Old Lace*."

Molly, wrapped in a blanket and nursing a cup of tea, looked up at me. "Seriously?"

"Seriously. I've wondered if the playwright got the idea from the actual case."

Martha sat quietly nonplussed for a moment. But she soon rediscovered her voice. "Heh, no argument there. Sometimes I think we'd be better off without civilization. Maybe the best thing Little Miss High Priestess got herself into and preached about when she could get the chance."

"I wouldn't align with that, though I'd also say that all things need us to approach them with moderation. It's an excess of anything that's a bad thing, not the thing in itself," Irena said.

"I was about to say, covering what happens when civilization breaks down ended my career in photojournalism abroad." I tried not to think of hunkering in a subway with a group of civilians in Sarajevo during an aerial bombardment.

"So where do we go from here?" Molly asked. "I feel like everything we tried to do to help was in vain."

Irena put a kindly hand on Molly's shoulder. "You made the effort. It's more than what some people would have done for her. She chose the darkness and the fire: these aren't your fault but hers."

I got up, checking my camera on reflex.

"Heading out so soon, Camera Man?" Martha asked.

"I got some loose ends to tie up," I said. Now that Hestia had ascended to whatever awaited her on the other side, I could pursue the lead without impunity.

I drove myself to the place where all this started, though a part of me felt like a dog returning to its mess.

When I arrived, I discovered a pair of police cars and several black SUVs with official plates along the street in front of the Whitford ruins.. Officers in blue uniforms and agents in blue windbreakers with FBI in large yellow letters on the back moved about the yard, carefully picking over the ruins. Wyzhard, spotting me, approached the yellow tape still ringing the scene.

"I thought they were tearing the house down after the neighbors complained about the eyesore?" I asked. A few houses on the street already displayed realtor signs from, Sotheby's.

"The city plans to, but we need to go over the last tiny bits as best we can with the place about to fall down around our ears," Wyzhard said. "Heard there was another fire at the shelter?"

"Yeah, I don't think the survivor from this place is going to survive this one." I said.

Wyzhard frowned. "That sounds bad. Please tell me she's not a firebug?"

"In a manner of speaking, she is."

Marshall Birch approached. "A firebug who didn't use an accelerant?"

I drew in a breath. "What would you say if she knew a way to summon unearthly fire?"

As I said this, a pair of agents approached, one tall and robust, who looked like he used to break kneecaps for the Mob, the other, shorter and glaring at the world through glasses like a cranky professor, the second perking up his ears.

"I'd say we're so out of logical explanations that fit, I'm ready to listen to the weird ones," Marshall Birch said.

"I mean, we know this group was into some ooga-booga stuff, but are you serious?" Wyzhard said.

I relayed everything I knew about Hestia, our High Priestess and her circle. The shorter agent took a notepad from his pocket, scribbling on it as fast as he could.

"You uncovered a fair bit of what we'd discovered about her circle," Agent Professor said. "I take it you never found out her full identity?"

"Never did, but I was hoping I would."

"Her name was Amanda Pelletier; she walked away from a group home when she was sixteen, about ten years ago. Whitford found her while he was trawling for 'sacrificial subjects'." He made air quotes with his gloved index fingers. "Read: vulnerable persons, generally unhoused or otherwise disadvantaged. He and his circle took her in, promising her a warm room and the chance to earn her keep, though they planned to make her the next victim to deposit on their sacrificial slab. We know this from a would-be victim who managed to escape before the fire, reporting her experiences to the police afterward."

"This is straight up Satanic Panic stuff," I said.

"That wasn't-isn't as widespread as the panickers among the press and on the pulpits would have it, but some of the crimes they feared have happened, just not on the scale they suggested," Agent Mob Enforcer said.

"The odd thing about power-hungry personages who attempt to harness the power of cosmic entities, or any power-maddened personages: sometimes they allow themselves a moment of clemency toward their victims," Agent Professor continued. "He saw something in Ms. Pelletier which inspired him to spare her, rather than throw her to the eldritch beasts. Maybe she was clever enough to keep him happy, maybe she played the innocent, maybe she was just as vicious as he. Maybe he just liked the way she smiled. Either way, he made her their High Priestess."

"At least until Whitford decided to sacrifice her,"

Wyzhard said. "Except, as you told us, she claimed to offer herself up in place of someone else."

"I almost wonder if she made that up to make herself look more like more selfless," I said.

"Which makes one wonder if she had worn out her welcome in the coven," Agent Professor mused.

"Leading to Hestia – I mean, Ms. Pelletier to summon that eldritch fire. Maybe she'd gotten more clout with the entities and Whitford envied her for that, and so she had to go," I said. "Do I want to know how many victims this bunch may have had?"

"We've found skeletal remains with signs of charring, buried under the dirt floor of a carriage house on the property," Wyzhard said.

"How many possible victims, or is it too soon to tell?" I asked.

"You'd be right for asking that," Agent Professor said. "From what I can see, there may be as many as ten."

"Why do I have a feeling there may be more than that?" I said. And Amanda was the last, though she died in a fire she called to herself to escape, maybe into something worse. She wanted only to take back her power, with something stronger to support her, only for that power to consume her."

The Kids Are Alright
Julie Aaron

In the upcoming weeks, when the trees shake off a few more of their leaves, the neighborhood parents will begin complaining about the eye sore in the woods behind the community. It's easily forgotten in the summer and spring when the greenery surrounding Pope Street is lush and thick with life. If you stand off the back porch of 118 Pope St. and squint on a clear breezeless day, you can see the edges of a nightmare.

Before the neighborhood was built, it was home to vagabonds and teenagers smoking pot, but before that, in the 30s and 40s, it was a thriving Baptist church for the growing East Coast community during the wars. That was until a sinister preacher moved into town, went crazy, and gassed his entire congregation one Sunday morning in 1957. Right down to the children's bible study class and the nursery. The bodies weren't found for days since most of the small town attended that church. The sheriff himself lay slumped, decaying in the summer heat, next to the banker and the baker. Some people say the murderous preacher was jealous that his wife had started to sleep with one of the deacons as soon as they settled into the parsonage. Others say he had become possessed. A victim of opportunity since the church was raised on cursed witch soil. Black blood still running thick as oil on crops under the floorboards since the witch trials of Puritan days. Some don't believe the rumors, dismissing the dark energy around the field; they just say he was a freak who went crazy, the worst kind of evil. Almost all agree his spirit lays restless behind the doors of the church.

The church sat just behind the line of sight for most residents on the right side of the subdivision. The exorbitant-sized backyards sat against the plush tree line that hid the remnants of what locals now called the cursed church. The wooden hull rotted with disregard due to grounds crews being too afraid to maintain the upkeep of the building. The metal steeple that once hung proud and beaconing now had shaken loose from rust and turned upside down, terrorizing those who caught sight of the blasphemy. The pulpit and pews had been vandalized beyond recognition over the years. Pentagrams were etched into the floorboards, and King James's version pages were ripped and strewn across the aisles. The walls were painted black like the soul of the murderous preacher, splashed to look like free-flowing blood with gallons of various shades of red by teenagers brave enough to accept the dares. Refusing to indulge in the mystery surrounding the decaying dwelling but still scared enough not to seek demolition, the city has yet to touch it. The Pope Street neighborhood begrudgingly accepted the atrocity resting on the outskirts of their homes.

Each year on Halloween, to the dismay of the HOA, the cliques around town would gather in the field behind the subdivision and take turns goading less popular kids to venture into the woods and collect a totem, a black rock, a page from a hymnal book, a cup from the offering tray, from the church and bring it back to the party for a chance to enter and challenge their low standing social status. This year was no different. Survive the cursed church and live like kings of the school for one night. Fail, and the football team would teepee your house. It's a risk worth taking.

Harrie, Nickie, and Charlie stood in the closet mirror, adjusting their thrift store-thrown-together Charlie's Angels costumes. The local radio station played softly in the background as the girls teased their hair, bathed themselves in White Rain, and drenched themselves in Estee Lauder perfume stolen from Harrie's mom.

"Does anyone think it's weird Jessica invited us to her birthday party this year? She never invites us," Nickie asked the group as they all adjusted the three bras wrapped around them in a weak attempt to create cleavage.

"Not any weirder than her birthday being Halloween night," Charlie retorts.

"Well. She is a witch, so it's fitting," Harrie jokes.

"Bitch is more like it," Nickie digs at the most popular girl in school.

Secretly, they craved what she had. Everyone did. She had a water slide in her in-ground pool, was captain of the cheer squad and the volleyball team, got her period first out of all the girls, and even though she was turning fifteen, her parents had already bought her a car. It almost wasn't fair. She really was a witch, casting spells on their classmates and teachers to adore her, cursing other girls to sit next to the AV club at lunch, and begging for the chance to be invited to her stupid Halloween birthday party. After a few more well-placed bursts of hairspray to keep their feathered bangs in place, the girls click the small radio off in the middle of "Another One Bites The Dust", and start the trek down Pope Street to Jessica's house.

Standing on the porch of 8 Pope Street, waiting for someone at the party to answer the door, Harriet looks around at the overstuffed pumpkin trash bags lining the driveway they had just walked up. They sat uneven, fat, and squatty. A stray twig puncture wound gaping gives an eye line into the dying brown leaves enclosed inside the bright orange plastic. Black balloons tied to the banisters hover just above their heads. A silver "HAPPY BIRTHDAY" banner stretched across the doorway, one side tacked lower than the other. The opening notes of *"Thriller"* can be heard from the field behind the house, followed by loud cheers and off-time claps. Nickie breaks Harriet's investigative glances as she says,

"Bet you my bike that she's dressed as Madonna."

Harrie cocks her head to the left and squints her eyes at her friend. Pursing her lips in quick thought, she replies, "No way. Dallas Cowboys Cheerleader."

Charlie shrugs from her spot against the porch railing as if to say she doesn't feel like playing. New to the group and new to town she was still coming out of her shell but had seemed to fit in well enough with the girls that they included her in everything, even their mission for popularity.

At that moment, the front door swings open, and the music from the backyard grows louder. There stands Jessica herself. Her pleather white cowboy boots are spotless as she taps her foot along to "Monster Mash", crossing her arms.

"Well, well, well. If it isn't *the yets*. Forgot I invited you, dweebs," the redhead in a too-short, too-sparkly blue skirt snarks, rolling her eyes.

"Hey, Jessica. Happy birthday. Please don't call us that," Nickie says without confidence, as she pulls at the tied-up flower blouse she borrowed from her big sister.

"Why not? Your names are Harry-YET, Nickel-YET, and Charl-YET. Plus, your boobs have YET to come in," Jessica says feigning innocence and poorly holding back a rude laugh.

"Right. Thanks for having us, Jess. Can we come in?" Harrie tries to mitigate the tension between the four of them. The girls shuffle towards the open door before Jessica roughly tugs it closer to her body, making the entrance a sliver of space.

"Actually, this party is a special invite only. You did get invited initially, but unfortunately, you need the designated special item to continue to the party," the redhead smiles saccharinely sweet and so obviously fake.

"Special item? Like a present? Cause we got you a coupon to the Lobster Shack. It's two free meals and a large shake to share," Charlie interjects.

"Are you sure you don't just want to take me to the Lobster Shack, butch?" Jessica bites back, causing Charlie to turn red and drag her tall, slender frame away to the back of the group, her eyes downcast. The birthday girl continues.

"No, not a present. The designated item is required for entry, and if you don't retrieve it, the football team will definitely be teepeeing your houses later."

The friends look at each other, afraid to know where this is going. Are they going to have to rob a bank, knock over the elderly couple down the street, or kidnap someone's pet? Their minds go wild, and Jessica, evil as ever, finally puts them out of their misery.

"You have to walk to the cursed church in the woods, go in, and bring back a flier off of the bulletin board. Survive the preacher's evil demon ghost and bring the flier back here, and you can come into the party," she says as though it's an easy task or a task they would ever agree to.

"No way!"

"Absolutely not!" Nickie and Charlie immediately voice their opinions at the same time. When they notice Harrie's quietness, they turn to her, talking over each other, begging her to not accept Jessica's demands.

"Or you could just not even attempt it, and I tell everyone you guys practice kissing with each other, and you invited me to your weird lesbo make-out game, and your reps will be ruined until you graduate and go off to play softball at an all-girls college upstate," she cocks her eyebrow and smirks, knowing a rumor like that would get back to their parents, and the only real friendship they cultivated in high school would be ripped away from them.

"Fuck you, Jessica. I know you got drunk off of spritzers and fell asleep with your hand on Mandy Masters' left boob at the homecoming party," Nickie says through gritted teeth. The threat is met with a half-effort eye roll as though Jessica knows she's untouchable no matter what she does.

"We get this flier, and you leave us alone. We don't want to go to your stupid party. You stop calling Charlie names and spreading rumors about us. Just forget we exist," Harrie counters.

"It's a win-win for me then. Leave the coupon. You have until midnight. Bye *yets*, so nice knowing you. NOT!" Jessica waves sarcastically before slamming the door in the girl's face as the chorus of "Karma Chameleon" plays behind her.

Harrie turns abruptly and storms from the porch, her two friends following frantically behind her. They call her name and trip over themselves, clutching at her flowing sleeves, trying to slow her down, trying to talk her into just returning home and forgetting all about this stupid dare, this ridiculous challenge. Unfortunately for calmer minds, all the blood in her head is currently pounding in Harrie's ears and behind her eyes.

"Who does she think she is?! I'm getting that flier, and we're crashing that party, and she'll eat her words!" Harrie mumbles as she trudges into the empty lot behind Jessica's ridiculous three-story house.

The parcel of land around them becomes thick with brush and branches each time they place one foot in front of the other. The grass around them stretches higher than their waists, itching at the spots where their ill-fitting crop tops rise. They follow Harrie deeper into the woods begrudgingly until Nickie and Charlie stumble to a sudden stop against Harrie's back as the taller of the three stands motionless.

Like stepping behind a curtain, the girls are alone, surrounded by dense forests. The infamous cursed church stares back at them. It doesn't look like much. Sure, the years of thick, layered Sherwin-Williams paint gave the illusion of a shadow or a void, but really, it was just a building in the woods behind a family subdivision. Had at least twenty people died inside of it? Sure, but that was America. It was a graveyard wherever you stepped.

"Harriet, we're not seriously going to do this, are we? This place is haunted," Charlie pleads, her eyes darting from her friends to the church.

"It's not haunted. It's just condemned," Harrie says. "Besides, you're not going in. I am."

Nickie interrupts the sudden, heavy quiet to respond to Harriet's dismissal.

"No, it's both. It was an old site for witch trials back in the 1600s when the town was first founded. There's so much blood buried here. My sister said everyone who goes in comes out wrong afterward. And some don't even come back out. So yeah, I won't be going in."

"If you're talking about that reverend, he was just a psycho, and your sister is a pothead bitch, so she said that just to fuck with you."

"I just think I don't have any business at church, much less a haunted one, if you get what I'm saying," Charlie adds quietly to dispel the tension between her friends. Harrie was a natural leader, but Nickie was fearless with conflict. It led to some intense conversations Charlie had learned.

"It's going to be fine, Chuck," Harrie comforts Charlie while eyeing Nickie pointedly. "What's the worst that could happen?"

The church stood menacingly against the dying trees and browning grass. Autumn had well and fallen on the town and, subsequently, the community. The night was crisp enough to warrant a jacket, but the orange glow of numerous bonfires in the distance meant the chilly air would be long forgotten. The church stood dominating the space around it. The upside-down crucifix warned everyone who approached what was possible if they dared step inside.

Something sinister leaked out of the ground underneath. Something old and vengeful. You could feel the heavy weight of it in the air when you approached. The feeling of pain seeps into your open mouth, leaving the taste of blood on your tongue. The longer you stand on this vile ground, the worse it gets. Paranoia bathing you as your eyes dance against the blackness. Attempting to shake it off, Harrie steps forward when a pair of hands grab onto her. Their eyes pleading, her friends shaking their heads frantically wordless, begging her to retreat to the safety of one of their comfortable homes. Harriet was doing this for them, though. For Charlie, who really did want to take Jessica out to share a shake and fries but could never tell anyone. And for Nickie, her oldest friend, who simply dreamed of fitting in. She would be in and out before she got the chance to be truly afraid. She could do this for her best friends.

A gust of wind cyclones around them, pulling the girls forward towards the busted and weathered double doors. The once brass handles were now spray painted black. Red hand prints adorn every reachable surface, the paint chipped and worn. With one last gasping inhale, Harrie nods resolutely. She steps towards the entrance, trembling hand reaching for the handle just as the smallest of clicks can be heard. The church welcomes her in, opening the door for her. She gulps and places one foot in front of the other. Her small frame crosses the threshold completely, her bright costume out of place amongst the dark night and even darker building. With her back to Nickie and Charlie, she turns to look at them one last time. Her once-over-done sandy, blonde bangs now fall loosely over her eyes.

"Be right back," she says with a tense smile as the door slams shut behind her.

Left standing by themselves, worlds apart, Nickie and Charlie resound themselves to waiting. Not long after the doors swallow Harriet, a stomach-churning scream echoes against the dismal night. The girls eye each other warily before shouting for Harrie, banging against the church walls and remaining windows.

"Harriet! What's going on?!"

"Harrie! I swear to god, come out right now!"

A current of air surges against the remaining girls' faces as the front door of the church swings open, revealing Harriet. She stands, her costume askew, her hair mused, and her eyes bloodshot as she cocks her head to the left, squinting at her friends.

"No God here, I'm afraid. At least not anymore," she growls.

Nickie and Charlie take an instinctual step backward, stumbling slightly, losing their footing in the unfamiliar surroundings. Harriet runs her palms down the front of her body, taking a large breath through her nose. She exhales with an open clack of her jaw, gnashing her braces-covered teeth at her friends. She strides towards them, rolling her shoulders and cracking her neck as if she's getting used to being in her skin.

"It's been so long since that stuffy preacher welcomed me in. It is *so* nice to be back in a fresh body," the voice coming from Harriet's mouth sighs.

"Harriet? What are you talking about?" Charlie stammers.

"Charlotte—shhh. We should go. NOW," Nickie frantically cuts her friend off, grabbing her hand and turning from the scene before them.

It's then that Harriet lunges after them, her hand swiping at the space where her friends had been standing. Her press-on nails skimming the top of Nickie's arm, but unable to close around her. Nickie and Charlie sprint through the dark, empty lot hand in hand, broken branches whipping against their faces, drawing blood and leaving angry raised welts. Hurried footsteps race after them, never letting up. They are too afraid to look behind themselves, knowing that whatever had spoken to them isn't their friend anymore. They continue running until they reach the neighborhood opening.

The quietness of the paved street and immaculate lawns welcome them back to safety. The girls slow from their pace into a brisk walk, still clutching onto one another for safety and comfort, and begin to make their way back to Harriet's house, thinking surely this was a prank gone wrong. The parties in the neighborhood continued to rage on around the girls; various top-charting pop hits blared down Pope Street, making it difficult to hear the screams coming from Jessica's backyard. They would've missed it if they hadn't been walking by at the exact moment. The panic-stricken, ear-shattering wails rang out against the thumping of the mixed lyrics and rhythms hanging in the night air. Nickie and Charlie freeze, looking at each other.

***

Seeing the two girls linger at a nervous amble, ducking out of the streetlights, and knowing she could hunt them down whenever the ringing between her ears quelled, Harrie thoughtlessly crept into Jessica's backyard. The party rages on around her. Every corner of the privacy-fenced space is filled with underage drinking, skunk-scented smoke, and couples on the dance floor pressed together as the ending of "Hungry Like the Wolf" fades into the next song.

She stands, eyes glassy and empty, taking in the sights and sounds. A tall, slender boy with shaggy hair breaks her stupor. He sways towards her wordlessly, looking as if he wants to speak, to say something idiotic. Harriet has no interest in stupid right now, the fever raging against her tongue, and her insides have no more patience to give. Without a word between them, she leans a fraction to her left and delicately picks up an abandoned pumpkin carving knife. Pumpkin juice still coats the blade. The handle is slightly slippery, but Harriet grips it tightly enough. She waits a beat until the shaggy-haired boy sways towards her again. Just as he begins to open his candy apple-stained mouth, she slashes the jagged carving knife silently through the air, slicing her classmate's throat wide open. Blood spatters as he drops to his knees before thudding face down into the grass near the snack table.

Harriet makes her way to the makeshift apple bobbing station set up against the side wall of the pool house. When Jessica mentioned bobbing for apples, her parents laughed it off until finally relenting to the unusually childlike wish of their typically sour teenage daughter. The day of, they lined a large wheelbarrow with a few leftover orange trash bags and filled it with buckets of water from the hose before leaving for their own Halloween party.

The entity inside Harrie brings her to stand behind a sophomore girl dressed as Wonder Woman. She has her hands clasped tightly behind her back, afraid to cheat even though no one is watching her. Her face is balanced carefully below the surface of the cool water as she chases down a stubborn green apple. With less of an internal fight than last time, Harriet grabs a handful of the girl's jet-black hair, wrapping the tendrils tightly around her nimble fingers. First, she shoves her further into the orange-tinted dark water for a count of twenty before she tugs harshly against the hair she's gathered in her fist and brings the knife against the soft flesh of her throat. Harriet saws the knife like a violinist, the bloody bath of apples her orchestra. She rises from her crouched position over the girl standing devoid of emotions while carelessly dropping the lifeless body into the tub to turn the motionless water a dark shade of crimson. With every pump of the girls failing heart, blood spills from her slit neck into the apple-filled water that swallows her heavy head. The girl's inky hair floats along the surface like Rorschach blots.

Harriet straightens, her spine clicking into place under the fever-hot skin that covers it. The knife hangs loose and dripping in her hands. Her costume is covered in sprayed blood, and her sleeves are wet from the apple water. From the corner of her eye, she sees Jessica standing still in the doorway to the backyard, watching her, gripping a Halloween-themed paper cup too tightly. Harriet flashes a fiendish smile as their gazes meet. Before Jessica has time to run, Harriet is upon her swinging her knife wildly, the blade barely kissing her white vest in a near miss. She finally frees a scream from her throat, and soon, a cacophony of cries joins her, swallowing the melodious chorus "Like A Virgin".

***

"What the fuck was that?!" Charlie asks, eyes widening and flinching at every high-pitched scream that reverberates from her classmate's party. They duck behind a row of nearby trashcans. The smell of stale beer and a week's worth of sun-cooked garbage swirling around them.

"There's no way she beat us here," Nickie whispers.

"Wait. There's no way she's actually evil, though, right? It's Harriet! She's our best friend! She's probably just playing a prank on us with Jess or something, and when we're good and scared, they'll invite us into the party."

"Chuck. I am good and scared. She tried to grab us and drag us into that hell hole. She fucking chased us through the woods!"

"I know it looks bad, but maybe it's all circumstantial. Let's go to Jessica's. If we catch them teaming up, then it's all over, right? We can call them out and go back to having a normal Halloween."

"UGH! This is so stupid! FINE! But if we die, I'm totally blaming you."

"Totally."

The girls step out of the shadows and head to knock on Jessica's front door. When no one answers, Charlie looks to Nickie and shrugs, raising her fist to tap against the ornate beveled glass one more time. Her knuckles hang suspended in mid-air as the door is yanked open in front of them. The heavy bass notes of "Killer Queen" thud against the home's walls. Jessica stands terrified in front of them, blood adorning her once stark white patent leather cowboy boots. Seeing who is at her door, her teary green eyes widen in fright as her skin blanches.

"It's ok," Charlie reaches forward, stepping in through the doorway to wrap her arms around the girl in front of her before she completely passes out.

Nickie quickly follows, shutting and locking the door behind them, looking around for something sturdy to barricade it with. Jessica begs under her breath, whispering words that sound too terrifying to truly understand, tears rolling from her eyes down her neck freely as she's held against Charlie's chest, paralyzed.

"Jess, what's going on?" Nickie asks beside them.

"She- she killed them," Jessica answers. "This wasn't supposed to happen. It wasn't supposed to be real."

"What are you talking about? Harriet? The church?"

"She killed them, Charlie; she ripped their throats out in front of me," Jessica sobs to the girl holding her.

"You did this to her!" Nickie shouts accusingly.

"I didn't think it was real, idiot! It wasn't supposed to be real. It's a scary story for scared kids. I didn't think she'd get freaking possessed and kill all my friends and ruin my birthday party!" Jessica retorts.

A thunderous rumbling sounds from above the girls, a rattling stretching over their heads. They crane their necks up when realization causes terror to wash over them.

Thudding and scratching, a scurrying noise, the sound of wood flexing under heavy feet. The sound of ugly hand-me-down clogs scraping against the attic's crowded floorboards and crawl space. Tears spring to their eyes collectively. Jessica tucks herself tighter against Charlie, using her shoulder to choke back a sob.

"She's in the house," Jessica whispers as her small frame shakes with panic.

"Do you have a gun?" Nickie asks, quickly opening the drawers of the entryway table and shuffling tchotchkes around to find something to protect herself and Charlie with.

"We're not shooting Harrie!"

"A gun?! Are you insane?!"

Charlie and Jessica hiss at once. The scurrying around upstairs gets louder the longer they stand around doing nothing. With Harriet seemingly either bored of the party goers outside or finished with them entirely, time is dwindling. Those thoughts sit heavy in the pit of Nickie's stomach, making her dry heave once before she straightens, brushing her auburn hair from her eyes, and leans into the embraced girls to stand her ground.

"That's not Harrie anymore," Nickie breathes. "I don't know what you want me to do. I'm hardly qualified to perform an exorcism! And you heard that thing. God isn't here anymore," she pokes her index finger into Charlie's arm, trying hard to make her point. "Plus. The last person it was inside was a freaking preacher! And look at what happened there!"

"Top left drawer of the entryway table," Jessica murmurs.

Nickie quietly pulls the drawer open and reaches in. The silver pistol was heavy and cold in her small hand. Before she can get used to the weight of it, Charlie steps forward, prying it gently from her grasp. Nickie lets her, suddenly feeling unqualified to kill her best friend. She silently thanks Charlie for bearing the burden.

Pink insulation rains down on the girls. Dust and screws and shards of plywood decorate their hair like confetti. The large crystal chandelier that hangs in the foyer to welcome guests is knocked loose above their heads. They duck away, covering their faces as their eyes squint and cloud with rubble from the crash. Crouched at their feet is Harriet. Her leg was broken from the fall, the shattered bone visible from a tear in her denim and blood drenching the material around it. Her nails were not the sparkly pink and green from the beginning of the night; now, they were a deep maroon. They had been soaked in the blood and wrapped around the throat tendons of every kid at the party that she could get her hands on. She stands slowly as if manually clicking her joints into place. It's jagged, her movements. It's so obviously not the Harriet they once knew.

"She let me in. Did you know that? So tired of her boring life of answering to others, she welcomed me in. She's here now, bargaining. Do you want to know what she's asking for?" the entity teases through Harriet's wind-chapped lips. The girls refuse to answer, too terrified.

Harriet inches closer and smiles. Her red-stained teeth shine in the flickering of the lopsided hanging chandelier.

"She's begging me to let her precious friends go. She's crying, throwing herself against the walls of herself, trying to save you. Trying to rescind my invitation, trying so hard to regain control. It's a shame she's so weak," she makes a show of shrugging sadly. "But you, Jessica, she doesn't care about you at all."

Harriet lunges forward, grabbing Jessica by her white vested shoulders, the glittery blue stars rough against the sleek material.

"She won't admit this out loud, but I know she'll enjoy this. You thought life would bend to your every want, didn't you?"

With one final snark to the sobbing mean girl, Harriet lowers her head to her throat, licking a broad stripe up the column, feeling the erratic pulse dance beneath her tongue. A genuine smile graces her lips as sobs rack the body clutched within her grasp. A disgusting crack dances between them as Harriet unhinges her jaw. The popping sounds like bones breaking, like every muscle has been torn to make room to latch onto Jessica's sinew-covered carotid. Before Harriet can clench her teeth around the young redhead a small click is heard. It's followed by a resounding and thunderous boom. The sound of flesh being dug into. The smell of sweet sulfur bathes the foyer. Gunsmoke clouds the air as Jessica and Nicolette scream. The body that drops to the floor unmoving is Harriet's. A gushing open wound adorns her sweaty forehead now. Jessica clambers backward, her fake leather boots sliding inefficiently, towards the front door, prepared to run for her life when the gun goes off three more times. Twice into Harriet's chest and once more into her already bleeding head. Silence engulfs them for an unending moment before Charlie speaks.

"The cops are never going to believe one kid killed all these people, and my fingerprints are on the gun now. We need to get out of here," she says evenly, though the slight shake in her right hand around the empty pistol betrays the calmness she's trying to convey.

"Do you know who my parents are?! I'm not getting in any trouble for - for this FREAK!" Jessica stammers, her confidence returning with the threat of death trickling away as the blood pools around Harriet's lifeless body.

Charlie makes a face of disappointment as hurt washes over her features at Jessica's words.

"We don't have important parents, Jess. Charlie's mom works at the Dairy Queen. My parents are on unemployment. We'll be tried as adults if the police really think we did this," Nickie steps in to say.

"Well, maybe you did do it. You three went out into those woods, and now all my friends are dead. And my totally authentic Dallas Cowboys cheerleader uniform has blood all over it!"

"We went into the woods because you made us! Harriet was good! She was kind and funny and good, and you did this to her!" Nickie screams as she steps towards Jessica menacingly. Guilt, fear, and regret manifest in unbridled anger: anger at the situation, anger at Jessica's uncaring words, anger at the unnecessary suffering and loss of her friend. Seeing Nicolette march towards her, Jessica squares her stance and readies herself to fight.

The bickering exchange of venomous words comes to a screeching halt at the sound of a whining creak above them. Once again, the girls strain their necks to the ceiling, their heart rates increasing as fear swallows them. Charlie cocks the hammer of the pistol still clutched tightly in her grasp, raising it to aim above them. It's then that the heavy crystal chandelier breaks its weakened hold and comes crashing down, crushing Jessica. She lays pinned under the polished brass and clear dangling Swarovski crystals. As Jessica lies gasping for oxygen to fill her punctured lungs, Charlie lowers the gun and laces her fingers with Nickie's sweaty hand, tugging slightly. With a tremble and tears in their eyes, Charlie and Nickie sidestep the fallen chandelier and Jessica's still body to kneel beside Harriet. The girls clasped hands gently brush the matted hair from her face before gently closing her eyes to give her one final moment of peace.

"Everything happened so fast. Nick, what if we made a mistake?" Charlie asks, her voice shaking unsteadily as she squeezes Nicolette's hand tightly, sweat gathering between their joined palms.

"Let's get out of here, Chuck. We can think about mistakes later. I'm sorry about Jessica."

"That's ok. She really was a witch."

With a glance at the gaping hole in the ceiling and the ugly mix matched decorations hanging haphazardly along the walls splashed in wet blood, Charlie sniffles before she says,

"This party looks like it sucked."

Their laughter surprises them—boisterous against the dead silence in the room. They couldn't help but laugh. This really was the worst Halloween of their lives. Tears slide from their eyes, smudging the heavy rouge of their cheeks. They take their first step toward the front door, their first step away from Harriet. The brisk early November night air hits them head-on. Without turning, they pause at the threshold. Their eyes set forward on the solitary road leading out of the neighborhood.

"Goodbye, Harrie."

"I'm sorry about shooting you, but you were being a real bitch."

With a final farewell, the two surviving girls step out into the darkness, never once looking back on the bodies that litter 118 Pope Street.

Comes in Threes
Danni Bowen

Calvert Daniels carefully dabbed his forehead with a cloth. One had to be careful about getting fiberglass dug into the skin after handling insulation. He was busy fixing up his new house when a gentle knock alerted him to a visitor. He practically jumped with excitement; his gramma had finally arrived. She was the entire reason he'd bought the house, so he had a place to take care of her. He loved his gramma more than life itself…

He practically tore the door off its hinges to find the gentle woman of seventy standing before him. She had no luggage; Calvert had already taken the liberty of moving all her personal belongings before she had been released from the hospital. He flung his arms around his gramma's shoulders tightly, taking in a deep breath of her scent. She smelled of antiseptic and cleaning supplies, just like the hospital, covering up her natural scent. She used to smell like Aussie hair products; she lived by Aussie ever since she was a hairdresser.

She felt just right in his arms, soft and fragile. Perfect. Just how he remembered. Tears started dripping down his face and splattering his glasses.

"I've missed you so much gramma," he breathed in deep again, trying to calm his shaky voice. "I was so worried while you were in the hospital."

"Then why weren't you at the surgeon's like you promised?"

She didn't say it unkindly, but the fact that she had yet to return his hug spoke volumes. Calvert stepped back, shame clinging to every inch of his face.

"Nothing I say would excuse me for not being there," the tears came down heavier then, "I'm so very sorry."

A sad smile spread across his gramma's face, "Is that why you're taking me in? Because of shame? And you're wanting to make it up to me?"

Vigorously Calvert shook his head. He knew for certain that, Lavon Daniels, would flat out hate him if he ever did something like that. "No, ma'am. I love you and I want to spend more time with you." He wrung his hands together in agitation, "The close call at the hospital made me realize that I'll only have you for a limited amount of time so I need to make the most of it."

Lavon nodded before entering her new home, satisfied with his answer. The house was an old Victorian; she had often spoke to Calvert about getting one like it but never having the time or money for one. These old houses took a lot of work. Thankfully though, Calvert's father Calvin owned a construction business. One he'd worked for every summer for thirteen years of his life. It was cheaper than getting a babysitter and Calvert always seemed to enjoy the work. That's why he'd gone into architecture in college.

And he'd done a fabulous job restoring the old place, so far. He'd probably put in months of overnights to get it this far in time. If anything, Calvin had probably dropped by to help. He knew how important this was to Calvert. She ran one of her wrinkled hands against the dark cherry wood of the staircase banister it was as soft as a flower petal. She could barely feel the grains at all. Very high quality. Not a sight of wallpaper anywhere. She hated wallpaper. Calvert had chosen to paint the walls in a rich burgundy.

She went past the elegant staircase into the hall, peeking into the living room, enjoying the dark blue jewel tones. Right under the staircase was a door to the basement, which is probably where Calvert had put the laundry. There was a single guest bedroom just past the basement door. She stopped at the double wide doorway that led into the kitchen, gasping in awe.

Below the deep forest green walls, the counters were set with copper cookware, real silverware, and China sets. Directly in the middle of all the supplies was a popcorn air-popper. A warmth touched her heart. Always, when they'd watch movies together, she'd make them popcorn this way. It was an essential part to their movie night ritual and the fact that he'd went out of his way to find an air-popper made her feel loved and wanted. For a little bit there, in the hospital, she had started questioning that.

Calvert watched his gramma check everything out and nearly burst into tears when she found the kitchen. She was indeed happy with it, he could tell. Her smile brightened up the lonely Victorian.

"This is amazing, how did you afford all this?"

Calvert had to stop himself from rolling his eyes. Gramma would have found it rude, but he had found it funny that she'd only think about the cost of things.

"Ebay, mostly. There wasn't much to pick over at garage sales around here."

Lavon nodded again with approval. She had always been frugal and was glad he'd picked that up from her too. Calvert showed her the rest of the house. She had some problem with stairs, but he was right beside her any time she needed him. His attentiveness and worry were touching, but she hoped he wouldn't treat her this gingerly the entire time she lived with him.

There were three bedrooms upstairs along with a full bathroom. Calvert had remodeled the bathroom downstairs for her with a walk-in tub that she could sit down in when she got tired, plus handrails to help get her up and down. He'd already put a small heater in the bathroom to keep the metal warm. He'd almost thought of everything…almost.

"Which is my bedroom?"

Calvert adjusted his round, black rimmed glasses. "I was going to let you pick." If he had picked the bedroom, he would have been in a sticky situation. If he picked the ground floor for her, he would be seen as treating her like she was too frail. However, if he picked a top floor without seeing her opinion about it, he might come off as insensitive. So, he had left her belongings packed and planned on moving them for her once she picked a bedroom. He could always get a chairlift built in if she picked the top floor.

Lavon thought for a moment. The rooms were nice upstairs, more spacious than the one on the ground floor. However, if she picked one of the top bedrooms then Calvert would have to carry her belongings up too many stairs. Either way, he'd already built the first-floor bathroom with the walk-in, and she didn't want to go up and down the stairs after a shower. Though, she was sure that if she picked the top floor Calvert would remodel it as well.

"I'll take the bottom room."

Calvert thought for a bit, humming to himself. "Are you sure? I want you to have enough room."

Lavon snorted, "I'll be fine. I don't have that much stuff."

Calvert raised an eyebrow incredulously before he went to the basement door to start bringing her belongings up. It took him two hours to maneuver every box into the small room. When he was done his shirt was dripping sweat. Lavon stared at the boxes a little bewildered.

"I guess I had more than I thought."

He chuckled in exasperation before sitting down on the floor and stripping off his shirt. For a solid minute he considered wringing it out like a dishrag but thought better of it, seeing as he had just put in new flooring. He glanced up at Gramma from where he had collapsed, wondering if she was taking everything as well as she seemed.

Sure, his gramma was a trooper. She rolled with the punches most of the time and yet…he couldn't help feeling like something was off. She'd been through a lot. The hospital was a traumatic experience, and she was bound to have some sore feelings about him not showing up. He was determined to work through it with her though, he was going to be there for her this time. He stood and asked, "You doing alright gramma?"

Lavon was a tad bit overwhelmed. There was a lot of unpacking to do, physically and emotionally. She didn't feel strong enough to deal with either at the moment, so she replied, "I'm tired. I think I'll take a nap."

"Do you want me to help with the sheets?"

Lavon shook her head; this was something she wanted to do alone. She wanted to prove to herself she could at least do that much for herself. She could tell that Calvert was put out, yet he didn't protest.

"If there's anything you need, give a holler and I'll come."

Calvert slowly turned away then. There were some blueprints he could be working on; he decided he should focus on those. Gramma would talk to him when she was ready. In his family there was no point in pushing; if someone didn't want to talk then they wouldn't. Rest would do her some good right now. Plus, he'd anticipated that she'd be tired for several days after everything.

Tonight, he'd make her a big dinner to celebrate being home. He'd even picked up a cake for dessert. Gramma probably would have preferred pie, but he wasn't good at baking pies yet. He wondered if she would teach him. Of course, he didn't mean for her to cook. He'd just need instruction. Like how they did Christmas cookies a few years back. She'd tell him what to do and he'd do it, asking questions if he didn't understand the directions.

He'd got frustrated, that was for sure, but the cookies were good anyway and it was the time with gramma that he cherished. All of his happy memories were with his gramma; now that she was living with him, he was sure they'd make even better memories.

Lavon watched as Calvert jogged up the stairs, probably to his home office. He worked from home more often than not, unless he had to visit a site. She forgot sometimes how hard he worked. After all, she'd grown up in an era where one had worked with their hands. They couldn't do across-the-world meetings over the internet before. Just because it didn't look like he was working doesn't mean he wasn't.

She rubbed her eyes from exhaustion before setting about making her bed. It was something she'd missed doing while in the hospital. It was nice to have busy work that kept her mind blank for a bit. One could say it was a type of meditation. Once finished, she crawled into the still chilly blankets, body shaking with weariness. Sleep took maybe seven minutes to set in, along with a singular thought...she was hungry.

***

After three hours slugged by, Calvert decided he should check up on Gramma. He pussyfooted down the stairs, not wanting to wake Gramma up if she wasn't already awake. He planned on softly opening the door to Gramma's bedroom, but it was already open when he got there. Odd, he thought, before peeking around the door frame. Gramma was sitting on the edge of her bed. Her shoulders bent forward making her seem much smaller than she was. She looked weaker than he last saw her, as if she was wilting away.

He shook his head of the macabre thought, then lightly knocked on the frame, "Gramma?"

She glanced up at him from the corner of her glasses. Calvert wanted to cry at just how haggard her face was. She had always been full of vitality; even when she was exhausted, she was a beam of joy. At least he'd always felt happy around her. Now, he felt sad.

"Feeling, okay?"

Gramma shook her head slightly, "I'm a bit hungry."

Calvert sighed in relief. Oh good, he thought, she's just hungry. Of course, she would be, she'd had a long day. Anyone would be a bit grouchy after not eating for that long. A small smile tilted his lips up, "Alright then, let's get you some food."

He went into the kitchen and pulled out some ground meat from the fridge (he'd moved some over from the big freezer in the basement that morning in preparation for Gramma's arrival), flattened in a zip lock baggie.

"Is Hamburger Helper, okay?"

Gramma nodded as she sat down at the breakfast nook in the kitchen. He pulled out his biggest cooking pan and slid the meat from the plastic bag. It made a clunk hitting the pan. The meat started sizzling almost immediately, filling the kitchen with a delicious aroma.

Lavon sniffed deeply. It was an old habit taught to her by her mother, it would help detect if the meat had gone bad, and while the meat smelled delectable, the scent seemed off. The meat almost had a pork-i-ness to it. Was it mixed in with ground pork? That could be it, but most Hamburger Helper directions were for beef only, which meant that Calvert may not be cooking it right.

"California," she gently drew his attention to her by using the nickname she'd given him when he was just a child wanting to make it big in Hollywood, "the meat smells funny."

Calvert chuckled as he nabbed a cooked piece and took it to her. Gramma had always been a nut about taste-testing the food; he handed the meat over on a fork for her to try. He watched her nibble it. Her eyes widened.

"This is really good, but what is it? It doesn't taste like beef or pork."

Calvert nodded going back to cooking, "It's deer."

That would explain why it smelled off, Lavon thought, but she was surprised that it was deer. Deer usually had more of a grass undertone. Then again, she hadn't had it since she was a young girl; her memory might be off. She assumed that Calvert knew how to cook this meat since his father often cooked with it himself. That's probably where he'd gotten it from too.

She quietly watched as Calvert added the other ingredients. She mused at the fact that he used to be such a clutz in the kitchen, but now he was maneuvering around it as if he was a professional chef. *When had he grown up?* She thought sadly staring at his scrawny back. Often, she had lamented on not being able to spend more time with him after his mother had moved him away. Afterall, he was the only grandchild she had. Well, the only one that spoke to her.

Technically, Calvert was her step-grandchild. Lavon had married his grandfather about two years before the boy was born. And by the time her own grandchildren were born, he was already five years old, with a very strong attachment. The other two never seemed to form that attachment; after they'd all grown up, they had stopped talking to her completely. They even somewhat detested her, but Calvert, he still had a very strong attachment.

She often considered if it was because she was more of a mother to him, since his mother had been out of the picture until he was about eight. He'd never really seen his mother and Lavon had raised him up till then. She had taught him how to tie his shoes, how to ride a bike, and how to mind his manners. There had been so much more she had wanted to teach him, but after he was taken away, she stopped having as much of an influence on him.

The distance hurt terribly for her, especially after Calvert became a teenager. He would tell of the fights his mother and he got into regularly. He'd call her almost every night in tears begging to move in with them. That stopped when they found out his mother had been listening in on their conversations. He became more and more distant the stronger his mother's grip tightened.

Anytime Lavon wanted to see Calvert, she would have to beg and say things she didn't agree with just to get her to relent. She had tried her best to get him away from all of that, and once he had started college he got to visit more often. He called every week, sometimes more if he wasn't busy with studies. Things started to feel as they once had when Calvert was young. She felt that their bond had started to mend. That's why when she was in the Hospital and Calvert hadn't showed up, her heart broke.

Now, here he was, cooking for her after having moved her into his house to take care of her, and there she was, conflicted on how she should feel. Should she act as if nothing happened? She had always been one to speak her mind. Calvert knew that, she reasoned, maybe she should just get things off her chest now.

Just then, Calvert set a large plate of cheeseburger Hamburger Helper right under her nose, distracting her from the painful thoughts. Her stomach growled rather aggressively, shocking her at just how hungry she was. She tucked into the steaming food and shoved it into her mouth. The savory flavor tingled her cheeks, she thought about the strangeness of it for two maybe three seconds before she pushed the thought aside and continued to eat.

Before she knew it, she was asking for seconds, which Calvert got without hesitation. He'd made enough for third or fourths for both if needed. Even though he wasn't eating. Lavon only noticed after getting half-way through her third plate.

"Why aren't you eating?"

Calvert blushed deeply, giving his cheek a light scratch, "I'm not hungry," he smiled nervously, "please, eat all you want."

He really didn't want Gramma to start plying him with difficult questions, so he got a jump on a different line of questioning, "How are you feeling after getting some food into you?"

Lavon paused to think for a moment. Oddly, she was feeling better than she had since before her first heart attack, more energized.

"I have enough energy to organize my room," as she smiled the sides of her eyes crinkled, "and then some."

Calvert tapped his fingers on the wood excitedly, "Excellent! I'm glad to hear it." He noticed that she was finished with her food, "Should I leave you to it then?" He went to lift himself out of his chair before Gramma stopped him, he sat back down, knowing what was coming next. He'd hoped to save this conversation at least until tomorrow, but Gramma hated leaving things to stew. Gramma stared at him quietly, seeming to consider her words, but he couldn't meet her eyes.

He loved his Gramma desperately and the guilt he felt for not visiting her in the hospital had eaten many a hole in his soul…some would even say mind. After missing the surgery, his grandfather had told him not to bother showing up. This caused him to spiral into himself, isolating from the outside world. Refusing to take jobs onsite or leave his (at the time) apartment. No one could reach him. Then he'd taken all his life savings to buy the house and fix it up. This caused talk amongst the family, they said he'd gone a bit mad.

Of course, he'd paid them no mind. He never had. To Calvert, his only family was Gramma and that's how he liked it. The other members judged or abused him, so they meant nothing. Lavon sighed heavily, causing him to jump in his seat, he'd lost himself to thought.

"Why weren't you there?" She asked softly, a bit worried that the question might break the poor kid in half. He'd always been a fragile spirit. She saw she wasn't entirely wrong with her concern as she watched Calvert bow his head.

"There is nothing I can say that would forgive what I did." His voice was barely above a whisper and even then, his voice cracked with tears.

Lavon could clearly see how painful this was for him, but she wanted to know. "Tell me anyway."

Calvert removed his glasses as he sniffed, trying to steady his shaking voice. "I had planned to be there. I had scheduled a few days off work, months in advance. I was even packing to head down the morning Grandpa called to tell me that your surgery was postponed, with no rescheduled date, so I couldn't shift the dates. I was onsite, several states away, when Grandpa called to tell me that you were going in for surgery, hours before you went in and this was weeks after the fact of the cancellation. I couldn't get the time off then and couldn't leave. It was essential that I was onsite for this job. When I contacted Grandpa next, he told me not to bother making the trip."

He took in a shuddering breathe, "I'm sorry…I should have dropped everything, got a plane ticket, and been by your side." Tears dripped from his chin onto his clenched hands.

Lavon could hear his teeth grind as his jaw clenched. She was stunned to hear that her husband had told Calvert not to come. The man knew she had wanted the boy there. Had he been that mad that Cal had missed the surgery? She'd figured that his absence had been because of work, but it makes sense that he wouldn't have been able to get the time off if he was needed onsite. Leaving would have got him fired; it probably would have been a black spot on his career. She sighed, as much as she had wanted him there before the surgery, she could understand why he was not. She'd felt so alone, with no one visiting her, that she wasn't sure she could get over the pain of it right away. Yet, seeing Calvert sitting across the table from her, sobbing, broke her heart just as much.

She reached across the table, taking his hands in hers. Giving them a squeeze, she said, "Thank you for telling me."

Calvert pulled his hands away, her sympathy hurt. He didn't deserve it and he dared not take it.

"I'm sorry," he whispered again, "After raising me as if I was your own blood grandchild and loving me through my teenage years, I should have been there for you. Even if it cost me my life."

Lavon snorted, irritated now. "You wouldn't have made the surgery anyway. There is nothing fast enough that would have got you to me before the surgery was over. You being there, *before* I went in, was the important part, not the after. You didn't even know when it was happening, how could I blame you for that?"

Calvert glanced up between his shaggy bangs. "But you did and that's fine."

"Then I was ignorant. I'm not now, and I'm mature enough that I can forgive. After all, I'm still here, and you're doing your best for me now. I think that evens things out a bit, don't you?"

Calvert sniffed before shaking his head again. "Not remotely."

"California," she sighed exasperated; the boy had a habit of clinging to pain, "for the sake of my health, let it go. I will. Just be the loving child I know you to be and everything will be fine."

This Calvert agreed to. He wanted more than anything for them to be Gramma and grandson again.

Lavon couldn't stay mad at him; he was her grandbaby and it wasn't his fault. His own grandfather had told him to stay away and knowing that man's temper, he'd probably alerted the nurses to the fact that Calvert wasn't supposed to go near her. Inwardly she shook her head. Corey was a stubborn man, who never really did right by Calvert. At least not to her standards. She remembered hearing him grumble about how weird the boy had turned out. Blaming it all on his mother. Not that she could disagree in the slightest.

She would scold Corey afterward, reminding him that a grandparents' duty is to love their grandchild unconditionally. That's the duty of a parent as well, but Calvert's mother had failed him, so he needed the extra love from them to fill that void. She insisted on it. She'd still hear his grumblings, but he'd do it a lot quieter afterward. There were more than a few times when Calvin, Calvert's father, had asked why she had married his father. She never answered him. How could she? How could she tell Calvin that she stayed because she adored Calvert, instead of loving his father? Perhaps that's why her own daughter had abandoned her.

Jen and Corey had never got along. Corey would often tell Lavon that she spoiled Jen, but tensions between them hadn't really blown up until three years after Calvert was born. She was attached by then, so she stayed, and Jen moved away. They had remained in touch for a while, but things went sour when Lavon had her heart attack. Jen blamed Corey for all the stress from his angry outbursts.

Lavon knew the real reason, though. It was because of Calvert's situation with his mother. The woman was a hag and treated Calvert despicably. When he would tell Lavon what his mother had done to him, she'd become so angry. How could someone treat their child the way she had treated him? Lavon just couldn't fathom that kind of cruelty. It disgusted her. She had felt so helpless, unable to do anything for him when she desperately wanted too. She had wanted to get him away from the bitch but found there was nothing she could do.

DCFS was a useless organization. They'd taken Calvert from Calvin and placed him in the care of his mother. Luckily, she had only got partial custody and Calvert would spend his summers with his father. That allowed him a semblance of safety, if one that would be shredded once August came around. Lavon shook herself out of her reverie. That was then and this is now. Calvert had fully cut his mother out of his life and now she was there to love him instead.

That is, if Calvert would accept the fact that he deserved it. She watched as he'd picked up and washed the dishes. He put them in a drying rack when he was done, then he put the leftovers away. He really had grown up, she thought warmly, as she watched him move nimbly around the kitchen.

That night, Calvert left Gramma at her bedroom door before heading back upstairs. He thought of what they had talked about and was hoping beyond hope that it would be exactly as it used to be. Just them at night watching old movies. Maybe he'd feel comfortable enough to curl up beside her again. A deep yawning sadness replaced his hope.

When he was a young boy, he'd often curl up beside Lavon in her recliner. He loved being tucked snuggly between his Gramma and her soft chair; it made him feel safe. This had always been a happy moment, spending time with each other. Yet, the first time he'd done it to cry his heart out about his mother the experience was tainted; he had stopped after that. He glanced back down the steps as he swore to himself that he'd make things better. Nothing in the world would stop him.

***

The next day, Calvert helped Gramma clean out her room. She had decided to throw a lot away. There were things she'd held onto for sentimental reasons that she no longer wanted to keep.

She watched as he'd haul things out to his truck, marveling at how much he'd changed. He wasn't buff in any sense of the word, but the husky little boy that had trouble lifting things was gone. That's what years of construction could do for someone, she guessed.

After much sweat Calvert finally collapsed onto the couch in front of a fan. Gramma was sitting in the new recliner he'd gotten for her. They laughed when they met glances. Whatever tension that had been between them was gone. They decided to celebrate by making several bowls of popcorn and have a Gojirathon. Calvert even became comfortable enough to curl up besides Gramma again. They discussed and heckled the acting, effects, and poor dubbing of the films. As the third movie of Godzilla tearing down buildings flickered across the screen, sleep started to overtake them. Before it had ended, they were out like lights.

***

They were happy for three glorious months, going about their days, cooking each other meals, and watching their favorite movies. Unfortunately, all good things come to an end and theirs ended when Calvert was requested for an onsite job. He was going to decline the offer, but the price tag was tempting so he brought it up to Gramma to see what she thought about it.

"Do we need the money?"

Calvert didn't want to say, he hated to think that he had worried her about their finances. They weren't in dire straits, but the Holidays were coming up and some more spending money would be nice. So, reluctantly, he took the job. He told Gramma that he should only be onsite for fourteen days, left instructions on how to cook the deer, which he advised she should have at least twice a week. He claimed it was for her health. She didn't argue; she rather liked the savory meat so no one had to tell her twice.

The first two days went by normally, if a bit slow. Lavon woke up, took her shower, made breakfast and coffee, then sat down to a Bonanza marathon on TCM. Around ten she was missing Calvert; she knew she couldn't call him since he was on a plane but the emptiness of the house was starting to make her skin crawl. She decided that she was going to text him even though he wouldn't get back to her until later. Then she turned up the tv as she started working on a wordsearch.

She had started doing them because Calvert said it would help keep her mind lucid. The medicine she was on could make her a bit hazy if she wasn't focusing on something. She continued this way until two when she got sleepy, so she took a nap. She woke up around six, when she heard footsteps on the floor above her. She blinked in confusion, was Calvert home early? She sat up listening closely, but heard nothing else. She chuckled at her silliness. She must have dreamed it.

However, the same thing happened the day after, but this time when she sat up to listen to the sound of footsteps they didn't stop. She walked up the dark stairs, quietly entering the darkness that engulfed the second floor. The air felt a bit crisp. That wasn't something out of the ordinary though, the house was old and drafty, especially with winter setting in. She stopped at the top, straining to hear through the thickness of silence. Nothing.

Lavon chided herself as she went back down the steps. She should know better than to go chasing sounds around the house. She'd seen enough ghost movies to know that it's better if she ignored the activity and went about her day. Why she went straight to thinking that it was a ghost, though, she had no idea. It just seemed logical. She believed in ghosts even though she had never come across one. It must have been the house itself, an old dark Victorian house at night. The perfect setting for a haunting.

So, over the next three days (five since Calvert had left) Lavon ignored the growing sounds of footsteps, the moving of doors and furniture, even the shadows she saw at the end of a dark hallway. She even refused to acknowledge it over the phone with Calvert when he called every night to check in.

It wasn't until the bruises started showing up that she began to worry (sixth and seventh day). Everything she knew about ghosts said that they wouldn't interact if they were ignored. This had obviously been the wrong idea. She had noticed that most activity was happening at night, so she stayed up during the night with lights on and slept during the day. This worked for about four days (eleven days since Calvert had been gone), then whatever it was started harassing her in the bathroom.

After a shower one night she saw the ghost standing behind her in the bathroom mirror. Instead of screaming and jumping to turn to physically see it, she just stared at its reflection. The ghost wasn't scary, if anything it seemed a little lost, as if it didn't know where it was. They met each other's' eyes before it vanished in the steam from the shower. Instantly, she knew that couldn't have been the ghost leaving the bruises.

She turned around then, only to be jumped by a rotting corpse with skeleton hands. This time she did scream as her back hit the sink, her eyes squeezed shut so as not to see the ghost anymore. Yet, it remained, and started sniffing her.

"You smell dead."

Its voice was scratchy and airy, as if its vocal cords were exposed. There was no accent to tell where it had come from, but it smelled. A rotting skunk in the middle of a ragging summer day would've smelled better. It cackled, "You must be one of us. One of us. One of us! One of US! ONE OF US! ONEOFUS!" It started chanting.

"ONEOFUS!   ONEOFUS!   ONEOFUS! Oneofus…oneofus…oneofu…oneof…"

She only opened her eyes after the voice started to fade. Immediately she ran to her phone to call Calvert, not caring that she was still in her bathrobe. Once Calvert picked up, she started rambling into the phone, telling him everything that had been happening after he'd left.

Feeling her distress over the phone Calvert knew he had to get home. He could no longer leave her alone in that house. He got on the last Red Eye home, not even bothering to explain to his boss why. He just said he was leaving and left. He was going to be by Gramma's side even if he got fired. That seemed unlikely though, the last three days that he was supposed to be there weren't crucial. When he reached the house, he flew up the porch steps, slammed the front door open (not even bothering to close it) and ran head long into Gramma's room.

"Where is it?"

Lavon was sitting on her bed (still in her bathrobe) blanket over her shoulders, sobbing. Calvert sobered at the sight. He knelt down in front of her, hands clasped over hers, trying to infuse some calm into her. He stayed with her until she cried herself to sleep and kept watch over her. He wanted to make sure she got enough rest.

The next morning, he cooked breakfast quietly as Gramma sat at the table. Now and then he'd glance over his shoulder at her. He wasn't sure what he should say, but he tried his best to comfort her.

"You're safe now. Please don't be so worried."

Lavon's head jerked up to stare at Calvert's back. "I want to call a priest."

Calvert dropped his cooking spatula on the floor as he whirled around. "Absolutely not!"

The kitchen went dead. Lavon was stunned at the vehemence in her grandson's response. After a few moments she came out of her fugue. "I know you have a dislike of the church, but having the house cleansed would put me more at ease."

"I can fix this," he snapped. "Just let me fix it." He left the kitchen and disappeared upstairs.

She shook her head, a whiff of something burning brought her attention back to the kitchen. She jumped up and removed the skillet from the burner before breakfast was completely inedible.

Later that day Calvert mentioned he was leaving for a little bit; "Running some errands. Do you want anything while I'm out?"

Lavon shook her head, still hurt after he snapped at her. As soon as Calvert was gone, she picked up her phone and dialed the local Catholic church.

Calvert sighed heavily as he drove back home. He'd got everything he needed to fix their "ghost" problem. Guilt ate at him as he thought about how he snapped at Gramma. She didn't deserve that. He knew she was Christian and should have expected that it was going to come into play at some point.

He pulled into the drive way, a bit confused to see that there was another vehicle parked there as well. He tilted his head suspiciously and left his supplies in the truck as he stormed to the front door. When he walked into the living room, he saw Gramma entertaining a Catholic Priest. He huffed angrily.

"Grandma, what is he doing here?"

Lavon stood then to meet him at the threshold of the room. "Don't be upset, I did this to put my mind at ease. Please, just let him look around?"

Calvert glared at the pudgy man wearing the usual fatherly outfit. He took several deep breathes clenching and unclenching his fists. "Fine," was all he said before he moved himself out of the way. He watched as Gramma led the man up the stairs to where she first started hearing the noise then back down to her room where she started getting bruises and the bathroom where she met the two ghosts face to face.

With every mocking 'hmm' or head nod the Priest gave, Calvert became more pent up. He wanted the man out. Rage seethed under his skin like worms wriggling in electrified mud. The man asked to be led to the basement and the attic which Gramma showed him willingly, even though Calvert protested the attic. That was his workspace and he wanted the Priest nowhere near it. Still, with a little coaxing Gramma got her way.

Calvert had to unlock the attic so that the two could enter. He followed silently behind, a mere shadow in his own home. In the attic he sat in his work chair as he watched the Priest go around searching the immaculately clean space.

"This is where the ghosts are coming from," the Priest said wisely. "There is a door to the spectral plane here."

Calvert's back went ridged. "How the *fuck* do you know that?" His eyes narrowed again with suspicion.

The Priest pulled out an amulet looking necklace. "This charm can find any nexus between here and the realm of the dead."

The boy sneered at the Priest, "What are you, part of the Watcher's Council?"

"The what?"

The Priest was obviously confused by this reference from Calvert so he waved away the comment, not wanting the man to stay any longer than was necessary and to explain Buffy the Vampire Slayer would take longer than he'd like. The Priest continued on with his spiel. "Unfortunately, this door is stable, which means it is strong. This is going to take a while to exorcise."

Calvert jumped to his feet then. "I allowed you to investigate not take action. Get out!"

"Calvert, you're being rude, let the man do what he needs to do." Lavon admonished firmly.

"No, Gramma," Calvert shook his head. "I want him out now."

"Do you wish me to be hurt again?" Lavon snapped.

Calvert whimpered then. He hadn't wanted to make her angry but he just couldn't let the house be exorcised. "No, of course not but—"

"But nothing," she said, firmly cutting him off. "Either this house is cleansed or I'm leaving."

Tears pricked Calvert's eyes and he grew quiet, letting the Priest move on with his blessing. Surprisingly, he had packed everything needed for the exorcism (he thought that Priests needed to get permission first) and he started right away. Calvert stood far apart from the other two, afraid of what might happen. Maybe this wouldn't go as bad as he was anticipating. Hours passed before anything started happening. It had gotten so quiet that he flinched when he heard Gramma's first cry of pain. She collapsed to her knees and he went to her.

"Gramma, what's wrong?" He cried out.

"My chest hurts," she whispered, grabbing where the pain was.

Calvert slung his arm over her shoulders bringing her in tightly. "Stop this. Her heart can't handle this!"

But the priest kept praying and splashing his holy water.

"I feel as if I'm being separated from my body," Lavon whined through ragged breathing.

"STOP!" Calvert commanded at the top of his lungs. At that moment though, a howling wind swept through the attic as a glowing purple aura in the shape of a rectangle appeared. "STOP IT!" He hollered above the screeching banshee that was the wind.

Lavon gripped his hand on her shoulder and looked up at him lovingly. He met her gaze intensely. "It's going to be alright. I'm already dead." Just as the last breath left her body, he saw a light blue figure in the shape of Gramma enter the purple door, right as it closed.

"NOO!" His cry was agonizing. "No!" He buried his head into Gramma's cooling shoulder. Sobs wracked his body as he begged for her to come back.

***

Father Paul watched silently as the young man grieved for his grandmother. He had not known that something like this would happen. His blessings shouldn't have given her a heart attack. He wasn't sure what happened, but he really didn't want to be there to explain this so he tried to leave quietly. The next second he experienced a sharp pain in his skull and collapsed, not completely knocked out. The boy leaned over him menacingly. "Oh good, for a minute there I thought I caused some brain damage. That would not do with what I have planned for you next."

The boy's glasses glittered in the light, only slightly hiding the fact that Calvert's eyes were glowing green, then the Priest passed out.

Father Paul woke with a start, his head pounding, he started screaming when he realized that only half the world appeared. One of his eyes had been blinded. He didn't see the slim figure sitting in a dark corner, a leg propped up on a knee; not until he heard laughing. He whirled to see who it was. The young man, Calvert, he remembered the boy's name, was grinning ear to ear.

"Good, you're awake."

The boy unfolded himself from his chair, stepping in front of the Father with a threatening aura.

"What are you doing? Why am I here?"

Calvert chuckled as he slowly knelt before the Priest. "You cost me a lot, old man. I figured you needed to pay me back for it. That's why you're here."

He stood then and grabbed a dagger from a nearby table. The Priest's eyes widened at the sight of the massive altar before him.

"Are…are you…a devil worshipper?" The Priest stuttered.

Calvert snorted softly. "No, not at all. Satan is part of the Christian mythos, which I loathe, so why would I worship anyone from it?"

"Then," the Priest asked confused, "what's all this?"

Calvert kneeled back down in front of the soon to be dead man. "You really want me to monologue, huh? Do you think it'll save you time? Figure me out, so you can talk me out of this? Or do you think you can record a confession of some kind?"

Father Paul glanced away from the boy; he was oddly knowledgeable about all this.

"Don't get your hopes up. I underestimated you once, not again, or have you not noticed that you're naked?"

The man caught sight of his naked skin before screaming at the top of his lungs again.

"Now, now. Stop that. You're starting to annoy me," Calvert said, leaning up against the wooden wall behind him. "No one is going to hear you."

"Where am I?" The Priest demanded angrily.

Calvert tapped his chin with the dagger's handle in thought. "If I said 'Your worst nightmare' would it be too cliché?"

The boy was mocking him, Paul realized. "Why are you doing this?"

"Oh, I need a form of payment for my grandmother's soul. The one you happened to exorcise. Simple as that."

The Priest started in shock, "What?"

Calvert cackled loudly, bending in the middle. "Wait, did you not know? Gramma was already dead. Well, more like living dead."

"What are you talking about? I witnessed her drinking tea and could touch her. She wasn't a ghost."

Calvert whipped away the tears from his eyes. "No, you're right about that. She was a ghoul. I paid one life for the body and another for the soul. I believe in alchemy they call this equivalent exchange. Luckily, I still have her very pristine body after what you did so the price this time will only be one."

With speed Calvert lashed out, slicing open the Priest's arm. He screamed again as he saw his blood pump out of his broken skin.

"You're going to kill me to bring your grandmother back?"

Calvert studied the ruby liquid spilling onto a chalk circle. "Well, yeah," he said in a matter-of-fact manner. "I mean, what would save you? I killed my own mother and grandfather to do it the first time. Why not you?"

"You're insane!" The Priest yelled so hard that spittle dripped down his chin.

Calvert admonished the man, by tapping him in the head with the butt of his dagger. "None of that. It gives a bad name to those that are actually mentally ill." He shook his head in disappointment at the man. He stood then and hoisted the Priest onto a hook that hung in the middle of the circle. He hummed as he made sure everything was just right for the ceremony.

"What about the door?" The Priest groaned from his hook, despite the fact his death was imminent, he was still oddly curious.

"It was where Gramma came through," Calvert answered simply.

"Why would you keep the door stable?"

Calvert shrugged glancing up at the Priest, "Just another price. It was a simple ceremony to do once a month during the New Moon. The only reason things started coming through was because I was gone during the New Moon. That won't happen this time."

Calvert walked up to the man then, far enough away so he couldn't be spat on. "You know. I never thought I'd go as far as killing someone in my life and yet here I am." He paused for a moment before continuing, "Well, you know what they say, right Priest?"

The Priest shook his head.

The boy chuckled once more before plunging the dagger into the Priest's gut and slitting him open hip to hip, "Everything comes in threes."

The last thing the Priest saw was his steaming innards spilling down his legs and the boy's glowing green eyes and twisted smirk.

Outside Cat

Colin Adams-Toomey

The statue was small, tucked under the well-manicured hedge by the front steps: a jolly, violin-playing frog. Marcy rolled her eyes at it. Even if she had not been instructed, it's the first place she would have looked. The first place *anyone* would have looked. She tipped the statue back, retrieved the spare key, and let herself into the house.

She dropped her bag in the front hall and flicked on some lights. It was late in the afternoon, but it was also late into October, and the shadows were already long. The empty house was dark. She found the pages of instructions left for her where she expected them to be and ignored everything but the Wi-Fi password. At this point, she didn't need to be told where the coffee was kept, where to find the extra blankets. This wasn't her first rodeo, or even her twelfth. Experience had taught her that people weren't that creative: they tended to find the same places to stash the same things. That was a good thing for Marcy. It made her life easier.

The house, though large and clearly expensive, was also absolutely suburban-typical. Colonial style, vinyl clapboard siding, nice hardwood floors throughout. The walls were painted a tasteful off-white, the furniture pricey but bland. She moved from room to room, closing curtains, switching on lights, working out the TV remote. Settling in.

Marcy existed almost as a scullery maid from another century would: on references and word of mouth. She had cat sat for Carol Johnson, who had told Clair Brown about her when Clair needed someone to look after her retrievers for two weeks while Clair and her husband were in Aruba. Clair had told Jamie Woodward, and so on.

The people who hired her, mainly women, liked her. She was vibrant and charming around them, competent and earnest. They liked hearing about her plans for grad school, the things she did with her friends. It didn't matter that none of those things existed. Marcy knew the game well.

She had a routine, worked out over her many jobs. Next up was to take care of the pet she was sitting, in this case, a cat. Locate food, water, etc. If possible, make nice with the cat early on, play a little, give it a treat. Establish good relations. Although from what Mrs. Jones had said, that might be easier said than done this time.

According to Mrs. Jones, "Baby" was a fairly independent animal. Marcy had cringed inwardly at the name. She felt insulted on the cat's behalf. As Mrs. Jones had been showing her the house, running down the list of instructions, Marcy had been casting looks around, hoping to see Baby. Hoping to get the cat to come to her, rub her leg. Demonstrate how good she was with animals to Mrs. Jones. But there was no cat to be found. Not only that, there was really no evidence that a cat existed in the house: no toys, no scratched furniture, not even a litterbox. Eventually, Marcy worked up the nerve to interrupt Mrs. Jones' litany to ask.

"Oh," said Mrs. Jones, "you probably won't even see Baby while you're here. She's an outside cat."

This struck Marcy as odd. She'd sat for outside cats before; they always came back inside eventually. Mrs. Jones elaborated:

"I love her very much, but we really need to keep her outside. She's a wild little animal, and if we let her in, she drags in all sorts of nasty dead things."

So be it. It was her dime. Marcy would never argue back with her employers. She dutifully turned to the refrigerator.

The kitchen was large, decorated in some faux-Tuscan style. The granite counters were wide, and it included a breakfast nook by the back door. Even with the lengthening shadows, the large windows made it warm and cheerful.

Marcy lived more of her life in other people's houses than she did in anything that could really be called her own. She liked it: it was a vacation where she could also fantasize about living in such big, nice places, far beyond anything she could ever afford. She did that often, walking from kitchen to living room, imagining the kind of settled life she had given up long ago, that could never be hers now. And, of course, she was alone. Alone in a big house where she belonged, had been hired to be, with no reminders.

Almost alone, but not quite. Which was perfect. She liked animals: they offered companionship with no true comprehension of who she was. They liked her, were happy with her, if she was just *there* and if she fed them on time. They couldn't ask her what she was doing there, they would never form impressions of who she might truly be.

She could handle that kind of relationship, that kind of responsibility. She'd sat for all kinds of creatures: dogs, cats, snakes, birds, even a tankful of stick insects once. But never babysitting. She'd been asked several times, but always politely refused. She never wanted that kind of responsibility.

Inside the fridge, she found Baby's food packaged and ready. Enough packages for the next few meals. This was a short job: just an overnight stay.

If Mrs. Jones seemed a little impersonal about Baby being in the house, she was certainly indulgent when it came to Baby's food. Marcy unwrapped tonight's package to discover what appeared to be a premium cut of some sort of meat. Pork maybe, or maybe even venison. She rolled her eyes again. It wasn't the first time she'd seen something like this: "pet parents" who had their animals on some sort of insane, high-end diet they'd read about. Damn cats that ate better than Marcy did herself, when really, given half a chance, they'd happily eat spiders and garbage. She sighed and sliced up the meat into the food bowl that stood washed and waiting by the sink.

She unlocked the back door, to leave the bowl on the stoop as she'd been told. She stood for a moment, looking out over the backyard as the evening crept in. The well-tended grass ended abruptly in woodland at the end of the property. It was a cold autumn, and many of the fiercely colored leaves had already faded and fallen. The trees were skeletal, clutching the setting sun with their branches. Marcy felt a bitter breeze and heard the cawing of crows. She shivered.

She didn't spook easily. She was fine with the dark, and with solitude. Indeed, she lived in those elements, at the bus stops, gas stations, and backwoods roads that made up a good deal of her nomadic life. Nevertheless, with one last glance down at the lonely food bowl beside her, she hurried back inside and locked the door.

She'd check back on the bowl later, maybe catch a glimpse of the elusive Baby. For now, she made her way back to her bag in the hall. She removed a plain blue bed sheet and went upstairs. It was time for the next part of her routine.

She admitted that part of her enjoyed this step because it involved snooping. It was such a strange thing, hiring someone to live in your house, live an approximation of your life for a while. Such an intimate exposure. In the past she had found evidence of hidden drinking, private fetishes, clues of a possible second family. It gave her a tiny thrill to have this secret knowledge. Here, she found photos in the back of a drawer: a man smiling, holding Mrs. Jones around the waist. She'd seen her share of divorce in these houses, too.

But she was no creep. She wasn't digging for her own perverted pleasure. She had work to do.

Her wants were few, but pet sitting was never going to pay the bills. She had an anonymous account on a website that allowed members to sell used upscale clothing.

Marcy was no fool. She stayed away from jewelry, cash, electronics: any of the obvious things her clients might check when they returned, just to be sure. She knew the game. If she were pet sitting in the summer, she would dig deep to the back of the closet to find that expensive pair of winter boots that would not be needed, or indeed thought about, for months to come. By the time the owner went looking for them and couldn't find them, they might think about the ski vacation where the boots could have been left, or the closet at work where they probably were. Or, sometimes, things just went missing for a while, who knew why? They'd turn up again eventually. The owner's mind would never go to that pet sitter back in June. Whose name the owner wouldn't even be able to remember off-hand.

If she were ever caught, Marcy wouldn't defend her behavior. She had no Robin Hood illusions of deserving what the rich had too much of. Simply, she needed money, and broken creatures such as her are led to broken decisions such as this.

She knew she could get a job as a waitress, but that would mean settling down. Besides, deep inside, she knew she didn't deserve it. She deserved the solitary life she had, and the kind of work she made herself undertake. She didn't want to make friends with coworkers, answer personal questions with lies. Alone was better. Even theft was better.

She spread out her sheet to hide the background. The rules were simple. She never took too many things, never enough to be noticed. Only two or three carefully curated items at a time. She laid out a pretty, barely-worn summer dress with an expensive label, and took a photo with her phone to post to the site. If no one liked it, back it went, exactly where it came from. It wasn't worth the risk unless she could sell it. She'd only take it if it got a hit.

She was back downstairs, carefully folding the dress into her bag, when she heard the noise.

She paused, listening. By now, she had gotten used to empty-house noises: the clunk of the refrigerator icemaker, the creak of settling walls. Though she always registered each sound. She lived her life such that when something made her stop, made her radar ping, she knew better than to ignore it.

It happened again. Not the creak of a settling house. More the creak of settling floorboards.

Creaking under the weight of something.

Or not. Marcy did not spook easily. She had seen worse, a lot worse, than a creaking house. Nevertheless, she stood and walked toward the kitchen, where the noise had come from. She had just crossed through there on her way to stow the dress in her bag. She knew it was nothing, but told herself it was always good to check, anyway. Even if it was a waste of time.

The kitchen was dark: she'd never turned the light on in the first place, and night had fully fallen. The light from the lamp by the front door barely made it this far down the hall. As people so often do in houses, she barely looked on her first glance, her arm already snaking around the corner of the doorway to find the switch. Then she froze, hand splayed against the cool kitchen wall.

The back door was open.

It was pointless for Marcy to tell herself that she had locked that door: from where she stood she could see the screwdriver that had been used to jimmy it open, still jutting from the deadbolt. The door yawned wide, and the back porch light cast a harsh yellow square onto the kitchen floor.

The spit dried up in her mouth and a pool of ice water formed in her stomach as she realized the well-worn and often-scoffed scenario had come upon her at last: she was the young sitter, alone in the house with an intruder. Her primitive brain locked in on the open back door, the escape it offered.

She stopped herself milliseconds before she moved a muscle.

The shape was difficult to make out, as it was on the other side of the shaft of porch light, which is probably why Marcy had missed it at first. But it was there: a patch of shadow crouched by the breakfast table, darker than its surroundings.

Large. Heavy. Man-shaped. Marcy stared at it with the wide eyes of a rabbit regarding an approaching snake.

A straining moment of terrified silence followed, and it slowly dawned on Marcy that the man was faced away from her. Inexplicably, all of his attention seemed to be centered on the open door. She could feel his singular focus from across the room.

She frantically ran through her options. Call the police? She'd stupidly left her phone upstairs, waiting beside the next garment she had intended to steal. To reach it, she'd have to cross back through the kitchen, a blank impossibility.

But the front door was behind her, back down the hall. She could run across the street, pound on a neighbor's door. But could she really make it all the way back there without him noticing? Could she get the front door open before he raced up behind her, grabbed her by the throat? She could see that picture with painful clarity. But it was that, or stay frozen here, waiting for the man to glance behind and see her.

She started to withdraw from the kitchen doorway. Slowly, so slowly, wincing at every quiet swish her clothing made. Then she stopped again in her tracks.

Through the open door, Marcy could see that a little girl was approaching the back stoop.

That something was wrong with this girl was immediately apparent to Marcy, and it went beyond the strange, nightmare scenario that was unfolding. Her age was hard to determine; maybe eight or nine. She wasn't walking; rather, she moved forward on hands and feet, like a primate might. She was far too thin; corded, wiry little muscles stood out on her forearms. She wore the remains of a filthy dress, and her lank, stringy hair fell over her face. It was then that Marcy noticed that Baby's food bowl had been moved: it was now perfectly centered in the open doorway. The little girl seemed to be approaching it.

Marcy struggled to cope with what she was seeing, whatever awful abuse this was. It quickly got worse. She looked on in horror and disbelief as the man in the kitchen raised his arm toward the girl. A large-caliber revolver caught the porchlight, glinted in his hand.

To say that Marcy chose to do what came next would be a little misleading. There was thought involved certainly, but her response was almost atavistic. Simply put, Marcy, of all people, could not, *could* not let this happen. Not her. Not this. She was moving before she was fully conscious of deciding to do so.

There was no plan of action, but Marcy found a kitchen chair in her hands as she rushed across the room. Both the girl's head and the man's turned toward her, as she brought the chair crashing down on the man's back. Marcy was dimly aware that the little girl had vanished, as though she had never been there.

The momentum of the chair carried Marcy down on top of the man, and she was reaching for his gun arm. The man swore, twisted beneath her, and kicked out. He was wearing heavy work boots and when he connected, Marcy went skidding across the kitchen floor, colliding with the center island. He got her in the stomach, badly winding her. She curled on the floor, gasping for air.

The man kneeled, facing her. "Jesus!" he said. Marcy could see him clearly now. Whatever she was expecting, it wasn't this: an average middle-aged man, looking terrified and unsure.

The man raised one hand, palm open to placate, though he still held the gun in the other. "Listen," he said, "I'm not going to hurt you. I, Jesus, I didn't think there was anybody here." Marcy coughed and struggled to sit up.

The man continued in a frantic, urgent whisper. The things he was saying were crazy. "Listen, you don't understand. It's not what you think it is. I have to kill it. I tracked it here, it killed my wife when we were camping last year–" The man broke off, staring at the back door.

The little girl had returned. She crouched, silhouetted in the door frame. She appeared to be watching the two of them curiously.

The man raised his gun again, and the little girl flinched back. Marcy screamed and lunged for the man's arm. She forced it wide, and the man struggled to push her off.

That was when the little girl charged.

She was impossibly fast, covering the distance in less than two seconds. She leapt fully six feet through the air, arms and legs splayed. She landed on the man's chest, wrapping her limbs around him. All three of them tumbled backwards, the gun spinning across the kitchen floor. Before he could react, the girl sank her mouth into the man's neck, and he started screaming.

Blood splashed Marcy's face, and she scrambled backward, her mind reeling away from what she was seeing. The girl yanked her head back, pulling up a mouthful of meat. The man's screams sank to gurgles. Marcy had never seen so much blood. It smeared across the kitchen floor as the man's struggles weakened.

It's a funny thing, but in the middle of horrific moments such as this, the mind often seizes on odd, prosaic little details, and those get burned into the memory with everything else. The man who survives the bear attack remembers clearly and forever how badly the bear's breath stank, for example. What Marcy noticed was that the girl appeared to be wearing a collar, and she realized she recognized it. She'd seen them before: it was the latest thing with pet owners. They were embedded with a little microchip that connected to an app on your phone, so you could keep track of your outside pet. The kind you left bowls of food for outside the back door.

The thought was out of Marcy's lips before she could stop it. "Baby?" she whispered.

The girl stopped, swallowed what she had in her mouth, and looked up at Marcy. Marcy saw her face clearly for the first time.

Her eyes were large, and a beautiful shade of bright green. The pupils were vertical slits, and they reflected back light like a nocturnal animal. She regarded Marcy and smiled happily. She had teeth like a piranha, razor points smeared slick and red. Red dripped down her little chin.

Marcy's nerve broke entirely. She fled out the back door, into the night.

She pounded across the backyard, mind all panic, only thought to get away. But she stopped short where the yard met the darkness of the forest. Marcy was terrified, oh yes she was. But she was also nothing if not a survivor. She wouldn't have lasted this long in her chosen life if she wasn't. She didn't want to believe in what she had seen, but she had seen it. She had no doubts on that point. She knew instinctively that the woods must be where…it, whatever *it* was, lived. Where it hunted. To run in there would be a fatal mistake.

But she was painfully exposed where she was, in this empty suburban expanse of backyard grass. The glare of the distant porch light felt like a prison searchlight pinning her down. The girl was fast, so fast, Marcy had seen. She could be anywhere now: crouched in those bushes, or up in those trees. Marcy dithered where she was, hating every instant that ticked by, which is when she saw the old garden shed. She ran full-tilt at it, colliding with the corner. She pulled at the door handle and mercifully found it unlocked. She slammed the door shut behind her and hunched against the wall.

Two small, dirty windows on opposite sides of the shed allowed dim light to enter. Marcy's eyes darted around the grimy interior and found it maddeningly empty. No rake, no shovel, nothing that could possibly be used as a weapon. Mrs. Jones probably hadn't done a day of gardening in her life; she probably paid a fucking landscape company every month. Marcy could have screamed. There was a cobweb-strewn badminton set leaning in one corner, and a cracked baseball mitt holding a scuffed baseball sitting on a shelf. That was it. She pulled a badminton racket out of the bag and clutched it to her chest. It was laughably fragile, wouldn't last one blow, but it felt better to be holding something in her hands.

It helped her breathe, to stop and think. She couldn't stay where she was, but at least she was hidden for now. If she could be quiet, if she could be slow…could she get to the house? If she could, she could barricade the door, find the gun…

A muffled thump jarred her back as something landed on the shed roof and began to move around. Marcy gasped and cowered into a corner. A shadow eclipsed the patch of light cast on the floor by the shed's window.

Baby had arrived.

She knew that if she were to crane her neck up to look, she would see that little round face, framed upside-down, lank hair hanging around it. Pretty green eyes searching the dark shed, a grin on that pretty little mouth, pretty little teeth…

Marcy's breath came in short, tiny bursts, her heart pounded in her ears. She pressed herself into the corner, gripping the racket so hard it hurt. Her gaze drifted to the old baseball mitt on the shelf. She had a crazy, likely suicidal idea.

She moved slowly, bending her arm to avoid the window, and scrabbled until she gripped the baseball. She snatched it back to her. She took a shaky breath and threw it as hard as she could at the opposite window. It went through the glass with a tinkling crash and thumped somewhere out in the darkness.

Immediately, she heard Baby galloping across the roof of the shed, in the direction of the baseball. Marcy didn't hesitate; she slammed through the shed door and sprinted in the direction of the house.

She didn't know if it was enough of a head start, probably, definitely, not enough. The girl was so fast. Marcy would feel little fingers closing around her ankle at any moment. But she forced this not to matter. She focused on the house, getting closer, twenty yards, fifteen, ten, until she looked up and saw a figure standing in the doorway, saw the figure of–

"Mrs. Jones!" Marcy skidded to a stop, panting. Mrs. Jones tilted her head, and Marcy reoriented. "Mrs. Jones, we have to get inside. I'll explain, but we have–"

"Yes, we do. It looks like things have gone a little off the rails."

"Please, I'll explain inside–"

"No need. I think it's clear." Mrs. Jones raised her hand. She was holding the man's gun, pointed at Marcy.

Marcy found, absurdly, that she was still holding the badminton racket. She dropped it and raised her hands. "What are you doing?"

"Get inside." Mrs. Jones' voice was cold, efficient. "Now." Marcy did as she was told. Mrs. Jones kicked the kitchen door shut behind them, keeping the gun on Marcy. Marcy licked her lips. "I don't understand," she said.

"You don't need to," replied Mrs. Jones, and brought the butt of the revolver down on Marcy's head. Marcy's eyes rolled toward the ceiling, and she crumpled to the floor.

She awoke to a pounding headache. The glare of light made her squint. Her first realization was that she could not move: she was strapped hand and foot to some sort of metal gurney. Her surroundings came into focus, and she saw that she was in the house's basement. Mrs. Jones had told her that the basement would be locked at all times. Marcy could see why.

It was a large, spartan-clean space, all concrete and cinder blocks, lit harshly from above by long rows of fluorescent tubes. It was covered in some sort of high-gloss gray paint, the kind that's easy to hose down. Marcy turned her head and saw a stainless-steel table.

The body of the man from earlier lay naked on the table. He had been brutally, efficiently dismembered. One leg and arm were missing at the joint, organs piled to the side in a glistening heap, and half his torso had been stripped of meat, down to the bone. Mrs. Jones leaned over the body. She was dressed in a blood-spattered plastic suit, with elbow-length rubber gloves. She was stripping meat off of the man's forearm with a long, gleaming boning knife. She stopped and turned her head toward Marcy. After a moment, she started up again.

"Damn," she said. "I was hoping you wouldn't wake up for all this."

Marcy was already trying to do the arithmetic of survival, though the equation here looked grim. "Mrs. Jones, I'm sorry. He broke in. I get it, I won't tell about the body."

"You don't get it." Mrs. Jones sounded impatient. "You saw her."

"What?" Marcy tried hard to catch up. "Baby?"

Mrs. Jones sighed. "This happens, every now and again. I try so hard, but sometimes there's mistakes."

Marcy was silent for a moment. She couldn't help but ask.

"Who is she?" For all this, Marcy genuinely found herself wanting to know.

Mrs. Jones paused again. "I guess there's no harm in telling you. We thought we were done; there was no chance. And then we had her. Our little Catherine. Our miracle." Mrs. Jones' face clouded, saddened. "But something was wrong with her. She was…so different."

Mrs. Jones brought the meat over to a stained butcher-block counter. The man's clothes were folded nearby, his gun neatly on top of the pile. "We tried to raise her as best we could, love her as best we could." She shook her head. "There was an accident and my husband…after that, I knew she had to stay outside."

"Why do you keep–" Marcy started.

"Because she's my *daughter*." Mrs. Jones' voice boomed through the basement. Then she smiled. "She's my *baby*."

Her expression hardened. "I take good care of her. I keep an eye. Even if I have to go away. How do you think I knew to come back so fast?" She picked up a tablet, turned it to Marcy. There was a network of hidden-camera feeds from inside and outside the house, and a pinging light showing where "Baby" Catherine was.

Mrs. Jones put the tablet back down. "She's better outside. She really is. And she's so shy. As long as she's fed regularly, she keeps her distance from people."

Mrs. Jones wrapped the meat she'd cut in butcher's paper and cling film. She brought it over to an open chest-freezer. Marcy thought about that meat she'd handled, cut into the bowl. Wrapped just the same. A lot like pork, but with that odd, gamey smell. She felt sick.

"But sometimes, I *do* have to go away. Every parent does," Mrs. Jones continued. "That's where people like you come in. I'm careful, of course. Most times, the sitters never see her. But if they do, well…" Mrs. Jones went back to the tablet. "I'm careful. I never hire anyone with a family, with anyone who'd come looking. And I'm not a monster. No one…*good* ever ends up down here." Mrs. Jones backed up the upstairs camera feed. Marcy, from above. Snapping pictures of clothes, packing up the dress.

Marcy licked her lips. "I can give it back," she whispered. "I don't need it. I'll give it back."

Mrs. Jones gave a little laugh. "Oh, that's not what we're talking about, is it? I do my research on anyone I hire. I have to. I *know* you, Marcy."

Marcy had never been good at "normal". She'd found it boring, felt more at home in places that were exciting, dark, dangerous. She'd had brushes with drugs and alcohol when she was sixteen, and those had gotten serious enough that her parents had intervened. Marcy rebelled against that, the way she'd been rebelling against everything, as long as she could really remember.

She had lots of friends who laughed along with her at her stupid parents, and their stupid, white-bread life. That wasn't where *real* life was; not like the high resplendent darkness where the streetlights were, where there were secret, breathless car rides to dim houses with loud music and loud, reckless, thrilling conversations.

Marcy knew she'd fly the coop as soon as possible, and she had a practical streak: she worked all the jobs she could, and hoarded cash like a bank-robber. She couldn't wait.

It was on one of those jobs – a babysitting gig – that life answered the challenge Marcy had been putting up, knowingly or not, for a long time. Marcy liked babysitting enough: parents trusted her because even then she had been good at appearances, and kids loved her because she was fun and let them get away with shit their parents never would. Rachel had been seven years old.

Marcy did everything right: made dinner, played the meandering pretend-world game that Rachel made up, watched a movie, read her a story. Rachel conked out around ten, *way* too late but who would know, and that was perfect. The party Marcy had been texting about with her friends was just getting into full swing. Marcy had her parents' car, she'd get there and be back around one, maybe two a.m. tops. Rachel, everyone, would be none the wiser. She'd done it before.

When she'd stumbled in, owlishly focused on being quiet and making plenty of noise, nothing had seemed amiss. Marcy had thought at first that she'd knocked over a coat in the front hallway, on her way out.

She'd had to call 9-1-1, though by that point, she already knew it was too late.

Near as they'd been able to tell, Rachel must have gotten up in the middle of the night, gone wandering (*looking for me, did she want a glass of water? Just to know I was there?*) and slipped in the dark on the stairs. She broke her neck.

"Didn't die right away, sadly." The paramedic had muttered it to his partner, out of what he thought was earshot, but Marcy heard. It's all she heard, then and every night after. She didn't die right away. She lay in the stairwell, alone, in the dark. Did she cry? Ask for Marcy? While Marcy sat a mile away with her shitty friends?

She didn't wait to watch the town turn against her, didn't wait to see the empty looks from her parents, at what used to be their daughter. She was gone the next day with all her cash, first bus out of town. She flew the coop, just like she wanted.

She got some calls at first from her parents, all of which she ignored. After a while, the calls stopped. To Marcy, that felt about right.

Mrs. Jones looked down at her. Marcy shook her head, and kept shaking. What was there to say?

Mrs. Jones leaned over the gurney, and pulled some lever Marcy couldn't see. There was a clunk, and then Mrs. Jones tilted the gurney upward, so that Marcy's world was suddenly upside-down. Below her head, a plastic bucket came into view. You have to hang the animal to drain the blood, before you butcher it.

Mrs. Jones brought the boning knife up to Marcy's neck. "I'm sorry," she said. Marcy guessed she was sorry, too. She thought about dying here, in this awful place. She thought it would hurt. She wondered if this was where the gray purgatory of her chosen life was supposed to lead. The tablet pinged: an alarm noise. Mrs. Jones paused, and her eyes flicked away from Marcy, toward the basement stairs.

Catherine was not supposed to be in the house. That was a rule. But the lock on the back door was broken. And there she was, crouched on the basement stairs.

She held the baseball in her hands, continuing the fun game that Marcy had been playing.

"Baby." Marcy didn't mean to say it; she couldn't help herself. Baby Catherine took in the scene, her slitted eyes flicking back and forth from Mrs. Jones to Marcy. Marcy on the gurney to the knife in Mrs. Jones' hand. Catherine's jagged-tooth mouth pulled downward into a frown.

"Cat, baby," Mrs. Jones was soft, loving, "baby–"

Catherine launched herself from the steps at Mrs. Jones.

The angle was bad, and both Catherine and Mrs. Jones went crashing into Marcy's gurney. The whole thing fell over, landing on Marcy's hand, crushing it. Marcy screamed.

So did Mrs. Jones. Catherine had sunk her teeth deep into Mrs. Jones' shoulder.

Marcy saw at once that her hand was broken. It sent sheets of agony up her arm. But Marcy was also a survivor. She saw what could be done. She pulled her hand through the restraint, gritting her teeth at the pain, and went to work on her other hand. Mrs. Jones had managed to throw Catherine off, but she had leapt right back on. The two of them spun through the basement, knocking things to the ground.

Marcy tumbled to the floor as the last restraint gave way. Mrs. Jones rose before her, boning knife clutched in her hand. But Marcy had already found the gun on the floor. She raised it in her good hand and fired.

Marcy had never shot a gun before, and the kickback was painful up to her shoulder. Her arm flung wildly above her head. But it was good enough: the bullet caught Mrs. Jones in the cheek, spinning her around and throwing a splash of blood onto the wall.

Marcy heaved herself to her feet and staggered up the basement stairs. Near the top, a noise stopped her.

It was Catherine. She crouched near the corpse of her mother, keening softly. She reached out a hand to paw at her mother's shoulder. She moved in a little circle, looked up with her pretty green eyes at Marcy, then back down at her mother's body. The noises she made had a question in them. And they were sad, so sad.

The noises any little girl would make when she was scared and alone.

Marcy was caught looking down, looking down at the outside cat, not knowing what to do. Knowing that the small figure crouched in the puddle of blood below her was, for once, more lost than she was.

Catherine took a small, hesitating step toward her, eyes wide, jagged mouth pulled down into a tiny moue of worry. Marcy took an involuntary step down.

Marcy was an outside cat, too. She was more at home under the streetlights at night, in the anonymous places in between safety. More at home outside of the houses she sat, the homes she had no real right to be in. In the alleys behind those houses, looking at the cracked concrete people forgot.

Where things that shouldn't grow, flourished. Where things that had no right to grow, did.

It was a bright afternoon in late January as Marcy wheeled the bins to the street. Mondays, she knew, were pickup day. She didn't even need the reminder on her phone anymore. She'd gotten into the rhythm of the routine.

Back in the house, she went down to the basement. She opened the chest freezer to a blast of cold air and checked the supply. She had a practical streak, and she was business-like about this. She had a clipboard hung nearby, keeping tabs. She checked off some boxes. The man, and Mrs. Jones, had lasted a good long while.

They didn't have to worry yet, but when they did, it would be ok. They could move if they needed to, Marcy was good at moving. Or maybe not; maybe they could find a way to stay here. No matter what, she'd never let anything bad happen to Catherine. Marcy was a problem-solver.

She was an outside cat, a weed in the concrete. But now, she'd been planted where she needed to be, she saw that now. She could take this responsibility. There was a child that needed looking after. And Marcy needed more than anything to look after her. She was up to that task.

OTHER HELLBOUND BOOKS
www.hellboundbooks.com

The Black Monastery

1866. Corpus Christi, Texas.

This deeply devout Catholic small town, still reeling from the wounds of war, has barely begun to recover when it faces yet another calamity. Under the cover of night, unknown assailants brutally murder local priests and abduct altar boys. Even the Saint Lucia Nunnery on the outskirts of town isn't spared by the merciless perpetrators.

Arisztid Wratiszlaw, the town's Hungarian-born sheriff, is left with only one blood-stained message on the chapel wall*: "Without the shedding of blood, there is no forgiveness of sins!"*

As the sheriff and his misfit posse set out to hunt down the brutal cult, but their mission is hindered not only by the tensions within their group but also by their living nightmares: Terrifying biblical stories brought to life before their very eyes and the haunting question of whether they're facing

Satan Rides Your Daughter Again

In our spine-chilling homage to the late, great Dennis Wheatley and the inimitable Hammer Horror films spawned from his works, HellBound Books presents twenty superlatively satanic stories guaranteed to have you fearing for your very soul?

A whole host of Hell's denizens skulk within these pages, waiting with growing impatience for brave of heart - or the relentlessly foolhardy - to make their otherworldly acquaintance, so please, do venture inside. If you dare?

Featuring hellish tales from: L. G. Merrick, Henry Myllylä, Alan Derosby, A.K. McCarthy, Brian James Lewis, C. C. Parker, Chisto Healy, Leo J. Winters, R.C. Mulhare, Henry Myllylä, J.B. Toner, Glen Damien Campbell, Nathan Blake, Gerald Dean Rice, Ricki Whatley, Carlton Herzog, Len M. Ruth, Vivian Kasley, Carson Demmans, Mark Towse, and Alexander Marai.

Anthology of Splatterpunk

splat·ter·punk
noun
informal
noun: splatterpunk

Definition: "A literary genre characterized by graphically described scenes of an extremely gory nature."

HellBound Books are incredibly proud to present to you horror most raw and visceral, two-dozen suitably graphic, horrific tales of terror designed to churn the stomach and curdle the blood.

This superlative tome is an absolute must for fans of Richard Laymon, Clive Barker, Monica J. O'Rourke, Matt Shaw, Wrath James White and Jack Ketchum – all put to paper by some of the brightest new stars writing in the genre today.

Featuring stories by: Nick Clements, Carlton Herzog, NJ Gallegos, Scotty Milder, Steve Stark, Frederick Pangbourne, Cristalena Fury, Amber Willis, Kenneth Amenn, Erica Summers, Allie Guilderson, Cory Andrews, Andrew P. Weston, Shula Link, Carlton Herzog, DW Milton, Brent Bosworth, JD Fuller, Robert Allen Lupton, C.M. Noel, Julian Grant, Jay Sykes, Phil Williams, and the incomparable James H Longmore.

Anthology of Horror

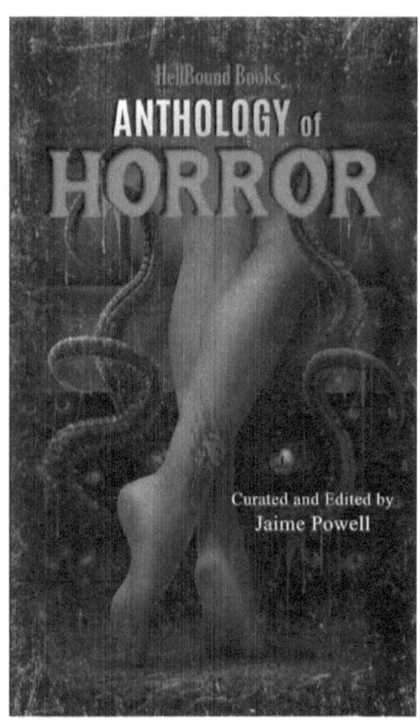

hor·ror
/ˈhôrər/

A literary or film genre concerned with arousing feelings of horror.

Rest assured, HellBound Books knows what scares you!

Skulking around in the deepest, thickest, darkest shadows of our authors' imaginations lies a whole host of terrifying tales to scare you witless and stir your greatest fears and, dear reader, we have compiled twenty-one such short stories for that specific purpose within the beautifully crafted pages of this very tome!

So, dig in – we dare you – and do remember to leave a light on…

Featuring short tales of terror from: Cory Andrews, Kathrin Classen, William Presley, John Schlimm. K.L. Lord, Jane Nightshade, K. John O'Leary, Dante Bilec, D. H. Parish, Whitney McShan, Keiran Meeks, Josh Darling, Paul Lonardo, Martyn Lawrence, Eric J. Juneau, Terry Campbell, Brett King, Sophia Cauduro, Christina Meeks, Kody Greene, and HellBound Books' very own James H Longmore.

A HellBound Books Publishing LLC Publication

www.hellboundbookspublishing.com

www.ingramcontent.com/pod-product-compliance
Lightning Source LLC
Chambersburg PA
CBHW061335310726
48974CB00001B/60